She put her hand through Hugh's arm, dreaming that they were on their way to a distant part of America on the shore of a vast lake where there was untold wealth to be mined. Looking into his quiet face, Catherine saw the hopelessness she had seen in other Irish faces like the stamp of the race. Could they so rob him of hope that he could not stand before her with pride?

"What will we do?"

"I know what I will do," he said, nodding at the ship disappearing in the night-time mists of Dublin Bay.

"You mean," Catherine whispered, "America?"

"Aye. We shall not look back from the shore that we sail from and the homes and families that we leave but ahead to the shore we shall sail toward and the home and the family the two of us will be founding."

Winds of Change

MARIE L. NOWINSON

BALLANTINE BOOKS • NEW YORK

Library of Congress Catalog Card Number: 79-83620

ISBN 0-345-27587-X

Manufactured in the United States of America

First Edition: July 1979

For my son, Peter

The Voyage I was born to make in the end, and to which my desire has driven me, is towards a place in which everything we have known is forgotten, except those things which, as we knew them, reminded us of an original joy.

The Harbour in the North
Hilaire Belloc

PART ONE

Chapelizod

(1831–1835)

Chapter I

CATHERINE MACAULAY opened her eyes at the sound of her mother quietly crossing the room and discreetly parting the window curtains to admit the pale daylight.

"Your father and I," her mother began in a voice which to her sixteen-year-old daughter sounded admonishing as well as informing, "are off to Dublin on a matter of business."

Catherine felt the well-known tightening of distress and the need to fight free of it. Sometimes she succeeded, succeeded even in bringing to life the laughing girl in her mother. It was always worth trying.

"A matter of business, is it?" she said, sitting up in bed.

Her mother was silent. Caught between her need to share concern and her wish to shield me from hurt, Catherine thought. And as always in moments like this, her mother was reaching back through the decades, past the horrors of the 1798 Irish uprising to her own childhood in Chapelizod. Catherine wanted to pull her out of that past twilight into the dawn of the present. She sought the needed bantering tone and went on, "And may I ask what business?"

"Business that concerns all of us," Mrs. Macaulay replied, managing both to answer the question and to convey an ominous hint at something else.

Catherine got out of bed. "Well, pleased to be included." Her laugh ricocheted about the room.

Her mother's answering laugh came at once, and Catherine triumphed at winning this round in their little game. But then her mother remembered the sorry state of affairs and said with a try at severity, "You are to take care of the house today."

"What is it this old house will be wanting today?"

"Look after the boys. You are older. They look to you."

"The three of us shall be cross-eyed by the day's end with so much looking to and looking after."

"Kate!" Ellen Macaulay drew in her breath. "You seem not to realize . . ."

This time Catherine had lost. She listened and dressed, and her mother went on with the litany. "The times are bad and growing worse. The Union of 1800 brought Ireland none of the promised and longed-for advantages. I dread going to Dublin today. Without an Irish Parliament sitting in College Green, Dublin is a gray ghost city. All our small businesses are failing."

But Catherine, ready now for the day in a blue blouse that matched her eyes, a purple skirt, and black stockings, was beside her mother, her arms about her, her young, fragrant face firm against her mother's soft cheek, her dazzling auburn hair dimming her mother's. "I understand, and I am sorry. But it is all that I ever have heard. It goes on and on. And now there is Daniel O'Connell. Might it not be that he has the answers?"

Ellen Macaulay opened and closed her mouth, then said, "Perhaps. But I dread any talk of uprising. I lived through the one of 'ninety-eight. I was younger then than you are, only fourteen. The artillery was right here in Chapelizod. I can still see my poor little mother. For the first time, I realized that she was English, and I wondered, Is she sorry she married my father? Her parents fought her doing so. There was a law in Ireland forbidding marriage between Protestant and Catholic. But they were determined, and so they married in England. Of course, as you know, he proved a fine man and good doctor. Ten years later, in 1792, the law preventing a marriage like theirs was repealed—"

"But all that was forever ago, Mother. This is the summer of 1831, and things are bound to come right. Go now to Dublin with Father. Do not worry at all. When you return, you will find the house still standing and me and the boys just as you are leaving us, only older, richer, and wiser by a day."

Her mother hesitated in the doorway, torn between lingering and leaving. It was as if she were on a bridge, suspended between the past she so often returned to and the future she feared to enter.

"Go now," Catherine said gently, and was rewarded by a quick lift of her mother's shoulders. Then with a wave of her little hand, Ellen Macaulay moved on.

"If things go better today than we dare hope, she said, "we shall come back in a bright new jaunting car. That is, providing the old one gets there without falling apart." Her laughter broke, and she was again the girl Catherine fought to keep alive.

That was all Catherine needed. Running down the back stairway to the kitchen, there was for her neither past nor future but only the blessed eternity of the July day. Despite its vexations, was not life wonderfully good?

In the kitchen, already dressed for a summer day's play, chubby five-year-old Jerry sat on a chair removed from the table.

"I do not want any breakfast," he announced, his brown eyes expecting contradiction.

Catherine's laugh rang gaily, heightening the shine on the pewter kettles that hung on the brown oak wall near the red brick fireplace. "Well, I see nothing to trouble us there," she said. "It is far easier not to have breakfast than to have it."

Jerry laughed his own quick, young laugh.

"The problem," Catherine said, "for people in Ireland and for some right here in Chapelizod is to have breakfast at all. That is a real trouble now—to wake wanting your breakfast and not be able to have it."

Jerry's eyes turned anxious. "I think I want my breakfast, Kate."

Catherine came over to him, solemn with concern. She put her arms around Jerry, hugged him hard, then kissed the pretty circle of pink in his round, firm cheek. "I am certain you do. Perhaps it was Mother and Father going off so early in the morning that made you think you did not."

"You will not go off, too, will you, Kate?"

"Do not worry about me," Catherine reassured her young brother. "I shall be here all day and likely forever. Now, let us see about breakfast."

"Did I hear you say breakfast?"

George, a slim, tentative thirteen-year-old in aging moss-brown breeches and lively grass-green shirt, came into the kitchen.

"Would it be dinner I would be talking about at this morning hour?"

George sat down at the table. In the sunlight from the high east window, his dark hair showed some of Catherine's red. "I suppose not," he said agreeably. Then his brown eyes lit teasingly. "Hugh been around yet today?"

"I do not know what you are talking about," Catherine retorted, and then her giggle and George's and Jerry's all broke together, for there in the opened kitchen doorway, his hair shining like copper in the sun and light streaming from his deep-set eyes, stood Hugh.

For Catherine the day began cresting toward a peak. She felt her heart flutter like the thrush Hugh had caught yesterday and given her to hold in her hand. But with her brothers' eyes watching closely for telltale signs, she managed not to depart too far from the brisk, authoritative Kate she pretended to be.

"Do sit down, Hugh, and make the lucky fourth for breakfast," she invited. "Let us not have any excuses, such as having had breakfast already."

Amusement twitched in George's eyes and undisguised delight stood in Jerry's as Hugh Condon unhurriedly collapsed his lanky frame in a chair, lifted his head, and smiled at them.

Catherine set four bowls of porridge on the table, then added bread and jam, milk for Jerry and George, tea for Hugh and herself, and sat down.

"Will you say grace, please, Jerry?"

Jerry made the sign of the cross deliberately, then rushed through the familiar prayer but did not forget to add, "May the Lord provide for the wants of others. In Ireland," he remembered. "Especially in Chapelizod." This accomplished, he turned to Hugh. "Our mother and father have gone to Dublin."

Hugh nodded. Even seated at the table, he seemed in a state of arrested motion. "As I started over, I saw them get into the jaunting car."

"Could things have happened the other way around?" George asked.

"Hard though it may be, George, let us try our best to talk sense," Catherine interjected.

"Well, then, what shall we talk about?"

"There are many subjects we might discuss," Catherine said. "For instance, just yesterday I was reading a book Mr. Whyte gave you years ago from the old Academy library. It was about a distant part of America, on the shore of a vast lake, where there is untold wealth to mine. Copper, they say it is; enough to supply the whole world and make any number of people as rich as anyone ever could wish to be. And I said to myself, If only the Irish could get over there and mine all that ore and grow rich, instead of staying here, where, from all reports, things are getting no better."

"The English will get there first."

"Now, that's a fine thing to predict, Jerry," Hugh said.

"Don't they always get everywhere first?"

"Still, there's no law that says they always will—"

"I was thinking I might go there myself—" Catherine interrupted.

"All alone?" asked Jerry.

"Well, it would be pleasanter, I think, to go with a husband."

"With Hugh?" Jerry demanded. This set George to laughing.

" 'Twould be a privilege," Hugh said, "to go there with your sister."

He paused, and the prospect of their doing so seemed to come alive in the warm kitchen. Catherine felt again what she'd sensed earlier. Life was cresting to a peak. Now there was something new in the promise, something she recognized as the forbidden stirring of sex.

"But for today," Hugh went on, "what would you say to my taking you all to the fair?"

"What was it I promised my mother?" Catherine wondered. "That by the day's end, we would all be older, wiser, and richer by a day?"

"We are bound to be older," George noted.

"You are right," Catherine agreed. "And perhaps I had better have said richer *or* wiser, for I guess it must be one or the other. Would you like to go, boys? I shall give you a pence to spend, Jerry. George, you may have two."

From a pewter pitcher Catherine shook out the coins. She held them and looked at them briefly.

"It is ten years now," she said, "that we have been using these English pence, and I still miss the look and the feel of the Irish ones."

"Aye," Hugh said. "So do I. So do we all."

She handed George his two English pence, which he took and spit on. Next she handed Jerry his one. He did as George had done and followed his older brother out of the house.

Then Hugh did what he'd been waiting to do: he opened wide his arms. Catherine stepped into them and felt them close warmly around her, drawing her to him. There it was again, that delightful quickening, longer now and with the hope of fulfillment. Once she found his lips sweet.

Hugh," she sighed, and deepened her kiss.

He pushed himself away, with something like alarm in his eyes. " 'Tis careful we must be, Kate. As you know, we've a long wait ahead."

" 'Tis ever so." She smiled. "With whatever we would like a little more of."

Emboldened, Hugh pulled her toward him again. But over his shoulder, Catherine saw the kitchen door slowly begin to open. A moment later George and Jerry burst in.

"What is keeping you?" Jerry asked.

"Are we interrupting anything?" George inquired.

"You, George, would be incapable of any such rudeness," Catherine said. "We are coming." She slipped her arm through Hugh's, dreaming that they were on their way to a distant part of America, then set out with him after the boys for the fair.

Chapter 2

SMILING A "GOOD MORNING," Catherine held open the door to the Chapelizod children. As they trooped past her into the house—Steven, Mary, Susan, Bill, Cathy, Peter, John, Michael, Joseph, Christopher, Joanna, Daniel, Mark, Jimmy—Catherine looked over their fair and dark heads and saw the apple tree just beyond the door shaking out its moist pink and rose blossoms against the tender blue morning sky.

Another spring. This is like all the others and yet like no other I have ever known, she said to herself. A gentle breeze lifted the branches, dispelling the fragrance of the flowers. It had happened just so last night. Hugh had opened the door, and they had stepped out into the blossom-scented evening. They had fallen silent. But had they not already said all there was to say about the coming day and the interview with Mr. Eldon that Hugh was resolved upon?

They had begun with Hugh practicing his address to the manager of the Dublin brewery, for whom he, ever clever with figures, had developed a new accounting system. One which, besides recounting income and expenses, would forecast the company's future. "Mr. Eldon, I have been testing my projections for a year, and I have waited a month to talk to you."

Catherine had played his employer. Mimicking first the fussy way Mr. Eldon buttoned up his coat and then the incongruous bull-like lowering of his head into his double chin, she had said, "Well, do not wait any longer." She had burst into a fit of laughter. No, that had been too easy. Reaching a second time for Mr. Eldon's gravelly voice, she had said, "Then you will not mind waiting somewhat longer."

Once the words escaped, she had gasped as though Mr. Eldon had actually said them. Suppose he did? Hugh and she had stared at each other. In the exchange, dismay stood out on their white, questioning faces. Then their heads had dropped, and they had laughed together at the alarm her acting had brought on them both.

" 'Twill go well," Hugh had stated with conviction. "Have no fear. But enough of this play-acting. It unnerves me."

Then he had opened the door, and they had stepped out into the fragrant, solacing dark and fallen silent with the hope that their long-deferred plans would soon come to pass. They had embraced and had felt themselves one with the spring night's urgency.

Now, as she closed the door after the children, Catherine questioned herself, Can this really be the fourth spring since I turned sixteen, and began to teach Chapelizod's children?

It had been her mother's idea.

"After all, we are better off than these others,

though not so well off as I wish we might be for your sake and the boys', Kate," she had said. "Your father and I were, despite all, able to teach the three of you. And George, like Tom Kemris and others, had those early years at Mr. Whyte's . . ."

Catherine had smiled. Hugh's parents had also sent him to Mr. Whyte's Academy.

"Then," Ellen Macaulay had continued, "there were the books." She had gestured toward the walls lined with leather-bound volumes. "You all took early to reading."

As did Hugh, Catherine had thought, and she saw him first a small boy, then a growing boy, then a young man còme into the book room to accept from her father some work to take home and study. "A good reader," her father would say, settling down to his work. "Learning. That, after all, is what counts. Life should be growth."

"But these children," Catherine's mother had gone on, "what have they? The places they live . . . you cannot call them homes! They are often hungry. They and their parents have lived so long in poverty, ignorance, and fear. We at least can lessen their ignorance."

"Let us try, Mother," Catherine had said.

And so they had begun. What had been a drawing room became a schoolroom into which timid children in tattered, fading clothes trooped willingly. In time they became perceptively less uncertain and more adventuresome. Often young laughter broke hesitantly, then more boisterously. Hearing it in his study, at endless hours on his history, Mr. Macaulay nodded approval. Catherine's mother, getting to know the children, responded warmly to the differing ones, laughing with them. But her special delight was in the teaching association with her daughter. How good it is for her, she thought. She is blooming again, more alluringly than at sixteen. Tom Kemris will come back this summer, and he will see . . .

As the children found their seats, Catherine murmured, "I shall miss all this in Dublin." Would this morning really be the last time she would hold open the door for the children and see the apple tree tremble in its pink spring beauty? How would her mother manage the school without her? She would miss her mother, miss George, miss them all. Ah, but there would be no time for regretting what she had known. In the mornings, soon now, there would be Hugh. Time had seemed to stand still, but day by day, it had been moving along. Four years of waiting, hoping, and teaching had passed. This very afternoon George would be driving her to Dublin to meet Hugh and to look for the rooms where she and Hugh would live together.

The children found their chairs with no more than the usual fuss and stood waiting. The silence stopped Catherine's wandering thoughts and signaled her to start the day. "Good morning."

"Good morning, Miss Macaulay."

"You may sit down."

Catherine waited for the noise of scraping furniture to subside. "Did any of you notice anything in particular as you came into the house this morning? Yes, Michael?"

"Johnny had mud on his boots."

Catherine turned aside to conquer her need to laugh. "John," she said, turning back, "please go outside and clean your boots. Is that *all* anyone noticed? Yes, Steven?"

"You were shmiling—"

Catherine waited pointedly.

"I mean *smiling.*"

"Did any of you notice something to make me smile? Did you, John, as you went out just now to clean your boots?"

"The apple tree is all pink and pretty as the divil."

"Oh, the apple tree," the children chanted.

But Catherine's upraised hand protested. "What did you say, John?"

Shamefaced, he confessed, "I said divil."

"And what should you have said?"

"I should not have said it."

"Probably not. But I am told—though I have never seen him, praise be!—that there is such a character. How do we pronounce his name, if use it we must?"

"Devil," one of the children prompted.

"Devil," Johnny repeated.

"Say it all together," Catherine urged.

Delighted at the freedom to do so, the class shrieked as one, "Devil!"

"That," Catherine observed with humor, "was enough to bring him right into this room. Or, at the very least, to blow the blossoms off the apple tree. She picked up a book. "We shall start this morning with our reading. But first, just to make sure that we are in tune with the spring and with one another, we shall sing. Mark, it is your turn to choose the song."

"Lave us sing—"

Catherine's imperious hand cut him off.

"Let us," Mark amended, "sing *Garry Owen*."

Through the mixed clapping and groans, Catherine sat down at the ancient harpsichord, which might long since have been sold except that no purchaser could ever be found, and struck an opening chord. The music released her. While the children sang and she played, her thoughts flew to Hugh.

'Twill be a treat to meet him in Dublin later today, she mused. There they were their true selves, no longer their parents' children. Though loathful about Kate's leaving the nest, her father's silence gave consent. He had always been fond of Hugh, finding in him something of himself and perhaps, Catherine guessed, also something that he lacked and recognized as desirable. True, her mother's silence was of a disparate kind and managed somehow to keep Tom Kemris among them, though for many years he had been with his family in London.

Some of the children called for *Garry Owen* again, and Catherine began once more.

What was behind her mother's strong preference for Tom over Hugh? His family's position? But how had they gotten their position? Tom's grandfather had apostatized, accepted money and a title which both their own family and Hugh's had disdained—and voted for Union. When Hugh was young, his father, Christopher Condon, had done well enough in the roofing business. He knew how to estimate and cut slate and to make a handsome durable roof. Yet with the passing of time and the continuing failure of Chapelizod incomes, few could afford a new slate roof. At best, those who had them managed their repair. "It is the will of God," the Condons concluded with a sigh.

But there was still the ancient skill of thatching, and Mr. Condon had turned to this. Whenever he drove through the countryside, he glanced with pride that was like a salute at houses whose roofs he had thatched. But a really fine thatched roof proved too time-consuming and expensive. And once again, it was "the will of God." In their acceptance, they were like many others in Ireland. The fight was finished; they had lost. There was little more to do. The Condons would farm their small acreage and look to Hugh.

In this, Catherine considered, they were unlike her family. Perhaps this was what her mother opposed. Her parents continued the struggle. Her father, always dressed neatly, and never doubting that his history would be published in time, went every day in the pale early morning to his study. The rents were poor; the business yielded little. No matter. He had his work to do. And her mother, she might admit mounting difficulties and deplore them, but there was always a way to outwit misfortune, a way to win. She had yet to become acquainted with defeat. It almost seemed to Catherine that a different God ruled the lives of the Condons from the God who ruled theirs. One God sanctioned humble surrender, the other defiant carrying on.

Would Hugh become like his parents? Catherine

shook her head. No sign of this showed. He was fighting today. Perhaps right now he was bravely accosting Mr. Eldon and saying, as he had planned, "Mr. Eldon, I have waited a month to talk to you . . ."

Catherine came to the end of *Garry Owen,* moved her hands, moist with concern for Hugh, over her knees, stood, and faced the children. She had to wait only till the afternoon to know what Mr. Eldon had answered.

The row of cloud-colored stone houses fronting Chapelizod's thoroughfare turned their high narrow backs on the Liffey to dream through the afternoon of a village history that went back to La Belle Izod, daughter of Ireland's eleventh-century King Aongus. The taunting spring sun came and went, and a wind with the smell of the ocean blew now and again from the river. George, seventeen, a youth bent now on being a man, brought around the jaunting car—alas, no longer the bright red it had once been. In an instant a coral-tinted door, like a streak of sunrise, flew open, and Catherine, in a high-waisted dress of checked blue, ran out and sprang into the seat across from her brother.

"Let us be off," she urged, "or there will be still more to remember." Sure enough, their mother and father came hurrying outside also. George lifted the whip but Catherine caught his arm. "No, wait. I shall go see." She jumped to the ground to meet her parents as they came toward her. Once more it was, "Yes, we shall remember. Adieu. Adieu. God go with you," and final parting hugs before she climbed back to her place across from her brother.

George whipped the little trotter, and she jolted the car into motion. Catherine blew a kiss to each parent. As always, they would watch them out of sight. The hoofbeats of the horse interrupted Chapelizod's dream. Curtains in front windows parted, and faces peered out. Soon, though, for the listeners, the sound of trotting faded, curtains swished to, and Chapelizod dreamed again.

Sitting opposite George, seeing the graceful lift of his wrists over the reins, the flood of warm color absorbing the few leftover freckles on his nose, and the sweet curve of his mouth in repose, Catherine gave herself up to the rhythmic sounds of the little horse on the country road and the onward movement of the car. There would not be many more such trips if her plans to marry Hugh Condon and to settle in Dublin carried through.

It was a year ago that marriage had begun to seem possible. Though for much longer than that the hope had lain in their minds and risen like an ache in their bodies through their parting caresses. Last spring Hugh had first had the idea of projecting into the future the figures which revealed the distillery company's financial condition during the present and past several years. Cautiously, he had confided his plan to Mr. Eldon. As Hugh anticipated, Mr. Eldon had listened doubtfully, but bit by bit his wariness yielded to Hugh's hardheaded thinking and fervor. In the end, Eldon caught his underlip in a bite, pondering what preferment such a showing might bring to him, and twin needlepoints of light danced in his eyes.

"Go ahead, Hugh," he had said. "You work it out. Let me see the proposal in writing. Then, for a year, we shall test your projections. See how they match current monthly figures. If your projections prove accurate, I'll see that your work is made worth your while."

That evening Catherine had paused in her walk with Hugh along the Liffey. "What does that mean, 'worth your while'?" She had lifted her face to his, and he had noticed how the pain of waiting had sharpened Catherine's earlier prettiness to a subtler sensitiveness.

"It means that we can plan to marry next spring."

"Ah!" she had cried, yielding to a kiss in which

desire stirred deeply, while Hugh pressed her to him so hard that she felt herself one with him.

For Catherine that spring had been a glorious one. The sky had taken on more beautiful colors. The sun had risen more brilliantly and set more gloriously. She had felt kindly toward everyone. So it had gone through summer and autumn and winter and into this second spring; the spring that promised fufillment.

"Heavens!" She turned abruptly to George. "Did we not have a time of it getting off?" What with Ellen Macaulay pressing upon her the letter to Jerry, currently at school in London because, since the closing of Mr. Whyte's Academy, there was no suitable school for Catholics in all Ireland. Jerry must have at least as good a start as Catherine and George had. And their father, never for a moment to be outdone by their mother, urging the box upon George for posting to Jerry. Then the warnings, blessed St. Patrick! the warnings—what to do, what not to do, as though she and George were but children still.

George chuckled amiably, his brown eyes lighting up warmly, as they continued to ride in silence. They were young, and the world, despite special difficulties due, as their parents said, to "the times," held out its wonders, ever fresh to each generation.

Suddenly Catherine exclaimed, "Goodness! Have I forgotten them?" She tore into her traveling bag.

Without a word George reined the horse to a stop.

"I have forgotten them! Oh, no, they are here," Catherine sighed. "Are you not the kind one, always to be finding whatever I lose?"

"Speaking to me?" George asked.

"I was not. I was saying a small polite thanks to Saint Anthony. But I do thank you for stopping and I thank you again for keeping silent."

George smiled, and Catherine was sorry to see how resignation was lately edging into his singularly agreeable smile. "What did you think you were missing?"

"The whole point and purpose of our trip. The addresses. Jimmy brought them to class only this morning. Lucky for him he remembered, or his mother would have come herself and Jimmy would have caught it. The addresses are those of the family's Dublin friends with rooms to let. Jimmy's mother thought they might have just what Hugh and I want. Or, to put it closer to the truth, just what we likely can afford."

George made no reply. This was another habit he had lately come to, the habit of not speaking when he had nothing to say to the point. In this he differed from some Irish who would go on forever, straying from the subject ever farther and farther.

"Well, let us go," Catherine said, for George still held the horse. "Why are we waiting?"

But her brother kept the rein tight. "Does this spot remind you of something, Kate?"

"Should it?" She looked about at the running Liffey and the weeds and rushes bent by the wind along its banks. As she glanced at George a skylark sang high above the river and trees.

"Oh, to be sure. The day we ran away to Dublin. We got this far when a skylark sang—"

"You said it was telling us to go home."

Catherine laughed. "Did I, now? Well, maybe it was a good thing that we went."

George relaxed his hold on the leather straps, and as the horse trotted forward, the minds of sister and brother recalled their return that day. Their mother had come forward to meet them, her hair then had been a dark warm brown like George's.

"How, may I ask, did you find the city of Dublin?"

It was almost as though she had wanted to run away with them, Catherine thought.

The swiftly trotting horse rounded a sharp turn, causing the light car to lean dangerously to the left wheel, almost turning it over.

"Do let us watch it!" Catherine said sharply. "Get us to Dublin alive."

George abruptly stopped the horse. "Is it that you would like to take the reins?"

"If need be, I can, as you know well. Let us get on. Only watch the turns."

George drove on, but Catherine regretted disturbing the sweet peace there had been between them. "It is not as though you are not one of the county's finest drivers," she offered. "Let us say even the finest."

"Let my rating be as it may. There are other matters that concern me more at this time."

"And what might they be?"

"They are matters that also worry our mother."

Catherine laughed. "Oh, despite some small differences, 'tis Irish you are, George, after all, with your wanting to make a deep mystery of quite usual things."

"Our mother does not find these, as you say, 'quite usual things.'"

Again, this time in the stretch where poplars, brought years before from Lombardy, lined the road like sentinels, George reined in the trotter, drew in his breath, and pressed his lips together. "Is it the case, Kate," he said finally, "that it is all finished between you and Tom Kemris?"

The poplars swayed with the wind like a metronome pendulum: tick-tock, tick-tock. The sound grew louder and clearer, and Catherine, six years old, was struggling through a duet with Tommy Kemris at the harpsichord in his family's drawing room. Pleased, Tommy's mother sat by. But with the years, her pleasure had changed to reserve as the childhood attachment ripened into first love.

George glanced at Catherine keenly, caught her remote look, and let the horse move slowly on. "Do you remember the time I played Father Aherne and married you and Tom in church?"

"I do. You were nine, and I can still see you there on the altar with the opened prayer book, scared to death that Father Aherne would come in and discover us. Tom had brought me roses from their greenhouse . . . The week after, his parents took him out of Mr. Whyte's Academy and sent him to London to school." Catherine looked at George steadily to let the truth sink in.

"You mean you saw a connection?"

"How could I not? After that, when home in the summer, Tom came like a fugitive from his parents. So I put a stop to his coming. George, it is the ancient feud—Protestant against Catholic, English against Irish. We may be neighborly, our children may play, but still, even though the law against intermarriage has long since been repealed, we must not marry."

"But our parents do not feel so."

"No. But they would expect a Catholic marriage and a promise that Tom would rear our children as Catholics. Perhaps the Kemrises took a longer look ahead."

"Then for you it has been long finished?"

"Yes," Catherine answered at last.

"Perhaps for you, but I think not for Tom . . ."

Catherine looked at him with surprise.

"We keep in touch, Tom and I. In close touch. His feeling for you hasn't changed. He is of age now and may do as he pleases. He is coming home this summer—"

"'Twill be to no purpose so far as he and I are concerned. All that is long finished. 'Twas part of our childhood days and is now but a memory, no more . . . Is that what our mother is wanting to know?"

"It is."

"Does she think I would be marrying Hugh Condon if it were not long over between me and Tom?"

Again George paused. "I judge she wishes it were the other way 'round."

To be sure, Catherine thought, I have known this all along. But hearing it put into words, something within her—well, what would it be but anger?—exploded. "Then I judge that that is the English in her."

"There is English in you, too, Kate."

"Perhaps there is just a drop in you? Since you have so kindly told me our mother's concern about me, I shall return the compliment and tell you she wishes that drop would keep you home at night and out of some possible trouble."

George was silent, reflecting.

But Catherine persisted. " 'Twas only last night I heard her say to Father, 'What is it, do you suppose, is keeping our George out late at night? You do not think, do you, that he has joined the Ribbon Men?' "

"What did Father say?"

He had said, quoting the Bible, "Sufficient unto the day is the evil thereof." But Catherine did not repeat this to her brother. He would only think it funny and laugh at their father's typical answer.

Getting nothing further from his sister, George tossed a covert glance at her. What did they know? What did Kate know? Dare he trust her? But the voice of their leader at the last meeting of the Ribbon Men roared in his ears like the North and South Bulls as the waves rushed over the sounds in Dublin Bay. "Talk to no one!" he had thundered. "No one! Not your sweetheart. Not your wife. Not your brother or sister." Perhaps he had erred already in mentioning that he was in touch with Tom Kemris. Still, George could not refrain from saying, "I always liked Tom. He and I—well, though he was more English than Irish, he and I saw the same way about things."

"And you and Hugh do not?"

"Hugh does not care about Ireland as I do . . . as Tom also cares."

"Hugh cares as our father cares—" Catherine stopped. For that was not quite true. Hugh did not have a historian's perspective. That made a vast difference in how her father perceived Ireland's conflict with England. Somehow, it also lifted him out of the conflict. He moved in a realm above it, considering causes, relating them to causes in yet earlier conflicts between ancient nations, working with unremitting industry and discipline despite the fact that his manuscript went unpublished. Due, he would say, "to extenuating circumstances." English publishers did not share his viewpoint, and there were none in Ireland who could afford to publish work such as his.

And yet in a sense, Catherine thought, Hugh did care as her father did. "Like Father," she went on to George, "Hugh hopes it will not come to yet another fight."

"And if it does?"

"No matter. He will not leave me to fight. We shall be married and living in Dublin. That is, we shall be if all goes well when Hugh talks today to Mr. Eldon."

"Suppose it goes other than well?"

"Why should it? For twelve months Hugh has tested out his projections—long months they have been—and they are no less dependable than he promised."

"Mr. Eldon may have reasons of his own for not seeing them as Hugh does."

Catherine did not answer, for now, through the late afternoon's diffused light, the Dublin Mountains stood suddenly close.

"Glory be!" she cried. "How is it that they are forever the same and yet always different?"

A truce fell like shared love between her and George. They were silent going through Phoenix Park, rounding the North Circular Drive, and coming down the road that led to Sackville Street.

"Have you no answer for Mother other than the harsh one you gave?"

"Aye," Catherine said gently, her anger having bubbled down, "I have an answer. You may quote to her what she has often quoted to me: 'Footfalls echo in the memory/Down the passage which we did not take/Toward the door we never opened . . .'"

When they passed Nelson's Pillar, George brought the trotter to a walk. Looking up at the General Post Office, Catherine said, "I wonder, what will you be doing this evening after you have mailed Jerry his letter and package?"

But there was no time for an answer, for they both saw Hugh at once waiting for Catherine on Carlisle

Bridge, and her brother already was tossing the reins to him. Once on the ground, George recovered the straps and let Hugh help Catherine down.

"Good luck to the two of you," George said affably. Then, clowning in a way that disguised his careful and good sense of balance, he jumped back up to the driving seat. Watching him, Catherine felt that his cheerfulness was a disguise. Did it not perhaps also cover a man who, alone among those closest to him, walks precariously in two opposed worlds?

"Please go with him, Saint Patrick," she prayed, and lifted her face to Hugh for his kiss.

Hugh's kiss was brief and did not stir her. Catherine searched his deep-set hazel eyes. But his eyes, gray now like the moist twilight Dublin sky, evaded her. Instead of asking if she would like to go at once to look for their rooms, he said, "Let us go walk on the Custom House Quay."

Down below on the quay with Hugh, and yet feeling more alone than if he had not been there, she leaned with him on the parapet, her elbows on the balustrade, her chin in her cupped hands, and gazed across the Liffey at Trinity College and to the bank that had once been the House of Lords. My English grandmother's father sat in that House of Lords when it *was* the House of Lords, Catherine recalled. Hugh's mother was fond of remembering that Hugh's grandfather's father, though Irish, had also sat in that House of Lords. They might have sat there at the same time, faced the same problems, but Catherine knew they would not have confronted them together, but each from his own differing point of view, each sure the other was wrong.

Well, had Hugh met with Mr. Eldon? And what had he said? Catherine tossed her head impatiently. How long must she wait? The muscles were flexing in her right foot, her "stamping foot," her grandmother used to call it when Catherine was little. Nothing in

Hugh's eyes or facial expression or in the bearing of his long-limbed rangy body gave a clue.

Farther up the Liffey, a North Atlantic packet, *Queen Adelaide,* outward-bound for America with emigrant passengers, stood with sails set, awaiting towing down the river and into Dublin Bay. No wind stirred her sails to suggest approaching departure and to call for the final farewells between those leaving and those remaining who stood on the opposite quay. It was as though time had stopped. As though both these groups were becalmed in some timeless place, freed from their troubled pasts and uncertain futures.

How different their setting out for America was from the blithe going forth she had imagined for Hugh and herself the day they had gone to the fair, when she was sixteen. These people aboard the *Queen Adelaide,* and the many others like them, were the hapless ones. They were real to her—as real as the families of the children she taught—and she pitied them. For the first time, understanding dawned as to how their kind felt toward people like the Kemrises who had apostatized and been well rewarded for doing so. Cleavages ran deep between the two kinds of Irish, deep as those between the English and the Irish. And was it so that George was now taking his stand with the luckless ones and perhaps drawing Tom Kemris with him into the Ribbon Men?

Until George, no one from her family had taken a stand against those who had gone the way of the Kemrises. It was cause for self-esteem that her mother's father had refused to convert at the cost of a title and fortune. Hugh's grandfather had also made the choice "to keep the faith." And she and Hugh had agreed they were proud of them. But now, aware of those departing in steerage and those saddened by their going, Catherine was less sure of her former approval. The faith had come down to these unfortunates as well, and they would have to rely upon it to see them through unknown distresses. Would it not have been better for them if . . . But that was a thought she dared not allow. Still, did not each class believe in its own way? These people? The Kemrises? And her family somewhat differently from both? Was not religion similiar to a dye, which various kinds of cloth took differently?

Then Catherine saw the tug. "Oh, look!" she exclaimed, pulling at Hugh's sleeve. "*Queen Adelaide* is beginning to move!"

The sailing ship was wrenched out of the timelessness in which she had been moored, returning Catherine to the present. The awareness of past and future was made evident by the wailing voices which floated from the *Queen Adelaide* to the quay and back again to the vessel. English soldiers, clubs in hand, were moving among the relatives and friends still on land. At times like this, riots threatened. Catherine wondered where George might be this evening in Dublin. A chill, such as evening brings sometimes, or like the change from summer to autumn, went through her. She stood transfixed beside Hugh as the *Queen Adelaide,* responding to the tug's impulses, with sails set for the Atlantic winds, glided in white beauty past Dublin's gray evening sky to the haunting accompaniment of voices crying, "Goodbye . . . Goodbye . . ."

"It is a strange thing altogether to be Irish," Catherine observed, regretting her earlier disavowal of her grandfather's choice. She did not bother to hide from Hugh the tears rinsing her cheeks. "I sometimes think you know *only* what you feel, and I ask myself, 'How can people who do not feel know anything at all?' "

Hugh put his arm about Catherine and wiped away her tears with his finger.

"Tell me whatever it is," she said. "Did you speak to him?"

"I did, Kate. He was making a sort of tour this morning, and when he came to where I was standing over my account books, I spoke up to him—"

"You had every right—"

"I had—"

"Did he appear to know you had?"

Hugh opened his hands to the question. "There is in him that which permits him to admit only what suits his own purposes. To be sure, I suppose there is a little of it in us all. In any case, I spoke up. I said, as we agreed last night I would, Mr. Eldon, I have been testing my projections for a year, and I have waited a month to talk to you—"

"Yes, Hugh?"

"And he said, 'You are talking to me now, are you not?' "

Catherine gasped. "The nerve of him, and you having done all you did!"

"Do you imagine I did not think of that, Kate? I could feel the blood hot in my face. There were those around who were watching and some who were wishing I might be losing my temper. He may have feared so, too. In any case—not at all in the way he spoke to me while I was working out the accounting system for him—he said, 'Come to see me at four o'clock.' With that, his own face turned bright red, and he walked away."

"Buttoning up his coat, no doubt, as he does," Catherine said, parading back and forth a bit and mimicking him with distaste. Suddenly she stopped. Moving as imperturbably as cause does to effect, the *Queen Adelaide* had come to where Hugh and Catherine stood on the Custom House Quay, and the solemn majesty of her set sails seemed to fall like a judgment on Catherine's mockery.

"My grandmother used to say I would be punished for making fun of my neighbor," Catherine recalled.

"Do you think your grandmother spoke the truth?"

Catherine laughed. "Indeed I do, with the ship's shadow upon me. But just let the *Queen Adelaide* go on her way, and I shall tell you what I really think. It was the English in her that caused her to see harm in such things, the same English that stopped her from immediately catching the point of our Irish jokes. To be fair, though, she would laugh minutes later, and then we would also. George would say that everything we used was made to do twice the intended service and that even our jokes must serve for two laughs.

"But tell me, did you go at four o'clock to see him?"

"I did."

"Perhaps he had had enough time to cool down a bit?"

"He had, though he did not invite me to sit down as when we were working together. He let me stand—"

"While you stood, did he tell you whom he dined with last night and mention someone with a title he looks to go shooting with?"

"Aye. He spoke of the Earl of Meath. He showed me his picture seated backward in his chair. But I said no word in reply and came to the point. 'Mr. Eldon,' I said, 'the new accounting system I worked out with your help'—I showed him that courtesy—"

"But you did it alone!"

"It is a manner of speaking, Kate. It is a thing men understand—"

"Then it must be a thing that *only* men understand!"

"Will you let me tell you my story?"

"Have I not been trying this past hour to get you to do so, and you going out by the back door every time I come in by the front one?"

"It is you who keeps coming in by the side doors. I never knew a house with so many—"

"Get on, Hugh. Get on. For the love of Saint Patrick, get on!"

"I said, 'I have tested out our accounting system for twelve months, and long months they have been. It is no less dependable than I promised—' "

"What did he say?" Drained of all color, Catherine's face was as white as the sails of *Queen Adelaide,* advancing from the Liffey's widening mouth into Dublin Bay, or as the sickle moon rising over the

bay like a beckoning finger, calling the vessel's emigrant passengers to America. *"What did he say, Hugh?"*

"He half turned his head, and without really looking up, he said, 'Your Irish co-workers will not thank you for your accounting system. For it tells me I am going to have to let half of them go. I do not like it. The forecasters tell us that 1835 will repeat the 1822 and 1831 famines."

"Why would he say a cruel thing like that?"

Hugh lowered his head. "It was cruel and unjust, yet in what he said there is also truth. The distilling business is shrinking. Because of Father Matthew, more and more men are taking the pledge. My accounting exposed the way things are."

"Is it not a good thing to know the truth?"

"For the company, but not for the men. Things might have drifted on for another year, two years, even three . . ."

"Whyever did you develop this system, Hugh? Is it a thing the devil put in your head to do?"

"No, Kate, it is a thing I thought of myself."

"Did you not foresee what the result might be?"

"I foresaw clearly that it would disclose the company's true condition, but I did not know then what that condition would be."

"Did you not guess that it might turn out as it has?"

"I did, but I had looked at it from the company's point of view and my own. Do you think I have been happy to wait another year and then another to marry you? I told myself that a company was doing its workers no favor if in the end it must fail. I did not ask myself then what the workers would wish. That is what I am asking myself now, and I know the answer."

"Can you be sure?"

"I can, Kate. I know they would rather stay on and wait out the company's failure. It is what I prefer, too, since I am in the same boat as they."

"You mean—" Catherine's hands flew to her mouth and her eyes widened with disbelief.

"Instead of an increase in pay, I shall be out of work, too. He must have someone to blame for letting them go. He can blame me."

In a small, quiet voice, as though from another world, Catherine asked, "Why does he do this to you?"

"He does what he does because he cannot help preferring his advancement to all else. With those above him, he will profit by my work, and I shall be made to take the blame with the workers, who otherwise might turn against him. And yet where there was no conflict between our interests, I believe he would do me a favor if he could. For I saw that he suffered in telling me what he did. I saw other things besides."

"Glory be to God! What more was there to see, Hugh?"

"I saw that hell may not be the blazing fire and brimstone we were taught as children, but that it may be living with what we have done. When Eldon goes shooting with the Earl of Meath, he will take with him his own little hell."

"Well, then, may there be a little old-fashioned fire and brimstone, too."

No answering laugh came from Hugh, and looking into his quiet face, Catherine saw the hopelessness she had seen in other Irish faces like the stamp of the race. Could they do this to Hugh? So rob him of hope that he could not stand before her with pride? But even as she looked, she saw something like a conviction tighten in Hugh's face.

"What will we do?"

"I know what I will do," he said, and he nodded at the *Queen Adelaide* disappearing in the nighttime mists of Dublin Bay.

Catherine followed his nod to the ship and then to the vast dark sky. As she looked, the sickle moon lengthened and reached down to them.

"You mean," she whispered, "America?"

Chapter 3

"AT LAST he is off!" Ellen Macaulay said. Through the dining-room windows she and Catherine watched until Jerry and the little sidecar disappeared around the curve of the road leading to the Kemris estate. The Kemrises had kindly brought Jerry back with them from school in London, and Ellen Macaulay was sending a note of thanks by Jerry's hand to Lady Kemris. Impulsively, she turned from the windows and the morning sun that fell on her geranium plants on the window seat below. A delicate pink flush suffused her pale cheeks.

"I wonder, Kate, did Tom return with the family?"

At the question, a fence, tall and divisive, went up in Catherine's mind between her mother and herself. More than a month had passed since the *Queen Adelaide* sailed, and her marriage to Hugh was timed to coincide with the date, another month ahead, when the *Independence* would sail. Already she and her mother had gone to Dublin and bought linen, lace, and ribbon. They had also engaged Miss Molly to come to the house to mend and lengthen Catherine's grandmother's wedding dress and to make new underclothing that must last who knew how long in America. Today they were to start the cake, rich with fruit and nuts, which must age not less than a month. Yet here was her mother, inquiring with undisguised, pointed interest about Tom.

"What if he has?" Catherine asked coolly.

Hope burned determinedly in her mother's fading eyes, and she persisted. "You played together so happily when you were children. Your laughter and his would come through this window to me—oh, look!" she interrupted herself. "Here is a bud!" She bent and caught between her thumb and middle finger the promise of a lovely salmon-colored flower.

Catherine disregarded the discovery. "We are no longer children, Mother."

"No, I suppose not. And yet, I cannot help wishing that we might go on in the usual way, Kate, enjoying the summer and looking toward teaching the children again in the autumn—"

"This autumn. and next, and for how many autumns afterward?"

Her mother sighed. "I know it cannot be. But there will be such an emptiness when you go. 'Whatever will the place be like.' your father said last night, 'without Kate's merry laugh?' "

"I know." Catherine yielded. If only her marrying were not taking her to America. The truth was that, as the time for the sailing of the *Independence* grew nearer, she herself shrank apprehensively from this adventure into the fearsome unknown. One evening at his home, Hugh had suggested that perhaps he should go on ahead and she should follow later.

There was no question about his going. None whatsoever. In the month since his talk with Mr. Eldon, the distillery employees had been let go week after week, and Hugh's responsibility for their loss of work was being ever more widely accepted. " 'Twas well," some said. "Hugh Condon was heading out for America. Otherwise . . ."

That "otherwise . . ." with all it implied, had been suggested to the Condons, and Hugh's mother, Josie Condon, managed to convey the threat to Catherine. " 'Tis go now he must, Kate, whether he wills it or no."

Catherine had seen with surprise that where Hugh was concerned, the "will of God" did not enter Josie Condon's speculations or those of her husband. From boyhood on, Hugh had ever enjoyed the right to choose his way.

"Aye," he had said, " 'tis certain I shall go. Perhaps 'twould be better were I to go ahead and Kate to follow later."

His mother had shaken her head. " 'Twas for Kate and the hope of marrying that you did this sorry study for the distillery, and I think Kate is the girl who will be wanting to go with you."

"I know," Catherine repeated now to her mother. Reassuringly, with her family she came first, as Hugh did with his. Still, it was best not to tell all she knew about Hugh's need to clear out. 'Twould only add to their anxiety. She fell silent.

Suddenly, the sound of the little trotter pulling the sidecar around the bend broke into the quiet, and looking out the window, they saw that Jerry had George and Tom with him.

"Oh, Kate!" Ellen Macaulay cried.

Somehow the salmon bud had gotten between Catherine's fingers instead of her mother's and snapped. "Never mind," her mother laughed gaily at Catherine's regretful extending of the bud. "Just put it in water. 'Twill do as well there."

Jerry tossed the reins over the hitching post, and the trio of young men started toward the house.

"How like old times," Mrs. Macaulay said happily. and hurried to the door.

"Why, Tom! How handsome you have grown!" she exclaimed, kissing him.

In her turn welcoming Tom with a kiss, Catherine saw with surprise that he did indeed appear a younger, slimmer version of his tall, distinguished father. Partly, to be sure, the resemblance lay in Tom's having assumed his father's manner, well-tailored country tweeds, and fashionable cut of his long, soft brown hair. But the expression which streamed from his light brown eyes was Tom's own and went back to his boyhood. What was it, Catherine questioned, George had said on their drive to Dublin that evil day? "Perhaps for you it has been long finished, but I think not for Tom."

"But nay," Tom gallantly answered Catherine's mother, "'tis not I but Kate whom time has smiled upon." Admiringly, he held her at arm's length and then pulled her to him again. "What a long time it has been, Kate."

"A long time indeed," Catherine's mother agreed as Catherine freed herself from Tom's warm embrace. "Would you not like a cup of tea?"

"Aye, if the soda bread I remember so well goes with the tea."

They trooped merrily into the dining room, and Ellen Macaulay made and poured tea, talking animately all the while.

"Tom, do tell us all about London and what you have seen and what you have done."

"Nay, I would rather learn whatever has been going on here in my absence," he said with a quick glance at Catherine. George's dark, expressive eyes dropped.

The talk turned inevitably to the frolicsome past they had shared as children, to the sometimes forbidden escapades they had ventured upon, to the long horseback rides they had taken through the country on the well-groomed Kemris animals, to the soda-bread sandwiches they had devoured on the banks of the Liffey, while their tethered mounts cropped the grass, and the three of them had chatted on and on through the leisured summer afternoons. Of what had they talked? As to that, with both sets of parents, they had been secretive. And they fell silent now.

Jerry broke into the quiet. "If I may be excused?" he asked, and color rose with embarrassment to his face.

"But why, Jerry? . . . Oh, to be sure," his mother said. "Because of the age you were then, you feel left out of these memories."

"No, Mother, 'tis not that. 'Tis just that I promised Harriet I would deliver George and Tom and return."

"A little young for that, are you not?" George inquired.

Blushing more deeply, Jerry took off.

"No younger than I was," Tom interjected, "when I first fell in love . . ." His eyes lifted to Kate and then moved to her mother.

Following his glance, Catherine saw hope burn determinedly in her mother's eyes, deepening them to their younger blue. With Tom's reappearance at this late hour, her mother actually looked for a last-minute, story-book twist to events. It was as if at her mother's bidding she accepted Tom's suggestion that they go together once again to explore the banks of the Liffey.

It was like being a child again, sitting there with Tom on the riverbank, and all the joy and well-being of those early days came washing back.

"Old rivers never change."

"Nothing real changes," Tom replied, moving closer.

Uncertain for a moment, Catherine looked at him questioningly. "What is real, what changeful?"

As if in answer, for the second time today Catherine saw Tom's boyhood delight in her stream invincibly from his eyes. It was here they had first kissed uncertainly. The early memories she had thought faded came back clear and bright. Here was the little boy she had fought during the harpsichord practice, and here was the older boy saying, "I do," in the marriage ceremony George was conducting. She had not dreamed, after the passing of so many years, he would come back, loving her still, wanting her for his wife. But unmistakably it was so. His enduring feeling recharged all, and they were children again together, loving each other.

She could not deny that there was pleasure for her in the recovery of their early life, a recovery that made those days more real than the recent ones full of Hugh's struggle, failure, and danger, and certainly more real than the unknowable future in America. Until now she had forgotten so much—forgotten awakening carefree in the summer morning, with no other thought than to run off with George and Tom, sometimes wickedly running from Tom's cousin Harriet and even—oh shame!—from little Jerry. How she took for granted that she was the favorite of the boys, alternately teasing them, sure each would forgive. She had merely to laugh to unite them in their love for her.

Tom's voice broke through her memories. "You remember those long talks we had here?"

"Aye, I remember."

"I never told my parents what we spoke of."

"Nor did we."

That talk was alive again, full of their young sympathy for the impoverished Irish they passed on their rides through the country; full, too, of their indignant judgment of the English and of their resolve to change Irish history.

"But your family has shared in that guilt," George had said one day.

Tom had dropped his eyes. "That is so."

Then, with a bitterly regretful glance at the cropping horse that was his for the day, George had said, "I can no longer ride your horses."

Tom had looked up, startled at so drastic an expression of disapproval, but ever George's loyal follower, had said, "Nor will I."

"Remember when we forswore riding our horses?" Tom was asking now.

"Indeed I do. I sorely missed our rides."

"When you feel as we do, George and I, you must be prepared to miss more than riding . . . You will marry me, Kate, will you not? For I am now on your side all the way. Forget about Hugh—George has told me—and this mad voyage to America. Do not leave us now. Stay here with us who love you well. Times will change. George and I—"

Catherine saw it was coming—what they, if they

had joined the Ribbon Men, were sworn not to tell—
and she pressed her finger against Tom's too ready
lips. One break in the chain might lead to another.
Ah, there was the hazard. Once taken, the step was
irreparable, and secrecy was sternly enforced. Tom's
family might get him to London, but who would save
George?

Resisting her attempted control, Tom got to his
feet and stood boldly before her. " 'Tis of age I am
now, Kate!" he cried. "Of age. No longer must I do
my parents' bidding. 'Tom, do this! Tom, you must
not!' " he mimicked his mother. "I am on your side,
Kate, the Irish side, the side my grandfather betrayed
and I shall redeem."

"But, Tom," Catherine said, weeping, as she also
got up, "there is no *one* Irish side. Even in our family
we are divided. My parents are more with yours than
with George."

"Then they are wrong, and they shall see, as my
father and mother shall see. I am with George and
against them. I am of age and I do as I please."

It was that last statement which gave him away, dis-
closing him to Catherine, despite his legal manhood,
as a little boy still, defying his parents, bent on having
his will. He was a child in childhood's world and strik-
ing out against the frustrations surrounding him. He
had taken her back to that world and she had loved
being there, but she could not linger longer with him.
Already she had stepped, partly by choice, partly—she
could not deny—by circumstance, into another, real
world, Hugh's world. That step was taking her from
all those she loved except Hugh. Her destiny and his
were as irreversible as George's and Tom's; different
but equally final. They would stay to fight, and she
and Hugh would marry and sail together aboard the
Independence.

"Ah, Tom," she said gently from her reluctant
adulthood, "I shall take with me to America the
children we were and the delight we shared, and I
shall try to give these children as playmates to my

own. They will never have any two better. And now
goodbye." She reached up and caressed him, and it
was long before she forgot—and perhaps she never
wholly did—the way his lips trembled like a small
boy's beneath that parting kiss.

"Then is it so, Kate," George asked, "that you have
said no to Tom and are resolved to go with Hugh to
America?"

They had come the next morning into the old book
room where so frequently as children they had been
together, each often reading silently and yet savoring
the other's presence.

"Aye," Catherine said, "though 'tis sorry I am to
leave you . . . and sorry I am for our mother." She
paused, regretting yesterday's scene on her return
from the Liffey.

"Ah, Kate," her mother had said, her cheeks
flushed that pretty pink and her eyes that young deep
blue. "I knew Tom would return."

"So he has, but it does not alter my plans."

"I do not understand."

"Because you do not want to," Catherine had responded with annoyance. "You have always preferred
Tom to Hugh. Why? Because marrying Tom would
keep me here, close by, in Chapelizod and maybe
in London. No farther than that. And because marrying Hugh takes me out of reach to America. Or is it
that you see my marrying Tom a step up and marrying Hugh a step down? Or is it your mother's English
in you turning, after all, from the Irish? I'm thinking
it is probably a little of everything. But whatever, it is
Hugh whom I am marrying and America we will be
going to."

"It is just that I—your happiness means more to me
than my own."

Catherine had hugged her mother warmly.

"Well, cannot we both be happy?"

"Aye," her mother had said. "We shall be."

Now Catherine asked her brother, "She has told you?"

He nodded. "And sorry we all are to see you go."

" 'Tis the decision Hugh made over a month ago."

"I am not quarreling as to Hugh's going. 'Tis go now he must—" George stopped, cautious, Catherine speculated, lest from his new, secret knowledge of his Ribbon Men membership he reveal what he ought not.

So, Catherine thought, the rumors that trouble Hugh's parents are not surface talk; they run deep.

"As to your going, Kate," George went on, " 'tis another question altogether."

"It is really one and the same, George. If Hugh goes, so do I."

They were both mute, caught inescapably in Ireland's old, unresolvable problem that so long had paralyzed their father and mother; brother and sister each seeking a separate way out. Catherine glanced at the ancient blunderbuss above the bookshelves. Once, when he was little, she had handed it to George, let him finger it. He followed her glance, and a faint shudder passed through him. Then, with the bravado of one who walks in two worlds, each denying the other, he said, "Well, I must be off to collect the rents so as to buy a cabin for you for the crossing. Tom said he would come along. Good of him, is it not?"

"Aye," Catherine answered. " 'Tis good of you both, and sorry I am to cause you the trouble."

" 'Tis no trouble," George said, clowning in order to dissimulate his emotions as he started out. Unpredictably, he turned and gently kissed Catherine's lips. "Pray for me," he said softly.

Later that day, in the kitchen with her mother, Catherine jumped at the harsh sound George made by throwing the rents he had gotten on the table. Knowing, in view of the poverty of their tenants, how bitter an undertaking collecting the money was for George, and how necessary if Catherine was really to go, their mother said nothing. Because what George had done was for her, to help pay the fourteen pounds for a Class One cabin to New Orleans, Catherine turned away, also silent. But unluckily for all, Jerry, returning from an afternoon spent with Harriet came in just then, saw the little pile of money on the table, and asked, in the new manner of speaking he had learned at his London school, "Oh, I say, is that all?"

George's answer struck like a blow between Jerry's startled eyes. "Yes, damn the English in you. That is all!"

"Oh, George!" Ellen Macaulay cried. "It is from me he gets his English."

"Maybe a little more English is what we need. The trouble with the Irish—" Jerry started to say.

"Did you say *the* Irish?" Enraged, George towered over his brother. "Is that what you are learning at your English school?"

Their father came into the room just then and looked from one to the other as if he sympathized with each and could not take his stand with one or the other.

"Suppose that he does *not* come." Lawrence Macaulay spoke out of his own fresh frustration.

"Who does not come, Father?" they all asked, curiosity uniting them for the moment.

"Father Aherne. He begs, if the Kemrises come to the breakfast, that we excuse him."

"That's Josie Condon for you," his wife noted with swift perception of Hugh's mother's interference. "Trust her to start something like that."

In the end, all went peaceably. Standing with her father at the rear of the center aisle, Catherine watched Jerry take their mother to the family pew in the hallowed small church into which all Chapelizod crowded, and sit down beside her. Then she saw her pupils Michael and Daniel, in white surplices, step out of the sacristy. Father Aherne, in weathered black cassock, white surplice, and green stole, followed them

out and knelt briefly before the altar, his servers bob-
bing down to the left and the right of him. Then he and
the boys rose and faced the congregation.

With George as his best man, Hugh crossed the
church just below the altar railing. He was wearing
the morning coat and striped trousers his father had
been married in, and George was wearing *his* father's
wedding suit. They waited at the head of the aisle before the altar, which Madge Dolan and Jerry had
covered with wild pink roses, yellow primroses, and
purple bellflowers.

Was it not Tom Kemris but really Hugh Condon,
Ellen Macaulay asked herself, watching, who was to
marry Kate? What wild life was Hugh bearing her off
to in America as though she were fitted for no better? Only God knew if ever they would reach New
Orleans . . . Even assuming they did, when would
news of their arrival reach Chapelizod?

At a signal from Father Aherne, the children in the
rear began to sing a cappella "Ave Maria, stella
maris." Little Madge, the bridesmaid in bright yellow,
started somewhat self-consciously up the aisle. Following in her grandmother's wedding gown and veil
with her father, Catherine thought that, like the crescent moon on the Liffey that night, light fell like hope
within the church, brightening a pathway.

Father Aherne's face was as a stone into whose
carving had seeped all that his Irish forebears had endured from the conquering English. There were those
stories he had told, passed on by his mother about "the
bad century," when clergy were hunted down with
the offer of an award of five pounds for the head of a
priest or a wolf. Studying his face, Ellen Macaulay
could see no sign of the softening she sought that
might after all bring him to the breakfast. A pity Jerry
had seated the Kemrises so near to the front of the
church. But there, except for Tom, now back in
London, they sat, excommunicated and alien—Lord
and Lady Kemris and her niece, Harriet. Mrs.

Macaulay turned to Jerry, and her quick disapproving nod said, "Stop looking so pointedly at Harriet."

But Jerry was diverted, for Madge was now passing by. "Such a dear girl, Madge," Jerry's mother approved.

Catherine passed by with her father. When they reached the foot of the altar, he gave her to Hugh and returned to the pew where his wife sat with their youngest son. Ellen Macaulay moved over a little to make room for her husband, but her eyes were on her daughter. In her white bridal gown, her hair under the transparent veil aflame, did she not look like a tall lighted candle?

Hugh and Catherine walked up the steps to the altar. Beneath their feet, the ancient, long-unrepaired stairs creaked loudly through the hushed church. George and Madge followed, and the stairs creaked again.

In the voice that, despite the years at Maynooth Seminary, identified him as a County Clare man, Father Aherne began, "Hugh Condon, wilt thou take Catherine Macaulay . . ."

Her mother, watching tensely, decided, there are, after all, but three possible courses: escape to America —that is Hugh's choice; putting one's life on the line in the fight at home—that is George's, I now know; and—. She glanced across the aisle at the Condons. . . . And acceptance, like theirs. For the first time, the hitherto resourceful Ellen Macaulay shook hands with defeat. And, she conceded, turning toward and including her husband, like ours.

With her distraction, she had missed Hugh's response, and Father Aherne was continuing: "Catherine Macaulay, wilt thou take Hugh Condon for thy lawful husband . . ."

Catherine lifted her delicate face—like a flower, her grandmother had once said long ago—and in a touching voice that seemed to her mother to embrace the whole unknowable future, answered, "I do."

PART TWO

The Atlantic Crossing

(August–September 1835)

Chapter 4

THE CRY "Visitors ashore" cracked like a gunshot over the decks of the *Independence*. Automatically people started away from the relatives and friends they were seeing off and then, their eyes brightening with fear at being caught aboard the departing packet, ran hastily back for one more "Goodbye, God bless you!" before scuttling across the deck and down the gangplank.

Standing close to his sister and her husband on the forecastle, from which he could see beneath the small covering poop deck to the main deck aft, George Macaulay watched the others on board with shame. They scurried about like rats. But he would not say so aloud, not even to Kate and Hugh. They were Irishmen all, and it was only a short time ago, the night he had driven Kate to Dublin, that he had confirmed his secret and total commitment to the freedom of the last mother's son of them. Until that evening, he might have dropped out. Others had. But since then, he was in the movement all the way, to the end. Still, he wouldn't hurry servilely as these emigrants were doing. He would take his own bloody time. And no one was going to spoil this leavetaking for him. He turned, smiling, to Kate.

"Goodbye . . . Goodbye . . ." Once again between ship and dock, as on that fateful night when Catherine and Hugh had watched the *Queen Adelaide* sail, voices were wailing in counterpoint. But now Hugh and she, husband and wife since that morning, were among the departing, their families among those being left behind. Below on the dock, a little apart from the crowd and waiting for George to rejoin them, were her parents, Jerry, and Madge Dolan. Though neither they nor Hugh and she joined in the crying, it persisted like a bleeding deep within Catherine.

She turned from the starboard rail to Hugh. "Your parents at least are spared this."

Hugh's father and mother had remained so that the breakfast guests who lingered would not be without hosts. All had gone pleasantly in the end. Father Aherne had relented and come, and Hugh's mother, far from snubbing Lord and Lady Kemris, had made a special play at being cordial.

Catherine glanced again at the sundered little group below. Would they, would she, would Hugh, survive this parting? She looked to Hugh for reassurance. God bless us, she thought, and could not suppress a small inward laugh; he looks least likely of all to survive.

George, bearing himself like a man who gives rather than takes orders, still stood by.

"George," Catherine said, "had you not better go? Or is it after all"—her eyes warmed with love and humor—"that you are crossing with us?"

George glanced from his sister to the grieving emigrants now crowding against the starboard railing of the main deck aft. "I am thinking without me the *Independence* has passengers enough."

"Aye," Catherine agreed, "and I do thank you for securing the cabin for us."

She thought compassionately of those in steerage. She knew their kind well from her teaching, and even before that; from childhood errands on which her mother had sent her to bring nourishing food, choice cuts of beef occasionally, to their poor Chapelizod huts, and to tell them to come get milk from their "friendly cow." When pregnant women were unable to look after their older children, it had become her after-studies duty, from twelve years onward, to care for those children. Every Saturday since she had been sixteen, she had gone to poor Mr. O'Hare, the widower down the street, to do the baking for him and his children. Their welcoming greetings and their parting thanks still rang in her ears, humbling her as she had hurried homeward.

Relatives of some of those people might be aboard. Perhaps she would know some. Hugh almost certainly would know some Dubliners. Might there not be even some who had worked at the distillery and, along with Hugh, lost out? Later she and Hugh must go see. Surely they would bear no grievance against him, now that they were all bound for America.

Again over the docks came the crack: "Visitors ashore!"

"George," Catherine said softly, "it is not that I . . ."

Still controlling any show of haste, George, in his droll, entertaining way, turned to Hugh. "The letter?"

Responding, Hugh acted startled and made a false, hurried search of his pockets. As if, Catherine thought, he would forget! The letter, she knew well enough, was Mr. Eldon's to Monsieur Gregoire Bienfaite, president of Bienfaite Brothers Brokers, recommending Hugh as accountant and manager. Hugh had been right. Mr. Eldon had gladly done him this favor since it did not conflict with interests of his own—indeed might even prosper those interests. Because once Hugh was out of Ireland, the legend might grow that 'twas Hugh Condon, not Eldon, who had caused the men to lose their employment. No matter. From Hugh's point of view, the letter was all-important and not a thing he would likely forget. But, like boys, George and Hugh must play their little game. For her benefit. She smiled, watching Hugh put the envelope he had pretended to discover back in his pocket.

A conclusive handshake with his brother-in-law, and George turned to Catherine for a farewell embrace. "Goodbye," he said, and his eyes lit with a subtle mockery at the repetition even as his voice broke on the words, "God bless you!"

At the gangplank, square-rigged in his American officer's uniform, Captain Eckhart stood up fully to his five feet eight. George stopped before him. "My sister and her husband, the Hugh Condons, have Cabin Number One, sir."

The captain, part owner of the *Independence,* gave little of himself away in his eyes, but his equable voice bespoke experience and competence. "We look for a fair sailing, sir. This is an American ship. There is no better afloat."

The captain thus brought the exchange to an end. George saluted.

Leaning over the starboard railing, Catherine watched George take the step from the gangplank to the dock and then melt into the little group waiting for him. Except for the final waving, the severance was done, the long two months' conflict and preparation had culminated at the nuptial mass this morning, and Hugh and she were off on their awesome adventure to America.

Catherine looked at Hugh. Tears were running down his cheeks. She had never seen her father cry, nor her brothers since they were tots, and her husband's crying was to her as if nature's order had somehow failed, the sun not risen with morning or set at day's ending. Then compassion stirred her, stronger than her need for his reassurance. Suppose, she thought, that he had gone ahead alone, without her?

"Are you not glad I have come?" she asked timidly. "Suppose . . ."

"Aye, I am glad. And let us not suppose." His arm tightened about her, and together they waved to those below who were waving to them.

For Catherine, her mother stood out. How valiant on her part to wave! Considering how unwillingly from the first she had heard Catherine's plan to marry Hugh.

Catherine waved back, stopping to blow her a kiss. But suddenly she was diverted. They were not, after all, leaving just yet. The last passenger, a milk cow, was being hoisted on board by means of a pulley connected to a band passed around the animal's body. There it was, poised in midair, its legs waving grotesquely. Catherine's gay laugh and Hugh's low, rumbling chuckle at the animal's ridiculous plight mingled with the roar of merriment that swept up from the emigrants and the crew and from relatives, friends, and workers on the dock.

Was it not the funniest sight under heaven? Wife looked to husband, young children to parents, older children to one another, and those who were making the crossing gestured to those on the dock, and the laughter blew like a not-quite-forgotten spring wind over them all, drying their tears, carrying off the sadness of leaving and being left, mysteriously freshening them for what was to be.

Catherine looked at Hugh, and then at once they saw George on the dock, doubled up in a very fit of laughter such as used to seize him as a boy. How agreeable to see him laugh so.

A screech tore unexpectedly into that scene, and Catherine looked about. As though to prolong and add to the gaiety, the pulley had stuck, holding the hapless animal aloft, and all attempts to jerk the rope into function resulted only in flapping the band about the cow's middle and seemingly massaging its abdomen. Gale after gale of laughter rose up and filled the air.

Finally, perhaps in response to the beast's own frantic movements, the pulley screeched again and gave, and the cow, amazingly escaping entanglements with masts and sails and rigging, descended amidships to the main deck, its legs still waving without coordination. Applause and a cry both of relief and of regret resounded. Some of the steerage passengers broke out in a jig. Friends and relations on the dock began to clap rhythmically. Others on the main deck aft took up the rhythmic clapping, and some began to sing.

"Look!" Catherine pulled at Hugh's sleeve and

pointed. There, on the dock, George was dancing a jig!

"Not since he was a boy has he clowned so," said Catherine. Tears brightened her dark blue eyes, and she clapped for her brother.

Abruptly George stopped, and his arm shot out in a farewell gesture. "We are moving!" someone shouted. Unnoticed in all the gaiety, the tug that had lain alongside the *Independence* had started to tow her slowly down the Liffey toward Dublin Bay. There ahead of the ship went the tug, steaming, puffing, and blowing as if asserting the power of little things to perform mighty tasks.

Catherine gazed at Hugh. He was stirred as he had not had time to be through the months-long preparation. Once again he was exultant, and his copper colored hair rose in the wind.

"For all on the quay this afternoon, our ship must make a fair sight as she moves down the river with her sails set," he said.

"Aye."

"Does it not seem that all the buildings of Dublin —the post office, Trinity College, the Custom House, the old House of Lords, the bank—are stepping right down to the Liffey to bid us goodbye? Is it not a fine sight from the river, our Dublin?"

"Aye," Catherine said again, "if your eyes be not blinded with tears. I can see but one thing in it all— those we love waving farewell." Suddenly she caught her breath. "I see them no longer!"

Hugh looked keenly at his wife. During the past weeks they had had less time between them than before that fateful night. It seemed he had almost forgotten, in the press of activities, how they could spontaneously be amused by the same things, forgotten her delight when he first showed her Mr. Eldon's letter, forgotten even the encouraging sweetness of her kisses. Was she now, after all, going to break like other women? To cry? He put his arm around her and spoke gently. "Let us go to our cabin, Kate."

Looking into his eyes, she thrilled to see there what she had seen many times before, so often and so stressfully repressed: his will to have her as his mate. "Aye," she said. " 'Twill be our home for this voyage."

"When we come out again," Hugh said, his voice exultant, "we shall not look backward to the shore we are sailing from, but ahead to the land we are voyaging toward, and to the home and family the two of us will be founding."

As Hugh and Catherine started toward their quarters, another cabin passenger who had escaped their notice came toward them.

Did he drag his right foot ever so little? Or did he merely fight the shy person's reluctance to take the initiative? Catherine couldn't be sure. But his unaggressive approach overcame her unwillingness to be delayed, and she smiled at him gently. He would be about Hugh's age, she judged, but no wise as handsome—of middle height, compact, with dark hair and eyes.

He offered Hugh his hand. "Nathaniel Avery. Call me Nat. I have Cabin Number Three."

"Hugh Condon," Hugh returned, shaking hands. "We have Number One." Then he turned to include Kate and said, "My wife, Catherine."

'Tis the first time ever he has called me wife, she thought.

Nathaniel Avery bowed. "Mrs. Condon."

Instantly Catherine knew the three of them would be friends. She smiled again and gave Nathaniel her hand. "They call me Kate."

"If I may suggest it," Nathaniel said, "I think we would like it better up above the bow than here at the starboard rail. We are already out in the bay. The tug will leave us soon."

Leaning over the rail, close to one another, they watched the tug go back up the river.

"Like a friend deserting you," Catherine observed.

Nathaniel's chuckle was as quick as approbation.

"So it seems, but more so, no doubt to you and your husband . . . My family home is in Boston, and I, after all, have been just a visitor in Ireland, and that only briefly, as a guest of some London acquaintances I had hoped to interest in a venture of mine—" He broke off. "Suppose we go fore?"

He led, and Catherine and Hugh followed the few steps across the small forecastle to a place above the ship's bow. "Look now!" Nathaniel urged.

All around the circle of the bay waves whitened and exploded against the shoreline. A cloud more vast than all of receding Dublin rose and blew overhead, beyond the enclosing peninsulas, out over the Irish Sea. Wind noisily filled the sails and the *Independence* seemed to rise up, up, up.

"I wonder, is it that cloud we are after?" Catherine asked. Then the *Independence* dove downward as if in response.

"Hold on," Nathaniel said, grabbing the railing himself.

Catherine and Hugh obeyed. "But what if she does not come up again?" Catherine asked.

Nathaniel laughed. "There are times in a storm when you think she will not. When she seems to head for the bottom."

Silently Catherine prayed they would not suffer a storm.

"That to the south is the Kingstown pier where I landed," Nathaniel told them.

"Aye; we call it Dunleary still," Hugh noted.

"Then would the island beyond with the martello tower be Dalkey?" Catherine asked.

"Aye," Hugh said. "And to the north, that one across the low isthmus of Howth is Ireland's Eye."

Up, up, up, they climbed once more, and then suddenly plunged again. This time they all laughed.

"We're good sailors," Nathaniel said.

"On whose say-so?"

With Hugh and Nathaniel, Catherine turned to face the unsmiling intruder, a man as tall as Hugh but dark like Nathaniel, except, Catherine noted, his eyes were pale blue. Her dislike for him was as instant as her liking for Nathaniel.

"Francis Byrne," he said. "My wife and I have Cabin Number Two."

"You boarded ahead of us?" Nathaniel asked when they'd exchanged introductions.

"This early morning . . . to avoid the others. We heard the commotion inside our cabin. What was all the laughing about?"

"I had my gear put aboard early, but I boarded late," Nathaniel said. "So I heard but the end of it."

Francis Byrne looked at the Condons.

" 'Twas a silly thing. Not everyone would find it amusing," Catherine said, for she felt she must shut out of her countrymen's merriment this man who, she saw, would not enter their hardships as her family had always done. She thought of her mother, called on at any hour, night or day, to relieve someone in distress. She, George, and Jerry all knew what a knock at the back door meant. Their father would say, "A cup of water in my name . . ." Had she not herself, these past four years, opened her schoolroom door to, among the others, the children who came scarcely dressed from Chapelizod's huts? Her mother, seeking clothing for the poor from the better-off families, would say, "Are we not in Chapelizod all but one family?"

Annoyed at his failure to win a response, Byrne addressed himself to Nathaniel. "We have been to London on business, trying to interest English investors in American railroading, and decided to return by way of Dublin. Were you visiting in these parts too?"

"I have had that pleasure," Nathaniel said. "A very real one." To Catherine, his response seemed a well-bred rebuke to Byrne's denigrating attitude. Nathaniel continued, resisting the other man's rude attempt to exclude them. "Ireland is home to the Condons."

"I see. What part of Ireland?"

"Chapelizod," Catherine offered. "We are but a little Dublin outpost on the Liffey, but we date back eight hundred years to the eleventh century."

"Ah," Nathaniel sighed, "if only the future did not pull so at me, I should bury myself in the past."

"Then you would be like my father, whose great love is history."

"I am not troubled by a love of the past," Francis Byrne declared. "I care only for the future and for what it promises."

Mr. Byrne has a way of putting an end to a subject by stating his point of view, Catherine thought. And so it becomes ever necessary to make a fresh start. She said aloud, "Perhaps my father is unusual, and it is more a woman's way than a man's to cherish the past."

"My wife interests herself in what interests me."

"Might she not like to join us?"

"Possibly. I will go see."

"Easy, now," Nathaniel Avery called with his good-natured laugh as Francis Byrne's right foot and then his left seemed to meet the deck floor too soon.

The more comical for trying to keep an air of importance, Mr. Byrne walked unsteadily toward the starboard ladder. Just as he reached it and the Condons and Nathaniel were about to applaud his success, Mrs. Byrne emerged from the port ladder, her hands gripping both banisters. Husband and wife stared at each other across the distance between them. Neither laughed, and this stopped the others from laughing.

Avery went to Mrs. Byrne's help. Even with his support she could not manage to cross the deck, so he led her to a nearby ship's chest and sat her down. She was a small woman, femininely padded, whose brown eyes were set in a round, smooth, warm-colored face. She thanked Nathaniel with an air of dismissal when her husband at last joined her.

She had come with news to share. After a brief talk with her husband, he signaled the others, who, with much jesting and laughing, crossed to the ship's chest.

Francis Byrne was matter-of-fact in a way that almost foretold reproof of any objections to what he had to say. "We have had an offer of help from the steerage," he announced. "A trio—husband and wife and the wife's brother. Between them, they will take care of the five of us; cook, keep our cabins and clothes in order for five pounds, a pound apiece for the crossing. What do you say?"

Seated together, the Byrnes assumed an air of implacable authority. As if, Catherine thought, the ship's chest were their throne. They were not asking the others to share in a common decision, but to agree with the one they had already made.

"Their names are rather humorous," Francis Byrne went on since no one had answered. "Patrick, Patricia, and Patrick."

Nobody laughed, and Catherine thought again of the poor she had known and loved and helped in Chapelizod. There had been many called by these names, and some had worked at her parents' place. "Their surnames?" she managed to ask.

"Surnames?" Mrs. Byrne seemed not quite sure of the word. "Does it matter?"

"I have a thought," Nathaniel suggested. "Let us leave this to the ladies."

"Agreed," Hugh said.

Francis Byrne nodded. "Roberta, you take it from here."

Roberta Byrne turned to Catherine. "I can summon them to our cabin tomorrow and we can make arrangements then."

"You are very kind," Catherine answered, "and I've no doubt we can agree as to arrangements." She hesitated. What Mrs. Byrne proposed was a kind of denial of her lifelong relationship with these people. "I think, however," she continued, "I would first like to seek them out and talk to them a wee bit myself. I believe my husband will take me to them."

"Very well," Roberta Byrne said, and she and her

husband stood as though putting an end to the audience. Nathaniel Avery bounced up from the deck, where he had been sitting cross-legged, and again offered Mrs. Byrne his help.

Catherine and Hugh sat down on the vacated ship's chest. Alone for the moment with his wife, Hugh put an urgent arm around her. "We are long on our way to our cabin . . ."

"Aye," she said. "Too long." She freed herself to face him. "Was I wrong not to allow Mrs. Byrne to do as she offered?"

"Why did you not?"

Catherine delayed answering, seeking to disentangle her motives. Besides her impulse to protect the emigrants, there were others. "For one thing," she began, "I do not like being told—"

"Aye," Hugh said. "In that you are like your mother."

Surprised, Catherine felt a swift rise of anger. "And proud to be."

"Aye," Hugh conceded. "I meant no offense. Go on."

"To be sure, the truth is, I do not like the Byrnes."

Hugh was silent for several minutes, and when he spoke he did so like one who had given much thought to what he would say. "In Chapelizod, Kate, you were free to do as you chose. In America you will not be so free. You must not show your dislike. You must try to like people."

"But I do like . . . nearly everybody. I like Mr. Avery very much."

"Aye. It might be well to like him a little less and to like the Byrnes a little more. We must get along, not going to either extreme."

Estranged by Hugh's suggestion, Catherine stared hard at her husband. What he proposed was destructive to her innermost self. How could she both pretend and deny true liking?

But Hugh was persisting. "Ask yourself, Kate, why you so dislike the Byrnes."

Catherine thought about this. The truth, she supposed, was that her dislike was in good part instinctive. The Byrnes were pretentious and arrogant. They had no sense of humor. They blighted the promise Nathaniel had aroused of a gay, companionable voyage. But beyond that, Francis Byrne had spoken condescendingly of Ireland as "these parts" and ridiculed the names of those who had offered to serve. And Roberta Byrne had assumed a social superiority that Catherine doubted she had long enjoyed. Nathaniel's credentials, she was equally certain, were valid. Her mother would judge him well-born and well-reared. Doubtless through his family in Boston, he was well-connected, too. And then he had spoken—not in Francis Byrne's braggart way—of interesting London investors in some venture of his.

Catherine turned to Hugh. "No matter what my reasons, Hugh, I shall try to do as you say. For your part, you do not mind taking me down below, do you?"

"That I do, Kate." He stopped. "For the purpose you propose . . . I do not think it is one they will take kindly to. Were there some real need for my going . . ."

Again her husband surprised her. Catherine probed his face. What was it George had said? "Hugh does not care for Ireland as I do . . . as Tom also cares." Had George meant Hugh did not care enough to risk danger? She asked, "Do you not care for these people?"

"Aye, I care. But you forget, I think, there may be some let out from the distillery who blame me for their loss of work. What good will our going at this time and for this purpose do them?"

"It helps them to know that we are concerned. In Chapelizod this was so."

"But this is not Chapelizod, and these are not Chapelizod people."

"That is so. Still, they may be like those I knew there."

"Some may be. Some may not. Many are ruffians,

and I have heard being trapped in steerage turns even the gentler ones into a mob. You have never seen a mob, Kate."

"Mob or no, among them might there not be some you and maybe George knew in Dublin?"

"There may be. But I should not care to meet up with any from the distillery. These may feel they have good reason to hate me. I should not like you to arrive in New Orleans a widow and without resources. No, Kate, I think it would be best if you would humble yourself a little. Go to Mrs. Byrne. Tell her I do not wish you to go to the steerage and you will be glad to see those she has in mind in her cabin."

Was this, then, her Hugh? The same Hugh she had known all these years and preferred to Tom? Dismayed, Catherine opened her mouth to protest. But just then Nathaniel Avery, his courtesy done, came up to join them.

Nathaniel threw himself on the deck beside the chest, and gazing straight ahead, said with mock seriousness, "When things go wrong, you must just make the best of them."

Catherine's laugh was the answer he sought. She had guessed that he, too, had been finding the Byrnes with their want of mannerliness a great trial. She welcomed his confirming this. His doing so subtly weighted her position against Hugh's, gave her confidence that she was right in wishing to go below. "We shall seek out this trio tomorrow," she said. "I have no doubt they will serve as well as any others."

"I judge this means that from tomorrow on, we must take our meals all together?" Nathaniel asked.

"Let it be only our meals," Catherine said, and Nathaniel shouted approbation.

Suddenly everything was again uproariously funny.

"Your husband endures them with better grace than we do," Nathaniel commented.

"Aye. To tell the truth, I think he is a bit on their side."

"Let *him* be the one to help her next time she comes

poking her head up the port ladder and her husband starting down the starboard one."

Now all three laughed as they had wanted to earlier.

"I think we shall have a merry enough time—between meals," Hugh gasped.

"Tonight let us have dinner, just the three of us, in my cabin," Nathaniel invited.

"No, in ours," Catherine insisted.

"Then first we shall have porter in mine. Do you realize, we are about to enter the Irish Sea. Let us go to the poop deck and watch from there."

From the poop deck they experienced in reverse the ship's wave climbing. As the bow rose on a wave, they went down; then, as the bow dove into the trough, they went up. From their new vantage point, close to where Captain Eckhart stood and turned the ship's big steering wheel, they could watch the ship perform. With the winds from the Irish Sea filling her sails, tacking a little to the east and west, rising and falling, she made her way out of the enclosing arms of the bay, through the roaring of the North and South Bulls, into the chopping Irish Sea. The cloud, which had flown ahead over the bay and out over the sea, dissolved, and in the pause before twilight the sun shone like promised happiness upon the chopping water. For Catherine, emerging from the bay to the channel was an awakening to new, unsuspected vistas.

Later that night, when finally they lay down together, timid at being at last husband and wife after their long courtship, stimulated by the eventful day's both joyful and sorrowful happenings, their unresolved conflict about going below held at bay until the morrow, Catherine knew a yet profounder awakening. It was as though Hugh, at last fully free to express his love on this, their first married night and at sea, caused her in some mysterious way, through his love, to be at one with the most secret impulses of nature, the movement of the sea, the orbiting of the stars, the very shuddering into life of the world at its creation.

Chapter 5

THE ABSENCE OF motion at first made Catherine believe she was awakening in her room at Chapelizod. Then she felt Hugh beside her, and rousing dreamily, she saw that he was still asleep. Her own drowsiness receded further, like darkness before day, and she vaguely realized they were becalmed.

So we are still, she thought, freed by the undisturbed quiet to remember. She turned on her side to watch Hugh as he slept. How young he looked, and yet even in rest there seemed to be a shadow of anxiety on his face from yesterday's experiences. She kissed him, and he awakened at once. She was glad. She wanted to talk.

Moving more closely against him, but resisting conversation about what they had known last night, she talked instead of their earlier evening.

"Did we not have a pleasant time in Nathaniel's cabin?"

"Aye," Hugh said. " 'Twas most pleasant."

"Those glasses he took from the fitted case, were they not pretty?"

"Aye, but I liked better the porter he poured into them."

For an answer, Catherine gave Hugh's toes a swift kick. "But best of all," she went on, "was the way Madge's skylark sang for our dinner."

"He's quiet enough now," Hugh said, and together they looked across the cabin to the cage in the corner where the bird huddled quietly. But how he'd sung

60

last night! As though on cue, he'd stepped up to the small wire orchestra in front of his cage, extended his little neck, craned his small head slightly, and sung his intoxicated song.

" 'Twas like being again on the Liffey," Catherine said, "and him singing high overhead."

Afterward, when the sun no longer warmed the air and brightened the water, and the stars and moon seemed to cast such light as they did only to disclose the darkness all about, they and Nathaniel had returned to the poop deck and, at Captain Eckhart's invitation, gone into the pilot house. The steering wheel was now in the helmsman's hands. The captain stooped over the ship's compass, which stood waist-high.

"The new Admiralty compass," he said, placing his right hand upon it. "It has overcome the influence that the magnetic pole and the ship's iron used to exert upon the needle. But we still use a sextant to measure the zenith of sun, moon, and star at a particular time, and then, with mathematical tables, compute the latitude and longitude of the ship."

He turned to the ship's chronometer. "This is also the result of studies the British Admiralty encouraged. Actually, it is merely the old one perfected, but it is now so accurate that it is possible to navigate a ship around the world and show only a mile's error in longitude at the voyage's end." Like a lover, he communed briefly with the chronometer before going on. "Until just last year, sails were pulled at sunset and vessels lay by until morning. With this, we can drive forward day and night, except when we must attend to some repairs."

They thanked the captain for the explanation and for his invitation to dine with him the next evening. A little later, while the *Independence* still climbed the night's dark waves, they had left the poop deck and gone to their separate cabins.

Catherine stretched beside Hugh, reaching for his toes with her own. "I wonder," she said, "what it is we have stopped to repair."

He did not answer. His hands were locked behind his head, and he was looking at her in a way that caused her to recall yesterday's unresolved difference. She flung a conciliatory hand to him, and he unlocked his and took it.

"You have a little hand, Kate," he said. "Very like your mother's."

It was as if, Catherine thought, he was again saying, and with displeasure, "In that you are like your mother." He could not forgive her mother's preference for Tom, so it seemed.

"Does that disappoint you?"

"I used to notice her hands."

"Well, since we are playing this game, whose hand do you have?"

Hugh held out his hand. It was neither broad nor narrow, but smaller than one might expect for his size, spare, and somehow an active man's hand.

"It is your father's."

Hugh nodded.

"Well," Catherine said with a laugh, "we have made a fine start toward getting things settled today."

"There is one matter I wish we had no need to settle."

Catherine waited, but Hugh's pause grew until at last she asked, "Are you then still opposed to our going below?"

"Aye. It goes against my view of things."

"We need not stay long."

"We may not ourselves decide how long we shall stay."

"They would not dare do us harm. Why would they? Are we not going as friends?"

"We may go as friends, but they may not receive us as such."

"Why would they not? Did we not share a merry time over the cow?"

"Aye," Hugh agreed, yielding. "That was merry, true enough."

The *Independence* was adrift still when the newly wed Condons started down the starboard ladder to the quarters below the amidships. "Look," Catherine said, stopping Hugh. The ship's sails lay in silhouetted idle beauty on the mirror of the resting Irish Sea. They went on down.

"Shure," someone below was orating, "on a calm day lak today, an' why canna we be up on deck?" Aroused, a group was enlarging about the speaker, jostling and shouting. A second man moved like his shadow beside him. Then—Catherine sensed it was already too late to turn back—the agitator saw her and Hugh. "Well, now," he said, "maybe ye be come with th' good news thit we may go above?" His tufted eyebrows seemed to Catherine at once to cajole and to threaten.

Then a woman about her age leaped out of the speaker's following and landed behind Hugh and Catherine, between them and the ladder.

"Shure," she said, "it be no sich thin bringin thim to us, but somethin else altogither."

The agitator came alongside the woman. Beneath his heavy brows, his eyes were menacing. Instinctively, Catherine stepped back.

With a natural skill at mimicry, the emigrant woman also stepped back. The man who had joined her laughed appreciatively at the pantomine, and his followers, laughing too, closed about Catherine and Hugh. Emboldened, the woman spread her skirts with mock respect and curtsied deeply. "At yeer service, Mrs. Condon."

Catherine tried to retreat again, but there was no room. "You are not—"

The other brightened boldly. "Patricia," she conceded. Then she saw that recognition of Mrs. Condon had not yet dawned on her husband and brother. "Allow me," she went on, mimicking the manners of those she had served. "Mrs. Condon, m'husband, Pathrick, and m' brither—Pathrick, too." But there was no need to introduce Hugh to the two men, for the eyes of both were narrowing with recognition and hostility.

"Mr. Condon," the leader said through toughening lips, "*the* Mr. Condon."

This time Patricia stepped back in authentic dismay, and her face, now without dissimulation, was expressionless. "Nat *thit* wan!"

Her husband nodded. "Thit wan." He raised his voice and finished with something of his wife's gift of ridicule. "An his system of accountin."

Catherine saw Hugh's lips straighten, heard him say, "I put myself out of work with the lot of you."

Suspicion worked in Patrick's eyes. "Did ye, now?" He stepped threateningly closer. "Be ye quite shure of thit?"

Hugh opened his hands in an equable gesture. "What would we be doing here? On our way with you and your wife and her brother to America?"

Suspicion loitered in Patrick's eyes like a guest unwilling or unable to leave. "Blasht ye, it be nat all so chummy as thit!"

Patricia stepped in front of her husband and spoke in his place to Hugh. "It be far from chummy. Should our water give out, as 'tis lak, would ye be aftir sharing yeers with us? An dinna ye ave a cabin to yeersels, th' two of ye?" She turned to Catherine. "An should th' ship go down, thir be lifeboats fir only th' cabin passingers—would nat thit make ye, an ye down in shteerage, unaisy now?"

"I—" Catherine began, but Hugh broke in quickly.

"Indeed it makes *me* uneasy for all of us. But I am thinking if the ship goes down, lifeboats or no, we shall all be taking our last bath together in the ocean."

Patricia laughed, but light leaped in her husband's eyes like a blue flame. "We shall be chummy in thit case," he said with some relish, "but nat entirely chummy yit." His eyes narrowed shrewdly. "Ye ave inshurance, perhaps, fir thim ye lave behind?"

Perhaps the mention of insurance and the thought of the money they were letting slip by made Patricia turn on her husband. "Will ye shtop it?" she cried. "Inshurance or no, 'twill be all th' same to thim in th' ocean. Will th' fish shtop to ask, 'Ave ye inshurance?'"

Patrick knocked his wife out of the way, and Catherine saw the blue flames in his eyes jet taller. He moved yet closer to Hugh, so close that their bodies met. "Maybe ye'd lak to try a bath out thir right about now?" With a quick turn of his head, he motioned to others to help him.

Patricia's brother, the other Patrick, silent till now, hesitated. "Wait a minute," he said, and he spoke to Catherine. "Be yeer brither wan George Macaulay?"

"Aye," Catherine said in a lifeless voice.

"Shure an didna I see 'im lit ye out th' jauntin car on Carlisle Bridge thit viry night—"

"Phwat night be ye talkin about?" his brother-in-law demanded, rolling up his sleeves for the work at hand.

"Why, th' night he swore iver to be a thrue Ribbon Man, provin himsel a thrue Irishman, ready if need be fir all, riskin his life, aye worse, riskin th' torture."

Now the agitator stepped up to Catherine, the anger burning soft and low in his eyes. "Why didna ye tell us?" He held out his hand to Hugh.

Hugh took it. " 'Twas to meet the three of you that my wife and I came down."

Patricia curtsied with respect. "Shure ye maum overlook our sheeming rudeness at th' start." She winked boldly at Hugh and said to Catherine, "We will report —th' three of us—come th' morning tomorrow."

Catherine went in ahead and slumped in a chair. Hugh closed the cabin door.

"Well, Little Miss Kindly, now that you have gone a-calling . . ."

His taunt aroused Catherine. She straightened in her chair, looked hard at her husband, and saw he was trembling with rage. At her.

Astounded, Catherine felt herself tremble, like Hugh, with wrath. "How dare you, Hugh Condon!"

"Ah, Kate Macaulay still," he said. "You Macaulays are a willful lot. And now, along, perhaps, with that Tom your mother was so partial to, we have George a Ribbon Man."

Fury lifted Catherine out of the chair, and she found herself shaking so that she tottered standing there. "If you but had the good sense to know, 'twas George's being a Ribbon Man that saved you from being thrown overboard—"

"And if you had the sense to know, 'twas you who came close to causing me to be thrown overboard—"

" 'Twasn't I," Catherine cried. " 'Twas you and your mischievous doings at the distillery!"

Hugh stared in disbelief at his wife. Then he swung around and went out. The cabin door slammed noisily after him, and as though at its slamming, the ship, which all the while had been quiet, shuddered into motion. An emptiness as vast as the ocean awaiting a crossing invaded the room. Into this void Catherine heard the startled skylark cheep its fright.

She moved to the bird cage, opened it, and took the skylark in her hand. Here, she grieved, was this little creature, torn from his native skies, on this voyage toward a strange land from which there was no turning back. The *Independence* was gaining speed, ascending the waves and dropping into the troughs, and its every impulse emphasized that she was indeed forsaking all she had lived among and cared for and that she was going toward an alien life. Worst of all, the one for whom she had gambled all and to whom she had given all had himself become a stranger. She pressed the skylark against her cheek and cried for the bird and for herself. "Poor little thing," she said, returning it to the cage.

What was it Hugh had said? "Well, Little Miss Kindly, now that you've gone a-calling . . ." Catherine shuddered with distaste. As if that had been the spirit in which she had gone. But worse, he had turned not only against her but against her family. "You Macaulays are a willful lot, and now we have George a Ribbon Man."

Ah, George . . . Had she but known his plans traveling to Dublin that day, she might have prevented his taking the irrevocable, final membership oath in the secret society, outlawing himself, bringing possible retribution to his family and to Hugh's, too, no doubt, but most alarmingly to himself.

Had Tom Kemris also taken that final oath? "That Tom your mother was so partial to," Hugh had said. Was her mother, after all, perhaps right? But no . . . Earlier on the deck, Catherine had thrilled to see again in Hugh's eyes his will to have her as his mate. But how stark the marriage promise "With my body I thee wed" was beside the reality. There had been that oneness with all life, as though through their love they were part of the rhythmic sea, the revolving stars, the very shuddering into life of the world at creation. Was it so, perhaps, that a new human life began?

The cabin door swung inward, and Hugh reappeared. " 'Twas a rough experience for you altogether, Kate," he said, "and I ought not to have spoken as I did."

But Catherine listened for no more. " 'Twas I who was wrong, insisting on going below. And I am sorry for the cruel thing I said."

"No, Kate, you said only what was true. It *was* my accounting system that put us in danger. And there are times when I cannot forgive my part in all that. 'Tis not Mr. Eldon alone who carries about a little private hell. What you said put me back for a while into mine."

"No, Hugh, no . . ." Catherine took his face in her hands. "You must not let my heedless words hurt you so." Then, aroused by the pressure of his hands and his mouth, she asked, "May we not miss the captain's dinner? I had rather be with just you and live last night again."

"No, Kate. We must give no offense to Captain Eckhart. And we must dress as the others are doing for his dinner. I will leave you now so you can hurry to get ready."

"I do not wish to get ready. I do not wish to sit with those Byrnes. And I will not have around me those dreadful people Mrs. Byrne engaged. I shall find others."

Hugh shook his head. "We shall have these. They are not dreadful. They were provoked and showed their ugly side. You would find others among them who also have this side. Indeed, there are few, if any, who do not possess it. We must not encourage the ugliness that lives deep down in people. We must behave so as to help them be the better selves they, too, may be. Now, hurry to dress, for I also must do so."

Hugh left the small cabin to her, and she swung about and looked at the dress she had hung out before they had ventured below. There, with its leaf-colored sash, was the ecru lace dress over its lining of soft salmon. Catherine took hold of both sides of the full skirt and spread it wide. Through the film of lace she saw her mother on the window seat among her geraniums, which had suggested the colors of the dress, sewing row upon endless row of lace . . . The light through the window was growing dim, and her mother had looked up. " 'Twill be all for today," she had said. The dress had been intended for other wearing than it was destined to have. Still, in the end her mother had said, "If you will take it from your trunk ahead of time, Kate, and let it hang, it will come unwrinkled."

When he returned to prepare for the dinner, Hugh's eyes applauded Catherine warmly. "A pity all Dublin cannot see you in that dress, but New Orleans shall."

"Indeed, 'tis enough for me that you see me."

However, at Nathaniel's compliment she responded with more than a little pleasure, Hugh thought, when together they stepped out of their cabin just as Nathaniel Avery came from his. "Mr. and Mrs. Condon," he said, bowing in the way he had of both doing the courteous thing and making light of it as he did so.

Then he added, as though he were commenting to others, "Catherine Condon looks radiant."

A cabin boy removed the bowls emptied of vermicelli soup, another began to present plates of cod with oyster sauce, and a third refilled the gentlemen's partly emptied glasses with sparkling hock. Catherine watched as he circled, filling first Captain Eckhart's, then Mr. Byrne's, Mr. Avery's, and Hugh's.

While she had dressed, she had reflected on what Hugh had said, and a world she had never dealt with until now had opened before her, a world inhabited by people unlike those amiable ones she had lived among. Then she had thought of George, a Ribbon Man, and of the threat he risked. So this ugliness lived in Chapelizod, too. It was everywhere, only she had been unaware. She had felt herself experiencing yet another awakening, a sorrowful one, but also expansive.

Currently, she was becoming aware that one need not like all the dinner company to enjoy being among them. She glanced at Roberta Byrne—her skin glowing warmly, her taffeta dress brown like her eyes—lively between the captain and Hugh. Roberta leaned toward her. "When you went below, did you find those people acceptable?"

"Aye," Catherine said. "I have no doubt they will do as well as any others."

The captain had seated her to his right, and she directed her conversation to him. "I see you paper your ceiling with charts. Do you sometimes show them?"

The captain bent toward Catherine, his eyes warm and approving. Through the ecru lace of her dress, the salmon lining seemed only a little less radiant than her hair. Captain Eckhart spoke slowly. "It would be a pleasure to show you."

Their eyes traveled toward the charts, rolled up and confined by tapes running from beam to beam on a ceiling so low that only under the skylight might a tall person stand upright. Space in the captain's cabin

—no more than ten feet square—was cramped. Nevertheless, Catherine thought the closeness lent a pleasant intimacy.

As the group finished dining, the three serving boys left, taking the dishes with them. In the draft that swept through the open door, the flames of the dipped candles, suspended securely in their holders over the table, wavered toward the wall above a recessed shelf on which a quarto prayer book lay; points of light fell upon the gleaming metal of a blunderbuss similar to the one in the Macaulay home. But it hadn't been in its place over the bookshelves when Catherine had reached for a few volumes to take on her voyage.

The dinner conversation was slow in resuming. However, Nathaniel broke the silence by speaking of his poor health, of a vacation from Harvard College, and of falling in love with the Lake Superior country where once prehistoric Indians had mined and smelted copper.

"Interesting," Captain Eckhart said. "Anyone tried there since?"

"Alexander Henry, less than a century ago. He was backed by the Duke of Gloucester and by the Empress of Russia's consul . . ."

The veil lifted over twin questions in the captain's eyes. "And?"

"He failed. But Henry was looking for silver mixed with the copper—"

"And now," Captain Eckhart interrupted, "copper has uses of its own."

Nathaniel clapped his hands. "Precisely. And the land is America's, thanks to Benjamin Franklin." He laughed explosively. "That wise old bird had the foresight at the Treaty of Paris to shift the northern U.S. boundary." A dream freed itself from Nathaniel's laughter and tossed wildly in his eyes. "There's already the Erie Canal. Why not another between the Superior and Huron lakes? It could begin at Sault Ste. Marie, where the St. Marys River—"

"What madness!" Francis Byrne cut in. "What the

country needs are railways criss-crossing from east to west and north to south. The Louisiana legislature—I am a member—has lately put through a bill incorporating a company to build a new one between New Orleans and Nashville."

Catherine observed that the veil lifted and dropped again over Captain Eckhart's eyes.

"That's so? My cousin, Martin Arnaud, is a legislator, too. He is building the New Orleans New Basin Canal."

This, Catherine judged, was the work the men in steerage were being brought to do. Apparently the others had reached her conclusion. From the look on Hugh's face, Catherine feared he had again stepped into his private little hell. The conversation lulled.

Of the men, Hugh so far had been the most self-contained, saying nothing of his own plans. It seemed that the others had spoken, in part at least, in the hope of interesting Hugh. Would he reveal his plans now? Speak of his letter? But instead, Hugh reached for a safe, neutral subject. "How soon will we enter the Atlantic, Captain?"

"With the wind we are having, probably tonight. Right now it is driving us southward along Ireland's coast."

"Then we are again in sight of Ireland?" Catherine asked.

The captain nodded. "The helmsman is taking us close by, close enough to show the farmsteads surrounded by crops, maybe even a sidecar jogging along a road. The emigrants are on deck for a parting look—"

But before he could finish, the cabin door flew open as though blown by the wind, and the three unsummoned serving boys broke in. "Man overboard, sir," they chorused unevenly.

"Excuse me!" the captain said hurriedly as he threw down his napkin and pushed himself from the table.

He went out, with the boys following him like mizzen sails. A draft swept through the room, and the candle flames flickered ominously in the direction of the prayer book.

One by one, the dinner guests rose to file outside. Before they could leave, however, the first mate appeared and said the captain wished them to stay.

"Rescue of a man overboard is the first law of the sea, and everything possible has already been done. Someone below tossed him a line with a life-ring and also a free life-ring. We got a dingy in the water right away and had it row to starboard. The sails were reefed also so the helmsman could maneuver more easily. I'm sorry to say no one has caught sight of the man. The dingy is working its way back toward us. With good seamanship, the officer and crew in it should be rejoining the ship shortly."

Ashen-faced Eckhart returned to the cabin and nodded dismissal to the first mate. He crossed to his chair and sat down as though by sheer force of will he meant to shake himself free of the place he had come from. It was impossible to ignore the unasked questions that probed the room's silence like the wind rising outside.

"The weather has changed," he said. "It is dark and raw. Weather," he hesitated, "has much to do with these happenings—and night closing in." Slowly the captain explained, "Without warning, an emigrant leaped into the sea . . . no warning at all . . . He is lost."

In the eerie quiet, each imagined himself alone in an overpowering, nighttime sea.

"I have ordered them all below," the captain said as though in answer to someone. "Later we shall hold a prayer service on deck. This seems to comfort the survivors."

"The man's name, sir?" Hugh inquired.

"Nolan. Patrick Nolan. He was crossing with his sister and her husband, Patrick."

"Then he was one of the three I had engaged," Roberta Byrne said.

Guessing what her husband was feeling and what he

would do, Catherine was seized with fear. "Hugh," she cried warningly. But he seemed not to hear.

"I knew this man," he said. "I must go to those he leaves."

The captain rose, reached for the quarto prayer book, and handed it to Hugh.

From the pilot house, the helmsman at the steering wheel, with the Byrnes and Nathaniel—and without Hugh—Catherine experienced her first storm at sea. Patrick Nolan, who had saved Hugh from being thrown overboard, had himself jumped into the roiling waves. Why? Catherine puzzled over this and prayed for his soul. "Eternal rest grant unto him, O Lord."

"Oh, oh," she cried, grasping for the nearest hand-hold to prevent herself from falling. The others did likewise. She saw it was everyone for himself now, and glanced distressfully at Nathaniel. His nod seemed to confirm this was so. In the name of God, where was Hugh? Even if he could leave those people below, how would he make it up the ladder in this raging storm with the ship floundering wildly?

The *Independence* wallowed in a rhythmic rolling and pitching movement, and the four cabin passengers listed and swayed from side to side, trying to brace themselves against the bulwarks. Nathaniel yelled, "Must have spun a quarter or a third of the way around then!"

"I fear 'twill never right itself!" Catherine cried back.

Indeed, they all were aware that the ship was at the mercy of the elements. Then Eckhart appeared to take the wheel from the helmsman.

"The ship's turned now to run with the sea," Nathaniel said after a while.

"And what may that mean?"

"The captain has given up trying to keep a course. They will throw out a sea anchor, which will sink and slow the ship's motion and make her less unstable."

Were I less distressed myself, Catherine thought, I

might be amused by Francis Byrne. The poor man has all but given up.

Suddenly the bow plunged into the trough of a wave that washed over the deck, and to Catherine it seemed that the ship was headed straight into the deep and would never come up again. She glanced at Roberta and guessed from the woman's blanched face that she, too, felt sick to her stomach.

At the wheel, the captain was but a blacker outline against the dark. Catherine shuddered for the sailors up in the swinging riggings and out on the swaying yards, hauling down the sails. Announced by a tremendous clap of thunder, lightning forked the sky, exposing the ship's every rope and spar. The *Independence* rolled, and all grabbed again for supports.

"She is listing forty-five degrees," Nathaniel shouted, and Catherine saw that the men and the boys on the riggings and yards were directly over the threatening water.

The psalmist had cried, "Thy lightnings lit up the world." To Catherine the lightning seemed to rend time as well as the enfolding dark and to expose the long timelessness of eternity. Was Patrick Nolan now in the strange unending present, where no clocks ticked time away?

Pitch-dark descended, and rain cascaded down. Then a luminous ball of lambent fire—steady, not flickering, very bright and dazzling, like a lump of phosphorus—fixed itself at the very top of the foremast.

"Saint Elmo's fire!" Nathaniel exclaimed. "So the philosophers call it. I have heard it is so rare that to see it once in fifty Atlantic crossings would be a fair average. They say it lasts as long as forty minutes." The ship dove into a wave.

"I think she does not like your Saint Elmo's fire," Catherine said dryly.

Would Hugh return from the hold to witness this wonder? Catherine dared not go down to get him. Besides, even if she were not afraid, she could never make it in this storm, with the ship tossing so. Catherine turned to Nathaniel. Perhaps if she asked, he might go. But she ought not ask. And the truth was, she did not wish to be left without him. Was she, then, so cowardly? Before she could answer herself, the fire burned itself out. Hugh had still not come.

At first imperceptibly, and then toward midnight, the ship's wallowing and spinning lessened, and the *Independence* seemed to Catherine to stay somewhat less long under water when meeting with a wave. And so, clutching at each other and at all stable fixtures, the group stumbled to their cabins. Alone in hers, Catherine removed and hung up the lace dress and lay down to recover.

Still later, Hugh, white-faced and grim, came in, bringing Patricia. Catherine got to her feet, and recalling the terror she had endured in the pilot house, she dared not imagine or inquire of Hugh what conditions had been in steerage.

"I shall leave Patricia in your care for what remains of the night and return to prevent her husband from committing some possible violence," he told Catherine. Then he turned to Patricia. "You will stay here for the night, will you not? You may rest in my bunk."

"Aye," the woman responded. "I be pleased to do so."

The vessel's wallowing and diving were abating further now. Glancing at the Celtic cross that George had hung in the cabin, Catherine said to Patricia, "Shall we kneel, then, and pray for your brother? And give thanks that this storm is passing?"

Patricia shook her head. "I be finished with prayin fir th' night. Down below Mr. Condon read prayers from th' captain's Protestant book. I doubt they be plasing to me poor brither. An aftir, we prayed th' Holy Rosary three times through. Joyful an sorrowful an glorious mysteries all. Thit be mich prayin fir wan night, an more prayers thin Pathrick had prayed fir 'im so long as he be livin." Her eyes came to rest on the hanging gown. " 'Tis a beautiful dress thir. Do ye min if I tech it?"

"No. Not in the least. Go ahead."

Patricia did so cautiously at first, and then she took a firm hold of both sides of the skirt and spread it wide, so that the salmon-colored lining shone through the ecru lace and made a lovely contrast with the leaf-colored sash. She continued to pull on the skirt. Then a thread snapped, and she let go.

"How long do ye thin I be in America before I git a dress as grand as this wan?"

"That is hard to say. But I am sure one day you will have one, and now I think we had better lie down."

"Aye."

"You do not wish to talk, then?" Catherine asked when she had stretched out on her bunk and Patricia had lain down on Hugh's.

"Thir be nothin to say."

Catherine hesitated. Suppose she spoke of *her* brother George, told how she feared for his safety? But she could not bring herself to do so.

She awoke later at the sound of a comforting voice and lay rigidly, awaiting recall. Then she remembered. It was Patricia in Hugh's berth, talking in her sleep. "Shure," she was saying calmingly, "ye be but a small bye still. Ye maum expict to git a black eye if ye fight with byes bigger'n yeersel. Can ye nat wait till ye be th' size of thim?"

In the early morning quiet after the night's storm, with only the sound of the waves and the lifting and dropping of the ship, Catherine saw George as a small boy, black-eyed and, for once, daunted. She had said much the same to comfort him.

Chapter 6

"No MATTER WHAT the mineral wealth," Francis Byrne said, "how could a man take his wife to that unsettled Lake Superior country?"

From the rug on the forecastle deck that she shared with Catherine and their husbands, Roberta Byrne, her short neck straining forward and her brown eyes intense, let go her embroidery hoop briefly to catch Hugh Condon's response. Hugh made no answer. Impatiently Roberta recovered the hoop and turned to Catherine. "Your husband keeps his own counsel, but surely he admits you to his thoughts?"

Catherine looked beyond their little group, out over the ocean. The early afternoon sun spilled all about, and the waves of the Atlantic threw the sparkling brightness skyward. She smiled at Roberta. "Aye, sometimes . . ."

Hugh had indeed shared his thoughts last night while they had lain together. "It appears," he had said, "that in America, as in Ireland, there are different worlds. I judge Nathaniel belongs to the world that in our part of Ireland is the Earl of Meath's. Francis Byrne belongs to a world that is just beginning to be in America —President Jackson's."

"And is there conflict, then, on both sides of the ocean?"

"The same conflict, I believe—between those who have property and those who lack it—only I think in America there is a more even chance that those who lack it may have it one day."

" 'Tis a fight, then, and the old question of choosing one's side?"

"Aye, so it seems. At home we stayed with the old order because our families' traditions lay there even while our inheritance dwindled away . . ."

Catherine spoke out of her feeling with seeming feminine irrelevance. "I like Nathaniel more than the Byrnes."

"Aye, so do I. Still, I ask myself, does it make sense in this new country for those who lack property to look out the eyes of those who have it?"

Catherine sighed. "Are you saying, then, that your side is chosen for you?"

Hugh surprised her by laughing. "What I'm saying may be but a great deal of nonsense." He laughed again. "For the truth is, Kate, neither Nathaniel Avery nor Francis Byrne has asked me to join in his venture."

"Is this because they judge you committed to Monsieur Bienfaite?"

"No. 'Tis a kind of commitment, 'tis true. Mr. Eldon also has written to Monsieur Bienfaite, so I am not altogether free. But until I see Monsieur Bienfaite, I'm not fully committed, either. Neither Nathaniel nor Francis Byrne knows of my letter. They may be merely fighting each other, contesting their opposite points of view."

"This may be, Hugh, and yet I have felt from the start that they vie with each other because each one hopes to interest you and each fears the other may do so."

This was surely what Francis Byrne sought to do, Catherine thought.

"My wife could not endure such hardships," he went on. Besides, she would miss New Orleans' parties and theater."

Roberta leaned toward Catherine and put her hand on the younger woman's arm. "Would you not enjoy these, too?"

But Catherine's reply was interrupted by Nathaniel's appearance. "Is there room on the rug for another?"

"Oh, to be sure," Catherine said, getting up and taking the smaller space between Hugh and Roberta so as to leave her former place to Nathaniel. 'Tis right I am, she said to herself, noting the Byrnes' annoyance at Nathaniel's intrusion, and unless I'm much mistaken, Francis Byrne was on the point of asking Hugh to share in some way in his business.

"The Byrnes were just telling us about the pleasures New Orleans provides," Catherine informed Nathaniel.

"Ah," he said, "but there are more meaningful rewards in life than pleasures. I have found them in the Lake Superior country."

"Up there, in that frozen land?" Francis Byrne questioned.

Nathaniel nodded. Catherine listened attentively. Francis Byrne seemed to say what was obvious, while Nathaniel often spoke out of fresh and original insights. "The eerie winter sunsets stir you in such a way that social pleasures are unregretted trifles. There is a mystery to beauty . . . Besides," he went on thoughtfully, "there is the chance up there to create a world of your own—"

Francis Byrne shrugged. "Why try to do that when New Orleans is already a great international port, someday bound to be the world's greatest?"

"Some of us," Nathaniel began in his deliberate way, "are out of sympathy—I have mentioned this before —with the direction our country is taking. The men and women—my own grandparents among them— who began this nation never meant it to go in the direction President Jackson is taking it."

"You talk of the early American dream," Byrne countered angrily. "That dream is just now beginning to be fulfilled under Jackson. The country is undergoing a revolution. Oh, do not misunderstand me"— he placed a reassuring hand on Hugh's knee—"not a bloody one, thank God. An economic one. Of course, like Nathaniel here, you can try to head it off. I prefer to jump into it. You talk of building a canal up in that frozen country with eerie sunsets. Well, I prefer to build a railroad from New Orleans to Nashville and eventually to the East Coast ports."

"But steamboats and packets already shuttle back and forth between those eastern ports and New Orleans and—"

Just then, however, Nathaniel saw Patrick at the top of the starboard ladder and let go a welcoming outcry.

At his welcome, Patrick started across the forecastle deck. In the past weeks aboard ship he had thinned, Catherine noted, and now, dressed in Hugh's former jacket and trousers, seemed a slighter and subdued version of his earlier burly self. Yet the alteration was more than physical. Even as he came toward them, Catherine observed an air of withdrawal about him, as though for the deeper needs of fellowship he had company of his own. Blessed St. Patrick! she thought. Is it not the dead man whom he keeps with him walking by his side?

Patrick let his eyes rove toward the sails, wind-filled and white against the blue sky in which cumulus clouds tossed.

"How do you read the sky, Patrick?" Nathaniel asked. "Are we due for at least one more storm?"

"Thir be no more storms on this thrip," Patrick said stonily.

"Can you guarantee that?"

"I can, sir." He stepped a little to the side as if to gain a better perspective of someone next to him, and spoke in a voice that had the hollow sound of the waves. "Th' ghost of th' dead man thit rides this ship with us will see to thit."

Catherine tried to divert him. "Perhaps you have news for us other than that of the weather?"

"I ave," Patrick answered, "though it no longer rightly be news. Th' shorry truth be thit phwat we— excludin mesel and m' wife, thanks to all of ye—air ateing an drinkin this past week be more fit fir animals thin people an nat really fit fir thim nather. I wonder th' whole lot dinna sicken."

All dropped their heads in embarrassment. Hugh was the first to lift his. "Another day or two, and we shall reach the West Indies. Captain Eckhart told me this morning that he has in mind stopping there for fresh water and provisions to last out the trip."

"Th' West Indies!" Patrick exclaimed. "Be it nat thir thit Cromwell shipped as shlaves sheveral thousand Irish, womin and girshas among thim?"

"Aye," Catherine said, "in 1649—to his everlasting shame and the shame of all who allowed it."

"But these," Hugh explained, "escaped with their lives. Others, the whole population of the town of Drogheda—men, women, and children—he put to the sword. Afterward, he prayed piously that all honest hearts give the glory of this to God."

Patrick turned a little to the side, as though to speak again to someone visible only to him. "So it be at th' West Indies," he said, "thit we shtop. Well, lave us go tell thim fir phwativer comfort it may be to thim."

Patrick left, and the Byrnes got up to leave, too. Before departing, Francis Byrne turned and said in a superior way, "Odd, the superstitions of the ignorant."

Nathaniel's head dropped, as though he were entering a realm apart from that of canals and railroads, and of differing views about America's course; a speculative area where he was at home, a world Francis Byrne probably never entered. When Nathaniel lifted his head, he said quietly, "It may be Patrick only entertains more confidently than most the quite common intuition of immortality."

Catherine put her hand on Nathaniel's forearm. " 'Tis an intuition my husband and I share with Patrick, though, as you say, perhaps with less confidence."

According to Hugh's reckoning, they should make the West Indies stop no later than today. He paused on the poop deck. The *Independence,* her sails filling with the warm air of the Gulf Stream, was running before the morning wind, climbing the waves like a toy ship released from the hazards of chance. At the wheel,

Eckhart looked like a make-believe captain steering his ship through a predictable daytime sea. He turned and motioned Hugh to join him.

"A fine morning, Mr. Condon." Captain Eckhart glanced from the wheel to Hugh and back again.

"That it is, sir," Hugh said, and he thought how in Ireland they would say of a day beginning in this soft, sun-filled way, "A morning to put dreams in your head." Indeed, dreams had been put in his head. Kate's intuition had been right, at least so far as Nathaniel was concerned. The next time the three of them were alone, Nathaniel had invited him to join in his venture.

"Running before the wind as we are," Captain Eckhart offered, "we can skirt the islands and enter the Gulf with a savings of as much as two days. We shall then make the voyage in seven weeks to the day, breaking my previous record."

Hugh stepped back in surprise and looked at a suddenly real-life captain grimly determined to make the crossing realize the utmost financial return. "Do you not plan to stop at a West Indies' port to pick up water and food?"

Eckhart delayed answering, and had Hugh not been sure the captain heard him, he would have repeated the question. "No," Captain Eckhart said finally, "I think not."

"But will we not, with the best of luck, be several days in the Gulf and perhaps several days more in the Mississippi before we dock at New Orleans?"

His hands gripping the ship's wheel, the captain looked straight ahead. Though Hugh could not see his eyes, he guessed the familiar veil had dropped over whatever secret they turned inward upon.

In the silence that pushed them apart, Hugh heard his own voice rise persistently. "Your passengers are without clean water and decent food, sir."

Eckhart's lower lip went over his upper one in overwhelming distaste. "They will have worse to endure once they have disembarked. Let them get used to it."

"But, Captain, whatever may happen to them in

New Orleans is not your responsibility. Getting them there alive is."

Captain Eckhart ignored him.

"Moreover," Hugh went on, a shrillness like the wind's rising in his own voice, "moreover," he repeated, "they are *expecting* to stop!"

Eckhart swung about, suddenly tough as if in response to an unlooked-for menace. "Expecting, do you say? Who has put this notion into their stupid heads?"

"It was you," Hugh roared, and above the wheel his own face leaned close to the captain's, "put the notion in *my* stupid head. I have passed it on to Patrick, and Patrick to all in steerage."

The captain spoke so quietly that Hugh could not decide whether his toughness of a moment before was feigned or real. "Since you have begun this," he said, "perhaps you will find a way to conclude it."

"There are but two possible ways."

"Let us hear them. And will you be good enough, please," Captain Eckhart added petulantly, "to stand a little to the side?"

Hugh moved out of Eckhart's range of vision. "The first is to take the longer necessary time and to stop—"

"And the other?"

"The other is to portion out to those in steerage whatever clean water and good food remain in the ship's supplies for yourself, the cabin passengers, and the crew, as well as from our own private supplies, in order to win the consent of those in steerage to go on without stopping."

"Suppose we are becalmed?" Hope brightened in the captain's eyes. "Do you not feel concern for your wife?"

"It is the chance we all must take."

"What have they to gain by shortening the voyage?"

"They are filled with a great longing to begin life in the new land," Hugh said. "Hunger may gnaw at them and the thirst for clean water thicken their tongues, yet they may consent because their hope is a stronger rage."

"I hold little confidence," Captain Eckhart said. "Still, if you wish, you may try what you can do."

Her sails reefed and her masts naked, the *Independence* lazed slowly through the tropical sunset to a halt. There was the sound of the anchor dropping. Alone on the forecastle deck, Catherine looked over the starboard rail. Beneath the tinted surface reflected from the painted sky, the Mississippi was pouring a muddy mass of waters into the deep blue Mexican Gulf. They would reach New Orleans soon. Yet so far as she could see, no land was visible, neither to the east nor to the color-streaming west.

She glanced down to the main deck midship. There at the drawn-up gangplank, as solitary and formal in his American officer's uniform as when George had saluted him, Captain Eckhart waited. For what? Catherine looked beyond him to the aft portion of the main deck and felt her question repeated in the up-turned sunset-purpled faces of the steerage passengers, excitedly crowding and jostling each other as they had done on departure. Uncertainty seemed to ignite gaiety. Their high-pitched laughter floated upward, and Catherine laughed with them as she had done seven weeks before when the cow had dangled precariously from the overhead pulley.

Then she saw Hugh approach Captain Eckhart. Soon after, Hugh's fair head, shining in the last of the dwindling light, appeared above the stern ladder.

"Did the captain say why we are stopping?"

Hugh nodded. "Aye, for the pilot who'll take us across the bar."

"Oh, then 'tis *the* sand bar."

"Aye, at last. But we must wait our turn, at least until tomorrow."

"Did he—" Catherine stopped, and then, in spite of herself, went on, "Did he at last thank you?"

"Aye, he did that."

"No doubt he was moved, seeing them amiable despite being hungry so long."

"Perhaps, but the captain had other motives besides . . ."

Catherine waited.

"He wishes to arrange a meeting between me and his cousin, Martin Arnaud, the contractor who has the New Orleans New Basin Canal."

Hugh spoke quietly, but there was a lift to his head and an expectant gleam in his eyes. A different Hugh, Catherine thought, from the man with whom she had watched the *Queen Adelaide* disappear into the nighttime mists of Dublin Bay. There had been hopelessness in his face then, the hopelessness she had seen in other Irish faces like the stamp of the race. But now he stood before her with pride.

"Hugh Condon," she said, " 'tis the promised miracle America is proving for you. Here we are not yet docked, and besides the opportunity with Monsieur Bienfaite, you have others with Nathaniel and now with Captain Eckhart's cousin. Unless I'm mistaken, there'll be one from Francis Byrne, and you free to choose from among them—"

"Look now!" Hugh interrupted.

An object reared itself above the eddying waters of the Mississippi's entrance: the mast of a vessel long since wrecked in attempting to cross the sand bar. In the twilight it loomed like a dark sign of something gone wrong, off course.

The sound, reassuring in the enfolding dusk, of a small boat moving through the water broke the silence surrounding the ship. Glancing down, they saw that the boat held three passengers, one of whom appeared to be a woman, and that it was drawing alongside the *Independence*. The first and second mates joined the captain at the gangplank, and the second mate threw down a rope ladder.

In the interval since the *Independence* had dropped anchor, seemingly all the boats that had since morning come within sight had moved shadowlike into the area. Drawn by the promise of excitement, Nathaniel joined Hugh and Catherine and began gaily to call attention first to one, then another: a British Indiaman, moving majestically, with her black, gloomy hull and her red ensign heavily unfolding in recognition of the *Independence*'s Stars and Stripes; a smart-rigged, rakish Portuguese polacca, whose dark-faced, red-capped sailors peered over the bow; a heavy Dutch sailing ship, and innumerable others at anchor, waiting for tide, pilots, wind, or towboats. Some of the sailboats had not yet reefed their sails, and these glowed pink in the fading light. From Europe, Cuba, and the islands, from Central and South America, and from Mexico they had come to New Orleans to unload cargoes and to reload their hulls with the Mississippi Valley's products. From across the waters, blown by the wind, came the mingled sounds of stern commands and the sonorous "Heave, ho, yeo" of laboring men.

"Look below." Unnoticed until now, Francis Byrne had come up and was calling attention to the figures coming on board.

In an audacious balancing of himself on the topmost rung of the rope ladder, one of the men, using both hands, lifted a colorful tapestry valise over the stern rail and passed it to the first mate. Then, without a break in movement, he leaped with incomparable jauntiness over the rail and saluted Captain Eckhart. Catherine gasped at the man's grace and glanced at the others, but neither Hugh nor Nathaniel nor Francis commented, so rapt was each in the figure presently climbing the ladder.

It was a woman, as agile beneath her dress as one of the sailors on the yards, and yet unlike them in their definiteness; she moved with suspenseful and feminine grace. A little distance below her, his left hand firmly on the rope and the right one free, the second man followed up the ladder. Then the veil covering the woman's head showed over the railing, and with another swift, dancelike movement, the first man reached an arm about her waist, lifted her high over the railing, and set her on her feet before Captain Eckhart.

The second man, the pilot, Catherine guessed, executed the railing, exchanged salutes and a few words with the captain, and then followed the first mate toward the poop deck.

With a wonderfully expressive stillness, the woman stood waiting. Was it the dying twilight, Catherine wondered, that enveloped her veiled face and young and narrow figure with mysterious sadness?

"Ah," Francis Byrne said, "the captain's mistress, no doubt. And unless I'm mistaken, she's a quadroon, with one Negro grandparent." He broke away to share his impression with Roberta.

Through the now expended twilight, the woman was strolling away with the captain toward his cabin. Though the woman was unknown to her, Catherine felt a sudden thrust of pain, for she understood that the captain's mistress was more vulnerable as a quadroon than she otherwise would have been.

PART THREE

New Orleans

(1835–1839)

Chapter 7

CAPTAIN ECKHART trusted the pilot to bring the *Independence* past the sand bar and up the Mississippi and remained in his cabin. With the ship under a change of command and the river's muddy waters replacing the deep blue of the Atlantic and the Gulf, everything suddenly seemed so uncertain to Catherine. She stayed close to Hugh. Together they leaned over the side of the port deck, searching for the river's flat, almost invisible shores, sharing in silence their first hungering glimpse of America.

Seven weeks ago, with the shores of Ireland receding, Hugh had said, "We shall not look backward to the shore we are sailing from, but ahead to the land we are voyaging toward and the home and family the two of us will be founding." But though she was resolved to do as Hugh had said, Catherine could see the Irish coast disappearing and with it her mother, George, her father, Jerry, and Madge. She swung away from the rail toward the ship, and the life she'd shared with Hugh in their cabin replaced that earlier scene. Lately she'd had a fantasy, one she was discreet enough not to reveal even to Hugh. He turned about, too, and followed her eyes around the ship.

" 'Twill be a wrench," he said, "leaving . . ."

Her eyes questioned him, for what he said touched on her fantasy that the two of them, ever young and sharing love, would never experience this pain, but ever be at home in their cabin which would cross and recross the Atlantic.

"Still," Hugh pursued his own thought, "we must

offer thanks for our safe voyage and," he added, his eyes seeking hers, "for one another." Then he turned her about toward America's coast.

They leaned over the railing again, searching the river's banks. First one, then another, then a cluster of queer, two-legged creatures, evidently great birds, helped define the shoreline they strode upon.

Catherine laughed. "Well, now, did you ever? Even the birds are peculiar. If those be birds standing over there at the river's edge."

"Pelicans," Byrne said, joining them. "We'll see a great many along here. Funny creatures."

"Aye." Catherine laughed again. "Funny indeed. But I welcome the sight of them. They are our first American friends."

A gratified smile—enjoyment of his role as informant —composed itself on Francis Byrne's face.

Is not he the one? Catherine thought. Ever so pleased with himself.

"Soon," he went on, "there'll be crocodiles."

Catherine gasped. "But they cannot be counted friends!"

The terror his mention of crocodiles had kindled further expanded Francis Byrne's self-importance, and he impulsively drew a card from his pocket and handed it to Catherine to give to Hugh.

"My business address. Come to see me," he invited grandly.

The address, Catherine noted with an inward gasp of surprise, was the same as Monsieur Bienfaite's. She quickly glanced at Hugh. However, he made no mention of this as he put the card away. "Thank you very much. I shall be happy to do so."

She and Hugh were silent, waiting. Why does not Mr. Byrne say whatever further he wishes to? Catherine wondered. And while he seemingly shaped whatever it was he had in mind, the *Independence* sailed past enormous bulrushes and, at last, came to the first sign of human habitation, a group of huts.

"Ah," Nathaniel said, enlarging the group, "the Balize."

Catherine leaned away from Mr. Byrne toward Nathaniel. "The Balize?"

"Home to pilots and fishermen and their families—" Nathaniel interrupted himself, for, as though there weren't room for both Nathaniel and himself, Francis Byrne was excusing himself.

On and on they sailed, with now and then, as Byrne had forecast, a huge crocodile luxuriating in the slime. How reassuring in all the newness, Catherine thought, to have Nathaniel sharing with Hugh and her the last of the voyage as he had the beginning. With him standing close, even the fierce creatures seemed somewhat less menacing. How they would miss "their Nathaniel" when he journeyed to the far northern country. The silence all three sometimes enjoyed held them together, and they watched without comment while great quantities of driftwood and enormous trees floated by.

Finally Nathaniel spoke. "We shall reach New Orleans late tonight."

"So Captain Eckhart promised," Hugh said.

"What accommodations have you in New Orleans?"

"None. We plan to keep to our cabin tonight."

"No need to do that. I've rooms at Madame Herries' on Canal Street. Come with me. You can leave your luggage aboard till tomorrow for her man Antoine, as I plan to do." He gave his exuberant laugh, which seemed to Catherine to open a highway on which all might walk without fear and with joy. "So what do you say?"

When they'd agreed and returned thanks, he tactfully left them together.

"Is not our Nathaniel kind?" Catherine asked.

"Aye. I did not know such kindness lived outside Ireland."

"I almost wish we might go on with him to his Lake Superior country."

"So, almost, do I . . ."

" 'Twould be the fulfilling of that early dream?"

Hugh nodded, and Catherine saw him and herself as boy and girl again in the Chapelizod kitchen with George and Jerry, the four of them talking about the remote place in America on the shore of a vast inland lake.

"But you feel you have a commitment to Monsieur Bienfaite?"

"Let me turn what you say upside down. Stand it on its head, so to speak. 'Tis he who, due to Mr. Eldon, has a commitment to me. But even if it turns out not all I might wish, I still think we must bide in New Orleans at least for a time. I cannot think it right to take you off to unsettled country to pass your days in loneliness while Nathaniel and I prospect for copper, and to bear our children with no woman by to help. No, I think we must bide at least for a time in New Orleans."

"New Orleans promises to be a great city from what Nathaniel says."

"Aye, does it not? French first, then Spanish, American now. Irishman that I am, I like well the fact that Americans defeated the English in their War of 1812 and kept the country American. Otherwise 'twould not be so happy a place for the Irish."

"There are English there, too, Nathaniel says."

"Aye, besides the earlier French and Spanish, English and Germans, Italians and Irish—but all Americans. Though his forebears were English, Nathaniel rejoiced when America triumphed over England."

" 'Tis a great city, then, Hugh, you bring me to, with much of the Continent I never knew mixed into it, and I am content to stay in New Orleans a while. Ought you not tell Nathaniel our plans? I believe he holds the hope that we shall go with him. You have said nothing contrary."

Hugh nodded. "Yet it is not because of Nathaniel that I've kept silent. You were right in guessing early that Francis Byrne also has an offer he wishes to make. But he will not make it so long as he suspects I have other choices, only if he finds I have none. I discover much of Mr. Eldon in this Mr. Byrne and do not like it that his office address is also Monsieur Bienfaite's."

Catherine's blue eyes darkened. "I did not look for another like that one this side of the ocean."

Hugh's laugh had an edge. "I think we shall find, besides Francis Byrne, there are a few others. But I do not mistrust our Nathaniel. You are right, I must tell him our plans. Let us go now and arrange for our luggage."

"The levee," Nathaniel said, rejoining them again later and pointing to a dike of earth six feet or so higher than the land and from twenty-five to thirty feet in breadth, thrown up on both sides of the Mississippi. In the distance, as grand as some English estates in the Irish countryside, great white pillared houses stood in tranquil dignity and beauty. "Sugar plantations," Nathaniel explained. Then at last, when Catherine had begun to doubt they would ever reach New Orleans, he indicated a curve of lights like the sickle moon and shouted joyously, "The Crescent City!"

A thrill stirred through Catherine, and glancing at Hugh, she saw that he, too, was exulting at the Crescent City's brilliance.

Strangely, there was something missing. To be sure, all those who had shared the departure . . . Why were they not on deck, holding their children high for this first glorious vision of the city they were bringing them to? Did Hugh know? "The others?" she asked.

"They wish to keep below until daylight. On arriving, fear has overcome them. Night adds to fear, and the children are crying, not wanting to leave the place they've grown accustomed to."

"The children," Catherine said aloud with great sorrow. And then to herself, How will it be for them in America? She thought of Chapelizod's children coming to her school every morning. She would miss them, miss teaching them, miss the schedule school imposed upon her as well as on them. At least they walked down known paths. These children . . . Life would unfold to their curious eyes in an alien place, in alien ways.

The mingled sounds from the shore separated and became the irregular tolling of a deep-throated bell, voices calling insistently and falling away uncertainly, the baying of dogs, and a bugle's rising note of hope. A tug came soon and moved the *Independence* in among a thousand masts whose riggings were penciled against the night sky. All happened speedily. Casting off the ship astern, the tug rounded to and left her alongside a Salem ship in a tier six deep.

"What now?" Catherine and Hugh turned toward each other uncertainly, immigrants after all.

With his sense of play, Nathaniel quickly dispelled the rising anxiety he guessed they might feel. Balancing himself with widespread arms, he led them in a mock game of Follow the Leader through various ships from gangplank to gangplank. A cabin boy followed with the few small necessary bags they required. When Hugh and Catherine at last jumped after Nathaniel to the solid levee nearly opposite Rue Marigny, Catherine looked up thankfully. Overhead, the moon that had reached like a beckoning finger out of the sky over the Liffey shone full and benign in the soft Southern sky over New Orleans.

With a glance toward the *Independence*, Catherine spoke softly to Hugh. "May it also shine kindly on them." Understanding, Hugh nodded.

A carriage was waiting, called by Byrne, who had somehow found a way to disembark with his wife and Patrick and Patricia, now in the Byrnes' employ. From inside the vehicle Roberta Byrne waved to the others, and Patricia winked boldly at Catherine.

"The only carriage right now," Byrne called to Nathaniel before he jumped in. "May we take your small luggage? We pass by Madame Herries'."

"Many thanks, if you don't mind pausing a bit to ring for Antoine."

And so Patrick lifted further pieces to the outside luggage rack, bade the Condons and Nathaniel goodbye with the wish to see them again soon, and sprang to the seat next to the driver, but only, Catherine saw, after he gestured goodbye to the ghostly friend from whom he was parting.

Well, and have not I a fantasy of my own? Catherine laughed to herself. Emboldened by Patrick's salute, she blew a kiss toward the cabin where she had left her own and Hugh's young selves.

"The question now," Nathaniel stated, "is whether to wait for another carriage, which may be long in coming, or to walk to Madame Herries'. It would be no distance for Hugh and myself, Kate, if you will not find it too much."

" 'Tis accustomed to walking I am," Catherine replied, "and I enjoy nothing more unless it be riding. Let us be off."

And so, Catherine between Hugh and Nathaniel, they set out for Madame Herries' through New Orleans's gaily lighted streets. The white moon poured its blessing over all, mysteriously restoring to the world its lost innocence, Catherine thought. She was like a child again with her parents and brothers in Dublin for the first time, seeing and hearing and identifying the city's nighttime sights and sounds.

At first a firm, smooth, graveled walk, about four feet above the street, with the primeval river to one side and trees to the other—India trees, Nathaniel stopped to say. In the moonlight Catherine saw that their leaves, like those of Chapelizod's lilacs, were shaped like pointed candle flames. The fragrance of those remembered lilacs filled the air.

A trio of animated young men passed, speaking French and exhaling tobacco smoke. In their gloved hands they held walking canes—sword canes, Nathaniel whispered, gesturing to them—and as they walked, they swung them in unison, and the canes glinted brightly. But with the white moon conferring innocence upon them as on all things, the young men seemed to Catherine but boys—George and Jerry, trying out new toys as they walked on that early occasion through the Dublin night.

"This is the market." Nathaniel opened his arms in a wide gesture. A massive colonnade loomed ahead, so long that Catherine thought it would take them forever to reach its end. When they did so at last, they paused to look back at the ships' masts rocking in the moonlight. "New Orleans turns up moments of sudden beauty," Nathaniel observed.

He stood entranced so long that Catherine found herself listening as well as watching, and said, " 'Tis a lullaby's rhythm they rock to."

Hugh answered, "Aye, I hear it so, too."

They turned then, and passing under the India trees, left the levee. When they'd finally crossed the esplanade, to Catherine surely the world's broadest and most spacious, she saw three Moorish-appearing towers. She tilted her head and followed their height into the night sky. "The cathedral, is it?"

"The cathedral," Nathaniel affirmed. As was the custom in Ireland, Hugh lifted his cap.

The next turn was into Rue St. Pierre. Here balconies projected from brick buildings, and Catherine saw with surprise that these New World buildings already looked old—though, to be sure, not so ancient as Dublin's. On that childhood night it had seemed to her that Dublin dreamed again of dimming times, of Norsemen coming early, Normans later on, and then inevitably the English . . . Walking through old New Orleans in the white moonlight, Catherine listened while Nathaniel reminded them that this city had its own past; French, Spanish, and already a war with the English. While Nathaniel and Hugh stood discussing that war, Catherine looked about, and it seemed to her that the old buildings grew slyly young again in the night and leaned toward one another, whispering about earlier days.

"Come, Kate," Hugh urged. "Do you not see Nathaniel goes on?"

"Aye, I see. But the city and the night have cast a spell upon me."

With Hugh pressing her onward, she hurried along. From Rue St. Pierre, they turned into Chartres Street. At a crossing, they glanced down a straight, long avenue whose lamps, as far as they could see, were hung by chains from house to house across the road. With its pearl-like glow, each lamp seemed to repeat the moon until the last one faded away.

Nathaniel turned into an entrance on Canal Street. Over the door hung a little bell with the sign "For Single Gentlemen—Belated." Nathaniel rang.

A boy about Jerry's age, as dark as Jerry was fair, appeared and greeted Nathaniel with an affectionate grin. When Nathaniel had introduced him as Antoine, Madame Herries' indispensable helper, Antoine bowed to Catherine and Hugh, then led them by a candle's light through dark passages and up darker stairways to Nathaniel's rooms. Closing the door, he lit an oil lamp and blew out his candle.

Catherine looked about the little parlor. How pleasantly it revealed itself bit by bit in the glowing light. The coal in the fireplace grate shone black. A red rose unfolded its petals in the floor carpeting. Dark blue grapes bloomed mistily on soft gray wallpaper leaves. A little writing desk offered itself. A gentleman's chair in blue and a lady's chair in soft yellow, like the curtains, emerged on either side of the fireplace. Finally, the white mantel gleamed over all.

Nathaniel opened a door to the bedroom, and there, Catherine saw, were her and Hugh's small bags. "You will sleep here," Nathaniel said. "There is only the one bedroom. I will use the couch in the study." Before they could thank him, he turned to Antoine. "Put the lamp in the bedroom. Bring the candle to me in the study. I will tell you what things to fetch from the *Independence* tomorrow, or is it already today? But first, if you will, bring Mr. Condon and me a nightcap in the study."

The bedroom door closed, and needing to rest before she undressed, Catherine threw herself on the bed. From the study adjoining the bedroom, Hugh's and Nathaniel's voices rose and fell. Was Hugh, at last, telling Nathaniel their plans? There were frequent pauses, some quite long, then the voices would continue. She ought to get up, kneel, say prayers of thanks to Christ's mother to whom she had entrusted Hugh and herself for the crossing; pray, too, for those who still slept aboard the *Independence*. But the day had been a lifetime, and the voyage forever, and with Hugh's and Nathaniel's voices going on between silences, she drowsed and soon fell asleep.

Chapter 8

"HERE IS Antoine now!"

Nathaniel stepped around Hugh and Catherine in the small parlor and threw open the door to the hall. Peering through the bird cage atop an armful of bags and packages was the black, triumphant face of the boy who last night had answered the doorbell.

Catherine couldn't help laughing. "Surely it is not *one* boy holding all this!" Is it not strange, she thought, that this Antoine, a slave, bought and owned by Madame Herries, performs his work with so much satisfaction?

"Did I not tell you Antoine is a man you can count upon?" Nathaniel asked.

"Do help him put the things down," Catherine urged.

Nathaniel took the cage and set it on a table near the window, and the skylark began at once to hop on and off its little stage. One by one, Nathaniel and

Hugh took from the boy the packages and luggage pieces until there remained at the end of his long, thin black arms only a single traveling bag. This he set down, and straightening himself, stood statuelike, waiting.

Nathaniel looked over the assortment and turned to Hugh. "He found the right things?"

Some of their bigger pieces, Catherine noticed, were missing. She looked at her husband. But Hugh nodded to Nathaniel. Had Nathaniel's long talk late last night changed Hugh's plans? Were their big pieces, like Nathaniel's, also to be moved directly from the *Independence* to whatever Mississippi River steamer would take them north? Well, Catherine thought with a rush of native recklessness, I'm just lightheaded enough to agree.

Then, like the slap of waves against the *Independence,* the outside shutters flew apart and struck against the house. At once Antoine, who had already taken the luggage to the bedroom and study, silently crossed the small parlor, opened the windows, and let in the sounds of a new day on Canal Street. Up and down the street, the cheerful slap, slap of waves was repeated as other shutters were thrown apart and other windows opened to the day.

Hugh followed Catherine to the windows. Black women, with huge baskets of rusks and rolls, and a roll in each outstretched hand, were calling insistently. Milk and butter criers followed. As they passed, they saluted one another gaily. "Boshoo, mundsal!" "Boshoo, mooshoo!"

Laughing, Catherine turned from the window to Nathaniel. "It has just come to me that they are saying, '*Bonjour*, mademoiselle!' '*Bonjour,* monsieur!' "

At her laughter, the lark stepped onto his tiny orchestra, extended his little neck, cocked his small head slightly, and began to sing joyfully. Then, quite as unpredictably as it had begun, the bird ceased. No one broke the silence.

Why, Catherine wondered impetuously while the

quiet grew, if Hugh has decided we will go north, did he not waken me last night to tell me? Or tell me this morning?

Then another thought occurred, a chilling one. Did Nathaniel persuade Hugh to settle me in Madame Herries' rooms for a time? Do the two of them plan to journey north together without me?

Catherine saw herself standing with Hugh on the Liffey Quay, heard him say, "I know what I will do," and followed his nod to the *Queen Adelaide* disappearing in the nighttime mists of Dublin Bay. Shaken, Catherine recalled Hugh's saying once, "Aye, 'tis certain I shall go. But perhaps 'twould be better were I to go ahead and Kate to follow later." Did he think now to go ahead without her?

Someone knocked, and Antoine moved noiselessly to the door and opened it to a black, slim girl with a yellow scarf over her head. She moved into the light that fell through the opened shutters, and Catherine saw that she was not really black, but a soft, warm brown. With what subtle rhythm she moved. Yes, like the woman who had come up the rope ladder. "A quadroon," Francis Byrne had said knowingly, "with one Negro grandparent." She must be Madame Herries' slave also, Catherine surmised, bought and owned, too. And, Catherine decided, equally agreeable.

She extended *Le Courrier de la Louisianne,* which Nathaniel took from her, and introduced her as Amelia, whereupon she offered Catherine a card bearing Madame Herries' name. Aloud, Catherine read what had been written. "Please take coffee with me this morning."

"Good! Good!" Nathaniel applauded. "That frees you, Hugh, to go first to see your Monsieur Bienfaite and me to hunt up a steamship to take me as far north as Galena—the first part of my voyage to the Lake Superior country. Ah," he added, and hastily tore a strip from *Le Courrier,* "maybe the steamship *Belvidere.* Wait, Antoine," he called to the boy, who was about to follow Amelia out of the room. "I want you to get us theater tickets for tonight. Mind you, get three, and the best they have."

Dumbstruck, Catherine watched Nathaniel blithely lead her husband from the room. Did he think she could be dismissed with a cup of coffee at Madame Herries', rewarded with a trip to the theater tonight, and then left behind? Had she so misread him?

Worse, what about Hugh? He had gotten into bed last night, their first in New Orleans, without waking her. She would not have been too tired for him. At Nathaniel's summons, he had just left without so much as a backward glance. Catherine crossed the room to the windows and gazed down. There below, at Nathaniel's uplifted hand, each went his separate way, Hugh no less than Antoine accepting Nathaniel's gesture of dismissal. Whatever had come over Hugh? This was not the husband to whom she had given herself. What was she to do with an ocean between her and her family?

Catherine lifted the card she still held. Who was this Madame Herries? She had no wish to join her. But perhaps she had better, she considered, too sorrowful to be angry. She might have need of a friend. Perhaps she had better dress more suitably for the call.

Catherine paused before the door. To the side of the gleaming brass knocker, fitted into a brass edging, was a card—like those on the doors of Dublin's Merrion Square—whose fine script read *Madame Herries*. To be sure, Catherine realized, it was like the card she had received earlier.

Catherine lifted and dropped the knocker. Amelia opened the door, saw Catherine in a full-skirted green woolen dress with soft blue threads running through, and smilingly led her into the still-darkened parlor. With mingled feelings of distress and anticipation,

Catherine seated herself in one of the room's high-backed thronelike chairs. With the shutters still closed, the windows down, and the draperies drawn, it might have been evening rather than morning. An oil lamp burned on a table near her chair and another on the mantel. In their light the room began to emerge contradictorily elegant and austere, as though possibly its final furnishing waited on more important under-takings or a fresh, long-delayed impulse. In the gloom, Catherine returned to her previous worrisome question. If only she'd had a moment alone with Hugh. And why was this room kept so dark? At home, no matter what the weather, the curtains were opened to admit the daylight.

Where was Madame Herries? As though to substi-tute, a glossy, cream-colored, close-coated cat, with a pointed long head, elongated, slender-lined body, and tapering tail, crept gracefully into the room, paused in the lamplight nearby to show its soft brown face, ears, feet, and tail, and stared fixedly out of blue, shining eyes at Catherine.

Catherine clapped her hands welcomingly. At the sound, with a force that nearly unsettled her in the chair, the cat leaped into her lap, circled about purr-ing noisily and then snuggled down. Catherine began to stroke it gently.

But a second cat appeared, and then a third, with the same blue, shining eyes. They stared fixedly at Catherine as though intending the same leap into her lap.

"You must wait your turn, each of you," she said, falling back upon the discipline she used with Chap-elizod's schoolchildren.

Muffled laughter sounded through the open door of an adjoining study, and a large, dark-haired woman, about Catherine's mother's age, came majestically into the room.

"Poo-poo," she said in a voice muffled like her laughter, "you naughty girl!" Hurriedly, and yet with no hurt to her dignity, she crossed the room, lifted the cat from Catherine, and held it lovingly in her arms.

"My dear," Madame Herries said, "will you forgive my bad-mannered children?" She laughed pleasantly. "Amelia!"

At her name, the maid came and took the other cats away. Down the hall a door opened, emitting the sound and smell of still more cats, and then closed on them all.

Still holding Poo-poo, Madame Herries sat down near Catherine in another of the regal chairs. "They are Siamese, you know," she said, stroking the pet affectionately. "I have five Siamese and four Persians." She paused to enjoy a better look at Catherine, sitting a little stiffly in the green dress with its long tapered sleeves and blue frogs that buttoned the closely fitted bodice up to the ribboned ruching about the high neck. In the lamplight, her brilliant hair shone in a subdued manner. Then, seeking a bond, Madame Herries added warmly, "You must have had cats."

"Aye," Catherine said, "we did have one."

"Only one?"

"Well, she would have kittens, you know, but we always gave them away."

"What breed was she?"

"I don't know her antecedents. Father called her a mouser."

"A mouser?"

"Aye, she caught mice. She would come to the back door and stand there with a dead mouse dangling from her mouth."

"How shocking!"

"Yes, it was, until you looked at it from her point of view. She was proudly reporting an accomplishment, and she would wait to take it off—you never knew where—until you clapped in applause."

Madame Herries looked about apprehensively. "You clapped just now."

Catherine laughed. "But there was no mouse."

Madame Herries' muffled laughter joined Catherine's. "I am grateful for that." The trivial task which could unite or divide had united them, she was sure. "I will show you my Persians. But," she paused, glancing at the glass-encased clock on her mantel, "you must wait for them until we have had coffee."

Amelia reappeared, set down a small water-filled basin containing a rose and a rose-scented towel, and took Poo-poo from Madame Herries.

"You will forgive me while I rinse the cat from my hands?"

"Yes, of course." Catherine's earlier distress was giving way to the pleasure of adventuring into a new friendship. And Madame Herries' approval was restoring Catherine's confidence in herself and in Hugh's devotion to her. Shame at her doubt of him warmed her as though she were blushing. How could she have feared he would go on without her?

"Forgive my not coming at once. I was writing a poem and needed only the two final lines."

While the coffee Amelia had poured was cooling, Madame Herries talked of the poem, whose subject was her husband's ancestor, the Lord Herries who had led Mary, Queen of Scots' cavalry at Langside, ridden with her into England in May 1568, and been one of her chief commissioners at the Conference at York.

Catherine listened attentively. Through her father, she knew before now of this Lord Herries. She also understood the need to lift life above its everydayness by searching its meaning. Doubtless poetry was Madame Herries' way of doing so. But she was puzzled that one who was an American and an heiress to a new way of life should reach into the past to claim descent for her husband from the nobility Americans denied. No matter. For friendship, she could accept this and other contradictions.

"But enough of my poem and me," Madame Herries said. "How do *you* find New Orleans?"

Catherine breathed deeply. "Of course, we have

only just come—and this morning proved unsettling. Yet I feel from my walk here last night that there are not words to describe it."

"Please try, though." Madame Herries laughed gently and grew young again as Catherine blended facts with her fantasies.

Madame Herries nodded. "There is much in New Orleans. There's the theater—"

"Ah, we go there tonight."

"I am glad. I have not seen either *Three Hunchbacks* or *Cinderella,* which are playing. You know, I love the omnibus trip down Chartres Street with its confusion of sights and sounds, the American Theater, and watching the ladies who come with their hair dressed à la Madonna and sit in the mirrored boxes or the crimson-cushioned parquet pews. You will love all this, too. You will adore New Orleans!"

Catherine, however, could no longer forbid the uncertainty about the future that rose within her like a strong wind at sea.

"But it is not certain even that we shall remain."

"Not remain? How is that?"

"I am not altogether sure myself. Though I believe there is the possibility we may go with Mr. Avery to his country up north."

Madame Herries put her coffee cup down firmly. "You must not go with him to this country. It is not a country fit for a woman. Besides," she leaned confidingly toward her visitor, "Nathaniel Avery is not a man to be counted upon."

Catherine put her hand to her throat to ease the constriction she felt there. "Not to be counted upon?"

"You may like him, but you must not count upon him. You must remain here in New Orleans. I will make your husband a special price for the rooms and meals, thirty-five dollars a month." Madame Herries paused, casting about for some special inducement. After hitting upon one, she smiled expansively, saying, "I will lend you Amelia when you wish to go shopping. You must do it today along Chartres Street, and

Amelia may go with you. Why don't you go now while your husband is about on business of his own?"

There had seemed no good reason not to do so, at least none that could be overridden by the self-trust Madame Herries had fostered and by Catherine's own strong wish to shop for gifts for those she had left behind. So she had set forth with Amelia, stopping first at the New Exchange, where she deposited the savings George had entrusted to her and withdrew ten silver American dollars. But the American money, so tangible and novel, had caused some misgivings. Had she the judgment, without consulting Hugh, to spend so much to the best advantage? Still, if it was true that they were going with Nathaniel, this might be her single chance to make purchases in this fabulous city. Will not Hugh be proud that his wife has such enterprise? No answer came readily, and Catherine glanced apprehensively at Amelia.

But Amelia, perhaps anticipating a gift for herself, said gently, "We need not be long."

Nevertheless, they were. The sky had darkened and the rain which had threatened earlier had begun when they returned in the late afternoon. Seeing the door to their rooms opened wide, Amelia smilingly took her gift of Odalisque perfume from the bulging shopping bag, handed the bag to Catherine, and hurried down the hall. Catherine went in, closed the door, and called merrily, "Someone left the door open!" Then she saw Hugh slumped in the blue gentleman's chair by the fireplace, his long legs stretched out, his cap tipped over his face.

Without looking up, he asked, "Did I leave the door open?"

Catherine glanced across the room. "And the windows!"

Hugh did not stir, and she put her package down before racing to the windows to shut out the rain.

Without looking up, he inquired, "So 'tis raining, is it?"

Catherine did not answer, staring transfixedly at her husband. Then she heard someone who could only be herself say, "Then you will not work for Monsieur Bienfaite?"

At the mention of Monsieur Bienfaite's name, Hugh lifted his head, and Catherine saw the desolation on his face.

Hugh pushed his cap back. "It appears I shall not. Though things at the start promised well."

"What happened?"

"Monsieur Bienfaite excused himself. Said he needed to talk with an associate. When he came back, he had had a change of mind. Would it surprise you to know his associate is none other than our voyage companion, Mr. Francis Byrne? You remember they both had the same address?"

"Aye, I remember." Catherine felt a sudden stab of pain and sat down in the yellow chair, not knowing if it was caused by disappointment for Hugh or by the baby she had not yet told him she carried. "But what might Mr. Byrne say?"

"That I am but an immigrant Irishman, unused to New Orleans and its ways, knowing only a behind-the-times accounting system, useful enough maybe in Ireland but of no use here in America."

"Why would Mr. Byrne do this?"

"I can but guess. But I suspect he still wishes to fit me into some plan of his own."

"Then why does he not say so?"

"Again I can but guess. Is it perhaps that he wishes first to destroy my every other chance so I have no choice but to agree to his?"

"You would never do that!"

Hugh gave a short, sour grunt.

Outside, Catherine saw, the rain was coming down hard, rinsing New Orleans's glamour away. She turned back to Hugh. "Shall we go, then, with Nathaniel?"

Instead of removing it, Hugh maddeningly shoved

his cap further back on his head and gestured toward the study. Catherine went and looked in and saw that it had been emptied of all that spoke of Nathaniel.

So . . . , Catherine considered, I had thought of the three of us going together, and even of the two of them going without me, but not of this, not of Nathaniel's hurrying off without waiting the outcome of Hugh's meeting with Monsieur Bienfaite.

She came back and sat down again. "I do not understand."

" 'Tis no easier for me than for you. When I returned here from my meeting with Monsieur Bienfaite, I found Nathaniel already gone and a note asking me to come to the steamship dock. I waited here for you; then, though I doubted you would still be with Madame Herries, I sought you there. 'It's no use,' she said, 'to search her out in the shops. There are many.' So I hurried next to the steamship dock.

"The *Belvidere,* with stops at Natchez, Memphis, St. Louis, and finally Galena, steamed off ahead of schedule. I got there just as it did so. Nathaniel was on deck. We waved to each other. No doubt from my delay he supposed I'd gotten the opening with Monsieur Bienfaite. I'd like in any case to believe he supposed this."

So it was she who by delaying Hugh had prevented his and Nathaniel's coming together. A low moan escaped Catherine.

Hugh raised himself in his chair and nodded toward the shopping bag. "Well, and what have you there?"

An immense sense of shame at what now seemed like utter folly overwhelmed Catherine. How could she show him in his present distress all she had bought with such pleasure but a short while ago? "I shall show you later."

Hugh stood and at last tossed his cap away. "I would like to see NOW!"

To be sure, Catherine thought, he is regretting bringing me to America. This is why his rage turns not against Francis Byrne for preventing Monsieur Bienfaite's engaging him, but against me. Without me, he would have been free from the start to go with Nathaniel.

But she could not unwrap and show the gifts now. She got up and walked past Hugh to the window. The rain was coming down in a solid sheet, like a theater curtain, Catherine thought, and remembered that she and Hugh and Nathaniel were to have gone to the play tonight. Only instead of separating actors from audience, the rain divided her bright excursion with Amelia from this time with her husband. In Chapelizod, she thought with a great pining for home, it rained gently. Never before had she seen it pour like this, except for that night aboard the *Independence*. She recalled the pitch-dark then, and the rain coming down, and the lightning that made past and future one unending present. But she had not guessed until now that an unending present could be hell.

Unable to bear any longer what she endured alone, she turned back to Hugh. He seemed to have an insane person's concentration upon one trivial purpose.

"I would like to see what you bought," he demanded.

"If you must see, you may look for yourself."

As though surprised by her refusing to yield, Hugh picked up the shopping bag, carried it to the desk, and spilled out its contents.

The first thing he picked up was the book bought for her father from Mr. McKeon at the corner of Camp and Common Streets, as *Le Courrier de la Louisianne* had advertised. Catherine watched while Hugh undid the wrapping. *"The Biographical Memoir of Daniel Boone, the first settler of Kentucky, interspersed with incidents of the early annals of the country,* by Timothy Flint,"* Hugh read aloud with expressive mocking inflections, and without comment laid the volume down. From the assortment, he chose another package.

This time it was the silver infant's cup, without a handle, that Catherine had bought in the English shop on the upper part of Chartres Street. Hugh undid the paper wrapping and came to the soft flannel casing. He removed the cup gingerly and whistled irreverently as he put it down.

Catherine forgave him. He does not yet know, she reminded herself.

Hugh came next to the fine Gothic sandwich tray she had found at S. & S. Brower at No. 17 Camp Street. With the same care he had shown through all the unwrapping, he undid this package and lifted out the tray. Then he gave not one, not two, but three loud, expressive whistles. "And this is for . . . ?"

Catherine struggled for her usual voice, but what came out was a whisper. "I intended it for Nathaniel."

It had seemed to Catherine that unwrapping the gifts had appeased Hugh's anger somewhat, but without warning he leaped from the desk chair. She turned at the sound of his fierce crumpling of paper and saw him standing there crushing with a passion of fury some paper between his hands. Then he turned, and with a force that lent the small, hard paper ball more than a paper's weight, hurled it into the fireplace.

It caught quickly and burned brightly, and Catherine knew then what it was. How often in their cabin aboard the *Independence* she had seen Hugh take from his pocket Mr. Eldon's letter, read it with hope. Catherine felt more sorrow than she had ever realized she could feel for another. She cried out her pity for him. "Oh, Hugh! But for me you might have gone with Nathaniel. Had I not been shopping when I should have stayed here, we might both have gone. . . ."

She felt his arms about her with such urgent need that at last she had the courage to ask, "You are not sorry I came?"

He moved away a little and looked out of his piercing eyes at her. "Sorry! How could I be sorry?" He gave a great dry sob and pulled her close again. "Ah, Kate, you do not yet know your husband. Forgive me for so unjustly turning my anger toward others against you."

" 'Tis the wrong time altogether to tell you our news," she began. "I have been waiting for the good fortune we looked for to tell you—"

"Nay, do not wait. Good fortune seems to have gone into hiding. Tell me now."

"Can you not guess?"

"That I cannot. Monsieur Bienfaite's change of mind and Nathaniel's steaming away on the *Belvidere* seem to have dulled my mind so that I can reach for little else. You must tell me."

She picked up the silver baby cup and brought it to him. "For what little one do you think I bought this?"

He took the piece from her, and beneath defeat and fear of the future, hope that was stronger than either lighted his eyes. "Ah, Kate, is it so, then?"

She could not believe in anything so everyday-like as the knocking that came at precisely that moment at the door. She hurried to answer lest Hugh go and in his initial excitement announce their news prematurely to whoever it was.

Through the opened door Antoine handed her a small envelope. The theater had been sold out, and he had waited until these tickets had been returned.

Catherine held out the envelope to Hugh. "Nathaniel's." She threw them down on the desk when Hugh did not take them. "What a pity. I had so looked forward to going."

Something tightened like a knot in Hugh's face, and Catherine remembered how once before, when they had watched the *Queen Adalaide* disappear in the nighttime mists of Dublin Bay, she had seen his face harden with resolve.

"We shall go anyway."

Catherine sat down at the desk. "Oh, Hugh, I cannot."

"Aye, Kate, but you can. Once before you could not go. Then it was to Captain Eckhart's dinner. But you went. And now we have special reason to go. Do we not have cause to celebrate? We shall go, and you will wear the dress you wore to the captain's dinner." He picked up another box from the desk. Undoing it, he held up a pair of pearl-gray evening gloves. "I shall wear these. They will not go a-wasting . . . Since there are three tickets, might you not like to ask Madame Herries to come with us?"

During the intermission that followed *The Three Hunchbacks,* while they awaited *Cinderella,* Madame Herries bowed and bowed again from the crimson cushioned parquet pew where she and Hugh and Catherine sat. It seemed to Catherine that their land-lady knew everyone. But she could not place the gen-tleman with Monsieur and Madame Martin Arnaud. Who was he?

"Ah," Catherine said, "to be sure, we know *him.* He is Captain Eckhart. A cousin, so he told my husband, of Monsieur Martin Arnaud."

Chapter 9

"DID YOU FIND the captain's card?" Catherine asked as she handed Hugh his cup of breakfast tea.

"Aye. 'Twas in the pocket of this coat." Hugh set down his cup, pulled out a card from his inside breast pocket, and read, "This will introduce and recommend Mr. Hugh Condon for work as supervisor. Your cousin, Captain Eckhart."

Catherine placed the basket with the two remaining rusks near Hugh and sat down with her cup of tea. Morning's fatigue had not yet shown through last night's excitement. "Does the card not give Monsieur Arnaud's business and address?"

Hugh turned over the card and read it slowly, as if

he were learning a lesson. "Monsieur Martin Arnaud. Contractor. Government House. Bourbon and Canal."

"Is he, then, like Francis Byrne, a member of the Louisiana legislature?"

"I do not recall. Monsieur Bienfaite, as you know, has offices in Government House, yet he is not a member of the legislature."

" 'Tis a mercy he is not and a great pity that other one is."

The kettle with the water she was heating for more tea began to sing, and as Catherine lifted it off the oil burner, the outside shutters slapped open so sharply that she nearly dropped the hot kettle. Hugh got up at once and hurried to open them. "Poor Hugh," Catherine sighed. She refilled his cup and put a kiss on his cheek before she sat down. Still they had had a fine time last night both at the theater and later at Madame Herries'. Afterward it had been with them as it had been in their cabin aboard the *Independence*. With such love as theirs ever growing between them, they surely could defeat whatever went amiss.

But it was morning now, and Hugh was in a hurry to be off so as to call early upon Monsieur Arnaud. A little later Catherine went with Hugh to the door, bade him goodbye, and watched him go down the hall. Was it truly but yesterday, with Nathaniel leading and Antoine following, that he had set off down that hall to see Monsieur Bienfaite? Catherine closed the door and crossed the parlor to the windows. Soon Hugh emerged from the foyer below. She watched him go up Canal Street until he was out of sight.

Yesterday, Catherine recalled, he had gone forth hopefully with, it seemed, many opportunities to choose between. All was different today. With the exception of whatever plan Francis Byrne still kept up his sleeve—surely Hugh's pride would not let him go there—there remained no one but Monsieur Arnaud. Catherine struggled for hope. In her mind's eye she saw him and Madame Arnaud bow to Madame

Herries at the theater and Captain Eckhart bow to Hugh and herself. So perhaps . . .

She turned from the window and looked about the room. Light fell revealingly about the small parlor, exposing worn places in the carpeting and upholstery and small breaks in the wallpaper. Silence pervaded the atmosphere. Last night's veneer dissolved, and Catherine felt her fatigue.

Someone knocked, and with slow steps she went to answer. Amelia smiled and extended Madame Herries' invitation to accompany her this morning before ten o'clock to the Academy, where, according to *Le Courrier,* Monsieur Duhertise wished to meet New Orleans ladies and to tell them about his handwriting course. Catherine took the newspaper from Amelia and read, "The Duhertisian system of writing, taught by the real inventor at the Academy, No. 43 Camp Street. The system promises, in six easy lessons of one hour each, that any writing will be reformed to a beautiful, free, expeditious, and permanent hand suited to Commercial Interests, the Counting House, and the Merchants' Ledger, while ladies are taught a neat and fashionable hand, truly elegant . . ."

Catherine's impulse was to ask to be excused. She was tired and she felt little desire to reform her handwriting. Besides, her thoughts were with Hugh in his search for employment. She could not go with Madame Herries.

Then, as last night, she heard Hugh say again, "Aye, Kate, but you can." Though he was also tired this morning, he had not put off calling on Monsieur Arnaud. Catherine smiled at Amelia. "Please tell Madame Herries I shall be ready before ten." Possibly, she thought, closing the door after the maid, her going would somehow help Hugh.

Hugh continued up Canal Street to Bourbon and paused before the small brick octagonal church, enclosed in its white paling. Had the church been Catholic, he would have entered, knelt, and spoken to the Christ he believed present out of love for men in the Sacrament of the Eucharist. But the church was Episcopalian, the same Anglican church that the rejecting, impoverished Irish had been forced to support throughout England's long, brutal conquest. In truth, though, here in New Orleans, with the entrance overgrown with tall grass, it looked more Catholic than Church of England. A white marble monument offered the melancholy comfort of the long view of time, in which all stress—even such as his own—comes at last to rest. Sure, he reminded himself, a hundred years from now . . .

But, as this morning, Catherine stood before him, bidding him goodbye, tiredness beginning to show through the excitement she had not slept off, fear instead of laughter brightening her dark blue eyes, and Hugh swung about and faced Government House. There it was, diagonally opposite, retired from the street, as suited the hospital it had formerly been, and imposing, though plain, with its snow-white front and detached handsome wings. Hugh started along the walk through the large green where orange and lemon trees were in fruit.

A male secretary read both sides of the card Hugh presented, disappeared briefly into Monsieur Martin Arnaud's office, and returned. Would Mr. Condon be good enough to wait until Monsieur Arnaud was free? Hugh nodded and sat down.

The Honorable Martin Arnaud was a larger man than his cousin, the captain, and more loosely built. Older, too, Hugh thought, shaking hands, perhaps by ten years. His eyes smiled, but there was some part of himself that Monsieur Arnaud did not offer with his cigars. Nor, when Hugh declined, did he insist a second time that Hugh try one.

"Won't you sit down?" With an expansive gesture,

Arnaud motioned Hugh to a chair. Like his body, his manner was more relaxed than the captain's and on the surface more cordial. Yet when he withdrew a small folded knife from his trouser pocket, opened one of the blades, and cut off the end of his cigar, his hands had a preciseness in action that seemed to bring the captain right into the room. He put the cigar in his mouth, and his lips closed sensuously about it.

"Well?" From beneath the contractor's lowered lids, appraisal leaped across the desk to Hugh. "You would like to work?" He pulled deeply on his cigar, set it down, and picked up the card Hugh had given him. "As a supervisor?"

" 'Twas the captain's idea," Hugh managed coolly enough. "I believe he thought such an arrangement would be gain to us."

"In what way?" Arnaud's voice harshened.

"I can but guess as to what the captain had in mind. 'Twas he who volunteered the introduction."

Monsieur Arnaud chewed his cigar's end. "Yes, well, I am somewhat at a loss, too. The captain was with us last night at the theater, but I've had no chance yet to talk business with him."

Before Hugh could comment, Captain Eckhart, in civilian clothes, walked unannounced into the room. His cousin jumped to his feet and reached over his desk to shake hands. "Welcome!"

"Thank you," Eckhart said. Then, looking somehow less than the medium height Hugh remembered, he turned and shook hands with Hugh.

Hugh sought to leave.

"No, no," the contractor said. "You must stay now that the captain's come. A cigar, Cousin?"

But Eckhart pulled his own cigar from a pocket. "Thank you," he said, waving it. With that familiar preciseness, he cut off the end. Before he put the cigar in his mouth, he sighed, "Good to be home."

"You should get married," Arnaud said. "Matilda has found the right woman for you."

Captain Eckhart laughed. "What, another one?"

The two men looked searchingly at each other, and the question each had for the other remained unanswered.

Eckhart spoke first. "Well, have they showed up?"

His cousin nodded. "Yesterday, around noon."

"How are they doing?"

Monsieur Arnaud glanced at Hugh and back to the captain, shrugged, and threw out his hands. "No worse and no better."

A silence excluded Hugh.

"How was the crossing?"

"All right." He turned to Hugh. "Thanks on two occasions to Mr. Condon."

Arnaud flicked the ash from his cigar. "You have had experience handling these men, Mr. Condon?"

"I have worked with some of them before."

"Do you know our problem here?"

"I know only that a canal is being dug and that a fresh shipload of men has been brought for the digging."

Martin Arnaud laughed in his earlier easy way. "I guess that's about it, except"—his mouth tightened about the cigar—"except that we've been delayed overlong what with hot weather, mosquitoes, yellow fever, cholera . . ." He leaned across the desk, and sudden passion inflamed his voice. "Every day's delay eats into profits! What we need, Mr. Condon, is a supervisor who will drive them. Do you understand what I mean —drive them?"

Hugh stood. "Suppose I walk out to the canal, look it over, and then let you know?"

The cousins communicated in silence.

"Very well," Arnaud said, standing also. "But don't take too long. We need someone today."

Captain Eckhart rose. "My greetings to your wife, Mr. Condon." He turned to his cousin. "You remember? In Madame Herries' pew last night?"

Martin Arnaud's eyes turned lively and speculative. "I do, indeed!"

"Is Monsieur Arnaud as pleasant as his wife?" Catherine asked hopefully. The meeting with Monsieur Duhertise was over, and Catherine had again climbed after Madame Herries into her carriage.

"My dear, you know people marry their opposites. Monsieur Arnaud is a monster."

"A monster!" Catherine gasped and sank weakly into the carriage cushions. "Poor Hugh, trapped perhaps this very moment . . ." Was there no way she could help him? Only one, she decided. She could pray. They had come a distance from No. 43 Camp Street and were nearing the cathedral. If only she might go in, and there, in the holy quiet, speak to Christ, pray for Hugh . . . But this was unlikely to fit in with Madame Herries' plans. She was much too bent upon worldly matters to take time out for so uncertain a thing as prayer. As their carriage reached the cathedral, Catherine could no longer restrain herself, and she cried out impulsively, "I must stop here!"

Alarmed at first, Madame Herries adjusted quickly and called to Antoine to stop. "My dear, I understand," she said. "You are a Catholic. You are devout. I will leave you and go on. I will return within the hour. Wait here for me."

"Will you not come in, too?"

Madame Herries shook her head. "My religion is within me," she said, pressing her hands expressively upon her expansive breast. "I do not find God in churches."

The front of the cathedral, as Catherine walked toward it, was thrown into shade and seemed to brood upon the surrounding scene.

"Mrs. Condon, is it?"

Catherine looked about and saw Patricia just leaving the cathedral. "Patricia! How are you? How is Patrick?"

"I be well enough, thank ye, and so be Pathrick, thank ye agin. 'Tis of th' ithers thit ye should be aftir askin."

"Then tell me about them."

"Do it matter to ye? Thin fir why dinna ye go yeersel to th' Irish Channel?"

Guilt at her failure to do so overwhelmed Catherine. Still, this was only her second day in New Orleans, and she had been concerned first of all about Hugh. But how had she busied herself in his absence yesterday and today? With Madame Herries, with shopping, and now with this trip to the Academy. Her mother had always placed her concern for Chapelizod's poor first.

"I should have done so, Patricia," she said. "Are things bad with them there?"

The dike of Patricia's self-restraint broke. Catherine listened, her eyes darkening with horror. She saw the tar-papered shacks, overcrowded, scarcely furnished, dirty, with the mosquito-breeding outhouses nearby and the children playing in the disordered litter all about. She saw the women struggling to prepare meals with the little they could buy at the market, and the men coming home at the day's end with their talk of death in the canal. She heard the bereaved family wail and someone say how in Ireland there would be at least a wake and a decent Christian burial. She understood how some among them grew angry at the false promises which had brought them far from Ireland's green fields and blue lakes, and why the men went for whiskey while the women withdrew to a more bitter loneliness than the daytime emptiness they had waited through.

At Catherine's shocked face, Patricia stopped. "Aw, aftir all, it be nat so bad."

"Not so bad?"

Patricia shrugged. "Thir be worse ways of livin. They can cry togither, an onct in a while laugh togither, an they niver lack fir someone nearby. 'Tis fir th' want of sich comforts thit Pathrick an mesel thin of laving th' Byrnes an goin to live in th' Irish Channel. I said to himsel last night, whin th' two of us were alone, an I'm shure 'tis thrue, 'Thir maum be more to life thin this iverlastin kapin clane.' "

As Catherine bade Patricia goodbye, after promising to come to the channel, she went into the cathedral. Besides Hugh, she took these other people to pray for. And what of yourself? an inner voice inquired. She knew she ought not to hate so. Yet what was it but hatred of Francis Byrne that had kept her from asking Patricia about him and his wife? Patricia had waited, expecting her to, when she had asked after Hugh.

"Tell Mr. Condon we'll niver forgit 'im," she had said, "an we wish 'im all th' Lord's best."

Hugh came out of Government House and followed the Mall along Canal Street. Not far beyond Canal, it formed a right angle and extended down Rampart Street to Esplanade, where it made another right angle and extended back again to the Mississippi, nearly surrounding the city proper with a triple row of sycamores. The morning sun brightened the leaves of the trees. Hugh passed Dauphine and Burgundy Streets and paused where the Mall turned at Rampart. He could see a great distance down Rampart, and as far as he could see, the leaves of the sycamores glittered like metal beneath the hot sun.

"Better take off your coat," someone, who had stopped to take off his, called to Hugh.

" 'Tis a day to make one do so," Hugh agreed, though he kept his on.

"Indian summer," the other volunteered.

"Is that what 'tis called here?"

"Whatever other name would you give it?"

"In Britain 'tis called Little Summer of Saint Luke when it comes in October, and Saint Martin's Summer when it comes in November."

"It only has one name here whenever it comes. Indian summer—and that's the right name for it. When you think summer has gone, with its heat and mosquitoes and yellow fever and malaria, it sneaks back treacherously, like an Indian." He smiled as he pulled a large handkerchief from his trouser pocket and wiped the sweat from his face. "Better take off your coat," he advised again, and walked on.

Hugh followed the Mall along Rampart Street. The buildings differed from those along Canal. Here they were French and Spanish, with entrances leading into flower-filled courts. In the bright sunlight, both buildings and flowers seemed to blaze with color. The brilliance added to the heat, and he decided to follow the advice he had been given and took off his coat. He went on, crossing Iberville and Bienville Streets.

As he passed Bienville, he saw that many waiting carriages reached in a long line to the next crossing. Before the Catholic chapel at the corner of Conti and Rampart Streets stood a hearse whose horses wore tall black plumes on their heads. Drawn by the reverent committing of the dead to God, Hugh stepped under the portico's shade and looked into the church. A dozen huge wax candles in tall candlesticks burned about a coffin beneath a black velvet pall on a high frame in the center of the chapel. There was no place to sit, and the mourners, each holding a long, unlighted wax taper tipped at the larger end with red and ornamented with fanciful paper cuttings, formed a lane from the altar to the door. Several priests and altar boys in black and white robes were chanting the Requiem Mass for the dead. Beneath surface differences, the service was the one Hugh knew in Chapelizod. He was comforted by the feeling of being at home.

"May the angels lead thee into paradise," he prayed as he had learned to do as a boy. "May the martyrs receive thee at thy coming, and lead thee into the holy city of Jerusalem. May the choir of angels receive thee, and mayest thou have eternal rest with Lazarus who once was poor."

Softly Hugh stepped away from the portico's shade, past the casual spectators and black servants, and continued on his way along Rampart. He came to St. Louis Street and finally to Toulouse, and there he turned left. At once he was assaulted by a noisome odor which mingled with the heat. He walked past another square and came to the basin from which the canal was being extended for six miles to Lake Pontchartrain.

He strolled beside the canal and above it, looking down to observe to what depth and width it had been dug at this end; the stink seemed to roll up from the gash opened into the swamp, the damp heat to press down from above. He stopped often to wipe his face, neck, and hands, and to shift from one arm to the other the damp weight of his coat. He could not say how far along the canal he had come when at last he saw them at work.

There they were, mid-deep in the swamp, among stumps of trees, bringing the axes in their uplifted arms down on the stumps. A little ahead of them, powerful steam engines were vigorously pumping the water from the swamp, aggravating the heat with their noise and steam. Hugh looked back at the workers. Some of them were waving their hands and swatting at the mosquitoes that swarmed all about. Even at the height from which he watched, there was something familiar about the men's movements and gestures.

He saw them again at the sight of the cow in the overhead pulley, breaking out into joyful jigs on the *Independence* deck. He saw them swing from hostility to affection when Patricia's brother said George Macaulay was a Ribbon Man; from confusion to calm when he began to lead them in prayer for the suicide Patrick; from rebellion to endurance of hunger and thirst when he promised an earlier arrival in America.

Remembering Arnaud's ruthless remarks, Hugh could feel his fists, first one, then the other, thudding into the putty of the contractor's face. His violence subsided, and to revive it, he glanced below to the men.

One of them toppled into the mud. Two others supported him for a moment and then, with the gesture with which the living let go of the dead, dropped him and continued their work.

"May the angels lead thee into paradise," Hugh began. But who was there to listen? Was there, indeed, anyone to hear a prayer for this poor man, driven forth in want from his homeland to this? A terrible retching tore through Hugh, and he leaned over and vomited into the canal. Was this, he asked himself, straightening, the New World to which he had come with such hope and to which he had brought Kate?

The fierceness was alive again in Hugh's fists when, freshened by a washing and clean clothes, he returned to Monsieur Martin Arnaud's office in Government House.

"Monsieur Arnaud," Hugh was told. "No, he has left for lunch and a siesta."

"Will he return?"

"Not today. Tomorrow."

"Very well." Hugh felt his hands relax, the fight going out of them. He turned and walked away. In the hall he paused and looked about at the doors leading to the legislators' offices. While he delayed, uncertain as to what to do, a nearby door opened and the Honorable Francis Byrne came out. The anger grew alive again in Hugh's fists. He waited to give Byrne time to leave without an encounter. But Francis Byrne saw him and came toward him smilingly, his hand outstretched in greeting.

"Roberta and I have missed you and your wife. How is she?"

'Tis but a game, then, Hugh perceived. Well, I shall play it and beat him in the end. He took Byrne's hand.

"Thank you, we both are well. And you?"

"Well, too. Will you not come into my office? I have been wanting to talk to you. Tell me first, how is Kate finding New Orleans?"

Catherine paused, then slid into a pew at the rear of the cathedral, awed by the contrast with the small Chapelizod church. She knelt and said an "Our Father" and a "Hail Mary" perfunctorily, after which the high altar ceased to confuse her. There, as in Chapelizod's tiny church, with the light burning before it, was the tabernacle, and she believed herself to be alone.

She was not, however. Three girls, about Madges' age, followed by a black maid bearing a rug, started up the aisle to the niche where a pensive statue of Mary stood. The maid spread the rug before the statue and withdrew. The girls knelt, put their hands together piously, and bowed their heads. After a while they got up, and each took an ornament from herself and put it on the statue—a sacrifice, Catherine understood, for an "intention."

There was something appealing in the brief tableau, the girls' youth, their need, their small gifts. But what had it to do with harsh reality? Was it her own psychic need to commune at some deep level of her being that created an answering understanding? Or was it, as she believed, Christ living beyond His death in the Eucharist? She felt a presence in the tabernacle; caring and, she might hope, loving and wanting a return.

Well, what was she to do? She could not help Hugh by herself, much less those in the Irish Channel. What, then? She came to it reluctantly. Perhaps she must give up as her "sacrifice" her intense dislike of Francis Byrne, her hatred really, since last night, for what he had done to prevent Monsieur Bienfaite from giving Hugh the work he had come to America to do.

"After all," Madame Herries interrupted Catherine's account of conditions in the Irish Channel, "we will not go to Monsieur Duhertise's class." The horses' hooves sounded rhythmically as Madame Herries' carriage rolled through the siesta hour's quiet. She leaned confidingly closer to Catherine. "Monsieur Duhertise is an imposter!"

"An imposter?"

"An imposter," Madame Herries repeated firmly. "The true purpose of his being here has come to light."

She tossed her head knowingly and pulled from her purse the clipping she had torn from *Le Courrier de la Louisianne*. "Here," she said, "read it!"

Testimonials include that of the celebrated O'Connell, M. P. styled 'Ireland's Liberator,' who declared, 'The Duhertisian system is highly worthy of the patronage of the people.'

Then, Catherine concluded to herself, 'twas some purpose the two of them, O'Connell and Monsieur Duhertise, shared. But who would have guessed O'Connell's efforts reached so far? And how much of his earnings from his handwriting courses did Monsieur Duhertise take back to "Ireland's Liberator"?

She handed the clipping back to Madame Herries. "I am sorry."

"No need to be," Madame Herries said, putting her hand warmly upon Catherine's. "It's no matter. Oh," she conceded, "some will take his course, but we shall not do so. We shall open our own school, you and I . . . for children."

Though she was becoming accustomed to Madame Herries' impulsiveness, this was almost more than Catherine could adjust to. "Our own school? How?"

"I shall announce it in *Le Courrier* just as Monsieur Duhertise announced his class. Did you not tell me you taught children in Dublin?"

"In Chapelizod," Catherine corrected.

Madame Herries waved the comment aside. "No matter. Did you not tell me that you missed teaching and that you wished you might work with the channel children?"

"But their parents cannot pay—"

"No matter." Madame Herries lifted her hand in dismissal. "We shall charge so much for the others that we can afford to take the channel children free of charge."

Catherine turned from her, but Madame Herries saw the tears and patted her friend's hand affectionately. "My dear," she said, "my ballroom will be our classroom, and our school will be quite the thing. You must have a title, however. Countess, perhaps . . . Yes, I believe Countess will do."

In the distance, the cathedral's three spires rose reassuringly through the siesta quiet. Catherine closed the curtains and returned to Hugh, leaning over him from behind his chair. "Were you fortunate, then?"

"I was. I am to be an assistant, so to speak, to a man of many interests who needs someone like myself to do a variety of tasks: keep books, direct others, follow the legislature . . ."

Catherine straightened. "Will he pay you well to do these many things?"

"Aye. I saw to that. I never let him be sure of me. We bargained, and as often as he might have beaten me down and gotten his way, I pretended an indifference I was far from feeling."

Marveling, Catherine walked around Hugh's chair and faced him. "However were you able to do so?"

"I do not know, Kate. But what I saw this morning made me both clever and hard, more so than I ever thought I had it in me to be. I was resolved that you and our child should not suffer like others."

"And so you settled things in your way?"

"At every turn in our talk."

Pride in her husband swept through Catherine, and confidence at being in his care. "You must feel very pleased with yourself to have done so much in one day."

"No, Kate, I do not. Those things I saw which made me both clever and hard also robbed me in some way of happiness. I thought they had robbed me of joy even in you. Then you came in and I heard you laugh with pleasure at finding me home, and I thought of the promise you are carrying and I knew the strangest thing of all—that joy can live beside sorrow. But I do not think this is true for those who cause sorrow . . ."

"Aye," Catherine said, and sat down on his lap, curving an arm about his neck. "I learned today of our friends on the Irish Channel. I wish what you gained for us today might also help them, but I doubt that it will."

"No," Hugh ageed, "but it may lead to my helping them later on. At least I know this. Those who drive them do not care what they, or others like them, think. But they themselves may care what those in positions better than their own think of what they do. I now have some hope of reaching people who can change things."

"Well, let us hope so." Catherine got up to make tea. "I have news for you, too. It concerns plans Madame Herries and I have for starting a school. But it must wait until you have told me the name of the man you will work for."

"Have you not guessed?"

"How could I?" She looked up from putting tea in the pot.

"His name is Francis Byrne . . ."

Catherine sprang back, dropping the container. "Not *the* Francis Byrne we sailed with from Dublin? Not the one who kept you out of Bienfaite Brothers? Not *that* one?"

Hugh came and put his arms around her. "Aye, Kate, that one."

Chapter 10

HUGH STARTED TOWARD THE DOOR, and his wife followed him heavily. She was by her own count near her time, and recently Madame Herries' physician, Dr. Ridault, had agreed: "Any day now." The doctor undoubtedly knew, Hugh thought, and wished he himself were less involved in the railroad bill.

"Feel all right?" he asked for a final time.

"Fine—in an abnormal sort of way."

"Today should tell the story, Kate."

"What story?" Catherine asked, though she knew what he was referring to. The New Orleans–Nashville Railroad urgently needed financial support, and getting it meant a great deal to her husband. Indeed, she sometimes laughingly said that between them they were undergoing two pregnancies—hers for the baby and his for the railway.

His had begun first, Catherine conceded, at Captain Eckhart's dinner when Francis Byrne had said, "What the country needs are railways criss-crossing from east to west and north to south. The Louisiana legislature has lately put through a bill incorporating a company to build a new one between New Orleans and Nashville." Since then, Hugh had become well acquainted with the Act of Incorporation, relating details to Catherine as she shared her physical changes with him. She knew—or should have known, for she had heard it often enough—that the act set capital stock at six million dollars with power to increase to eight million dollars, conferred an exclusive privilege to the Mississippi state line and an exemption from taxes for twenty years after completion, and allowed rates of transportation that would provide annual dividends of up to fifteen percent upon the stock from the time the stock was paid in. And Hugh realized she thought their child's birth could probably be more conveniently achieved.

Catherine was aware that all the concessions of the incorporating act had been inadequate and that the slave labor, by last November, had completed only one mile of track on piling, extending from the intersection of Canal and Robertson Streets out toward the Metairie Ridge. While the baby was growing within her, Hugh's projected cost system, developed for the Dublin distillery, was at work, forecasting that activity, lacking further funds, must stop on the railway before the end of May, about the time the baby was due. In every way, the baby's birth and the railway's seemed to Catherine inextricably connected.

Hugh opened the door just as someone came down the hallway—the tall, dark-haired Senator Cambon.

"*Bonjour,* Senator," Hugh greeted him.

"*Bonjour,*" Senator Cambon answered, bowing to include Catherine. "Let us breakfast together, Monsieur."

"Aye, save me a place next to you."

Hugh waited until the senator, with his long, still-youthful stride, had gone down the steps; then he closed the door quietly.

"Is it Senator Cambon you are not sure of?" Catherine asked.

"No. We can count on him."

"How can you tell for sure those you can count on from those you cannot?"

Hugh smiled at his wife. Perhaps her teaching the channel children right up to the time of delivery kept her mind quick while her body slowed. "Francis Byrne calls it the sixth sense of the Irish," he said. Then his smile faded. "I will tell you about that sixth sense. It is always to know what means *most* to the other person. Senator Cambon hates Senator Isaac De Guerre. He will vote *for* the railroad because, indirectly, it is a vote against De Guerre's shipping interests on the Mississippi and Ohio river's route . . . Say a prayer that all goes well."

Catherine's mischievous grin was meant to remind her husband of how she had agreed, at his bidding on that Indian-summer day months before, to give up her hatred and to accept his going to work for Byrne.

"Am I to pray for success founded on hate of another?" she asked. "Will the Lord hear such a prayer?"

Hugh chuckled at his wife's turning the tables on him. "It is somewhat different from how you put it, Kate. For one thing, it is not Senator Cambon's vote we need."

"Still, he is on your side and he hates Senator De Guerre."

"But that is not the question."

"What is it, then?"

"It is simply whether or not the New Orleans–Nashville Railroad will be built. You remember we feared at one point it would not be."

Catherine nodded. She had listened in bed to Hugh's story of bringing his projected accounts to the second-floor office in Government House. "The figures spoke for themselves," Hugh had said, "and Francis Byrne, for once, had nothing to say. His face went empty." It was then, Catherine remembered, though Hugh had forgotten, that she herself had suggested the loan. In the end, the agreed-on bill required the State of Louisiana to loan the New Orleans Railway Company five hundred thousand dollars on condition that the company execute to the state a first mortgage on its road and property for the payment of the principal and interest at six percent. It was this bill, with its further stipulations, that the Senate would vote on today.

"The House voted the necessary help," Hugh continued now. "Byrne saw to that, once he was head of the Standing Committee. You remember what work I had to get him the spot?"

"Aye. 'Twould take the railroad itself to pay for all you have done."

Hugh stopped as though a new thought had struck him. But he merely said, "We must win first, and much as I dislike to leave you, I must go or Jean Cambon will wonder."

"And here comes Amelia with my breakfast. I and my child are as hungry for food as you and your railroad are for financing." Though she agreed to his going, she threw her arms about his neck, detaining him a bit longer. "Go now," she said after a while, "and battle while I prepare for my channel children."

At Catherine's mention of the channel children, Hugh's head dropped, and he walked down the corridor reflectively. Months had passed, and Christmas come and gone, since that Indian-summer day when he had observed his countrymen at work on the New

Basin Canal and sickened. In the interval, many of those who had shared the crossing aboard the *Independence* were finding their way into other work, serving the river and the cotton presses, driving the drays and carriages. However, living conditions on the channel remained inhuman. In the summer, people there died of yellow fever, smallpox, and cholera. Some argued that the infectious diseases started and spread from there. He had tried unsuccessfully to interest Francis Byrne. He must try someone else, maybe one of the senators, but not today . . . Today he had all he could handle.

As he made his way through the dining room to the place Senator Cambon was holding for him, Hugh acknowledged greetings. Jean Cambon half rose from his chair. "Anyone would think it was you, not I, who was senator." His eyes glinted wistfully.

"Such an error would be corrected by a trip to Government House."

The senator laughed and clapped Hugh on the back. "Nevertheless, you might like to run for office." Cambon's eyes narrowed. "Do you sometimes think of this?"

"I think of one thing at a time." Hugh paused to greet Antoine and to permit him to put down the breakfast plates of cornmeal and bacon. "Today I think of getting the Senate to approve the loan to the New Orleans–Nashville Railroad."

Cambon's eyes brightened, revealing imaginative depths. "This means a great deal to you?"

Hugh opened his hands disarmingly. "My livelihood is tied to the railroad's success. If this bill fails, the railroad stops."

A question filled Jean Cambon's eyes, but he stared down at his plate and silently speared a piece of bacon. After a short period, he said, "Senator La Bruyere knows he can count on my vote. I've assured him he can also depend on Senator Maintenon's. Senator Isaac De Guerre has had it his way long enough. His blue-blooded nose isn't big enough any more to stand in the way of railroad development."

Hugh gestured doubt. "It still casts a shadow. Three are bound to vote with him."

Cambon nodded. He knew who they were and how their interests tied in to De Guerre's.

"Then there's Senator Pascal."

Cambon nodded again. "He'll vote with De Guerre every time in the hope of tucking his feet one day under De Guerre's table. Pascal controls the votes of two more. And there's still Senator de Joinville, head of the Senate Standing Committee—"

"But that's it!" Hugh broke in. "Pierre La Bruyere has his three brothers, you, and Henri Maintenon, as well as Jacques Necker and Delos Faguet, who also believe in the railroad!"

Uncertainty tormented Cambon's eyes. "Why? Are they tied in in some way?"

Hugh shook his head. "They think the country's future depends on the railroad's development. They believe the country needs both river routes and railroads."

"Hard to understand men like that, men without personal motivation."

"They would find it hard to understand others."

Cambon's eyes again filled with a question. "And you, which kind do you understand?"

"It is my business to understand all."

Senator Cambon laughed. "Well, we have eight of the seventeen, and we need nine. That leaves Senator Guillaume Faguet."

"Right. With his vote, we lose or we win."

As Hugh sought an excuse to break away, little sandy-haired Senator Maintenon came in late for breakfast, greeting all on his way in the buoyant, effusive manner he affected. Hugh returned his *"Bonjour,"* gave him his chair next to Cambon, and excused himself. As he hurried through Madame Herries' place and stepped out into the New Orleans May day, it struck him that Kate was right. For all he had done and had still to do, it would indeed take the railroad itself to compensate. Why not take stock in it instead of the promised bonus if all went well today?

From the window above, Catherine watched her husband start up Canal Street. Ever since Hugh had accepted the job working for Byrne, she had tried to adjust to the fact that Hugh's and Representative Byrne's plans were now the same.

Well, I must accept the real world, as Hugh says, she thought, and this is real enough for me. She sat down to her breakfast tray. Pain struck suddenly, and, unwarned, she cried out. Was this the onset? She waited, but the pain did not recur. She found she had appetite only for coffee. Perhaps she ought not to teach today? But the children were coming. She would take them this last time and at noon tell them not to come again until they heard further. They were used to birth in the Irish Channel. They would understand.

The channel students were late again. They were at present Catherine's only pupils, for, with the approach of warmer weather, the parents who paid had withdrawn their children out of fear of yellow fever. Who can blame them? Catherine thought while she waited.

Still, she knew, as did all informed people, that the disease was transmitted by mosquitoes that carried it from one person to another. But what panic warm-weather fever brought to the affected one and those concerned! Might this be yellow fever? More often than not, it seemed, the dreaded developments followed quickly, sometimes within hours. There would be the flushed face, congested eyes, red nostrils and lips, scarlet tongue. Then came the unspeakable vomiting, dark with blood, and the hemorrhaging, and finally the feeble pulse, cold skin with lemon-yellow tint, and, all too often . . . death.

Catherine shook herself free of last summer's stories—and thought of the children who must surely arrive soon. Awaiting them in the large chilly room that had been Madame Herries' ballroom and which the landlady could not afford to heat for the nonpaying channel children, Catherine saw her pupils tumbling out of their disordered shacks to await their uncertain trip by dray to school. She sat down on a backless bench with frayed, soiled, rose-colored cushions from which young ladies had once risen to dance, and pulled out of her skirt's deep pocket the letter she had gotten yesterday from her mother.

Kate, dear,

It was with relief that we learned from your last letter, written ten days before Christmas, that the yellow fever had subsided. Perhaps the iron pipes that have replaced the old wooden ones will improve conditions this coming summer and lessen the dreadful contagious disease which unsanitary conditions are known to cause. Let us hope so.

We are happy to know also that Tulane University has opened a School of Medicine. A medical school should help not only by training physicians but by checking the spread of these terrible illnesses. As you know, your grandfather was a physician, and since the penal laws limited his practice, he did research in the very diseases you mentioned. Take every precaution again this summer with water and with milk and avoid all unnecessary contacts for yourself and for the baby who may already be with you by the time this letter reaches you. How I hope so! I need not say how sorry I am not to be with you at the time of birth.

Indeed, your father and I sometimes talk of coming to visit. Besides our great desire to see you and Hugh and the baby, we cannot help wishing to escape here for a time. We are now feeling the worst effect of last fall's poor potato crop. There is much suffering. I am sorry to write that your father's health lately has not been as good as usual. Even so, he insists on working on his history.

He was most pleased to hear that President Jackson is losing popular support, since he understands from you that it is to Hugh's advantage to have a President who is opposed to Federal investment in public improvement so as to leave open opportunities for local undertakings like Hugh's railroad. (I confess I myself do not quite understand this.) Moreover, your father is concerned about Jackson's destroying the National Bank. The poor man, with so little means of his own, to be worrying his head over this.

Jerry appears to be making good progress at school. While in England, he sees much of the Kemrises. We suspect it is Harriet. Please keep our dear George in your prayers.

The longing to have her parents come for a visit pulled Catherine up from the bench. If Hugh's bill passed the Senate today, besides his monthly pay he was to have a large bonus. Hugh had said it was to be hers to do with as she wished. Often he asked, "Well, and have you decided?" Her answer had always been, "I have not, not as yet." But now at last she had. She would use it as a down payment on a house, perhaps not as large as the one in Chapelizod with rooms to spare, but large enough to allow her mother and father to visit in comfort their grandchild, her, and Hugh.

All through the morning's classes—during prayers, singing, writing, doing sums, and reading—excitement buoyed up Catherine and inspired her in resolving difficulties. When the children complained the room was cold, she led them to the empty fireplace and imagined with them a tremendous fire roaring in the grate. "Do not move so close to the fire, Norah, lest your dress catch! Stand back a little," she cautioned, and the children laughed merrily as, pulling her dress closely about her, Norah stood back. "And now you are warm," Catherine said, "make a big circle, slip off your shoes, and skip about the room three times until you have come back to your own pair of shoes."

She stood aside, seeing with sorrow how poor the shoes were they had removed and set down. Perhaps Madame Herries or her friends . . . But no, she must take care not to ask for too much. With only the poor students coming nowadays, Madame Herries spoke less often of "my school." Indeed, it was generous of her still to allow use of the room and of her friends to provide the books.

A quick, sharp pain caused Catherine to turn her thoughts to herself. There could be no mistake. She was relieved it had come when she was alone, and forewarned her so that she could control any outcry before the children.

When the students had gone, she tried to wait patiently. But the pains recurred with decreasing intervals in between. Amelia looked in and ran in alarm for Madame Herries. Over her protests, Catherine was installed for the event in the huge bed in her friend's room.

Madame Herries, her sense of drama alerted, prepared to take charge. "Amelia," she ordered, "get Antoine. Tell him to go at once for Dr. Ridault."

With longing Catherine thought of her own mother's wholesome sanity in a crisis. How often she had hurried off to help at a birth. And now her daughter was to have instead Madame Herries, who lived a flight above reality in the make-believe world she conjured up and presided over.

"Now, little Countess," Madame Herries said, "you have only to wait for Dr. Ridault. He was educated in Paris, you know, at the university there—"

The door to the bedroom opened, and Patricia walked in.

Madame Herries drew herself up and without speaking demanded to know who this woman might be. Patricia passed by her and went directly to Catherine. "Shure it be th' children told me, an I made Pathrick to forgit his lunch. 'Git me thir right off in yeer dhray, Pathrick,' I said.

" 'Ye mane without me ateing?' he asked.

"An I said, 'Thit be me viry maning, clare an plain.' "

"Madame Herries, this is Patricia," Catherine said.

"Patricia? Patricia?"

"Th' midwife to ye, Madame Herries," Patricia explained, "an heer to see Mrs. Condon's child into this world safe an sound."

"But Dr. Ridault is sent for."

"Lit 'im come, thin, an welcome so long as he dinna intirfere!"

Madame Herries looked at Catherine, but her mouth was wide in a silent outcry of pain. "If you'll excuse me," she said, "for just a moment."

"We'll ixcuse ye, but ye maum plan on more thin a momint," Patricia said to the exiting Madame Herries. In an undertone, she added to Catherine, "Biteen she know about this—her as ave niver had wan."

There was a pause between contractions. Catherine could not resist asking, "But, Patricia, are not you and Madame Herries alike in that?"

"Her an me air no ways alak, Mrs. Condon."

"I mean you also have not had children."

"Th' Lord niver seen fit," Patricia said stonily. Clearly hers was a case of an altogether different kind. "An now ye'd best give over takin up fir yeer Mrs. Herries and lave thins to me. 'Tis miny a wan I helped into this world, an ivery wan safe an' sound."

An unrepressed outcry at a more intense contraction brought Madame Herries running back into the room, Poo-poo following.

"What is it? What is it?"

Patricia's weighted pause indicted Madame Herries of folly. At last she said severely, "'Tis th' customiry thin. Th' infant be on th' way. Lave her scrame. She canna help it. No more could yeer mi—"

Madame Herries drew herself up and began, "My mother—"

But Patricia had seen Poo-poo. "Niver min yeer mither jist now. An I'll thank ye to git thit cat out of this heer room and to kape it out. I'll have no cat ocastin a spell."

"Poo-poo." Madame Herries stooped and picked up the cat. "This is not your moment. Later—"

"Nat so long as I be heer an in charge," Patricia interjected, and closed the door after Madame Herries.

When Catherine could relax again, she wished for Hugh to share her amusement. In all the world were there two more disparate women? And here they were, joined in her care. I must count myself fortunate to have them, she thought. Otherwise . . . An immense loneliness invaded her. She was back in Chapelizod, and her mother was imploring her to wait on developments rather than leave immediately with Hugh. No doubt her mother had anticipated out of her own experience. For the first time, Catherine thought with awakened compassion of her mother's giving birth to her. She also had been a first child. The channel children seemed to march before her, each somehow more precious. Had each cost agony like hers? Worse, she knew, seeing the immigrant women give birth amidst squalor. Even in the steerage there had been births.

The door opened again, and a slender, ascetic-looking man followed Madame Herries in. With the victor's conciliatory smile, she announced, "Dr. Ridault."

Nodding considerately to Patricia, he moved swiftly to Catherine. "Mrs. Condon!" Authentic concern broke in a smile through the doctor's native austerity.

Catherine thanked him with her smile. From the first she had liked him. "Aye," she said, and reached for his hand.

Dr. Ridault turned to Madame Herries. "We . . ." He nodded to Patricia.

"Patricia be me name."

"Patricia and I," he amended, "shall both want freshly laundered overall garments. Something from the kitchen will do very well. And separate basins of heated water. Antisepsis, you know. I have brought a calcium chloride solution."

"I know indeed," Madame Herries said. "Your years in Paris—"

"'Tis not in Paris we be now," Patricia interrupted. "But heer in th' New World an' an infant fightin to git into it."

"How right you both are," Dr. Ridault said equably. His dark, deep-socketed eyes flashed amusement at Catherine.

From the adjoining room, Madame Herries was heard passing on Dr. Ridault's orders to Amelia.

"Oh," Dr. Ridault thought aloud, "and we shall want many copies of *Le Courrier de la Louisianne.*"

"We shall nat be wantin thim yit fir some hours."

"You are right, but it is best that we have them on hand. You'll excuse me." He was heard adding this request to the others, and Madame Herries passing it on to Amelia.

"Niver min thim." Patricia took advantage of being for the moment solely in command. "Jist remimber 'tis all up to ye. Brathe aisy, aisy as ye can. Kape barin down mich as ye can so ye'll help yeer baby to come. Remimber if 'tis a hard time ye be havin', th' biteen wan is havin a yit harder time. An ye do be wantin to help, do ye nat now?"

"Oh, Patricia, I do. You know I do. And you know I thank you for coming."

"Niver min thanks. They be out of place now, as mich as yeer Madame Herries. Thir she be now, iver thinkin up somethin disturbin."

"Dr. Ridault," she was heard saying, "do you not think we should send for Mrs. Condon's husband?"

With a groan, Catherine turned to Patricia. "Oh, no—no—no."

"Ye dinna want 'im?"

"Yes, I do, I do—but we must not send for him. He

is fighting his own fight today, a fight he must win . . ."
She was ready now, she felt, after he had won, for the
question "Well, and have you decided?" The answer
was "Aye." And 'twas a house of their own she
wanted, one to which *they* could come . . .

Patricia had marched to the door. "Mrs. Condon
says plase nat to disturb Mr Condon jist yit."

"But I think he would want—"

"Lave us do as she wishes jist now."

"For the time being," Dr. Ridault agreed, reenter-
ing the room and making ready to close the door after
him. "A first birth. It will be long, many hours yet."

And it was long. Though no longer than usual for a
first birth, Dr. Ridault said. Still, fourteen hours had
passed since the first early pain. It was night now, after ten o'clock, and through the partly open windows
came the stirrings of revelry. Inside, Madame Herries,
alert to the impending drama despite her flouted authority, kept to her drawing-room sofa. In the room
with her was Hugh, long since returned from Government House, rocking back and forth on his feet in
his restless way, staring toward the door which kept
him from his wife, stopping and standing dead-still at
her screams, his hands pressed to his ears.

A final anguished cry reached him, "No, I can no
more!" as the infant squeezed and pushed against the
walls of its mother's bony outlet. Catherine was
alone in a world that excluded all others, a world of
suffering, wholly her own.

Seemingly from afar she heard Patricia shout, "Ah,
at last, th' bag of waters!" and felt the baby's head
emerge.

A glance passed between Dr. Ridault and Patricia
like a contest of wills. Out of character though it was,
Patricia yielded. Quickly, with his adroit, fine hands
Dr. Ridault grasped the infant's head, slowing delivery
momentarily. Watching judiciously, Patricia understood he was minimizing any tearing. She drew herself
up authoritatively. Would she not herself do the same?

"An lave us see phwat more they taught ye in Paris," her posture demanded.

Gently Dr. Ridault maneuvered. First one shoulder, then, after a pause, the other, and finally the small body eased out. His glance yielded to Patricia, and she stepped forward and received the baby.

Catherine heard a slap and a cry, then Dr. Ridault marveling, "Ah, another miracle!"

Still remote in a world of her own, Catherine hazily recalled earlier moments of triumph . . . The *Independence* moved out of the enclosing peninsulas into the Irish Sea . . . and later that night Hugh and she, in some mysterious way, were one with the most secret impulses of nature . . . But no previous experience matched giving birth to another human soul, Catherine thought as Patricia handed her her little daughter. "Safe an' sound!"

Hugh entered the room and stood beside the bed, looking down at her and the baby. The loneliness Catherine had known in pain so short a time before was already quickly retreating.

"Aye, Kate," Hugh said softly, "you have won."

"And you?"

"I also, but I doubt not that your fight was the harder."

She waited, but he did not ask, "Have you decided?" She was too tired to remind him. Dozing, she thought, We have begun.

Chapter II

IT WAS THE AFTERNOON of Christmas Eve, their third in the Crescent City, and Catherine knelt to arrange the nativity figures on the parlor's deep windowsill. Emily, nineteen months old, hovered by companionably. Hugh was due any minute and indeed should have returned earlier.

Catherine glanced up Canal Street, hoping to see him hurrying home. She could recognize him some distance off by his swift, excited walk. But there was still no sign of him.

"Daddy?" Emily asked. Catherine turned from the window to the child. How enchanting she was with her small, delicate face and the dark hair and eyes George and Jerry had.

"Aye, Daddy," Catherine said. "Soon now."

What was detaining him? To be sure, she realized, it was the railroad again. The act passed by the legislature the previous year had helped, but not enough. The railroad was in fresh difficulty. She rearranged the creche figures and Emily tried to help, moving them about this way and that, seemingly with a plan of improvement. Her mother laughed and let her. "I must get a candle."

From the mantel, where she now displayed the Gothic sandwich tray bought that early day for Nathaniel, she took one of the candles and put it on the windowsill. In Chapelizod they always did so. When it turned dark outside on Christmas Eve, they lit the wick, hoping Mary and Joseph would see it and feel welcome to come in.

She seemed to drift back in time to when she and her brothers were children. As she, George, and Jerry peered into the dark, their mother blew out the lighted taper. "There, now, and welcome to you."

"Might they not like it better at the Kemrises'?" Jerry asked.

"And why would they?" George demanded.

"It is . . . far grander there."

"As if," their mother said with mingled scorn and gentleness, *"they* care for *that!"*

"Care for what?" their father asked, coming belatedly from his desk.

But no one would tattle on Jerry.

"No matter," their father said; " 'tis a good thing to be able to hold one's own counsel."

At their father's favoring a stand which just now worked against his wish to know, they all had laughed heartily.

Remembering, Catherine laughed again, but not without regret. She had hoped this Christmas that she, Hugh, and Emily would be in a New Orleans home of their own, and if not the boys also, at least her mother and father with them for a visit. But the bonus last March, a substantial sum which Catherine had thought to apply toward a house, Hugh had used instead to buy shares in the railroad. Dismayed when he had told her how he spent the money, she had gasped with shock.

"But it was you, Kate, who gave the idea to me when you said, 'Twould take the railroad itself to pay for all you have done!' "

Well, she supposed, no doubt this was not the first time lightly spoken words had been taken literally. So instead of a house, we have a railroad that is partly ours.

But in Chapelizod tonight, Catherine thought, standing back and looking over her and Emily's nativity arrangement, her mother would also be lighting a candle in the window, and as all drew close to the

Christ Child, they would somehow also grow close to one another.

Though they were lacking the home she longed for, had they not much this Christmas to give thanks for? They had again come safely through another New Orleans summer of yellow fever, smallpox, and cholera, unlike so many others. Hugh had withdrawn their savings from the bank last spring before it, along with other New Orleans banks, failed. This, Catherine conceded, had been done on Francis Byrne's advice.

A knock at the door ended her reverie, and Catherine went to answer it.

"Merry Christmas!" Madame Herries was as gay as a child. "Plan to come to my Christmas Eve supper! I am again—reckless woman that I am—inviting all who will be here over the holidays. Supper will be late, late enough to allow you to go to Mass first." She came close and spoke confidingly. "Do you know the second coming of Christ draws near? My dear, I cannot wait. But I see," Madame Herries laughed her muffled laugh and shook her long forefinger, "you have a closed mind about this. *Your* church is not open to His second coming. But no matter; you must come to supper after the service."

So they would, and with pleasure, Catherine acknowledged, returning to Emily.

Hugh held Emily high overhead until her delight squealed itself out. Then as she went back to the nativity scene, he turned to Catherine. "You have been busy, I see."

"Aye. 'Tis Christmas Eve"—mischief crept into her eyes—"though there be some who take no heed."

"Do not count me among those, Kate." Nevertheless, he looked out the window to where the railroad was building and added, "We had a good talk."

"You and Francis Byrne?"

"Aye, and a number of the senators besides, and some of the Crescent City's business leaders as well."

"You talked of the railroad?"

"At first. Then another idea came to me."

He was rocking back and forth on his feet in his restless way. As he teetered before the windowpane, staring outside, the eagerness to know what he was thinking began to pound excitedly within her.

"This new idea . . . is it one that anyone may know?"

He turned and smiled at her as though, for the first time since he came in, he saw her instead of the plan that was filling him. He enfolded her affectionately, pressing his cheek against hers. "Not anyone, Kate," he said, letting her go. "But 'tis one *you* may know."

"Let us have it, then . . . before I die with waiting."

"No, you must be patient. Do not look so anxious, for when you do know, I fear all the rest of you will disappear into your eyes!

"It happened this way. Everyone was complaining that the railroad could not get anywhere so long as De Guerre keeps pounding it through *Le Courrier de la Louisianne,* which, as all know, he controls—"

"Is not that what everyone has been saying for months?"

"Aye. They were saying so once again. 'Twas right in the midst of this talk that the idea struck me. 'Why do we not start a paper of our own?' I asked. 'One that will hammer away at the river route as the *Courrier* hammers at the railroad, and that will boost the railroad as the *Courrier* boosts the river route.'

"Did you ever hear a silence noisier than talk? The silence that followed was such a one. Finally, Monsieur Bienfaite spoke the thought everyone had. 'This is war. And I know no better way to win. In fact, I know no other way.' Senator Cambon wanted to know what we would do for money. Everyone laughed. Then Monsieur Johnston said, 'Let every man here'—there were ten of us—'contribute or raise five hundred dollars, the price of a single female slave.'

" 'And let us meet in this coffee house again in a week, each with his five hundred,' Senator La Bruyere declared.

"With that, after a drink to toast your husband's idea, we broke up."

"So now we shall have not only a railroad but a newspaper."

"Aye, 'tis understood each man of us will also own stock in the paper." He went on after a pause. "The paper will also be a means of helping those still in the Irish Channel, though my partners as yet do not know this. I intend to use it as well to attack conditions there."

"I am glad for that. May we then perhaps have a home of our own and invite those we love to visit us?"

"We may, Kate. 'Tis America, where each man has a chance to prove himself and to grow rich."

"Yet it seems to me not so different, though I do not doubt there are some who will grow rich."

"You may put your husband at the head of those lucky ones."

Once again, as always before, Catherine put her faith in his words. Delighted to hope anew, she grabbed up the wondering Emily, lifted her high, squeezed her hard, and then put her down. An unresolved question had assailed her. "Hugh, where will you get your five hundred?"

" 'Tis Christmas, Kate," he said, merry as a boy. "The Christ Child will bring an answer."

The knocker fell against the door, and Hugh started to answer it. "That will be the Byrnes."

"Perhaps Patrick and Patricia." Catherine went with him.

It was neither couple. Before their doubting eyes stood the one person in the New World they were happiest to see. "Nathaniel!" they cried together. "Nathaniel! Is it really you?"

Nathaniel looked himself over as though he, too, needed to make sure, and laughed explosively. Then the arms of the three were about one another, and they stood there crying and laughing foolishly. Emily had tried to join in also, had fallen, and sat clapping her hands with delight.

From one bulging pocket Nathaniel pulled two small, brightly beaded deerskin slippers. He got down on the floor beside Emily. "We must see if the size is right. A little Indian girl from far up north sent you these. She said they would fit. And they do!"

"But where," Catherine exclaimed, "is your luggage? For, of course, you will stay—"

Nathaniel's head dropped, and Catherine noticed the slight drag of his foot as he moved back from fitting Emily. "I was not sure there would still be room."

Alternating with endearing hilarity was the remembered diffidence still. Perhaps, Catherine thought, the solitary life in the North . . . "But of course there is room!" she said. "My grandmother, for whom we named Emily, used to say, 'When there is room in the heart, there is room in the home.'"

"In any case, my luggage will not crowd you. I have but one piece. I sent the rest on ahead to Boston and came the roundabout way to see you."

He sat down and went on. "Many things urged me. There's this copper outcropping which surely indicates good ore below. Then, too, Michigan's come into the Union last January, and people are discovering the Upper Peninsula. Our old friend Captain Eckhart now sails the Great Lakes during the summers. It was he who told me of Emily. But we will talk later of what I hope for."

"Aye," Hugh said. "We will talk of whatever you please in your own good time."

Something like a sigh escaped Nathaniel. "I am sorry I have been delayed so long. But I am glad to arrive on Christmas Eve. You cannot think how different it is here from Christmas in Boston. Apart from the weather, there is such a coldness there, as though people have not quite made up their minds to let the Christ Child in. Here everything is gay, like a true birthday celebration." Nathaniel's head drooped moodily, and he looked up out of troubled eyes. "I say to myself, 'Either He came or He did not come.'"

"He came," Catherine said gently, conclusively, as

her mother would have said. "To me it seems your coming this Christmas is simply fresh proof. Do you not think so, Hugh?"

Suddenly Christmas had come to the street below, and they ran to the window. With a clatter, a horse-drawn omnibus was traveling down Canal Street, its driver and passengers jovially chanting, "A Merry, Merry Christmas." The driver swayed on his perch as he sang, and the whip danced in the holder beside him. Even the horses' hooves beat out the joyful refrain on the road.

The omnibus stopped, and Catherine saw Patrick and Patricia climb out, wave goodbye, and stroll down the street, still singing in unison with the passengers who drove on.

When Catherine opened their door, Patricia sang Merry Christmas again, and then, bearing aloft a large box with Emily's gift, she led Patrick into the room. They both stopped abruptly, surprised by Nathaniel, and Patrick drew back. "Is it yeersel thit we see, thrue enough?"

"Myself," Nathaniel answered, and went to shake hands with them. "You did not take me for the ghost?"

"Dinna make jokes of thit wan," Patrick said warningly. "Dinna all of us owe our safe, aisy crossing to 'im?"

"Were he here," Catherine said, "I believe he would want all of us to be happy."

"Aye," Hugh agreed. "That he would, and I must pour a glass of wine for each, and perhaps Patrick will drink a glass for *him* as well."

" 'Twould be fittin," Patrick acknowledged, "an I will be plased to do so."

Nathaniel was his rollicking self. He lifted his drink in a toast to Christmas, to the Crescent City, to the *Independence,* which had first brought them together. His laughter broke from him, unrestrained as a boy's. At the sound of it, they were all children again, with life's problems their parents' concern. Catherine's laughter rang as brightly as at home in the Chapelizod kitchen. Emily looked up in delight from the floor, echoed her mother's laugh, and rolled her new, big red rubber ball, which she had discovered in the box Patricia handed her.

"How have you found the New World, Patricia?" Nathaniel asked.

"Th' Christ Child forgive me if I say so, an this His birthday, 'tis but a shorry mess."

"Aye." Patrick followed his wife's straightforward lead. "Beggin His pardon an beggin yer own."

Nathaniel sobered. "I assumed you had found happy positions with the Byrnes."

"An who'd be happy with thim," Patricia asked, "who dinna know how to be happy thirsels?"

The merriment went out of Nathaniel's eyes. "Patricia, you have just spoken a deep, philosophical truth."

"I ave spake th' truth, an as for th' rest, ye maum jedge."

"Then you are not with the Byrnes now?"

"Nay. We be in th' Irish Channel with our own, an we lak it better thir. Though we dinna lak it thir nather. Fir this be truth . . . one or th'ither of us may catch yellow fever or cholera thir nixt summer, an who will thir be to care?"

"That's a sorry thought," Nathaniel sympathized. "Going out of the world unmourned . . . I used to entertain it, too, sometimes, up in the North, alone, at night . . ."

" 'Tis a shorry thought," Patrick agreed. "It maum throw a shadow on yeer welcome into th' nixt."

"What work have you been doing here, then?"

"I dhrive a dhray whin they lave me. Patricia heer cooks whin they lave her."

"Did himsel ask ye phwat I do?"

Patrick dropped his head like a child who had misspoken.

"Well, when spring comes again, how would the two of you like to come north? I will send you your steamship tickets for the river trip. And from there, you can choose one of several routes to Ontonagon, on Lake Superior's south shore. I will tell you the one I like best. There's copper up there waiting to be dug. I need a man to drive and care for a horse, and I need someone to cook."

The husband and wife looked at each other out of light blue eyes full of the abiding hope that life might yet take a turn for the better. Could this be that long-awaited turn? Patricia glanced about defiantly. Did anyone dare to say it was not?

Then, a second time, Nathaniel began. "Perhaps now that I know where to look for the copper veins— As you know, I have hoped . . ." He paused, for Patricia had stood.

"Lave us go, Pat, an break our good news to th' channel."

"But—the books," Catherine objected.

As she handed them to Patrick and Patricia—a volume for each boy and girl who would come again for lessons after Twelfth Night—she saw last year's little group about the imaginary blaze in the fireplace and said, "I wish a gift of warm clothing went with each book."

"Shure, th' wish will kape thim as warm," Patricia said, and led her husband from the room.

Silence caught the three who were left, and then Nathaniel asked, "Is it as bad as they say? And are people doomed to stay there?"

" 'Tis," Hugh said. "Though some are breaking away, many seem doomed to stay. But I think I now have the means to work a change there—"

Again a knock fell against the door, and this time the Byrnes came in, Roberta bearing a gift.

"Merry Christmas," Francis said authoritatively, as though the decision that it should be merry was his, and Roberta echoed the greeting. When they saw Nathaniel they stiffened in surprise.

Nathaniel crossed to them promptly. "Welcome to the company of the good ship *Independence*," he said, shaking hands.

"Thank you," Francis said, and with the air of holding court, he and his wife seated themselves as they had done on the ship's chest. Roberta held out the gift to Catherine. "For Emily."

"I shall open it now. Come see, Emily. This is a present from Mrs. Byrne to you."

It was a little girl's white, beruffled dress. "It is lovely," Catherine said warmly. "Emily and I both thank you." She turned over the embroidered ruffles while Hugh handed wine about. "I regret that I did not allow you to teach me to embroider aboard ship."

"Who of us does not repent his misspent youth?" Nathaniel asked with hilarity that sounded more like delight than regret. He lifted his glass to be refilled.

Byrne, however, had more pertinent things to say. "Has Hugh here told you our new plan?"

Nathaniel shook his head. Hugh glanced at Nathaniel and cleared his throat. Catherine thought, well, if it must be told, perhaps it is better told before Nathaniel puts hope into words.

"It is really quite simple," her husband began.

"Was there ever a good idea that was not?" Nathaniel asked.

"In any case, it is this. We have been trying for more than two years to build the railroad we need from New Orleans to Nashville. Yet New Orleans sits on its hands and refuses to hurry. We must have a newspaper to push our idea. To the public, it will be another New Orleans newspaper, and we hope one the people will like. But every day or two there will be a story telling of New Orleans' need of railroads, or one that will raise questions as to what is holding them up."

Hugh stopped to catch his breath, and Byrne, with the confidence of the victor, looked toward Nathaniel.

Like a man loathfully seeing the point of another's argument though it warred against his interests, Nathaniel asked, "How will you finance your paper?"

Francis Byrne disposed of the problem. "We'll have the money. Those of us who are in on this are all"—

he glanced at Hugh—"or nearly all, ready to put up five hundred dollars apiece."

Had Nathaniel missed Byrne's implication about Hugh, as Catherine wished, or had he caught it? Nathaniel's face was averted. His head dropped moodily, and he glanced up out of troubled eyes, as though, Catherine decided, he were repeating, "I say to myself, 'Either He came or He did not come.' "

Soon after the Byrnes had left, Nathaniel turned to Hugh, and slowly, as though resolving the near two-thousand-year-old question and fitting his own action to his answer, said, "I will lend you your share for the investment. I make but one condition. Should the paper not prove the answer, you are to come north and join my venture."

It was dark outside. Catherine got up quickly to light the window candle. She picked up Emily. Hugh and Nathaniel followed. Through the open window came the distant song of the black choir in Congo Square singing of Christ's coming. "Noel, Noel . . ."

His face warm with reminiscence, Nathaniel turned to Catherine. "I would hear this sometimes when I lay awake up there under the stars."

"Noel, Noel."

The singing took Catherine back to Christmas Eve in Chapelizod. For she perceived that the voices, though different, were the same—the voices of the deprived escaping into song, rising to the aspiration of a changed and happier life.

Chapter 12

"WHATEVER IS IT this morning, Hugh, that puts you in so great a hurry to be off?"

"You would know, Kate, had you but listened last night."

It was true. As Hugh had talked on the previous evening, her mind had kept jumping away from what he was saying to the home she craved. Whenever she had attempted to give him her attention, it seemed that the same happenings were forever repeating themselves. This August—their fourth in New Orleans—had not yet come to an end, and the money, delivered by legislative act to the railroad in the early spring of 1838, had been spent in the year and a half since, so that, once more, work threatened to stop. Had something now gone wrong as well with the newspaper Hugh's friends had been publishing these nearly two years? Yes, it was of the paper, she remembered, that Hugh had been speaking last night.

"Did you not say that Kendall Johnston had given the money to pay off the bills, and that, thanks to him, the paper would be coming out as usual today?"

"Aye, Kate, you listened rather better than you seemed to have done. Then you no longer wonder why I am in a hurry to be off. You must know it is to pick up an early copy."

"Can you not go first to see whether the letter I have been awaiting has come, and if so, bring it to me?"

Hugh half turned away. "I went yesterday, Kate, and the day before, and the day before that. What word are you expecting from your mother?"

Catherine hesitated. She had not yet told Hugh that she had written her mother early in the summer, when all was going promisingly, that she hoped to be in a home of their own before long and trusted that her mother and father would visit. Rather than go into a long explanation, she merely said, "Her answer to my letter is long overdue."

"Was there ever a letter from home that was not? Antoine will go for the mail at his usual time. Only be patient."

'Tis a bigger order than he knows, Catherine thought, when the door had closed after him and his steps were fading down the hall. Emily, awakened by the door's closing, and with the remoteness of sleep about her still, came dragging her daytime clothes into the room.

"So you would like to be dressed and get on with the day?" She picked Emily up, hugged her, and set her down. "I've news for you," she said, laughing. "We are both to be patient today."

"Ah, we have been patient, and here is our reward!" Emily looked up from her blocks on the windowsill as Catherine waved the letter Antoine had just brought, and crossed to the little desk to sit down.

Dearest Kate, Catherine read eagerly,

> You must know there has been good reason for my delay in answering. I write to tell you your father has found the way to be with each one of us.

"Oh, no!" Catherine exclaimed, dropping the note. Frightened, Emily knocked over the blocks and raced to her mother's side. Catherine caught the child up in her lap and pressed her lips against the dark, soft hair. Emily looked at her mother wonderingly.

"Grandfather . . ." Catherine said, and paused as her father's presence seemed to invade and fill the room, "has died."

Emily continued to gaze at her mother wide-eyed.

"Grandmother," Catherine continued, seeking to hold back tears, "says that he will be here with us now."

Emily gazed about the room searchingly.

I wish I could speak with him and hear him talk again, Catherine thought. But I believe I'll remember more clearly some of the things he used to say . . .

Emily lifted her pretty face and gently kissed her mother's cheek. Then she slid off her lap and ran back to her game.

Catherine picked up the letter and read slowly on to the end of the page. Strangely, mysteriously, her father was alive, going into his study to work on his history, coming out to communicate, to whoever would listen, some new discovery he had made that no one else had noted yet. "Is it not an astonishing thing?" he was asking, his eyes luminous with a light that burned inward.

His daughter got up, went into the bedroom, and closed the door between her child and herself.

Alone, she gave way. Had she not come with Hugh to America, would she not have been there? Aye, that was so. Did she wish, then, not to have come? No . . . But neither had she known until now the full cost of emigrating, and she felt the payment was dear. Her parents might have come if she had had a home for them to come to. Instead, her husband had used his bonus for railroad stock. How often since had he taken stock in lieu of money?

"How is it," she had asked him the last time, "they are ever so ready and willing to give stock away?" He had not answered. But she would force an answer now. They must have a place of their own so that at least her widowed mother could stay with them.

Did the door to the hall open and close? Catherine waited. Then she heard Emily prattling to someone, and Catherine went out to see.

She stopped abruptly. There was Hugh, slumped in a chair, his legs stretched out, paying no attention to Emily, who hovered about him. On the nearby table was his purse where he had thrown it. With a questioning glance at her mother, Emily picked it up and sought to open the clasp.

Realizing immediately a business disaster must have occurred, she believed the paper had failed to go to press. But no. A fresh copy lay on the floor where Hugh had tossed it. It had to be the railroad again. Instead of pay, Hugh had probably taken more stock. Little he cared for a home. But she cared. And now she had fresh reason to. She went to him, and when he took no notice, said, "The letter from my mother came at last."

"So . . . ? For your sake, I am glad."

Catherine waited. Without his asking, she found herself unable to tell him what the news was, and he did not ask. Oblivious to her sorrow, he lifted the paper from the floor, and the large, black headlines leaped out: NEW ORLEANS–NASHVILLE RAILROAD DOOMED. Below, somewhat smaller letters that were also somehow less black announced, "Traffic increases on river route."

Catherine sat down and faced her husband. "I do not understand . . ."

"It should be plain enough to you."

"All the same, it is not."

"Is it not? Well, strangely, neither was it quite plain to me . . . until today. Kendall Johnston, who so obligingly put a little more and still a little more money into what we thought was our paper, was all along De Guerre's man. The last sum he contributed made him a majority owner. The paper is his. That is, De Guerre's. He will keep it going at least long enough to convince any readers who believed in the railroad that they were mistaken."

With a discordant jangle, the contents of Hugh's purse came down at last on the table. Uncertain whether to be frightened or pleased at what she had managed, Emily held up the emptied pouch. Hugh took it from her crossly and began to scoop up the scattered contents. Emily snatched up a key that had fallen to the rug.

"Give me the key," Hugh demanded.

"To what is that key?" Catherine asked.

"I do not know."

"Then let her keep it since it is of no consequence."

"I do not say it is of no consequence. Only that I do not recall at this moment what it is to."

"Then until you do, let her keep it."

Hugh took the key from Emily, and she began to whine.

"There is no cause to cry," her father said. "It is mine, and you have given it back to me. Go and play with your toys."

Emily ran back to the windowsill. Catherine went to her desk, picked up the letter, and began to cry. Hugh rose from the chair and came to her. "What is it, then?" She handed the letter to him.

At the second sentence, he stopped, shocked. "Why did you not tell me at once, Kate?"

"I have been trying to do so all this while. But always there is your railroad, and lately your newspaper! You think first of them."

Hugh did not answer, and Catherine looked up. He stood with his back to the window but was not rocking impatiently. He was standing quietly. "I no longer think of them, Kate. They are not mine to think of."

Dismay smote Catherine, and deep within her, compassion for Hugh began to build. But still she drove on. "Then perhaps you may think of my father."

"I do think of him, Kate," Hugh said, his head bent. "I think of how he lived at peace with everyone and went on with the work he had chosen to do. Perhaps it would have been better for him and for his family had he done otherwise. But I believe he did what he felt he had to do, and did it as well and with as much happiness as he could. I feel in some way he will always remain with me. At least I will never wholly forget him."

Catherine relented. "Aye, I am glad there was understanding between him and you. Perhaps now," she added, taking her mother's letter from Hugh, "you may think also of my mother and provide a home for her here to visit."

"I have not finished her letter," Hugh said, and Catherine handed it back to him. He read to the end and then turned it over and read on.

"What is that you are reading? I did not know she had written on the other side." Standing beside Hugh, Catherine read what her mother had brought herself in the end to put down.

Kate, you must not doubt that more than anything I would like to come for the visit you have set your heart on. But I must tell you that, with conditions as they are, I cannot encourage you to hope.

Stricken, Catherine walked to the window and looked out over the city. All the landmarks were still there, but for her, all was changed. She knew at last that the separation from her family was final. She would not see them again.

Turning from the window, she saw Hugh lonely in defeat. Her heart went out in compassion to her husband. "Perhaps," she said, and at her voice, Hugh lifted his head, ". . . perhaps you and Francis Byrne may think of something further."

Hugh's chuckle had a raw edge. "Perhaps he may, and perhaps I may, but we'll not do so together."

"Why not?"

"I have seen Byrne. For all we have been through together, he cares nothing for me."

"Then at last you must hate him!"

"I did so for a while. But my hate is gone now. For it has come to me that maybe he is no more careless of me than I was, when all promised well, toward those others who crossed with us."

"That is altogether different. He owes you much for all you did."

"It seems to me he does . . . and yet, now that I am

cut off from all I hoped, it also seems to me there is a deeper debt than his to me which we all owe one another. I hope I may not soon forget this."

"But you tried to help, Hugh. You tried—"

"Nay, Kate. I was ever about to and never quite getting to it, and now I no longer can."

"What will we do, then?" Catherine's voice was small, beyond feeling, the voice in which reason struggles for an answer.

Catherine saw something tighten like a knot in the despair of Hugh's face. "This is not Ireland," he said, "where men—and good men, too, men like your father—could do no better than dream. This is America, and we will do what others here do when one place fails them."

"And what might that be?"

"We will move on. America is big."

"You mean," Catherine asked, "to Nathaniel's country?"

"Aye. Those were Nathaniel's terms when he loaned me the money. You shall not have your New Orleans home, Kate, but I promise you a fine one up there."

Weeks later Catherine was at the desk in the small parlor they were leaving on the morrow, reading over the letter in which she told her mother that a second child was on the way, and gave their new address, "Care of Mr. Nathaniel Avery, Ontonagon, Upper Michigan, United States," when she heard her husband's key in the lock.

She glanced at the mantel clock, observed that it was just past twelve, looked about, and saw Hugh. He was changed. Or was it that he was himself again? He had come from the farewell dinner Senators Cambon and Maintenon had given him, and the earlier wounded look was wiped away from his face.

"I see you had a merry party."

"Aye. 'Twas that, and better than that. 'Twas a toast of real friendship, the like of which I have not known since before we sailed down the Liffey."

His eyes were remote with a deep content, and gone

from his voice was all the tension that had plagued
him these past weeks about what they must leave
and what they must take, what they needed to buy in
New Orleans and what they would wait to buy at
Galena, where they would change boats for the trip up
the upper Mississippi. Standing before Catherine, he
drew out his pocketbook and took from it a five-
hundred-dollar note. "Their parting gift," he said.
" 'Twill replace what I put in the newspaper. 'Tis
yours to use as you wish. Let us go to bed, Kate, for
we must be up early tomorrow."

Madame Herries, both awkward with her great size
and dignified with serene self-importance, climbed into
her carriage, sat down on the right, and leaned toward the door. "Please hand me Poo-poo," she ordered. "She must adjust gradually, you know, to this
change."

Catherine handed her the cat, stepped into the carriage, and sat beside Madame Herries. Hugh swung
Emily up, got in after her, and sat beside Catherine,
lifting Emily to his knees. Antoine closed the door,
raised to the floor beside the driver's perch the small
traveling bag he had not taken to the boat earlier,
and positioned himself on the coach. Soon, through
the sultry September morning, the horses' hooves began to beat out a familiar rhythm upon the cobbled
stones along Canal Street and down Common toward
the steamship dock.

Like bells, the hoofbeats rang out echoes for Catherine. That first ride of hers and Hugh's with Madame
Herries along Chartres Street, past the public square,
along the esplanade, and then back to the American
Theater . . . The early drive with Madame Herries to
Monsieur Duhertise's class . . . and afterward to the
cathedral . . . Catherine lifted her hand to her throat,
where a great ache grew for Madame Herries, whom,
despite her pretensions, Catherine loved and would
miss . . . and for the Crescent City she was leaving

with all that it had promised and had not had time to fulfill.

Soothed by Madame Herries' affectionate stroking, Poo-poo purred amiably.

"I fear you shall miss her," Catherine said.

"Who would not? But I shall be comforted knowing she is with you. Besides, who knows, one day I may follow you." She lowered her voice confidingly. "Society in New Orleans is no longer what it once was."

Not to betray amusement at Madame Herries' little fiction of rejecting the society which, in truth, no longer took her seriously, Catherine turned her head. Emily, tense with expectancy, caught the humor in her mother's eyes and responded by kicking her feet joyously. They struck against her father's shins. Hugh dropped his hands over the girl's legs and firmly held them still. Over Emily's dark head, Hugh's and Catherine's eyes met with understanding. Their first night in the *Independence* cabin now seemed to them but a prelude to their last night's love. "Aye," Hugh had said, holding off sleep, "the love between us grows ever better. If only our fortunes improve . . ."

From between Hugh and Madame Herries, Catherine caught a glimpse of a river steamboat. As Antoine turned the carriage and they drove alongside the dock, swarming with carriages and people moving in all directions, Catherine picked out, one after the other against a white siding, the dark letters of their steamboat, *A l g o n q u i n.*

Along with the other steamboats that crowded the Mississippi, all with their warning bells jangling incessantly, the *Algonquin* had a flat and shallow hull, for her boilers and engines were on the main deck, the boilers forward and the engines in the waist between the paddle wheels. There was a second deck with a promenade, and over its foredeck still another; atop all this, between smokestacks at either side, the pilot house reared.

Antoine drew to a stop. "My dear," Madame Herries said, "did you notice her? No, the small, dark-haired woman with her maid. I'll tell you who *she* is. She is the Miss . . . oh, I can't think of her name. The one who plans a school in the wilds near Memphis for Negro and white children, to prove that black children can learn as well as white. Fancy that!"

Catherine was silent. Some might have thought it a waste to teach the channel children. But she had not thought so, and she was glad they would still have a school. Madame Arnaud was taking over. If only she and Madame Herries did not fall out. Madame Herries insisted on her little fictions, and Madame Arnaud as determinedly would not allow them. But Catherine took hope from Madame Arnaud's sense of humor.

"Goodbye, little Countess," Madame Herries said, kissing Catherine.

Hugh, Catherine, and Emily got out of the carriage. It is true, Catherine thought. We really are going.

The band on the *Algonquin*'s deck squawked tentatively before beginning, and from the deck and levee voices sang.

It rained so hard de day Ah left, de river here
   was dry,
Ah thought Ah'd sholy freeze to death; Susanna,
   don't you cry.

Madame Herries leaned out the carriage, handed her prized cat to Catherine, and blew a kiss.

"For me? Or for Poo-poo?"

Madame Herries' gesture mingled annoyance and affection. "For you all. I shall miss you." She waved. "Goodbye, my dears."

Her words rang in Catherine's ears to the rhythm of "Susanna, don't you cry" as Hugh, carrying Emily, and she, carrying Poo-poo, went up the gangplank and into the steamship. The years in the Crescent City had been but a four-year stopover in the journey, which Hugh and she had dreamed of eight years ago, to that distant part of America with copper enough to supply the whole world. It was the autumn of 1839, and they were on their way.

PART FOUR

The River Voyage North

(Autumn 1839)

Chapter 13

A GHOST OF A MOON opened a shifting vista, and in its wake the *Algonquin* advanced on its paddle wheels up the Mississippi into the continent's unsettled interior. Catherine sat holding Emily outside their stateroom beside Miss Julia Warren and her black maid, Rosalie. This was the second night on the river, and moving through the dark into the unexplored wilderness without Hugh next to her, Catherine felt an immense loneliness and uncertainty. She shifted her drowsing child, pulled her shawl more tightly about herself, and smiled at her fellow voyager.

Miss Warren had been standing along the gallery with her maid yesterday when the Condon family first stepped out after settling into their cabin. Catherine had recognized her as the woman Madame Herries had called attention to; she was on the short side of medium height, with a compact build that spoke of physical stamina, and a determined set to her dark head. They had introduced themselves. A moment later, the *Algonquin* had lurched forward and Miss Warren had dramatically closed her eyes. When she reopened them, Catherine saw they were wide-set, hazel, and expressive. She could not be more than a few years older than herself, Catherine judged. Perhaps they might be friends.

She had assured Hugh he might leave and go to the main cabin, forbidden to women, where there was much raucous life and men's rough, speculative talk of making fortunes. Hugh was eager to go, but it seemed to Catherine that he was also reluctant to leave her and Emily. She had reached for his hand and squeezed it tenderly, recalling that this was, after all, the second time failure was sending him onward and that he had grown to like New Orleans well. Still, they must hold themselves open to this new experience. Was there ever a more challenging one than entering this new, little-inhabited land? Hugh must acquaint himself with these other adventurers, learn their ways, probe their thoughts. She could do so only indirectly through him. So she had pulled away her hand and said encouragingly, "Do not worry about us. You can see for yourself we have found good company."

On this second night, Catherine laughed to herself at her previous day's concern that Hugh share the life of his fellows. He had returned from that first sally to the main cabin with an excited, quickened gait and with hints of stimulating stories from men who had gone up the great "Father of Waters" before. Since then, it seemed to Catherine, he was eager to get back to that cabin—to the boisterous life and talk—and quite willing to leave her to Miss Warren. Though her association with Miss Warren was in its second evening, they still were not friends.

"We reach Natchez soon," Miss Warren said, interrupting Catherine's reflections. "We stop there, you know."

At her words, Rosalie asked to be excused.

Miss Julia, as Rosalie called her, hesitated briefly, then nodded. When Rosalie had gone, she leaned toward Catherine. "I cannot think why that girl must leave so often." She shook her head, and settling back, shrugged beneath the weight of forbearance.

She seemed to imply furtive motives, but Catherine could only guess as to what they might be. "At least she never stays long."

With heightened exasperation, Miss Warren replied, "That's *just* it!"

Just *what*, Catherine could not surmise. She tried a diversion. "You are not getting off at Natchez?"

"No, I am going beyond—to Memphis."

"Oh, only to Memphis."

"*Only* to Memphis!" Miss Warren shrugged once more, this time with irritation. "What woman in her right mind would go beyond Memphis?"

The temperature seemed to Catherine to drop and the night to turn cold. How desolate it was without Hugh. Missing him, she was aching with doubt about this venture of theirs into remote country with the ruffians who sat and roared and spat in the main cabin and whose company Hugh seemed to prefer to her own. She shifted Emily again—how heavy she was— and tightened her shawl—how inadequate it was.

Was she not in her right mind? They were going beyond Memphis to St. Louis, another two days' and nights' travel, and beyond there to Galena, two days and nights more. There, for the trip up the uncharted upper Mississippi to Prescott, they would board a smaller steamboat, the *Chippewa*. And from Prescott, they were to go by canoe.

"Yes," Miss Warren said shortly. "Memphis is my destination. We should be there in another day and night if we do not run into a snag, and if our boiler does not explode, and if the *Algonquin* does not catch fire . . ."

"Merciful heavens!" Catherine exclaimed, and at her startled voice, Emily stirred and whimpered. Catherine wondered whatever had possessed her to go off into the wilderness with her young child and a husband who seemed to have forgotten their existence, to give up her secure, easygoing life in the rooms at Madame Herries'. She forgot the summer-long fear of contagious diseases and her drive to leave Madame Herries for a home of her own. Her overriding thought was, How pleasant it was there. She glanced timidly at Miss Warren.

Miss Warren nodded sternly. "On the Mississippi these things happen daily." She sighed. "I hope I may prove equal to my undertaking. You see, I am on my way to a Tennessee estate in the western world's most impenetrable forests, to devote my fortune, time, and such talents as I have to aid the suffering Africans."

Awe at so altruistic an undertaking gave way to guilt at her failure to recognize Miss Julia Warren's stature, and Catherine quickly yielded to curiosity. "But why?"

"Why?" Miss Warren spread her hands and lifted her shoulders in an expressive shrug which seemed to inquire, "How can one do otherwise?"

"Why indeed?" she asked. "To show that nature made no difference between Negroes and white men, excepting the complexion."

"How will you show this?"

"By giving the same education to a mixed class of races—"

She was interrupted. The *Algonquin's* paddle wheels churned slowly to a stop. She stood and flung her arms up and out. "Look! The lights of Natchez!"

From the bluffs which leaned back from the wide river, pale yellow rectangles gave shape to stately white plantation homes. Catherine felt heartache. Was life going on gently in those homes as it had in hers in Chapelizod, from which she was traveling farther and farther? Still, she consoled herself that in the deepest part of memory life went on for her—and ever would. However questionable the future, the past was hers to return to and wander about in at will.

"We are docking," Miss Warren proclaimed. Even as she spoke, men vaulted through the dark from the steamship to the pier. "Kentuckians. Flatboat men. You know the saying, 'Half horse, half alligator'? They earn their trip back up the river by gathering wood to feed the engine."

While the Kentuckians diverted Catherine, a Natchez official had come aboard and found his way to the gallery. He lifted his hat and bowed. "Miss Julia Warren?" Without awaiting her assent to her identity, of which he seemed certain, he pulled from his pocket papers authorizing him to search the *Algonquin* for one Washington Coleman, Negro, twenty, a slave, run away from New Orleans.

"Do you suspect *me* of stowing a runaway slave?"

"You have a Negro girl, Rosalie?"

At her name, Rosalie appeared beside Miss Julia. But the girl's smiling, soft denials did not dissuade the official. To Miss Warren, he said, "We have authority to search her cabin. Do you wish to come?"

"Certainly not!"

At this vigorous disclaimer, Emily woke and got off her mother's lap. Miss Warren turned to Catherine, who now stood behind Emily with her hands reassuringly on the child's shoulders. "You see what I am subjected to?" She threw open her arms. "It is all because of what I propose to do!"

She stopped, for the official and Rosalie were coming back down the gallery. The official bowed. "I beg your pardon, Miss Warren. We have made a mistake."

"Do be more careful next time," she advised, dismissing him.

Catherine remained standing. She wished more than anything to leave the woman and to put Emily to bed. To go to sleep herself. But she dreaded to go to their stateroom without Hugh. Would he never take leave of those rowdying men and return to her and their child? Then, glancing down the gallery, with overwhelming thankfulness, she saw Hugh coming toward her.

Ignoring Hugh's return, Miss Warren sprang to her feet. "That girl has gone again! But where? And without my consent!"

From the dimness into which she blended, Rosalie reappeared, smiling her compliant smile.

Miss Julia Warren threw her compact, vigorous body into her words. *"Where* have you been?"

There was a splash, the sound of someone falling into the river from the stern of the boat. Hugh picked up Emily, and he and Catherine ran after Miss Warren and Rosalie. Transfixed, they saw a head emerge from a deep underwater dive, and a powerful arm, black in the white moonlight, reach out over the water in a shoreward direction.

Miss Julia turned on Rosalie. "Where did you hide him?"

Whether from the moonlight or from a light fused in an inward triumph, the black girl's face shone, transfigured, in the dimness.

In her unaggressive voice, she said, "In mah stateroom."

Her dark head forward, Miss Julia moved closer. "You lie! He was *not* in your stateroom at Natchez. *Where* was he?"

Rosalie stepped back. The brightness still lay on her face. "In Natchez he were in yuh stateroom."

Miss Julia pushed closer. "Where in my stateroom?"

"Under yuh bunk."

The resounding slap sounded more loudly than the splash of water, but Rosalie made no noise or motion.

So as not to waken Emily, Catherine got up from the bunk and walked quietly across the cabin to Hugh's. He lifted his arms and pulled her in with him. " 'Twas time you left the child and came at last to me."

"Aye, and long past time. I thought the evening never would end and you never would return to me. You seem to be content with those boorish men."

" 'Tis not a question of being content, Kate, but we are traveling the same way, and perhaps I can learn from them. 'Tis a rough life, Kate, I cannot deny it, and for your sake I have felt again my old misgivings about it."

Hugh fell silent. Being too explicit about those misgivings might frighten his wife. There was good cause for a woman going where they were going to suffer fear. Life was cheap in the area they were headed toward. Men took it without a qualm. He dared not think what it might be like for a woman whose husband's life had been taken, for a woman left alone . . .

"Aye," Catherine said as though divining his thoughts, "but I have you, and so long as I do, I am not afraid. Indeed, now that I'm with you again, it seems to me a most tremendous experience to be adventuring both into life and into a New World. Married couples go on honeymoons, but how tame such trips are compared with this one we've begun. To me it seems full of wonder and majesty. I do not forget the eerie beauty our Nathaniel promised up north in his country."

Catherine pressed closer to her husband, inviting the love he had yet to begin. He turned, pulled her close, pressed his lips into hers, and within moments she again knew the rewarding stir of awakening desire. Then, consoled by Hugh's love, her joy restored in their journeying, she murmured, "Was not Miss Julia Warren cruel to her Rosalie?"

"Aye . . . she was that."

"I wonder that one who wishes to educate Negroes and to prove they are equal to white men should strike a girl who has but set one free."

"You well may wonder. Those who claim lofty purposes may often be less human than those who do not profess such purposes. So I have found . . ."

" 'Tis strange. Why do you think this is so?"

But Hugh had slipped away from her into sleep, and Catherine was left alone to answer her question. She puzzled about it; years later, looking back to this first part of the long and arduous trip to Ontonagon, she would still be unsure of the answer, and she would wonder at odd moments what had become of Miss Julia Warren's school.

They had transferred at Galena from the *Algonquin* to the smaller *Chippewa* and were traveling up the uncharted upper Mississippi. Catherine had just taken Emily for her after-dinner rest to the women's cabin aft when the *Chippewa* stopped abruptly a second time. She hurriedly led the little girl to the gallery. They arrived there in time to see the square-framed Captain Cadotte, megaphone in hand, clamber quickly up the ladder, despite his considerable weight, from the forecastle to the boiler deck and beyond to the hurricane deck, with the pilot house and Pilot Silas Smith his unmistakable objectives.

From the twin tall smokestacks at the *Chippewa*'s sides, gray plumes of smoke unfurled against the blue, benign sky. The vessel's paddle wheels churned the Mississippi fiercely, but the little steamboat did not budge. At once a disorderly throng of men, calling one another "General," "Colonel," "Major," and "Judge," spilled out of the main cabin and about the ship, shouting, gesturing, swearing, and laughing. Among them Catherine picked out her husband. He did not look quite like one of them, but neither did he appear ill at ease among them. She saw that he sighted her and was forcing his way through the others toward her. Below, the poorer deck passengers, eager to share the free-for-all excitement, were scrambling to their feet.

"Another sawyer?" Catherine asked.

Hugh was beside her, his eyes, reminiscing the love they had known the night before, seeking hers. "Aye. 'Tis only the lower Mississippi, as you know, that has been dredged." He stooped and lifted Emily.

Standing there beside him, with Emily clasped tight in his arms, Catherine glanced happily at the commotion. "What with one sawyer and another," she said cheerfully, "I believe we may be as long on the *Chippewa* as on the *Algonquin*, though you tell me the *Chippewa* travels but one-third as far."

"So I judge by the fares. 'Twas twenty-six dollars and ten cents each from New Orleans to Galena, and eight-seventy from there on to Prescott."

"A pretty penny to pay," said one of two passengers joining them, "and maybe in the end to be dumped in the river."

"Come now, Judge," the other said. "Do not frighten a woman and child."

" 'Tis not to frighten them, Colonel, but to warn them," the first replied.

"I cannot think what help any such warning would

be should the tree that is holding us here tear a hole in this steamboat."

Catherine glanced at her husband and read his reservations toward these two. Still, she saw he treated them amiably, and she would, too.

"On a voyage like this . . ." She laughed and gestured acceptance of mishaps.

In an instant the scene brightened. A southbound upper-Mississippi boat was steaming toward them. In contrast to the pinioned *Chippewa*, her freedom to maneuver made the sister steamship look buoyant. Approaching with the promise of help toward the disabled *Chippewa*, she somehow appeared even gay, as though with good will.

On a signal from Captain Cadotte, in a frenzy of extroversion, her crew tossed out grappling irons, and in a few minutes the business was done. Again the abrupt bluffs, tree-covered or crowned with limestone or sandstone, which had replaced the banks of clay with their drooping willows and curiously shaped cottonwoods, began to slide by. The *Chippewa*'s passengers let go a hearty shout of thanks. From the deck of the other, the passengers waved with the captain and crew in pleased acceptance of the tribute. The steamer stood by briefly to see whether the *Chippewa* had sustained damage, and when it appeared she had not, continued on down the Mississippi.

The colonel chuckled. "Nothing to it, it seems, when you know how."

"Well, then," the judge dug at his companion, "may we all of us always know how."

They laughed at the judge's wit, and Captain Cadotte, passing by, paused to share in their merriment. "This time we laugh." He waved the megaphone he still carried.

"Aye," Hugh agreed. "It is ever the next time we must think upon."

Captain Cadotte shook his head. "There will not be a next time." He gave a short, authoritative chuckle. "There's a man aboard—Jonathan Harding—who has been a pilot before. He'll serve for the rest of this trip."

So here as elsewhere, Catherine thought, mistakes cost their proportionate price. It seemed that the sun, so bright on the water moments before, had dimmed, and the southbound boat disappeared in the shadowing.

"What was Pilot Smith's fault?" Hugh inquired.

"It's fault enough to strike a second sawyer. There's no excuse for these mishaps in the afternoon sunlight. That tree threw its shadow upward."

"Will Pilot Smith leave the *Chippewa* at Dubuque?" the judge inquired presumptuously.

The captain affected not to hear and walked off like one in command, leaving them to deal, each in his own way, with the image of the tall discredited man they had known only as pilot.

After the next morning's stop at Dubuque, with Jonathan Harding in the pilot house, the *Chippewa*'s side paddles turned once again and the boat headed for La Crosse, the next stop, and the last before Prescott. On the deck, the cornetist played,

It rained so hard de day Ah left, de river here
    was dry,
Ah thought Ah'd sholy freeze to death; Susanna,
    don't you cry.

In his cabin on the hurricane deck, Silas Smith sulked. He had elected not to leave at Dubuque and stood on his contract right to travel to Prescott and back to Galena.

Catherine was sitting in her favorite place, enjoying the sun and entertaining Emily, when the inseparable colonel and judge strode down the gallery, halting before her.

"Good day." The colonel saluted in his jaunty way, and the judge bowed formally. "We do not wish to intrude."

They had come by design, not by chance, Catherine felt. She mistrusted them. But Hugh was at ease, or appeared to be, with all this uncertain company. And so, Catherine decided, she would act accordingly.

"Oh, not at all," she said. "The days are long, and I hear only such news as is brought to me."

The men exchanged a look meant only for each other. "Then have you heard what is brewing between Pilot Silas Smith and Pilot Jonathan Harding?" the colonel asked.

"I know only that Pilot Harding has succeeded Pilot Smith."

"You have not heard, then, that Pilot Smith struck Pilot Harding when Harding refused Smith's company in the pilot house?" the judge asked. "We cannot vouch for its truth, but it's rumored that Smith challenged Harding and that the two pilots will fight it out at La Crosse."

"Let us hope it is only a rumor."

"Yes, let us hope." The judge's eyes brightened oddly, and Catherine's mistrust deepened.

With an abrupt change of subject that somehow seemed to his point, the colonel said, "You are a brave woman!"

Catherine chuckled. "I, brave? Indeed, I should like to be. But why do you say this?"

"The travel that lies ahead would frighten many men. By canoe up the St. Croix, is it not?" Catherine caught an urgent expectancy in his pause and observed that the judge was also listening intently.

"Indeed, I take the journey but a day at a time and leave the planning ahead to my husband."

"Your husband is well able to plan," the judge observed, "and we wish him success in his quest for copper."

"Then wish him success only, for it may be something other than copper he seeks."

"No, Kate, I told them nothing of our intended route or our purpose." Hugh spoke softly, for they were sitting together on his bunk, and Emily was at last napping on Catherine's.

"Then they thought to trick me into revealing our plans?"

"Aye. They are a pair of rascals. 'Tis they who are promoting the fight between Smith and Harding tomorrow. They are collecting bets from one and all—the judge for Smith, the colonel for Harding. The money's to provide a purse for the fighters—a bigger share for the winner—and the rest is to be divided among those who bet on the winner."

"And does Captain Cadotte allow this?"

"Captain Cadotte plays Pilate. It may be he has reasons of his own for letting the fight go on." .

"And the betting?"

"The betting livens the trip. 'Tis said the captain's betting on Smith."

"I cannot believe this!"

"Nor could I at first, but one comes to the point of believing strange happenings. Some say there's no puzzle. The captain simply thinks Smith is a better fighting man. Others hold the captain now fears the action Smith may take against him on the *Chippewa*'s return to Galena."

"But you are not betting?"

Hugh quietly got to his feet and stood smiling down at his wife. "Aye, Kate, that I am, and on Smith, too."

" 'Tis a wrongful thing you are doing, Hugh Condon. Do you not yourself feel it to be?"

"Then what would you have your husband do tomorrow when all go to the clearing at La Crosse? Stay aboard the *Chippewa* like a tenderfoot and be scorned by one and all? No, Kate, 'tis a rough situation we are entering, and there's danger in being soft . . ."

"Shall I, then, be left alone with Emily on the *Chippewa?*"

"Nay. Captain Cadotte is required to stay aboard so long as you and Emily are, and I have informed him you will be."

"Does this disappoint the gallant man?"

"Nay. He made no complaint, and indeed, I think it suits his purposes well."

Except, Catherine supposed, for the captain, she and Emily were alone on the *Chippewa,* docked now in midmorning at La Crosse. "We shall take a look around," she said to Emily. "Maybe even go to the men's cabin, where Daddy likes to go. Who is now to say we cannot?" Catherine giggled merrily, and Emily echoed her mother.

At the cabin's far end, Catherine pushed open a door. The judge and the colonel sat at the cabin's opposite end, counting and arguing over money. Surprised at the sound of the door opening and closing, the two men sprang away from each other, and the box over which they contended dropped, spilling coins and notes across the floor.

Terrified at coming upon the two, Catherine picked up Emily and raced to their cabin. Inside, she locked the door and hid the key behind her.

Before long, there was a pounding at the door. Catherine held the child tight, pressing her finger over Emily's small mouth, imploring quiet with her eyes. Emily's body quivered and strained against the unfamiliar harshness of her mother's clasp. Fright leaped questioningly into her eyes, and her mouth pouted uncertainly. But she obeyed, and Catherine waited out the pounding.

"Perhaps she is climbing up to the captain's quarters?" the judge said.

The colonel chuckled knowingly. "Much good that will do her."

"Then she has started for the clearing. Overtake her!"

"Nay, *you* overtake her!"

"Better that we both escape now. We may get some small craft at the dock and work our way down the river a bit."

"Agreed," the colonel said.

From the gallery, Catherine sighted the two below

on the dock, negotiating for a canoe. They were again judge and colonel, the judge aloof and lordly, the colonel debonair. Soon they would be on their way and out of reach. Catherine grabbed up Emily and hurried through the *Chippewa*. The gangplank was still down. She stepped across and started toward the clearing. It was no problem to know what direction to take. She followed the shouting. The alternating cries of the partisans came, exulting, complaining, mixed, and exulting again. As she drew closer, the two factions seemed to roar with victory and groan with defeat more and more evenly. Then the voices rose all together, increasingly piercing, and ended in sudden silence. Into the silence Emily screamed.

The crowd broke apart. Hugh emerged and started toward Catherine. She put Emily down and waited. She could not help laughing inwardly at the expressions which chased over Hugh's face: disbelief, annoyance, alarm. There was no telling which one would triumph.

"We are sorry to intrude on so lofty an event," Catherine said, "but the colonel and the judge are at this moment escaping down the river with the betting money."

The silence had greeted Pilot Jonathan Harding's failure to rise, and the fight had come to an end. But there was no purse for the fighters and no return to the winners who had betted on Smith, and Captain Cadotte refused to delay any longer so that a search party might go after the culprits.

Twin plumes of gray smoke signaled departure at midday, and the *Chippewa*'s paddle wheels turned again. The cornetist failed to play. No one missed his solacing notes. A strange new peace gripped the boat.

In the pilot house, Smith turned the wheel. Beside him, both eyes puffed and closed, Jonathan Harding sat in comradely silence. Now and again one of the two would curse and then laugh and the other would join in. They both had lost the promised purse. What did it matter now that one had been defeated and the other had won?

In the men's cabin, between the former two factions, both equally outwitted, all was camaraderie, and a fine, impartial discussion of the fight alternated with joined recriminations against the scoundrels, who, as someone said, "took us all."

As though on moccasined feet, Captain Cadotte walked the gallery softly, pausing to blow meditative smoke from his pipe. Each trip brought its rogues, and this one had turned up the judge and the colonel. He'd seldom had two who had enlivened a voyage so greatly and, so far as he personally was concerned, so profitably.

In their stateroom, where Emily listened big-eyed with excitement, Catherine told Hugh of the discord between the men before their precipitate flight.

" 'Tis the way with rogues," Hugh said. "And they were a pair, true enough!" He laughed, recollecting, and hurried off to the men's cabin.

Catherine did not seek to detain him. Instead, feeling the morning's strain, she lay down for a midday nap with Emily. She would deal on her own with her fear that the judge and the colonel would one day reappear. Somehow her race to the clearing had given her the confidence that she could meet future dangers. Hugh was right. They both had to adapt to a different life. Hugh was doing so. He had changed more during the days aboard the *Algonquin*—and especially the days aboard the *Chippewa*—than he had in all the years in New Orleans. There he had somehow remained Hugh Condon of Chapelizod. But here on the Mississippi, Catherine was aware, he had confronted the frontier, where every man was what he proved himself to be, and had given up the restrictions of his former life to accept the frontier's challenge, to be an American.

Chapter 14

THE INDIAN CANOE route Nathaniel had recommended to Hugh as the shortest north-south pas-
sageway to the Lake Superior region began where the
St. Croix flowed into the Mississippi at Prescott. Here,
on an early September morning, the Condons bade
goodbye to Cadotte, his crew, and the passengers who
had voyaged with them the whole distance from
Galena to Prescott. There were loud and jovial cries
of good wishes, the more vigorous, Catherine suspected, for the knowledge that beyond Prescott danger
menaced success. But all were adventurers, she realized, who did not anticipate reunions, and if parting
was cordial, it also was easy.

It was a comfort, therefore, to her and even more so
to Hugh to find true Nathaniel's prediction that they
could depend upon voyageurs for the canoe trip up the
St. Croix and beyond to La Pointe on Madeline Island
in Lake Superior, where, a century and a half before,
Pierre Charles Le Sueur had built a fur-trading post
for New France. An already assembled party welcomed them. Among the party were two traders, Pierre
Balthazar and Christopher Lawler; scientist and explorer Joseph N. Nicollet; three half-breed guides
and interpreters; and a company of Chippewa Indians.

Tragedy lent them the Indians, Monsieur Nicollet
said, and for them the journey was two moons delayed.
They had started northward from Fort Snelling early
in the Thunder Moon and been attacked the second
day, while yet asleep in the deep, cliff-lined ravine of
their encampment, by a greased, decorated band of

182

Sioux warriors. The survivors had fled southward in
their canoes back toward Fort Snelling to complain to
Indian agent Lawrence Taliaferro. At Prescott they
took counsel. Was there any use in going on to the
fort? No one there had heeded their early summer protest against the Great White Father's changing the
place where they received their payments from St.
Croix to remote La Pointe, and before long the Hunt-
ing Moon would wane. So, with ranks thinned, as
they foresaw the trees would soon be of leaves, the
Chippewa braves, with a few squaws and children,
were starting a second time for La Pointe. From the
half-breed in charge, they had secured the promise to
stop at the ravine to bury their dead brothers and to
put maple sugar in little houses over the graves. Ironi-
cally, the Indians' disaster was the white men's good
fortune. Though they welcomed the Indians' services,
neither the white men nor the half-breeds sorrowed
with the Indians. Catherine puzzled at the half-breeds
especially. In New Orleans she had seen the mixture
of slaves and whites and observed that even the
quadroons remained partly black. It seemed to her the
half-breeds were somehow closer in sympathy to
white men. Later she would ask Hugh if he judged
this to be so.

After both some discussion with Monsieur Nicollet
and Hugh's payment to the half-breed in charge—not
without trepidation on Catherine's part—the canoe
carrying her, Hugh, and Emily moved into position for
the long trip through the wide, placid, lower St. Croix
and beyond. Their canoe was fourth in a line of six,
each perhaps twenty-five to thirty feet long, and she
and Hugh sat with Emily, cuddling Poo-poo, between
them. One of the three half-breed guides and interpreters was their bowman. He and four Indian
middlemen paddled on their knees. A fourth Indian
steersman stood and paddled in the stern. With an unaccountable thrill, Catherine saw their canoe was
holding its position in the line, gaining speed in unison
with the others. She glanced over Emily at Hugh and

saw that he shared her excitement; indeed, she believed it was heightened in him. Nothing in their earlier venture had so delighted him. Her own spirit lifted to meet his.

She glanced back through the swirling morning mists to the fifth canoe, following them and carrying a single white man, Monsieur Nicollet, who was as well pleased with the company of Indians as that of white men. Actually, he seemed not to require either, so absorbed was he in checking his map of the area for his 1836 observations of latitude and longitude. All the same, Catherine was thankful for his gentlemanly bearing, and she had noted and enjoyed the extraordinary understanding his dark eyes held. If men like the colonel and the judge were probing America's interior, there were also men like Monsieur Nicollet!

Just behind his canoe, the sixth and last in the line carried traders Pierre Balthazar and Christopher Lawler, bound for La Pointe to barter the Indians' sacks of wild rice and kegs of maple sugar for flour and corn sent there from Detroit and for tallow and pine gum from Michilimackinac. They had been somewhat less agreeable than Monsieur Nicollet and had grumbled because her and Hugh's household goods from Chapelizod, and the new warm clothing, gun, ax, and adz, bought at Galena, crowded out a last keg of maple sugar. But the half-breed Hugh had paid for their passage told Mr. Lawler to dispose of the keg at Prescott. Still, Mr. Lawler's question "And where will you be putting all you have brought?" had made Catherine wonder.

Over Emily, she asked her husband, "What do you think, Hugh? Will we crowd out our Nathaniel with all we are bringing?"

"Nay," Hugh responded. "He will make room for our equipment, and 'twill be only until next spring when I will build our own cabin."

Catherine nodded, then soon she inquired, "Do you not think your letter pleased him greatly?"

"Aye," Hugh said, "if he has received it."

Monsieur Nicollet had advised that beyond Fort
Snelling, mail was carried twice a month by canoe and
foot up the St. Croix Valley. Beyond there— *"Mais
oui,"* he had said, "out there it is a matter of chance."

"If not," Catherine went on to Hugh, "we may
surprise him as he surprised us last Christmas."

But she needed not to look back or ahead. The moment itself was full of delight. With what skill and
grace the bowman and the Indians all paddled. She
saw that Hugh was observing this, too, and with pleasure. Undiverted by the *Chippewa*'s passengers, she
welcomed being again a close little family. The last of
the morning's white mists lifted over the water and
swirled away. In the distance, framing the St. Croix
where it widened to a lake, long, rolling, tree-topped
hills rose, fell away, and rose again. How beautiful
this America was. As beautiful and so much vaster
than Ireland. God was everywhere, here as well as
there. The day began to fill with gentle sunshine.
Through time and distance, Catherine saw her
mother smile.

They stopped at dusk that first day at one of the
long, narrow islands near precipitous sandstone cliffs.
With relief Catherine rose from her cramped day-long
position and stepped from the canoe to the ground.
With words of praise for their fine little traveler, Hugh
lifted Emily to her, and Catherine hugged and set her
down. Then the bowman retrieved Poo-poo and put
her in Emily's arms. Only he, Jacques, and the other
two half-breed bowmen, Michel and Henri, came
ashore, along with the Condons, Monsieur Nicollet,
and the traders. Indian middlemen and steersmen
from the last three canoes leaped into the other waiting canoes, and the Indians paddled away to keep
their tryst with their dead.

With lagging movements the half-breeds pulled
in the three canoes left behind. Did they, Catherine
wondered, all suffer the divided allegiance of men of
mixed races?

"Dépechez-vous," Monsieur Nicollet said, and the

half-breeds moved somewhat faster to empty the canoes' contents and upturn the boats over the cargo.
They built a fire next and, from a tripod of sticks, hung
a kettle of water over it.

Appetite would push them. Monsieur Nicollet
turned to Hugh, Catherine, Emily, and the two
traders and lifted his arms to the beauty all about. In
the setting sun's light, a flower—"the red lobelia," he
said—burned over the land, and among the green
trees atop the cliffs, gold and crimson leaves shone
here and there.

"Ah, *oui*," he said, following their glances, "the
aspen and birch. They change to gold and the maple
to red." He gestured to the sandstone cliffs where the
early Sioux had carved and painted vermilion figures
and images. Love made the country his own. Love
and intimate acquaintance.

That night, lying with Hugh under the stars, long
after Emily, a little papoose in her warm nighttime
garments, had gone to sleep, Catherine felt an impulsive yearning to be at their destination.

"Aye," Hugh said, "at times I also feel this longing."

Though the Indians returned at dawn, their requiem accomplished, and the party moved on, Hugh's
desire was to be tested. They had come another day's
paddle, struggled through a rocky pass against the
rapid current, and taken family accommodations for
the night at St. Croix Falls, where Seth Ferguson and
other would-be lumber barons had bought land from
the Chippewa and built a warehouse and two log
cabins among the rocky cliffs at the foot of the rapids.
On hand, brought from St. Louis by the side-wheel
steamer *Palmyra,* were millwrights, carpenters, ma-
sons, lumbermen, teamsters, and laborers to build a
sawmill and shops, and the needed tools and supplies.
While the falls roared outside and Emily slept and
Catherine waited in bed for Hugh, Seth Ferguson
talked to Hugh over drinks before the fireplace in the
room outside.

"Here we are," he said, "with elm, soft maple, birch, and ash all about, a dense forest of centuries-old white pine to the north—ours for the cutting—and the river to float the logs."

"Aye," Hugh agreed, "'tis a chance for a fortune such as seldom comes in a lifetime."

The key turned in the lock, and Catherine raised herself on her elbow. "Hugh?"

"Aye." He locked the door and stepped over to his wife. "Why are you not sleeping? Is the bed so poor?"

"'Tis a bed. What has delayed you?"

Hugh sat down on the hard edge. In the moonlight from the high window, Catherine saw again the excitement that had lighted her husband's face when he spoke of the New Orleans railroad and, before that, of his accounting system back in Dublin.

"Well, and what now?"

"Oh, Kate"—he bent like one in great suffering—"'tis such a chance as I doubt will come to me again. Oh, Kate," he moaned once more, "Seth Ferguson wishes me to take a position here as sutler and has offered me a share in the business."

"Is that a reason to suffer as you appear to be doing?"

"Aye."

"Why is it so?"

He looked at her in surprise. "You remember the Christmas before last when I took that loan from Nathaniel?"

"I remember well."

"Then maybe you remember that it was on condition that if the newspaper should fail, I would join him?"

"Can we not stay here a while and go later?"

There was no humor in Hugh's laugh. "'Twas ever a woman's habit to seek to have things both ways."

"Since you are a man, how, then, will you have them?"

Hugh stood, and the moonlight shone full on his

face, austere with denial. Pride in her husband's integrity stirred her, and she felt again her last night's yearning for the country up north. But now her yearning for her husband's love was even greater, and she pushed the future away for the present. He, too, reluctantly at first, then with overwhelming willingness, put regret behind.

They left early the next morning, climbed the portage past the falls, then fought their way, sometimes by canoe and sometimes on foot, through the upper St. Croix rapids. From there, struggling against or circumventing rapids all the way, they traveled by successive rivers, whose names Monsieur Nicollet would call out, to the St. Croix headwaters, where they took Le Portage des Femmes to the Bois Brule, which flowed northward into Lake Superior.

Except for herself and Hugh, Catherine noticed all took the portages almost as easily as the canoeing. Weighted with their loads, the Indians still walked at a fast pace. Hugh, carrying Emily on his back, labored to keep up. Catherine could see that the portages were hard for him. The more so, she was sure, because his heart yearned back to the opportunity he had renounced at St. Croix Falls. Toward the end of each portage, Catherine herself could but stumble along, and she ceased attending to Monsieur Nicollet's announcing where one river portage ended and the next began. Snake, Yellow, Namekagon, and Eau Claire, to her, were all alike.

More distressing than her own fatigue and accompanying indifference to their route was Hugh's progress, blunted by misgivings. Faltering along, Catherine perceived what she had not before fully grasped: that for Hugh, unlike most men, it was not enough to make a living. For him it must be a fortune. Even back in Chapelizod, Catherine had recognized this possibly insatiable instinct. His experiences in America had whetted his drive. There had been his agitation over his early accounting system, then it was America, and

the railroad and the newspaper. Always he was striving
to amass a fortune. Indeed, it was of this that most
men venturing into America's interior seemed to
dream.

From Monsieur Nicollet, who lifted her when she
fell and then lent her a muscled, sustaining arm, Catherine was to learn of a man whose goal in this area
was other than material gain. One, Monsieur Nicollet
said, all in their company ardently hoped to see in La
Pointe. His name was Père Baraga.

As Monsieur Nicollet talked, his formal English
breaking into French, Catherine saw Père Baraga,
bent under the weight strapped to his back, plodding
on foot from one Indian village to the next, sometimes
five walking days apart. She saw him going in the
spring when the miry swamps swarmed with mosquitoes. And she saw him going on snowshoes in the
bitter winter through driving blizzards as blinding as
sand in a desert storm.

"Why does he do this?" Catherine managed to ask
as she faltered along.

"Ah, *pourquoi?*" Monsieur Nicollet threw up his
unengaged hand. "A profound love of God's Indian
children, such as few white men know, brought him
and keeps him here."

"What does he do for the Indians?"

"Ah, what does he not do? He baptizes, hears con-
fessions, visits the sick, anoints the dying, teaches in
the wigwams, has built a church, and translates Bible
stories and prayers into the Chippewa language. Besides French and English, he came knowing German,
Latin, Greek, and, of course, his native Slovenian.
To these he has added Chippewa. He has also taught
himself the sign language which Indians developed so
that one tribe might speak to all others. In this they
are ahead of us Europeans, for whom differing un-
learned languages remain a barrier between nations."

"Is Père Baraga all alone in his work?"

"No. No longer. He has the company of his widowed

younger sister, Antonia. All rejoiced because she returned with him last year from his trip to Europe."

So work in the name and love of God went on here as in Ireland. Catherine would tell Hugh of Père Baraga. She lifted her eyes, which had been focused on the ground to avoid stumbling, to Hugh, who seemed to her still to move ahead somewhat unwillingly, and saw him flounder. Even as he fell, he kept a tight hold on Emily. Monsieur Nicollet sprang to his aid.

"Permettez-moi," he said. "We have come almost to the end of Le Portage des Femmes. For what distance remains, I shall carry *la petite.*" He lifted Emily to his back. *"Non, non,"* he said to Hugh's protests. "She is but a feather."

Somewhat shamefaced at letting another carry his child, Hugh fell back. "Do not regret his help," Catherine consoled her husband. "In the days ahead I doubt not we may need to accept as well as give help."

"Aye," Hugh said. Then he voiced aloud what he had been telling himself all along. "Oh, Kate, 'twas such a chance at St. Croix Falls as I doubt will come to me again!"

But to those who endure, all distances are at last accomplished, and finally they came to the end of Le Portage des Femmes. Catherine climbed into the canoe once more for the paddle on the Bois Brule. She sank down beside Hugh and lifted Emily to her lap. Poopoo, who had trailed the long, intermittent portages, leaped joyfully into the vessel after them. "Ah, Poopoo," Catherine exclaimed, "what would Madame Herries say could she know what we have put you through?" She laughed at her friend's imagined consternation.

Like eternity, glimpsed from the narrow entrance-way of time, Lake Superior lay before them, shining and immense. Their canoe moved out of the deep woods shrouding the Bois Brule and, like the others, headed east toward the ancient Chippewa capital of

La Pointe on Madeline Island. The lake spread all around, a vision such as one dreams.

Catherine turned to her husband. "Are you not now glad we did not linger at St. Croix Falls?"

Hugh glanced from the bold shoreline out over the blue distances—calm, clean, and cold under the late September sun—and Catherine saw excitement again light his eyes. " 'Tis a fair sight, this," he conceded.

But Catherine wanted more, so she pressed further. "A fair sight and more. Do you not feel we may grow to share our Nathaniel's love of this country?"

"We shall need to share more than his love of it," Hugh said, and Catherine knew he still brooded over the opening he had renounced.

Chapter 15

WHERE THE SHORELINE ROCKS gave way to a pebbly beach, the travelers climbed from the canoes to La Pointe's long dock and looked about. In the softening sunlight, the island buildings stood aged and weathered, as though sun, wind, and rain had completed them and made them as invulnerable to change as was the landscape. Here the Jesuit missionary Claude Allouez spent four arduous years, from 1665 to 1669, waiving in turn to his brother Jesuit, the scholar-missionary Jacques Marquette. "Ah, Père Marquette," Monsieur Nicollet said, lifting and dropping his expressive hands. "He once led his Chippewa, starving and freezing, three hundred miles to the Straits of Mackinac, with the hostile Sioux chasing. After nearly two hundred years, the Chippewa still tell the story." He stopped to listen, putting his hand to his ear. *"Écoutez.* The Indians say the lake is a woman and talks to herself." He laughed, and in his laughter Catherine heard his acceptance and love of the Indians.

Awaiting the travelers on the dock before the large warehouse and the fur company's buildings stood a diminutive white woman of authoritative bearing. When Monsieur Nicollet led the way to her, she lifted her hand in a gracious welcoming gesture.

"Bonjour, Monsieur Nicollet." Her alert dark eyes were smiling into his, but they were also instantly inquisitive. *"La femme et la petite?"*

With a circling arm, Joseph Nicollet swept the Condons in front of him. "Madame von Hoeffern, the sister of Père Baraga. *Permettez-moi . . ."*

"But here I am Antonia. Madame von Hoeffern gave her warm smile and assuring handclasp to Catherine and Hugh. Then she stooped to Emily and said promisingly, *"Tante* Antonia." She greeted in French Monsieurs Balthazar and Lawler and Jacques, Michel, and Henri, then welcomed the Indians in Chippewa.

"My brother is away," she said regretfully. "He has gone to Ford du Lac on the *Crescent City. Quel dommage!* But the *Crescent City* will return him to us tomorrow."

And so she did, toward twilight, and all hurried to the dock to greet Père Baraga. Her sails white against Lake Superior's pure-toned sunset, the *Crescent City* strained against her mooring upon the rough-ridged water. To Catherine, waiting with the others on the dock while Hugh and Monsieur Nicollet walked Emily about, the sailing ship seemed a tethered wind-borne bird, eager to take flight. She was stopping but briefly for passengers bound for Ontonagon and the Sault.

"Since you cannot stay," Antonia was saying with her kindly concern, "I am glad Monsieur Nicollet is going on to the Sault and that you will have his company as far as Ontonagon. But how sorry my brother will be that you'll have only a few minutes' time for him."

Catherine glanced from the *Crescent City* back toward the island with its roughly hewn community of buildings. The island, so bleak yesterday, seemed now, like Antonia, to smile at Catherine.

"Ah," Antonia said, "here comes my brother."

Catherine caught barely a glimpse of a man under medium height, with dark brown curling hair, like Antonia's, as he jumped from the gangplank to the dock. At once all of La Pointe—men, women, and children—hemmed him in with a welcoming babble and outreaching hands. From all parts of the island, innumerable dogs came running.

"Will the crowd not overcome him?" Catherine asked.

Antonia shook her head. "He seems never to tire, and I must remind myself that he is as glad to see them as they are to see him."

"He is still young, Father Baraga."

"Forty-two."

Suddenly he sprang to one side and then vaulted in the opposite direction, out of the circle. From the voyageurs, half-breeds, and Indians came a roar of laughing acceptance. Catherine and Antonia laughed, too.

"Somehow he manages this every time," Antonia said.

But now, no longer the prankster boy but moving deliberately and with dignity, Father Baraga approached them on short, stoutly built legs that, Catherine thought, perhaps had been bent beneath the back-pack his sister said he so often carried. His skin was weathered almost to a half-breed's tan.

"Ah," he said after Antonia's introduction, "then you have kept my sister company, and this, I can see, has brought her new life." He greeted Monsieur Nicollet, who had brought Hugh up.

"Ah." He nodded when Hugh told him his purpose. "Copper is there without a doubt. The Indians mined and smelted it four thousand years ago, and they tell me it still lies underground in long bars. Make friends with the Indians and find those bars, and you may come upon rich veins of ore. White men make a mistake when they scorn the Indian. Theirs is an ancient culture. I have caught this in their language—all goes by rule."

Including Catherine in the conversation, he said, "'If you listen as well as the Indians, you may hear Saint Joseph's new bell ring." He laughed. "The Indians tell me they hear it wherever they are. One day we will build a church in Ontonagon for you and those who will follow. We must spread the Kingdom of Christ in this part of God's world. As soon as God wills, I shall come in my canoe to visit you and the Indians." His speech was slow, cool, and distinct, but what Catherine never forgot was the loving gleam that emanated from his eyes.

"As though," she said later to Hugh on the *Crescent City*'s deck, "I counted for more than I ever dreamed I or anyone could."

"With me it was also so," Hugh responded. "He looked at me, and I felt myself become the one I was meant to be. It seems to me we have come to the place we are destined to be."

At her husband's words, Catherine felt hope fly free as a bird. Father Baraga had found the exact words for Hugh, freed him from his obsessive backward look to the falls, focused his vision ahead to where they were going, made him a whole man again. "It must be he looks so at each one, whether he be Indian, or white, or half-breed."

"Aye, I think it is the soul in each he sees, and sees with great love."

Emily reached into the pocket of her coat and pulled out a piece of maple sugar.

"Now, where—?" Catherine began, but there was no need to ask. Père Baraga had somehow managed to tuck it in there.

" 'Twas a wonder I was not more afraid," Catherine would answer years later when her children asked what she had felt when she first sailed on wind-disturbed Lake Superior. "I suppose the truth is, I had not the sense to be. To be sure, I was still young." She would pause, remembering. But what she recalled of that propelled flight through the waves, which at night darkened to black, was something other than fear. It was love she recalled, in the cabin bunk with Hugh; love dispelling loneliness and fear of the great bullying lake they rode; love uniting her and Hugh and keeping ever alive their hope in the future.

It was true she had not yet the judgment to know the peril of this lake, into whose awesome, cold deeps through the years uncounted ships descended. But Captain Eckhart had. By now, along with the seamanship of many ocean-sailing years, he had acquired an overmastering respect for Lake Superior's storms, which, he said, came with less warning than the Atlantic's. In a river harbor midway between La Pointe and Ontonagon, he halted the *Crescent City*'s flight. There, on diminished waves, with sails furled, she rocked to the booming winds through the evening.

All that night and the following day and the next, the wind frenzied, tossing waves so high that the line between the downpouring sky and upthrusting water was lost. They kept to their cabin, delighting together in Emily, or freeing each other to read or to write letters, and rejoicing in each other.

Still, there was time for Catherine to question why Captain Eckhart's quadroon wife had never made an appearance; time to envisage Père Baraga voyaging in his canoe in all kinds of weather, rising at three o'clock on summer mornings to meditate and pray uninterruptedly in the hours before daylight, and working winter nights, with the wind howling about, in his cabin on his Chippewa dictionary and grammar, on his Chippewa sermon book of the Epistles and Gospels, or on his Chippewa Bible history of the Old Testament. Often Catherine's thoughts turned to her father and the American history in the making that he had not lived to know even through her letters.

On the third day the wind abated and the waves grudgingly subsided. Aboard the ship there was a mighty stir to ready her for sailing. "The wind is right," the captain shouted, and hurried along the deck. "If it holds, we can make the Sault in good time."

"Does he not mean to stop at Ontonagon?" Catherine asked Hugh.

"He agreed to do so before Jacques and Michel put all aboard."

Monsieur Nicollet, enjoying with them the first of three days on deck, nodded. "It was agreed in my presence."

Though at Hugh's gesture Captain Eckhart stopped on his next turn, his impatience was evident. "It has been a long delay," he said. "One I had not counted on. We must regain lost time while the wind is right."

"Even so," Hugh persisted, "you *will* stop at Ontonagon?"

Captain Eckhart stared at Hugh, the veil over his eyes lifting and exposing them. Looking into their depths, Hugh remembered that earlier time when Eckhart had wished, despite his steerage passengers' lack of water and food, to take advantage of a fair wind.

" 'Tis but a short distance from here to Ontonagon, and you have your canoe. Can you not disembark here?"

"That we cannot. Nor was that our agreement."

Catherine looked at their companion, who spoke quietly, as though he were observing that the land lay one way instead of another. "I also regret the delay, but maritime law requires a captain to keep his agreement."

Captain Eckhart seemed suddenly tired. "Very well, we will stop. But please," he added petulantly, starting off again, "do not delay me further."

A final obstacle, a sand bar, forbade the *Crescent City* entrance to the Ontonagon's mouth, and it was necessary "to lighter." The ship dropped anchor well outside the bar, and from the deck, standing beside

Hugh and Emily, Catherine watched the ship's deck-hands lower the birth-bark canoe, bought from the La Pointe Indians and containing all Hugh and she possessed, including poor, cowering Poo-poo, to Lake Superior's wrinkled cobalt blue. When the captain offered no further help, Monsieur Nicollet descended the rope ladder to steady the lurching canoe. From the deck, Catherine watched while Hugh, with Emily fastened to his back and her arms tight about his neck, climbed slowly downward.

She saw them safely into the canoe. While Monsieur Nicollet unfastened Emily and put her in the middle-man's seat, Hugh moved to the stern with his steersman's paddle. Catherine glanced shoreward. There, on the east side, but a short distance up the Ontonagon, through October's trees she saw with immense thankfulness Nathaniel's log cabin. Now it was her turn to descend.

"Were you not afraid, Mother?" the children would gasp years later at this point in her story.

"I must have been, I am sure. For I believe, even then, I had some little sense in my head."

The rope ladder danced in the wind and she felt herself dancing with it. The wind tossed her bright hair, and more than one of the sailors watching her wished he were her husband waiting below. Hugh and Monsieur Nicollet gazed up fearfully, but Catherine giggled and called down to them, "Catch me if I fall."

All the same, she was glad for Monsieur Nicollet's muscled arms about her and his help to the bow, where she knelt Indian-wise. She sought a paddle, searching for the remembered feel of her brief St. Croix River practice.

"As soon as I am on the ladder," Joseph Nicollet said to Hugh, "give a good push from the ship to get clear of her and begin to paddle at once. I shall mount slowly to allow you time before the *Crescent City* sails to make your way into the Ontonagon. Do not depend upon his waiting."

Unaccountably, Captain Eckhart delayed long

enough, not just to allow them to make their way into the river without having to fight the moving ship's suction, but long enough even to permit them to reach the small river dock in front of Nathaniel's cabin. With the canoe secured, they waved to Monsieur Nicollet. When Hugh bent to tie the canoe more closely, Catherine saw Captain Eckhart standing apart on the starboard deck, looking solitary in some new and suffering way. Moved to compassion, she waved to him.

When Catherine heard, the ensuing year, that on a first spring voyage the Sault-bound *Crescent City* had gone with all hands, its captain, and his wife into Lake Superior's awesome, frigid depths, she would remember Eckhart's final wave like a touch of grace.

Now Emily was looking about for her uncle Nathaniel. It was apparent to Catherine, however, as it already was to Hugh, that Nathaniel was nowhere around. The canoe on the dock, the *Nat,* was turned over, and an almost tangible atmosphere of desertion exuded from it. Hugh led the way to the cabin door, from which a closed padlock dangled. He withdrew the family purse from his pocket, opened it, and picked out a key. Catherine noticed it was the same one he had yelled at Emily about some time before.

Hugh fitted it into the padlock. With a click, the lock fell apart. Hugh pushed open the door and they all stepped inside.

Desertion lay like a vapor over everything. Yet Catherine saw immediately that the interior offered comfort and more. Her eyes went to the shelves upon shelves of books, and then to the windows through which Lake Superior sparkled brightly. They rested at last upon a mighty chimney which rose in the cabin's center over a hearth with a partly burned log.

Shadows, not their own, fell through the doorway. "Indians," Emily said, clapping her hand to her mouth in the gesture she had caught from her mother.

"Shure we may look lak Indians, and so may ye whin ye ave bin heer as ave we fir more thin a year. But we be nat Indians no more thin ye."

It was Patricia, and beside her, grinning with familiar helpless appeal, was Patrick. With startled insight, Catherine saw what until now had somehow always escaped her. The two were children . . . and always would be. They would always react in terms of others' approval or disapproval, never wholly out of themselves. With a rush of affection, Catherine knew further that they somehow were her children—hers and Hugh's—to provide for. Deep within her the hope, the prayer, stirred that she and her husband would prove equal.

When the surprise and greetings had passed, Patricia said, " 'Tis more compiny we ave had today thin any day since th' Ontonagon Indians lift fir Big Iron River fir th' winter. First it be a judge and a colonel on thir way up th' river aftir th' copper rock. We gave thim thir breakfast in our cabin up th' Ontonagon an sint thim on thir way."

"A judge and a colonel?" Catherine asked, dismayed.

"Aye. Is it so thit ye know th' pair of thim?"

"We have met," Hugh said.

"I tak it ye didna thin well of thir laks. Nather did we, but we welcome any white persons—since Mr. Avery lift us so suddin-lak, due to word his father had died."

PART FIVE

The Ontonagon Country

(1839–1844)

Chapter 16

THE CONDONS FELT obligated to journey by canoe up the Ontonagon River to assure themselves that the cabin built for Patrick and Patricia the previous summer held adequate supplies. They found the cabin on a smaller, simpler scale than Nathaniel's, but on the same plan with the essential large central fireplace. In the storeroom they discovered wild rice, corn, preserved blueberries, and tea. These, they judged, plus what they'd brought from La Pointe and would share with Patricia and Patrick, the river's fresh carp, sturgeon, and trout, and wild fowl would suffice for a while. As Nathaniel had promised, the Ontonagon's water ran pure and untainted.

Through the early days that followed, Hugh and Catherine held to the belief that Nathaniel would return before winter. Yet as time progressed, they spoke of this less often. From the start both had doubts, which each withheld from the other, of his early return. They assumed Hugh's letter had reached him, because hope forbade doing otherwise. And so, abandoned to their own ingenuity, the Condons set about coping. The days were even more desolate because the friendly Chippewa had already left for their wintering site.

Hugh had previously done little physical work, having from boyhood been "bookish," as his mother, not without Irish pride in the "taste for learning," used to say. It was peat, not logs, that burned in Chapelizod fireplaces. The saw and ax, however, were first-rate, and so with hesitancy but also with instinctive relish in experimenting, Hugh began sawing already felled trees into logs, splitting these, and stacking the firewood in great piles.

The first day Hugh was at this, Patrick arrived and greeted him with a sweeping wave and resounding "Top of the mornin to ye." Instead of pausing for companionable talk, Hugh handed Patrick a second ax, with the promise of going up the river to lend him the same help.

The next day Patricia came, too, and Catherine sought her assistance in heating kettles of water Hugh had carried from the Ontonagon and in washing the family's traveling clothes.

" 'Tis America, and heer we all be equal," Patricia observed.

Catherine was taken by surprise. She had expected their relationship to endure on former terms. What was behind Patricia's thrust of assertiveness? Perplexed, Catherine did not reply.

"Ye didna expict himsel before winter?" Patricia inquired. But this inquiry, Catherine caught, also had a thrust—to defeat her hope. Why would Patricia wish to do this? Again Catherine was silent.

When the two, with the droop of dejected children, set off up the river, Patricia's question seemed to hang in the air.

Still, Catherine could not bring herself to raise the same question to her husband. Through the days and long evenings that ensued, the silence between them expanded, and even Emily chattered less in her struggle to learn how to speak. All the while the yellow and red leaves fell quietly, until at last the aspen, birch, and maple were thinned of foliage, and the sun shone through their nakedness, clear and shrewd as an old woman's eye perceiving life's truth.

"Our Nathaniel will not come before spring," Catherine stated.

Hugh nodded, agreeing, and with nothing to deny for the sake of the other, they again talked freely.

One night soon after, Catherine awakened with the awareness that Emily was missing from her bed. She found her sitting at the window, puzzled by the white, unfamiliar scene. It was Catherine's first glimpse of winter's austere spell in this new country. Holding Emily tight, she wished Nathaniel were with them to share their experience.

It snowed repeatedly, enveloping the cottage. In the evenings a mystic quiet hugged the land. Absorbed, Hugh sat and read from Nathaniel's geology books, lifting his head now and again to read a paragraph aloud to Catherine, who saw excitement glint in his eyes and ring in his voice.

So she should not have been surprised when, early one still morning, he said he had thought of asking Patrick to go with him to look for the copper out-cropping he judged he could locate. "Unless," he added, "you do not wish me to leave you just now . . ."

Catherine could not deny to herself the dismay she felt at his willingness to desert her. Their second child, conceived at Madame Herries' before leaving New Orleans, would come before winter's end. This time there would be no Dr. Ridault—only a changed Patricia—and Hugh wished to go off prospecting . . . Was she, then, so unattractive in this pregnancy? Through her first, he had remained attentive. But lately, living their solitary life and for the first time undertaking the hard work of pioneer women, Catherine realized she had become undesirable. She glanced at her husband, who stood waiting for her answer, prepared for her denial, tension standing in his eyes and straightening his bearing, even seeming to lift his copper-colored hair upward.

Seeing his despairing endurance of further inaction and his overmastering need to be off, Catherine let her natural merriment break free, and she laughed.

"Nay, Hugh, I'll not detain you," she said. "Go with Patrick. Patricia will bide with Emily and me."

So, equipped for winter prospecting, and shouting a final order to keep front and back doors locked, Hugh set off with Patrick up the frozen Ontonagon, and Patricia settled in with Catherine and the late-sleeping

Emily. When the front door closed after the men and she had bolted it, Catherine offered another cup of tea to Patricia. Teacups in hand, they sat down before the fire.

Patricia held her cup at arm's length for a better look. "Be this Mr. Avery's?"

"No. These are mine."

"But Mr. Avery lift iverythin heer. Thir be some of his, too, be thir nat?"

"Aye, but I prefer not to use his so long as I have my own."

Patricia reflected briefly. "Folks as has thins comes to all manner of notions."

As on the earlier visit, Catherine caught self-assertiveness beneath the comment. She was distressed and this time sought to turn aside her companion's combativeness. "I think you would feel so, too, in my place."

"Should himsel nat return nixt sprin, would ye thin feel free with his thins?"

Catherine glanced at the long icicles hanging from the eaves and glinting through the windows. Winter had brought acceptance of Nathaniel's delayed return, and now she and Hugh always spoke of his coming with the spring. Patricia's question had a thrust as pointed and chilling as the icicles.

"Mr. Avery will return. In the spring. We have come at his request to share in his plans to discover copper and develop this country."

"We be heer fir th' viry same raison."

"Of course. We are all here together."

"An gone from bad to worse in laving New Orleans an comin to this shorry land."

And so, to Catherine's regret and confusion, the conversation continued with Patricia's will to destroy hope gaining momentum.

After lunch Catherine would always read to Emily, and now from Nathaniel's shelf of American books she took Washington Irving's *Sketchbook* with "Rip Van Winkle," from which she liked to improvise as she went along, bringing the story down to Emily's grasp. She sat down at the table and waited for her daughter, who usually came running but who was now following Patricia about.

"Perhaps Patricia will join us?" Catherine tried.

Patricia clanged kettles she had brought in. "Lave thim as has time fir to read do so, an lave me git th' apples ready for cookin aginst thir spoilin," she said, and, Emily still trailing, went toward the storeroom.

The cabin's back door closed. There was a delay and then laughter before they came back, Patricia bearing a heavy load of apples and Emily carrying a small one in her wake.

"Did you lock the door?"

"I canna be lockin an unlockin an lockin th' door all day. I will lock it onct an for all at th' day's end."

Catherine glanced at the rifle over the cabin's front door.

"Ye air nat expicting someone to call?"

No, she was not. Who indeed was there to call? Even to her, Hugh's admonishment seemed exaggerated. She closed the book and returned it to the shelf. "Come. Bring the apples to the table and let us work together."

For a time all went well, quartering and peeling the apples and removing the cores. The women were absorbed in their task and the silence was unstrained.

"They be but wastin thir time, th' two of thim," Patricia broke in suddenly.

"They?"

"Miss Antonia an her brither, Père Baraga. Ye canna tame Indians. An why should ye? Lave thim be as they air, an lave thim to thirsels."

"Père Baraga thinks otherwise. He sees no important difference between them and us."

"Thin I ave no wish to meet 'im if it be an Indian he would be aftir takin me fir."

Catherine laughed. "Oh, it is not quite so." She saw again the look that came like love from Père Baraga's eyes. "But he believes that Indians, too, have souls."

"Aye," Patricia muttered, "Indian souls."

And so, with Catherine repeatedly stepping aside to avoid conflict, the day passed, and the next.

Over breakfast the third day, Catherine suggested, "Is it not a comfort to think our men will be starting homeward this morning?"

"Aye, if it be thrue. But lave us nat forgit they be gone yit firther north to where danger lurks."

"Danger?"

"Do ye niver heer th' howlin whin th' dark comes? 'Tis wolves . . ."

Involuntarily Catherine shuddered. Seeing this, and seemingly taking encouragement from it, Patricia got up abruptly and came back dressed to go out.

"You are not leaving?"

"Aye, I be goin to my cabin."

Emily ran for her coat. Patricia laughed and glanced at Catherine. "Aye, if yeer mama be willin, I'll tak ye on yeer biteen slid."

"You will not be long?"

"Nay, we shall be comin right back."

Catherine's book dropped to her lap. She was unable to read. The tension with Patricia stood between her and Washington Irving. What was behind the hostile attempt to destroy hope in Nathaniel's return? Was Patricia at heart a fighter with a need for ascendancy? Catherine recalled their first meeting aboard the *Independence*. She saw her leap out of the hectoring group and land behind Hugh and her, cutting off their access to the ladder that was their escape, then mimic her own movement away, and finally, with mock respect, spread her skirts in a curtsy. That was all so long ago, and long since then they'd been friends—good friends, Catherine thought, recalling her coming for Emily's birth. Why did she wish to fight now?

Catherine looked out the window to the north. Against the austere landscape a pine stood tall and self-assertive. The chill she had felt at first coming face to face with the eerie beauty here stirred through her. In the peace that followed, she lost and found herself. She would not surrender to Patricia's will to make her despair but would continue in silence to hold to her faith. She picked up her book and read on.

Absorbed, she barely heard the back door open and Patricia and Emily come in. She looked up and saw Patricia hold out a faintly recognizable letter. She was curious. There had been no mail. "You have a letter for me?"

" 'Tis not fir ye. 'Tis fir himsel."

Catherine waited, her curiosity mounting.

" 'Tis fir Mr. Avery."

"May I see it?"

"Ye may. 'Twas fir thit raison I brought it."

Catherine got up and took the letter, folded over and addressed in Hugh's handwriting.

"Shure 'twas thit litter as kaped Pathrick an me, th' two of us, from moving back into this heer cabin. An why would we nat thin of betterin oursels any way thit lay opin? We laked this heer place well thit first summer heer with himsel. 'Tis America, an heer we all be equal, be we nat?"

Ah, Catherine thought, grasping at once the basis for Patricia's hostility. 'Twas our coming robbed them of their dreamed-of equality and made us enemies to their hopes.

She turned over the letter and saw the seal had been broken. "Then he . . . saw . . . this?"

Patricia tossed her head. "How could he, an 'im alridy on his way thir?"

Hope of Nathaniel's coming in the spring drained slowly away, and, defeated at last, Catherine sank down again.

Patricia watched craftily, awaiting the other's surrender.

"You may be right. I fear now he will not return."

They both looked up with disbelief at the sound of someone's knocking at the cabin's front door. Catherine got up, and they went together to see.

"Who is it?" Catherine called through the bolted door. Patricia reached for the rifle.

A voice, familiar but not quite recognizable, asked, "May I come in?"

"Ye may not. We air nat receivin callers this day."

They waited, their eyes searching each other's. Then over the snow came the crunch, crunch of a man's boots.

They stared again at each other. Then they swung about and saw in the opposite entrance, his earlier jauntiness displaced by desperation, the reduced figure of the colonel. Was the judge waiting outside? No, Catherine intuitively knew, he was dead, killed by his friend. Emily cried out, and Catherine felt herself sicken.

With a ringing call on all God's saints for help, Patricia leaped from Catherine's side and landed before the colonel, blocking his way. Catherine saw him shift to one side, saw Patricia swing toward him, heard the rifle go off, and felt the discharge fill the cabin with noise and the smell of powder. Emily cried again, and Catherine slumped to the floor.

Through the dark that lifted and then closed again, a voice was saying calmly, comfortingly, "Shure, ye had a fright. For yeer own sake and th' sake of th' wan ye be carryin, ye maum lie quietly now an lave all to me. Thir be no one now to fear. He be runnin still—away from heer."

In a single act of sudden violence, Patricia had found a way to be equal. Due to another's need, she had been able to stoop in kindness.

Catherine, however, had gone down in defeat, despairing of Hugh's achieving. She had seen before what failed prospecting could do to a man, even to someone like her husband, and understood that men and their families could be as adrift on land as at sea.

When Hugh sat down beside her on the sofa, she did not wish to look into his face, dreading to see failed confidence there. Trying to block out the image, she covered her eyes.

Hugh pulled her hands from her face, but she turned her head away.

"Look at me, Kate. Kate, look at me!" Gently, but firmly, he moved her toward him. She kept her eyes tightly shut.

"Tell me what is wrong, Kate. Tell me what happened."

At that she opened her eyes. "You do not know? The colonel was here. I think he killed the judge." She covered her eyes again.

"You're right." Hugh again removed her hands, and again she closed her eyes. "The fight you saw begin in the *Chippewa*'s cabin ended up on the Ontonagon by the copper rock . . . I will not leave you again, Kate. Kate, look at me."

"I saw the colonel's face. I am afraid to look at you!"

"But I am not him, Kate. I am your husband, Hugh. Look at me, Kate!" He pressed her lids open, and she stared at him out of eyes filled with fear.

"We must leave here, Hugh. Your letter did not reach Nathaniel! He will not come. We must go and leave this cottage to Patrick and Patricia."

From somewhere came the sound of Patricia's soft weeping. "Nay, dinna go. Stay. 'Tis yeersels we prize more thin this heer cottage, fine though it be . . . Stay, even though himsel dinna come."

Hugh spoke with authority. "Have no fear about Nathaniel. He will come with the spring. Before they broke with each other, the colonel and the judge had cleared the ice and snow from the copper rock and the ground nearby. Not only the giant rock but the veins in the surrounding earth glowed red in the winter sun. I have seen what Nathaniel saw. Believe me, 'tis a sight to bring a man back."

Determination seeped into Hugh's radiant, confident face. Catherine lifted her hands, pressing her palms against his cheeks. Even as she did so, she knew that what she saw was within and could not be felt.

"Believe me," her husband went on, " 'tis a sight to keep you and me and Emily here. We have only a few months more to await our new baby. Winter will be nearly over then. Can you not be patient?"

Crying, Catherine said, "Aye, I shall try."

Hugh got up and put a fresh log on the fire. Coming back to the sofa, he began to wipe away her tears with his finger. Between sobs, she managed to say, " 'Tis a strange thing altogether to be married to you, Hugh Condon. And the queerest thing of all is, I believe you."

"Well, now," Hugh said gaily, "we shall wait and see who will come first, Nathaniel or—?"

"Larry," Catherine said. " 'Twill be a boy, and I wish to call him for my father."

"Larry, is it? Well, then, we shall see who will be in the greater hurry, Larry or Nathaniel."

Larry arrived first.

Hugh had put Emily to bed and was immersed in a geology book. It was February, and to Catherine the month seemed to go on eternally. She tried to settle down close by Hugh with reading of her own, but she could not contain her restlessness.

"I cannot abide it, Hugh," she sighed, breaking into his concentration.

Hugh looked up. "But you have not long to wait now, Kate."

Catherine gestured annoyance. "Nay, Hugh, I do not mean *that*. What I cannot abide is another evening shut up here in this cottage. I must get out. Go somewhere!"

Loathfully Hugh put down his book and made a try at humor. "Where would you like to go, Kate? You have only to name it. Is it out somewhere to dine late? Or to the theater?"

Catherine jumped up, throwing down her book. "I must get out, Hugh. Out of this cottage!"

Hugh heard the deep urgency in her cry and came to her. "But where can we go, Kate? There is only one other cottage hereabout—Patrick and Patricia's."

"Then let us go there!"

"Up there? This cold night?"

"I must go somewhere, if 'tis only there." She led him to the window. "See how the moonlight lies on the snow? 'Tis a bewitching night. Let us go out into it. Do not dawdle. Let us hurry."

"But Emily? What of her?"

Catherine waved her hands impatiently. "Of course we shall take her—on her sled, wrapped in a fur covering."

Yielding his judgment over to his wife's whim because he caught her oppression and remembered— indeed, had never quite forgotten—how she had behaved on his return from the copper rock, Hugh went for their outer wear and laid it all before the fire. Catherine did not wait for hers to warm. With the awkwardness of the last stages of her pregnancy, she began to button on her leggings and pull Indian moccasins over her shoes. Hugh brought a sleeping Emily before the flames.

"Here. Let me." Catherine took the little girl without waking her and began to put her into her warm outdoor wraps while Hugh banked the fire and dressed himself for the bitter night.

And so they moved up the frozen Ontonagon, Hugh supporting Catherine with his right arm and, with his left, pulling the sleeping child's sled. Their feet crunched in the snow, firmed almost to ice by the long cold. Catherine sighed with contentment. The air seemed to her nearly palpable. She swung her unengaged arm back and forth.

"Whatever are you doing?" Hugh inquired.

"This winter air—'tis like none other I have ever breathed. I thought perhaps I could divide it like water. Ah, Hugh." She stopped. "See that lone pine tree yonder? Is it not majestic against the white land?"

"Aye, 'tis so. I like the birch trees, too, white like the snow, a fair contrast to the pines."

"So they are. But do they not shiver with cold in their winter nakedness?"

They moved onward.

"Perhaps. But see this one nearby? It does not forget to point heavenward."

Catherine followed Hugh's glance, saw how the birch aspired toward the sky but stopped short of the heavenly canopy which receded, boundlessly remote. The stars, though, strangely enough, burned close—close enough, she thought, for her to reach up and touch. The moon poured its blessing on a land asleep in white and primal innocence. Catherine tottered and stood still.

"Is the walk tiring you overmuch?"

"Nay, but the night is making me drunk, and I am possessed by all manner of notions."

"What might they be?"

"Ah, they are such as do not fit themselves into words . . ."

"Can you give me no inkling?"

"Aye, that I can." She lifted her face to Hugh's and pressed his lips with an ardor that she had not shown him for a long time. He met hers with yet greater urgency. Warm then, she unfastened her coat, and he let slip the rope to Emily's sled, holding his wife to him as closely as possible. "Ah, Kate, 'twill be only a little while, and then . . ."

He kissed her again, gently this time, buttoned her coat, caught up the sled rope, and they went on.

No one came to the door to answer their knock, but two faces peered in wonderment out the window. Then, seeing Hugh and Catherine, Patricia threw up her hands in joyful welcome and rushed to the door ahead of her husband.

"Come in, come in," she said, and he stood by, his grin seconding her cordiality.

Hugh stooped to pick up Emily and handed her to

Patricia, who, shushing her husband with a glance, carried the child to the adjoining room.

" 'Tis delighted we be," Patricia said, returning, "but phwhat brins ye this cold winter night to give us sich pleashure?"

" 'Tis the moon," Catherine said. "It bewitched me."

"Aye, I felt it mesel, an I said to Pathrick, 'lave us go visit th' Condons this night.' But himsel said to me, 'Be ye foolish, womin? Phwhativer would thirsels thin an we arrivin sudden-lak?' So ye felt it too, did ye, now?"

"Aye, but I feel something other just now."

"Be they pains tellin ye th' new biteen wan be comin?"

"Aye, and I think this one is in a great hurry!"

And so he proved to be. On the couch over which Patricia laid fresh covering, before the fire with the brimming kettles set to boil, and with Patricia all the while announcing, "Dr. Ridault knows naught thit I dinna know," Catherine in a single hour gave easy birth to a son. Shortly afterward, Patricia handed him to Hugh, who this time could not be kept outside. Wondering, the fatherless Patrick reentered the room, marveling with Hugh, while Patricia declared, "Anither miracle, Dr. Ridault would say, did he be heer."

Chapter 17

FOR THE MONTH after Hugh brought Catherine and the children home to the cottage, Patricia stayed in full charge, and for a time afterward she came in the morning and did not leave until evening. While Patricia kept Catherine company and cared for

Emily and the new baby boy, Hugh and Patrick hunted and fished. The wild fowl were flocking back north from their migration and it was no problem at all to bring one down, so that Hugh and Patrick vied with each other as to who had more at the day's end. The cold would provide storage for another month ahead, and the fowl would be welcome again. They had lived for quite a while on the deer Hugh had shot and divided between them. Now, with the ice loosening from the shore and drifting out into the lake, the men ventured out a little way in Nathaniel's canoe, seeking the trout that lived in Lake Superior's cold water.

Both men found the change to out-of-doors a happy one. Through the winter, besides keeping the kindling piled high for their fireplaces, they had worked to make furnishings for Patrick and Patricia's cottage. Although they were rough-hewn, Patricia exclaimed happily over the table and benches they put together for the kitchen. With these and some of the pieces Nathaniel had given them after their first summer in Ontonagon, their cottage began to look like a home.

The first day on her own again Catherine was triumphant because she could feel April unknotting winter's stranglehold on the land. At her husband's outcry, she turned from the crib where Emily rocked her infant brother and rushed to Hugh at the window.

"See?" he said. "There . . . Now it has gone . . . Ah! There it is again. See?"

With all her might she strained to see out over Lake Superior through the morning's breath of haze.

"See, Kate? Can you not see it?"

"Is it mad altogether you have gone, Hugh, with the long, lonely waiting and hoping? I see nothing beyond the Ontonagon Indians putting up their tents below the river's mouth."

"Aye. Like the birds, spring brings them back. But out yonder. See now? How it moves?"

Catherine strained fiercely toward the east. Then

she saw, white against the blue and unmistakable, the sail of the season's first trading ship and felt herself overwhelmed with joy.

Hugh swung away from the window. "I will take the canoe and go out to meet her."

"Suppose she does not stop?"

"She will. See now O-Kun-De-Kun is already off in his canoe?"

Sure enough, with expertise the Ontonagon Chippewa chief was paddling out to the sand bar. Activity was stirring again in their little world. 'Wait then," Catherine cried, and ran to get a letter to her mother.

"Let us hope the captain has a message from her," Hugh said, taking Catherine's. " 'Tis a long while since you have heard—"

"Aye . . . Her last letter told of my father's dying," Catherine recalled, "and my last to her told of our coming here. With it I endorsed to her the money order from your New Orleans friends."

Hugh straightened pridefully. "I hope it served her well. And 'tis money I am needing right now." He started for the drawer and the pocketbook with the money that remained. Midway he paused and looked down at his son, still red of face.

"Little Indian," he said, "you are slow to turn a respectable white. What do you say, Emmy? Will you come with me to meet the ship? We may at least buy some fresh meat and other supplies." Then, afraid to name the hope that had sustained him and Catherine through the winter, he went for his pocketbook.

At the window, seeking to follow the sail that alternately dipped and rose advancing like a dancer over the waves, Catherine felt a tug at her belt and turned to see Emily rubbing tears from her eyes.

"No matter," she said.

"No matter?"

"I think we should keep him."

"Keep who?"

"Keep Larry, even if he is an Indian."

Catherine's old merry laugh broke free and startled the baby. Picking him up, she said, "Aye, this is one small Indian we shall keep!"

Hearing his wife's laugh, Hugh came back and, at her explanation, joined in with a roar of his own, so that Emily, though not quite understanding, giggled with them, too.

When Emily had buttoned herself into her warm coat, she put her hand in her father's and they went outside to the dock and the waiting canoe.

From the window where she stood, holding Larry, Catherine watched them float down the Ontonagon.

The ship had anchored. Was Nathaniel even now descending the rope ladder? She could not see. But how briefly the ship tarried. Already it was moving out into the blue, bound next for La Pointe. There on the dock, Catherine thought with a rush of affection, Antonia would wait, small and authoritative. And unless he had answered some need, taking him elsewhere, Père Baraga . . . "Well, what do you think, little one?" Catherine said to the baby. "Has our Nathaniel come?"

Swiftly O-Kun-De-Kun moved his canoe up the Ontonagon. The other canoe, sunk deep in the lake water, came slowly on. Was Nathaniel weighting it so? What new gear might he be bringing? Wherever would they place it? The morning's haze was dissolving, being mastered by the bright sun. Catherine shielded her eyes, but Lake Superior sparkled blindingly blue, and she could see only the canoe moving slowly toward the river's mouth.

Hurriedly she laid Larry down in his crib, picked up a wrap, and ran out to the dock. The cool day stirred with living freshness. She could sense sap running in the trees and all nature tossing and turning in disturbed wakefulness. The canoe she waited for made its way up the Ontonagon. At last she could see that it carried no one besides Hugh and Emily. He had not come . . .

She watched her dispirited husband climb to the dock and could think of nothing to say. From an inside pocket he drew out a letter and without a word handed it to her. She turned it over, saw her mother's handwriting, and gave a cry of joy.

"You have waited long," Hugh said. "Go, now, and read it. Emmy will help me put these supplies away."

It was his *not* speaking of the hope that had sent him hastening to the sand bar that made Catherine suddenly blind, so that she stumbled toward the cabin. At the door, like one in a trance remembering some long-past happening, she turned and called to Hugh, "We must not forget he does not know we are here."

"Nor do I know where to write him."

Catherine read greedily through the letter like a person gone too long without food, and after her first hurried gulping, she stopped in astonishment. It was almost as if night and day alternated no longer, or that the seasons had reversed their sequence. Could she think of Chapelizod in the same way again, with her mother no longer going about in the old house and sitting down among her geraniums on the dining-room window seat to read the letter just come?

From the storeroom came the disordered sounds of Hugh and Emily at work. Catherine was sure nothing was being put where it should go. No matter. Afterward she would rearrange it all.

Hugh returned, dusting his hands. "Well, that is done!" Then with forced, harassing good cheer, he asked, "Any news?"

"Aye. Jerry has married!"

"Has he now? Madge?"

"Harriet."

"Hmm . . . Well, and what else?"

But Catherine was not ready to dismiss lightly so considerable a piece of news. "Like you," she said, "I liked Madge better . . . and so, I think, did my mother."

"Apparently Jerry liked Harriet. Anything else?"

"Jerry and Harriet will live in the Kemrises' Chapelizod place the year round."

Hugh whistled. "Not bad for Jerry. What will the Kemrises do in the summertime?"

Catherine didn't hear. She was thinking . . . So in the end Harriet was to be mistress of the Kemris place.

"What will the Kemrises do in the summertime?" Hugh asked again.

"They apparently have elsewhere to go." Hugh's question was somehow irritatingly beside the point. "Mother is renting our place and moving in with Jerry and Harriet."

"Then it is so that your prayers for her have been heard."

Catherine hesitated. In some way hard to define, a great deal more than she had prayed for seemed to have come about. "In any case," she went on, "she has drawn this note on her Dublin bank in our favor. 'Tis in the same amount as I sent her." She handed Hugh the note.

He looked at it, put it down as though he would have liked better to have her keep it, and started to move away.

"Wait! That is not all. George came for the wedding—Tom Kemris, too. It seems that he, not George, was Jerry's best man. And right afterward, Tom and George left together." Catherine looked up, but Hugh was out of hearing.

Were Tom and George still friends? Such friends as they had been as children, not needing to speak, each reading with a glance the other's mind? How close the three of them had been . . . There was that day George had played Father Aherne and married her and Tom in church. Afterward, George's brown eyes had lighted teasingly, and his merry glance had endowed her with a title and a mansion.

From the remembered elegance of the Kemris place, Catherine turned to the frontier cabin that, since fall, had been home. In the letter now on its way, she had described it blithely. Would her mother perhaps read from this letter to Harriet? Catherine looked about and saw Nathaniel's cabin through Harriet's eyes.

Catherine returned to the letter. Now, why was the Kemris place Harriet's instead of Tom's? Intuitively, Catherine knew. There could be but one answer. Like George, Tom had turned from his family, remained a Ribbon Man, and, since the wedding, was again off and about with George on revolutionary business. And she—oh, she, once at the heart of their lives—guessing only now how much she was loved by them all—perhaps she might have changed all that. But she had left them all to go her own way.

Hugh returned, dressed once more for the out-of-doors, and Catherine saw him now not as the Hugh whose earlier image she always kept. For the first time, she saw him as he had become, a frontiersman, accustomed to laboring, owning nothing but courage, and graceless in his urgency to be off.

"Where do you think of going?"

"For Patrick and Patricia—so they may share the fresh food with us."

Catherine got up mechanically. "Then I must go see what you have brought and prepare dinner."

"Aye. They also will be disappointed at having no sight of Nathaniel."

But they were as merry as larks or as children over the meal, caring as little as either for the next day, trusting all to Hugh and to Catherine. They listened wide-eyed when Hugh repeated O-Kun-De-Kun's story of finding the white man's body and giving it an Indian burial. No one doubted the dead man was the colonel, pursuing the trail to the Indians' wintering place, collapsing and dying of hunger and exposure; a death the Indians knew better how to avoid.

And so the colonel now lay between the Chippewa's summering and wintering places in a shallow Indian grave, covered over with a quilt and a mound of birch bark to keep off the rain, and with tobacco and maple sugar provided against his awakening.

As Hugh told the story, Patrick spoke of the judge they had left beside the copper rock in the frozen country. They had but said a brief prayer and left with the plan to bury him when the ground thawed.

Hugh nodded. "We shall go as soon as can be." He glanced at his wife. They had not spoken of this since he had returned and found her in a state that gave him reason to fear for her sanity.

But now, in her normal and agreeable way, she said, "Aye. We must not let the Indians outdo us in mercy."

Still, Catherine noted the easy acceptance of death on both Patrick's and Patricia's part, and their far greater appreciation of the provisions Hugh bought and shared with them.

"That is so," Hugh agreed when Catherine spoke of this while they lay in bed that evening.

He gave a moan, but when she lifted herself on her elbow to look at his face, she saw that he was already asleep.

From the crib in a corner of the room came her baby's cry. She got up and put on her woolen robe and beaded Indian slippers. Then she picked up the baby and went out to such warmth as the banked fire gave. She sat down to nurse Larry and looked about.

Because of her mother's letter, she had seen the cabin through Harriet's eyes, had begrudged the transfer of the Kemris place from Tom to Harriet and so to Jerry, had begrudged Harriet her mother's company, had regretted anew George's course—and Tom's, too —and had looked at Hugh out of disparaging eyes. Had the witch that her grandmother used to say hid in every woman come alive in her then? Catherine smiled to herself at the possibility. Holding and nursing Larry, she understood that her mother's letter had sent her back in time, had briefly made her young and inexperienced again, putting life with its choices ahead ... And now with deepened poignancy, she recalled:

Footfalls echo in the memory
Down the passage which we did not take
Toward the door we never opened . . .

Then she was again the woman she had become,
not the girl she had been. In every life there were
turns not taken, and only the one chosen was real.
She looked down at Larry and at the soft spot that
pulsed reassuringly beneath his brown, fine hair, hair
like George's. He was real.

Chapter 18

NATHANIEL CAME a week later on the next
sailing ship from the East. Since morning that day a
torrential downpour had discouraged their usual look-
out for a promising sail upon the horizon. Instead,
they were huddling about the fire, relieved that for
the moment both Larry's fretting and Emily's restlessness were quieted in sleep, when the front cabin door
was thrust open. Jumping up, they saw O-Kun-De-
Kun toss in wet pieces of familiar luggage. In the
instant before the departing chief slammed the door,
Nathaniel, his mackintosh dripping, hurtled in out of
the rain.

Hugh and Catherine went toward him joyfully.

"Oh, I say . . ." Nathaniel backed toward the door,
his voice ringing with surprise—but not, Catherine
thought, pleased surprise. ". . . is it you?"

Catherine stopped where she was, and Hugh took
but a step or two further. "Were you looking for others
besides us?"

"No." When he took off the mackintosh and hung

it by the door, Catherine observed a black mourning band on his sleeve. "I thought perhaps Patrick and Patricia . . . I had no word of your coming."

Like a sober stranger in place of the Nathaniel they had awaited, he came toward them to shake hands.

He was looking about the cabin and seemed to note with dismay each small change he found. "When did you arrive? I trust it was in more decent weather."

"Aye," Hugh said. "The day was fair." He turned away, and Catherine knew he sought his letter to Nathaniel.

" 'Tis there. On the bookshelf."

"I have it, Kate."

He handed it to Nathaniel. "Perhaps this will make everything clear."

"Let us sit down while I read."

Nathaniel saw that the seal had been broken and unfolded the paper. "But this was written last summer, before—"

He spoke not to them but to himself, as though, for him, last summer's life and all that had gone before had come to a sudden stop.

"Before?" Hugh echoed.

"Before—" Nathaniel's tone bespoke his irritation, as if no one could possibly fail to understand. Suddenly, without reading the letter, he folded it, put it in his pocket, and stood. "Excuse me." He took down his mackintosh. "I must be alone. I must think."

Catherine cast an appalled glance at her husband, but he did not stir from his chair, so she got up and followed their friend to the door. "Where will you go? Not out into the rain?"

"Aye, out into the rain!" Nathaniel shouted. "Like O-Kun-De-Kun." He laughed on a wild note, and as the cabin door closed loudly after him, Hugh and Catherine looked at each other, astounded. Was this the note they had heard and not fathomed in his old hilarious gaiety?

He returned in a more accountable mood, like one who has had his outburst and seeks acceptance.

"Ah." Catherine looked up from setting the table before the fireplace. "You are in time for supper."

"I hurried back so I would be."

"Back? From where?"

"I went up the river. I saw Patrick and Patricia."

What of your need to be alone and to think? Catherine wondered. But she said, "You found all well there?"

"Aye. All seemed near the same as when I left."

Once Catherine might have said, "I am sorry for the changes you find here," but a new attentiveness, nurtured through the long and solemn winter, made her hear, beneath Nathaniel's provoking words, his anguished need for some small unchanging area in which he might resolve a mortal conflict.

"I am glad you found it so," she said. "When the rain stops, you will see that outside all is as before also. It is only in here that change has come."

So lost was he in himself that he did not inquire what change there might be beyond the surface ones he saw, and Catherine was glad that the children were in bed for the night.

Hugh came in without Catherine's hearing his tread. "I have put your bags in the bedroom we judged to be yours. Perhaps I can help you further somehow?"

"No, no," Nathaniel said. "You must give me time."

"Speaking as the cook," Catherine teased, "only a little just now."

She watched him go toward one of the two partitioned rooms at the cabin's end, and as she watched, she remembered how her brother George would clown to hide from those close to him that he walked at once in both the conforming and the rebelling Irish worlds. Though Nathaniel was not clowning, perhaps he also walked in two different worlds. But no man could go on forever so. He must choose—or break.

At breakfast next morning, Nathaniel was his pre-

vious rollicking self, attentive to Emily, marveling at
Larry, laughing appreciatively at Emily's wanting to
keep the baby, Indian or not. But Nathaniel's jovial-
ity ceased as abruptly as it had begun when, the table cleared, he and Hugh sat down there to talk.

Moving about at a little distance, sometimes out of
range of their voices, Catherine could catch only
threads of their conversation.

" 'Tis rich mineral country beyond a doubt," Hugh
observed. "I have been to the copper rock, and I have
seen the veins of copper ore roundabout it. I have
heard that the Indians thousands of years before
mined copper here and smelted it, and that copper
bars still lie on cribbing underground."

"I, too, have heard of that, and it *may* be so."

"What is this, it *may* be so?"

"What have we to prove it beyond rumors and reports of attempts at mining, all of them failures."

"Aye, but it was you who first pointed out to me
that some of these reported attempts were for silver.
Copper had but few uses then."

Nathaniel sighed gravely. "That is true. But we are
still wanting the proof that copper exists in commercial quantities here. We must have a competent geologist's word for it. I hear such a one—Douglas
Houghton—is making a study. So far he will not com-
mit himself."

" 'Tis well that he will not. We can make good use
of the time until he does."

Nathaniel laughed a new chilly laugh. "Let us take
care not to presume an advantage which does not
exist. Suppose the copper *is* here, and other minerals
besides? We still don't have the right to take it."

"Not the right?"

"No. The United States must first acquire this land
by treaty with the Chippewa."

"Did you not once tell me that General Lewis Cass
made a treaty with them—in the 1820s, I believe
'twas?"

With an impatient gesture, Nathaniel pushed this

aside. "Aye, that gave the right to remove minerals, but it did not go far enough. There must be an outright treaty with regard to the land so that authoritative surveys can be made. Only then will it be possible to locate areas and secure the right to mine them."

There was something strange in his talk, Catherine thought, strange and altered. Always before, Nathaniel had sought Hugh's agreement. Now Hugh was seeking his.

"Besides the ore, if there is ore," Hugh was saying, "there are the forests here for undergirding the mines, and the lakes, natural waterways—"

"Do not overlook the barrier at St. Marys Rapids."

"You spoke once of a canal."

"So I did—once." He hesitated. "I know now how the men in Washington look at this place . . . and my own acquaintances in Boston, too."

Hugh stood. "You also once spoke of the chance to create a world of your own, unlike another."

"Another man—Major Robert Rogers—dreamed such a dream and made his own treaty with the Indians. They put him in chains at Michilimackinac and tried him for treason."

Afterward, when Hugh had thrown up his hands at the uselessness of further discussion and gone out to draw fresh water, Nathaniel sat alone. Catherine came and sat with him. He lifted eyes so gravely wounded that Catherine thought of the news that had taken him from Ontonagon shortly before she and Hugh had arrived.

"I am sorry for your father's death," she said.

He dropped his eyes, and she went on. "My father also died last year, and I have found that in time the dead retreat tactfully. But we must let them . . ."

His reaction was vehement. "But he will not retreat! He will not allow me to carry out my own plans. He has tied up everything in his will, and I am no longer free!"

So this, Catherine thought, was the explanation—

but there was more to it. Control of the family fortune had already adjusted Nathaniel's sights and substituted caution for adventuresomeness. Then she saw Hugh through the window, his shoulders stooped with the twin pails of water he carried, and something within her toughened, too. "You must make yourself free," she said.

At her words, bewilderment settled into Nathaniel's hurt eyes. He did not answer Catherine's challenge, but his bewildered expression seemed to accuse her of failing to understand.

"Forgive me for all I do not understand," she said gently, "but there are also some things you do not know."

She told him of the opportunity Hugh had had at the St. Croix Falls mill site and of how, in great travail, he had turned this down rather than break faith with his friend.

"How would this break faith with me?" Nathaniel interrupted.

"How? You do not remember you lent him money in New Orleans on condition that, if the newspaper failed, he join you up here?"

"No. I do not recall exacting any promise. I seem to recall lending money, but only vaguely."

"Then the difference between your fortune and ours must be greater than we thought, for Hugh did not take the loan lightly."

The confusion in Nathaniel's eyes grew to a look of terror, and as though shaking himself loose from some physical hold, he broke without a word and rushed outside.

Catherine watched in panic from the open door. Was it in an irresolvable conflict like this that men killed themselves? Or destroyed others? Ought she run to find Hugh? But she dared not leave the children. How tragic to fear the friend she and her husband loved beyond all others in America. But she was afraid even for herself. She locked the cabin's doors, both front and back.

Larry's cry came like an echo of her own distress. Hurrying to the crib over which Emily bent, Catherine asked sharply, "Whatever is the matter?"

Surprised at her mother's tone, Emily straightened and replied in a like manner, "*He* cannot tell you."

"To be sure, *he* cannot. But perhaps *you* can."

At the implication that she was responsible when she had been doing her best to keep Larry happy, Emily sniffled and turned away.

Catherine picked up the crying baby. She would have liked to cry herself.

Whatever Nathaniel had rushed off to do, she felt responsible for his actions. She had told what Hugh had withheld—about the offer at St. Croix Falls. Why had she taken this upon herself? Why had she not left the telling to Hugh?

It was not until midafternoon that she heard Hugh's whistle at the back door and went to let him in. "What of Nathaniel?" she asked.

"What of him?"

"You have not seen him?"

"Aye, I have seen him. We have been together this long while. With O-Kun-De-Kun we fished for trout. We cooked our catch over a beach fire, and ate our fill there."

"There was no opportunity for Nathaniel to speak?"

"Aye, when O-Kun-De-Kun left, it happened there was."

"Of what did he speak, then?"

"Of many things. He has inherited a vast fortune from his family, and with it, weighty responsibility. He no longer is free to do as he chooses. He must return to Boston."

"What shall we do?"

"We shall stay here."

"To live as the Indians do?"

"Nay, Kate. I shall not be an Indian, nor you a squaw. There is much I must do. I must seek out this Douglas Houghton, discover firsthand what his findings are, and assist him in all ways I can. I must also travel to the Sault and speak to the United States Indian agent there about the need for a final treaty with the Chippewa. I must also look into this question of surveying—perhaps I can share in this work. And somehow, with Patrick's aid and such further help as comes this way, I must try to locate the copper ore."

Catherine saw that Hugh's eyes were remote with the deep content they had showed once before when his New Orleans friends had proved true.

"Though Nathaniel cannot stay, he will not leave us alone in all this. He will do all he can through men in Washington to promote the treaty and the survey. Later, when we see the outcome, we shall make our plans for sharing."

Catherine glanced about. "And will we remain here in this cabin?"

"No. We are to go farther up the Ontonagon, nearer to the copper rock, where we will build a bigger and better cabin, one large enough to make room for Patrick and Patricia for those times when I must go away. On Nathaniel's advice, we will choose one hundred and sixty good acres, so that when the United States owns this land and puts it up for sale—as Nathaniel says will happen—we can bid on it at whatever low figure Congress provides." He paused, and the outside silence invaded the cabin. Then he spoke again. "In some way that is not altogether clear, Nathaniel's dream is now mine . . ."

"Is it so, Hugh, that you can do all these things you speak of?"

Humor, long absent, leaped into Hugh's eyes. "There is an advantage to being disadvantaged, Kate. Disadvantage forces you to do whatever you are required to do. It is in this that Nathaniel and I differ. He may do as he pleases. I am required to do what I must. And yet it is through having to do what I must that I shall win out."

Catherine laughed happily. "I am glad you have

found an advantage here. It is one that escaped me."

They were all merry over the fresh trout Nathaniel cooked on the fire's embers before he left on the returning supply ship, bound now for the Sault. Patrick and Patricia joined them, and there was jollity enough that night to last out the many days to come. Nathaniel, his problem resolved for the time, was as Hugh and Catherine had known him first. His blithe spirit made the world expand and all things seem possible.

All else that Nathaniel and he had agreed on seemed to Hugh to depend first of all on the existence of copper. The Indians reported that farther north a white man was seeking copper. This white man, Hugh decided, must be Douglas Houghton, the geologist who could say with authority whether the peninsula had copper in commercial quantities. So, shortly after Nathaniel left, both Patrick and Patricia moved in with Catherine and the children, and Hugh, with O-Kun-De-Kun, ventured by canoe up the Keweenaw Peninsula's west coast to seek out the geologist.

Dr. Douglas Houghton, explorer and physician as well as geologist, was able to converse in the language of the Chippewa, and when O-Kun-De-Kun, whom Hugh sent in as emissary, told the little scientist that Mr. Hugh Condon was there to speak for Mr. Nathaniel Avery, Dr. Houghton at once offered to see Hugh.

"Yes, indeed," the geologist said affably, "I know the Boston Averys well. What is Mr. Avery's interest here?"

"Copper," Hugh answered directly. "He wishes proof that it exists here in commercial quantities."

"Proof?" Dr. Houghton leaned his head sideways, and twin points of light seemed to pause inquiringly in his eyes. "What kind of proof?"

"Nathaniel is of the opinion, sir, that your word as geologist would be proof enough."

Dr. Houghton modestly inclined his head and stopped a gratified smile by pushing his lower lip over the upper one. "That is kind of Mr. Avery. Very kind."

Hugh had not missed the arrested smile. "I am confident he speaks the truth."

"Then you may tell Nathaniel for me that it is my unqualified judgment that copper does exist here in commercial quantities."

A more ravaging inner commotion than those he had experienced in the promising hours of his previous failed enterprises assailed Hugh, and it was with surprise that he heard himself ask coolly, "Would you be good enough to put this in writing?"

"Why, yes. I'll write directly to Nathaniel, though there really is no need to do so. Next February I'll release my fourth annual report to the legislature—I made my first in 1838—and then," the gratified smile spread unstopped, "all the world will know."

Dismay drowned Hugh's brief elation. "The legislature?"

"Why, certainly. The appropriation for my study is from the Michigan legislature."

"I see, I see . . ." Then, Hugh thought, there would be little time in between to take advantage of, as he'd hoped. They must hurry.

When Hugh sought Dr. Houghton's help toward getting the needed treaty with the Chippewa, the geologist threw up his hands. "I've no idea at all about this. You are taking me beyond my competency. I'm a scientist, not a politician."

You are politician enough, Hugh thought, to have secured the appropriation; but he dared not presume further. The rest, he told himself, must lie with himself.

Catherine was overjoyed at the report her husband brought home. "And 'tis cheer that I need, Hugh Condon," she said. "For you have me pregnant a third time. And I cannot say I am as pleased as I was the first time or the second."

But Hugh was elated. " 'Twill be another son, I

think. And since you have taken our Larry for your very own, I shall claim this one for myself."

"Is it not a little early for that?" Catherine asked, dismayed at what she must undergo again.

But for all that, she was very pleased by the geologist's assurance of copper and satisfied that Hugh's undertaking was at last fairly launched.

"Nay, Kate," Hugh said. " 'Tis but the beginning. Now there is more need than ever to hasten. I must be off again soon . . . this time far inland."

"And leave me and the children once more?"

"I am sorry for that."

"But not so sorry as I."

"Aye, Kate, I'll miss you sorely."

"Still, you are off and adventuring . . . and I . . . I am shut up here closely with the children and those two."

"Did all not go well?"

"Aye, all went well. They dote on the children, and sometimes I think the children are fonder of them than of us. But 'tis crowded we are here, Hugh, the five of us, and I wonder when we are to build that bigger place of our own that you promised."

"On my return we shall make a start. We shall at least choose the site."

"I am glad to hear that, for I should not like to be here still when Nathaniel comes again."

They were silent, remembering Nathaniel's behavior on finding them there. "Nor," Hugh said, "would I."

"We are agreed, then, and so you may go again."

In the end, Hugh delayed setting out, for he could see Catherine was no longer the robust Kate who had carried Emily and then Larry with so little distress. The months dragged on for him as for her, and there were days when he shared her doubt that she would make it. The children, with whom she was normally so companionable, distressed her one February day almost unbearably.

"I shall take them to Patricia for a bit to relieve you," Hugh offered.

"Aye, please do," Catherine responded shortly.

When he returned, he found Catherine in bed and already in labor. Stunned, he stopped at the foot of the bed. "I shall go back for Patricia."

But Catherine shook her head. "Nay, Hugh, do not leave me now. This one is in an even greater hurry than Larry."

God Almighty, was all up to him, then? Alarm rode Hugh's face like a frightened rider on a runaway horse. Seeing his dismay, Catherine could not stop the laugh that rose in her.

Hearing her laugh, so natural and everyday-like, he moved cautiously toward the bed. She held out her hand. "Dr. Ridault knows naught thit ye dinna know," she mimicked Patricia.

And so this time, on a cold February day in 1841, and recalling step by step all that Patricia had done at Larry's birth, Hugh was the one who eased the new infant into the world, tied and cut the umbilical cord, caused the first outcry, and afterward, when Catherine was resting, laid their second little boy in bed beside her.

They called him Christopher Macaulay. The Christopher was for Hugh's father, which greatly pleased Hugh, but soon he noticed that Kate and Emily were calling the baby Mac.

No matter, Hugh decided, seeing his family's looks in the infant, this one is mine, even to the copper-colored hair. And always he remembered that he himself had delivered this second son.

In the spring O-Kun-De-Kun and Hugh set forth on foot far inland, following Indian trails, in search of Captain Jefferson Cram. After many days' walking, they found him at Lac Vieux Desert. He reported that he had just finished the War Department's survey from the mouth of the Menominee River to Lac Vieux and was about to pursue his efforts to the Montreal River's headquarters.

The captain was cordial, glad to tell what he had accomplished, open to sharing with another his participation in the frontier experience. Though in temperament Captain Cram was as unlike the versatile and imaginative Dr. Houghton as two men well could be, he held the same disinclination to step beyond his own competency. When Hugh sought his aid in securing a War Department treaty with the Chippewa, the captain shook his head. "Sir," he said politely, "some men give orders. I take them."

This time Hugh returned to Catherine with hands empty of success and uncertain as to what to do next.

"No word from Nathaniel?" he inquired.

"No, but there were other letters." She handed them to Hugh, and he opened first the one from George, addressed to Catherine in New Orleans.

"Does he not yet know your address?"

Hugh read, in George's sharp, slanted handwriting, two paragraphs from Lord Byron's "Childe Harold's Pilgrimage," ending with: "Arm! Arm! it is—it is— the cannon's opening roar!"

"Still playing war games," Hugh said.

"I fear so." Catherine shared her husband's concern for the danger to their families as well as to himself that George presented, but she kept her own unalterable love for her brother. "The other letter is from Madame Herries. 'Twill not please you, either."

Hugh took it and read:

Madame Bienfaite says that her poor husband is quite beside himself, for he trusted and loved Francis Byrne as a son. That was why Monsieur Bienfaite did not act until there was no longer any doubt. Had he not acted when he did, he would have found himself out of his own company and Francis Byrne sitting in the president's chair. Even so, Monsieur Bienfaite did not prosecute, and Monsieur Byrne left New Orleans, some said for Texas, but in any case a free man.

"What do you think?" Catherine asked. "Did I not always say so?"

"Just so he stays far from here," Hugh observed, and read on.

> What with the scandal in New Orleans, I think sometimes of following where you have gone. Still, I believe I must stay at least through the spring of 1844. That is when the Reverend William Miller predicts Christ will return to establish the Kingdom of God on earth. Think of it, we have only a few short years to wait!

Catherine clapped her hand over her mouth to stifle her laugh. All knew that Christ would not come again until the world's end, and then as its judge.

"The poor benighted soul," Hugh sighed, and without further reading, put down the letter. "And no word from Nathaniel . . ."

Spring moved into summer, and no word came from Nathaniel. But Captain Cram had reported that the Whig Congress had included in the Land Act of that year the pre-emption clause which enabled a family to settle on one hundred and sixty acres of public domain at the minimum price of one dollar and twenty-five cents an acre. So one summer day Hugh and Catherine took the children and canoed up the Ontonagon to choose the site for a cabin of their own. They left their three youngsters with Patrick and Patricia and went on from there. The place Hugh chose just below the Ontonagon Falls was proof, Catherine thought, that in spite of himself, his thoughts returned now and again to the mill site at St. Croix Falls.

"Does this location please you?" he asked.

"Aye. I like it well."

"Then we shall take the one hundred sixty acres

extending north and west from here, as Nathaniel advised us to do."

The summer of 1841 ended early, and snow flew again. Cut off from the world by winter, Hugh and Patrick trapped, hunted, fished through ice, hauled water, cut and brought in wood. And in the evenings, guided by Dr. Houghton's early 1841 report, Hugh drew a map of the Ontonagon country and sketched in the areas where the copper deposits were thought to lie. Emily and Larry were growing, Larry struggling into speech, and little Mac was trying to walk. All were thriving happily.

And then—no less a miracle for its recurrence—spring came again, and the first sailing ship of 1842 brought Nathaniel's long-awaited reply to Dr. Houghton's and Hugh's letters.

Over Hugh's shoulder, Catherine read;

"Dear Hugh: I am sorry to tell you that I am unable to come to Ontonagon this spring . . ." Catherine looked up. Not until now did she realize in how many small ways she had begun to look forward and to prepare.

Business keeps me here. But to be truthful, I do not see how my coming will help matters along unless and until the treaty is made with the Chippewa. It is now over a year since Dr. Houghton made his promising final official report, but the United States is still not free to survey and sell this land for mining purposes.

I share your disappointment that the War Department survey, begun before Dr. Houghton's final report, has not extended further into the interior. But of course there is no point in the War Department's surveying territory to which the United States still lacks title.

Also with regard to last year's pre-emption law, it is indeed operating to the advantage of those elsewhere in the west, but it is of no use to you with regard to acreage there, and for the reason I already have mentioned twice. Until a treaty gives this land to the government, it cannot be put up for sale.

There is but one remedy to all this, and that is the long-awaited and necessary treaty. I look forward to hearing from you on this.

As always, Nat

Please excuse the haste with which I have written. And please tell Kate I have become engaged to Miss Lucinda Parker of Philadelphia. We look forward to marrying later this year.

"Well!" Catherine exclaimed. "I declare!"

Hugh tossed aside the letter and went alone to the dock. But he was not long alone. Emily and Larry, with Mac toddling between them, followed.

Catherine reread Nathaniel's letter, her indignation growing as she recalled all Hugh had done, and tried to do. She walked slowly out to her family. But all were gone—the canoe, too. Those imps have prevailed on their father to go down the Ontonagon, Catherine thought. Well, who could blame them?

The day was full of clear, fresh air and softened sunshine. Standing there Catherine felt the surprise and the promise of spring. How good it was after the long white winter to sense the approach of the budding, delicate green. Farther north, at the site they had chosen for their cottage, the falls, full from the heavy snow, tumbled to the river and reawakened the vibrancy of living. She felt like a girl again. The Indians already had come from their quarters on the Big Iron River. Perhaps even now they were pitching their summer tents on the beach at the Ontonagon's mouth.

But no. Had they been, Hugh and the children would have lingered. Instead, they were already returning, fighting their way upstream against the river's strong current. Beside them came another canoe. Was a single day to bless them with both spring and a guest? Her hand shading her eyes, Catherine strained to see who it might be who dipped and pulled his paddle with so easy, even gay, a rhythm. Père Baraga! So he had not forgotten his promise of three years ago to visit!

He was traveling the one hundred eighty miles from La Pointe to L'Anse on Keweenaw Bay, and the trip from Ontonagon, on the western side of the peninsula's base, was more quickly made overland than by canoe. Apparently he hoped to find the Condons still in residence and planned to leave his canoe with them, traveling the rest of the way on foot. The chance of meeting with her family seemed to him another instance of the Lord's provident kindness. And he had need just now of that help. For a new vision was taking excited shape in his thoughts, kindling his blue, benevolent eyes, hurrying his movements, so that when walking, he would break impetuously like a child into a short, urgent run.

The plan, he explained to Hugh, Catherine, and Emily while Larry and Mac napped after lunch, was really not new. The Jesuits had tried it in Paraguay, and also in Canada during the seventeenth century; the Franciscans had tried it late in the eighteenth century in California. It was simple. He looked about him, relishing with delight his option of sustaining the suspense or revealing his secret. He chose the latter.

He wanted to build a mission at L'Anse—a church, a priest's house, and a school for the Indian converts, as at La Pointe. At L'Anse he would collect the Indians in one village near the church and build for each family a small log house with good windows and doors and a brick or stone chimney. Each home would be on its own lot and would have a cooking stove and furniture. Every family could have provisions and clothing to begin life in a civilized manner and would be taught to garden as well as to do all else they needed to know to live decently. In this manner they would be better able to heed the teaching of Christ and to practice their duties as Christians. A great deal of money would be needed, and he had the promise of some to begin with.

Père Baraga looked about but did not find a response to match his own enthusiasm. He saw that Hugh and Catherine sat in some shadow of their own that prevented them from realizing that the sun might shine elsewhere upon others.

"I have talked too long of my Indian children," he said. "Too long. Now what about you?"

Hugh told him their problem.

"Eh, *bien.* But the man you must see is Lewis Cass."

"Lewis Cass? He has left the area."

"Mais oui, but he has returned, and there is talk that he might make a distinguished President."

"President? I know only of his early treaty with the Indians, which has not proved to be the answer."

"Mais non, but it was along the right lines. He has done much besides. From 1813 to 1831, he was governor of the Michigan Territory, and during his tenure he opened a land office in Detroit for the sale of land in the lower territory. While governor, he arranged for the treaty with the Chippewa you speak of. Later he went to Washington to serve as President Jackson's Secretary of War, and then to France as the United States ambassador. Now he is back among us—in Detroit. Go at once to see him."

After baptizing Larry and Mac and giving his blessing to all, he was off with a gay parting wave early the next morning. At first he walked in a dignified way, but then, while still within their sight, he broke into a carefree run. How was it, Catherine wondered, that even Antonia's departure to open a girls' school in Philadelphia left him undefeated? He had said only, "For her, it is better so. Our winters here are severe." His gift of cabbage, corn, and onion seeds in her hand, Catherine turned from the doorway. Whether invaded by the bright day that was beginning or by fresh hope, the cabin seemed to fill with space and light.

Hugh spaded a small lot in the acreage he planned for his own and planted Père Baraga's seeds carefully. Then, on the first Sault-bound trading ship to stop at Ontonagon that summer of 1842, Hugh, following Père Baraga's advice, left for Detroit to see Lewis Cass. This time Catherine went with him, and Patrick and Patricia took charge of the children.

Chapter 19

THEY SAILED ALONG the Keweenaw Peninsula's west coast, where, two years before, Hugh and O-Kun-De-Kun had canoed for the meeting with Dr. Houghton. They rounded the peninsula's tip and followed upper Michigan's northern boundary to the Sault, gazing upon Lake Superior's immensity out of eyes which held memories of their voyage from Madeline Island to Ontonagon. "She is a woman and talks to herself," so Monsieur Nicollet had quoted the Indians. And she has much to talk of, Catherine mused, and thought of Captain Eckhart and his quadroon wife, dead in the lake's icy depths, while Hugh and she sailed its surface shining beneath the summer sun.

On this eastbound voyage no storm surprised them, and they changed at the impassable Sault to another ship for the voyage into Lake Huron, down lower Michigan's eastern coast. There were moments when, unpredictably, an image of Emily or Larry or Mac would appear, asserting a claim upon Catherine. She would remind Hugh of something one of their children had said or done. "Aye," he would say pridefully. And yet it seemed to her that, without the youngsters, they were a newly married couple again. She had thought she had left the bridegroom and bride in the *Independence* cabin, forever crossing and recrossing the ocean. But they found them again as they sailed down Lake Huron.

"So once again," Catherine observed as they lay together in one of their cabin's twin bunks, "we are young and in love."

"Aye," Hugh agreed, "but we are also what we have made ourselves."

"That is so. We are more than we were then. And our love is greater, too. Do you not feel it so?"

"I do," Hugh said, raising himself on his elbow. Gazing down at his wife, he added, "You are more beautiful than ever."

They changed vessels a third time at Port Huron, to a twenty-foot ship that carried them down the St. Clair and Detroit rivers to Michigan's capital, the city of Detroit.

"Does this not put you in mind of our trip up the Mississippi?" Catherine asked.

"It does," Hugh agreed.

They fell silent, sharing memories.

Then Hugh said, "I still remember our first sight of New Orleans."

"Detroit is older than New Orleans," a woman named Madame Gratiot remarked, joining them.

"Aye," Catherine said, "so you informed us at lunch, and we are much interested."

From Madame Gratiot, a handsome woman Catherine guessed to be in her forties, and proud of her French descent, they learned a bit more of Detroit's early history. Founded in 1701, it had first been French, then British, and had not come firmly under United States control until after the battle of Lake Erie, the year after the War of 1812.

"Then it has a history somewhat like New Orleans," Catherine observed. To which Madame Gratiot gestured in a way that suggested perhaps greater differences than similarities.

"I see," Catherine said. "Like and yet not alike."

"*Mais oui*," Madame Gratiot commented.

Her carriage was waiting for her at the dock, and she kindly offered to have her coachman drive Hugh and Catherine to the Mansion House on the northwest corner of Jefferson and Cass, where they intended to stay and where Hugh hoped to see Lewis Cass.

"Cass is named for Michigan's statesman Lewis Cass," Madame Gratiot told them. "And," she could not resist adding, "Gratiot for my husband's family."

Catherine recalled Madame Herries. The two women, she decided, were like New Orleans and Detroit, alike and yet dissimilar.

The coachman drew up before the Mansion House, and pleasure tingled through Catherine at the prospect of staying at so handsome a place. While the driver dismounted and took down their bags, Hugh stepped out and reached for Catherine's hand.

"Tomorrow, while your husband sees to his business, you will want to go shopping," Madame Gratiot said as she pressed Catherine's unengaged hand. "Go to the F. T. and J. General Store, named for the three Palmer Brothers, Frank, Tom, and John."

Outside the carriage, Hugh held his hat high in salute, and Catherine bowed graciously to Madame Gratiot as she drove on.

Already dressed for his morning call on Lewis Cass, Hugh looked at Catherine, still abed. "You will not be lonely, Kate?"

"Nay, Hugh. As soon as I can pull myself out of the comfort of this bed and away from the pleasure of breakfasting in that fine room below, where we dined last night in such elegance, I shall take Madame Gratiot's advice and go to the store she recommended. After such a long time, there is much I am eager to see —and some things I wish to buy. I shall look today, and perhaps tomorrow we can go together and decide on these purchases."

"Aye . . . if all goes well when I meet with Lewis Cass."

"Hugh Condon. Irish, is it, now? Then let us shake once again and vow our shared enmity of England."

Sixty years old, his black hair silvering, Lewis Cass stood powerful and smoldering; a man with unfinished fights still to win against an old enemy.

Hugh answered guardedly, "I come as a citizen of the United States."

The man who had dealt persuasively with both Indian chieftains and the King of France waved aside Hugh's response. "Still, you must hate England, and for graver and longer-standing grievances than mine, though mine go deep enough." A man unafraid to speak his own mind, he moved toward a chair in his Mansion House sitting room.

Hugh felt his caution slipping. All the praise of Cass he had heard on the voyage from Ontonagon had failed to prepare him for so courageous and comradely an individual. He himself would like to speak out, but both his inheritance and his experience had bred discretion. "May we not hope one day for a peaceable settlement of Ireland's differences with England?"

His shoulders lifted like those of the Ohio frontiersman he had formerly been, and Lewis Cass swung about. "It will never come peaceably! O'Connell knows this. A mighty man, Daniel O'Connell . . ."

There it was, the inescapable Irish memory, like a swamp on an Indian trail which must be circled to avoid sinking into. "Aye," Hugh said, still carefully withholding full agreement, "a man of many gifts."

"You know him?"

"Who that is Irish does not?"

"I know him well." Cass seated himself, and with authority but without arrogance, motioned Hugh to an opposite chair. "We met and talked in Rome last year. He has re-created the Catholic Association of 1828 and 1829, through which, as you know, he won emancipation. From Rome he returned to Ireland to organize meetings for the repeal of the Union."

All that had grown remote for Hugh was suddenly close again. When stronger nations tangled, Ireland might yet count for something. But there was always the danger that she would be but a pawn. Was she preparing to try again? Was this the meaning of George's strange letter to Kate? The two had been very close. Had he, then, wished to forewarn her in the event he fell in this fight?

"I am sorry to learn this," Hugh said slowly. "I doubt O'Connell can win this one, and my wife has a brother, still in Ireland, who must ever be fighting."

General Cass's dark eyes pierced Hugh. "And you?"

Centuries of losing had conditioned Hugh against further useless fighting. Unlike George, who was going into the fight expecting to lose. Hugh answered cautiously. "When I fight, I like at least a fair chance to win."

Cass sucked in his lips speculatively. "Still, there are times we must fight—win or lose." Confidence beamed from his handsome features. Twin needle-points of light leaped into his eyes.

"I fought England with sword and rifle in the War of 1812, when I was about your age. We defeated her, but she did not know she was beaten. This is a problem with England, a lesson she finds hard to learn. As governor for eighteen years of the Michigan Territory, I fought and beat her again and again.

"As ambassador to France, I also fought and beat her. The Quintuple Treaty between England, France, Prussia, Russia, and Austria was negotiated to suppress the slave trade. But in fine print England provided for her 'right to search.' I caught this, wrote a pamphlet in Paris attacking this 'right to search,' and the French refused to ratify.

"But as I say, when it suits her not to learn, England is the world's biggest dunce. Things came to a head all over again in the Webster-Ashburton Treaty, and once more England refused to give up her claim to the right to search American vessels. That is why I resigned as ambassador to France. That is why I am home. But I am home to continue the fight.

"Enough of me. Let me hear about you. You say

you have come from upper Michigan. How did you get there? By way of the Erie Canal and the lakes?"

"Nay, by steamboat from New Orleans, then by canoe up the St. Croix and the Brule, and by sailboat along Lake Superior's south shore to Ontonagon."

Lewis Cass's voice warmed. "I know the area well— as the site of the copper rock. Plover, then chief of the Ontonagon Indians, first called the rock to my and General McKenney's attention when we were negotiating a treaty with the Chippewa at Fond du Lac in 1823." Cass paused reflectively.

"Three years later, on a treaty-making expedition, I went up the Ontonagon to see the rock myself. We made the treaty then, but it granted the right only to minerals. The Indians were unwilling to cede the land, and I did not wish to push them further than they were willing to go."

Impetuously Cass leaned forward. "I understand Julius Eldred of our city was up there a summer ago, that he tried and failed to carry off the rock, and that he plans to return better equipped to try again." His eyes turned defensive. "Is it about the rock you have come?"

Were this the case, Hugh was sure Lewis Cass would oppose him. He spoke thoughtfully. "No . . . for all I care, the copper rock may rest always where the Great Spirit put it."

The other man relaxed. But his dark eyes stayed alert. "What, then?"

"It is the copper that runs deep into the ground that interests me. The time has come for a treaty by which the Indians can cede the lands. Without such a treaty, surveys cannot be made, and without surveys, it is quite impossible to locate mineral permits."

The former governor's expressive face turned meditative. "That is so. I left some work unfinished when I answered President Jackson's call to be Secretary of War."

He was silent, looking back, perhaps aware even then that his richest years of achievement were past.

For it was as governor of the Michigan Territory, when in the full flood tide of his manhood, that he had turned a wilderness into a civilized, self-governing American state. If he had left behind in that wilderness the young man he had been, it was also in those solitary years there that he, a New Hampshire blacksmith's son, had found a self to match the King of France or any other man.

He sighed and resumed the conversation. "I do not like unfinished business. But there is much else just now to keep me busy. Perhaps you have heard? The Pennsylvania convention at Harrisburg passed a resolution favoring me as the next Democratic candidate for President. The *New York Herald* has endorsed me as a new Jackson who would lead the party in triumph. The people like my anti-British stand. But I see that the issue of the day is the annexation of Texas. Is this not so?"

Was Lewis Cass, then, consulting him? Did great men, no less than ordinary men, need others to advise them?

Cass did not wait for Hugh's answer but continued, thinking aloud. "The South favors annexation, the North opposes it. Though a Northerner, I am inclined to say let us annex Texas. Then let the people of Texas decide themselves whether they will be a slave or a free state." The general looked straight at Hugh. "You have lived both in the South and in the North. What is your thinking?"

Hugh hesitated. He could not forget that runaway slave on the *Algonguin* who had dived into the muddy Mississippi. "There is that on slavery," he said, "which goes against the grain."

"So it does. But are we to stop the nation's expansion westward to the great natural Pacific Coast ports? I prefer to see Texas free, but I wish first to see Texas a state. Is this wrong?"

Hugh hesitated again. Somehow in the central core of self, where a man is most truly himself, he believed slavery to be wrong. But the general's eyes were boring him, repeating his question. In the end, Hugh said, somewhat unwillingly, "I can see no evil in it."

"Good! I shall issue a statement to that effect. And since you have helped me to clear up this pressing problem, I shall see that that unfinished business in upper Michigan is taken care of. I know which man to speak to, and I know him well. You will have your land treaty, and you will have it promptly."

The candidate for the Democratic nomination for President stood and held out his hand. "Tell everyone you speak to that I will be ever loyal to the great State of Michigan and to its future."

Hugh hurried to their room in the Mansion House to tell Kate his good news, but she was not there. He could not wait for her there. He had to get out in the open and walk!

The sun shone and the breeze blew fresh and sweet through Detroit's parks and open spaces, down the main thoroughfares radiating from the city's center, and out along the territorial roads. Hugh's mood expanded. Had the rebuilt city been less open and roomy than he found it, his mood would have made it so.

He, Hugh Condon, had talked with one who had sat with presidents and kings, one who might himself succeed Harrison as President of the United States. Hugh's steps lengthened in his stride. They had talked man to man. Like himself, Cass had been a frontiersman, clearing and planting, knowing and defeating loneliness in study.

The treaty would be made. Who could say what might come of it? In this immense and open country, all things were possible. Before he sought return passages, he would write to Nathaniel.

But first he would tell Kate. He turned about and started back to the hotel. Surely by now she would be there, waiting for him, eager to tell him what she had seen and wanted to buy, more eager still to learn how he had fared. He hurried into the Mansion

House, ran up the stairs, and from outside their room heard Catherine moving about inside.

"Kate!" he called. She swiftly unbolted the door and stood before him in her chemise and petticoats. He closed the door behind him, slid the bolt in, and stood gazing in wonder at his wife. She was still the enchanting girl he had courted in Chapelizod, still the radiant bride he had brought to New Orleans, but a more subtle quality, perhaps something of the Ontonagon country's mysterious beauty, had entered and ennobled her looks. Later, he promised himself, she must put on her lace dress and they would go to dinner in the handsome room downstairs. Maybe General Lewis Cass would also be dining there. How proudly he would introduce him to Catherine.

"Kate," he began, but there was no need to tell her. One glance and she knew, and was in his arms, trembling with relief and happiness. He held her close, running his hands up and down her back to quiet her shaking. Sometimes in the past it had been with a sense of failure that he sought her, and it would be her love which consoled him. But today it was otherwise. Now, as all men desired to do, he would possess his wife in triumph.

Chapter 20

CATHERINE GLANCED OUT THE WINDOW at the November sky, dark with unspilled snow, and felt yet another winter clamping down upon them. On mornings like this, their trip to Detroit and the events at the Mansion House that summer of 1842 seemed unreal. Was it possible that two years had passed since then? There was proof enough that they had. Little Macaulay, nearly four now, conspicuously his father's favorite, ran about after Emily and Larry. They had been settled in their own cabin at the foot of Ontonagon Falls long enough for the children to feel it had always been home.

Since the treaty with the Chippewa, which Lewis Cass's friend had negotiated in the spring of 1843, an enormous change had come to the Ontonagon country. Prospectors swarmed over the land, and some had found their copper mines. There was much talk of other mines, some farther north near Eagle River. But though Hugh went each day with Patrick in search of the vein he was certain from his study of Houghton's report lay somewhere about the former site of the copper boulder, he had yet to discover his mine. And each day Patrick arrived later and Hugh waited with greater impatience. He was waiting now.

"Listen to this, Kate," he said. He was sitting at the table, from which she was removing the breakfast dishes, and where, to restrain his mounting tension at Patrick's delay, he was rereading Houghton's report to the Michigan legislature. " 'With a single blast I threw out nearly two tons of ore. With this there were many masses of native copper, from the most minute specks to one of about forty pounds in weight.' "

"Aye, I remember." Catherine nodded and went on with the dishes.

With an angry clap, Hugh slammed the book shut, nearly causing Catherine to drop the dishes and startling the children, who played at the far end of the room. He got up. "Where is that man? Why has he not come?"

The trouble, Catherine knew, was that each day Hugh feared Patrick would not come. At the time of the Eagle River discovery, Patrick had hinted that perhaps the true place to seek the red metal might be somewhere other than where they were looking. At each successive discovery of a copper vein or at the unearthing of an ancient Indian mine—or the rumor of either—he spoke vaguely of going to the new and more promising site. But going presented problems beyond Patrick, and always he ended by staying.

Now, however, a new development threatened. To protect the rights of those who located copper mines, the United States Government had opened mineral agencies at Ontonagon and elsewhere on the Keweenaw at which a prospector might present his permit and record a description of his claim. Though Hugh did not yet have a claim to record, he had recently gone to the agency at the Ontonagon's mouth. After introducing himself and chatting a while with the government man, Hugh had walked the short distance to the nearest saloon, where all was much as he had understood it would be.

Here were the men who looked to profit without exploring and digging. "White Pawnees," they were called, and they filled the flimsy saloons that now cluttered the once-undisturbed country. Hugh saw that it was here that the business went on. The White Pawnees were getting prospectors drunk and sometimes succeeding in prying from them the supposed location of copper veins. While he had watched, Hugh noticed more than one of the Pawnees leave the man he had gotten drunk and hurry off to the agency to record a description of some explored area and obtain a permit to work it. Soon the man would make his way to another saloon and, with luck, sell the permit, more than likely to another White Pawnee. So the travesty went on, and with winter's approach drawing a halt to the prospecting, it grew livelier. Some of the Ontonagon Chippewa who had failed to follow Chief O-Kun-De-Kun to the tribe's wintering place also lounged about, drunken as well. The life that had come to the Keweenaw Peninsula would not make Père Baraga's work with the Indians any easier.

Someone had come up from behind and put a compelling hand on Hugh's shoulder. He had swung about, and with the intuition that this was in truth what he had anticipated, saw Francis Byrne.

"We meet again," Byrne had said, and held out his hand in much the same way as on that day outside Monsieur Arnaud's office in the Government House.

Once again Hugh had taken his hand.

"Let us drink on our meeting," Byrne had invited, and Hugh had caught in his eyes the furtive gleam he had seen in the eyes of the White Pawnees.

"Aye," he had said, reversing their former relationship with his invitation, "I shall stand you a drink."

They had moved to the bar, and Hugh had ordered for Byrne and himself.

"You have not forgotten my drinking preference," Byrne had observed.

"No," Hugh had answered. "I have not forgotten."

"It is a long time since you left New Orleans. I suppose you have since lost touch with everyone there."

"Kate hears now and again from her friend, Madame Herries."

"So. Well—" Byrne had lifted his drink. "To our future."

And lifting his own drink, Hugh had said instead, "To *the* future."

There had not been a great deal more, and Hugh had not told Kate of the meeting. Still, she sensed this morning that he was more than usually upset by Patrick's tardiness.

"Indeed," she remarked as the hour grew later and Patrick still had not come, "I, too, fear the White Pawnees may have gotten him."

Hugh began to put on his warm outer clothing. Catherine watched apprehensively. Last night, for the first time this fall, the distant howl of a hungry wolf had broken into their sleep. "You will not go alone?"

Hugh did not answer and continued getting ready. But before he had finished, to Catherine's immense relief Patrick arrived.

" 'Tis a hard pull up th' river," he said, "an th' day

as cold as it be." He glanced out the window at the snow-burdened clouds and then stared longingly at the fire and at the chairs he had helped Hugh make the previous winter.

"May I offer you a cup of hot tea?" Catherine braved her husband's scowling disapproval.

"We are already late, Kate," Hugh said brusquely.

Patrick moved defiantly toward a chair. "Aye," he said, sitting down, "an we be later still, fir I ave thit to tell ye thit may intirest ye, an I ave a min to tell it to ye now."

Watching her husband, Catherine felt him tense. "Speak, then," he said. He remained standing.

Patrick shook his head unhappily. After all, they were not to sit down together in comradeship. It was not to be easy. He sipped several times at the tea Catherine brought him. Then, with a story-teller's sense, he began, "An auld acquintince has come our way agin."

"Who?" Hugh asked.

But before Patrick could answer, Catherine had guessed.

Patrick sipped his tea again before answering. "Mr. Byrne," he said finally. "An 'tis a thrivin business he be doin at th' Ontonagon's mouth," he added, watching Hugh slyly all the while.

"Is this your news?"

"Aye."

" 'Tis not news to me. I have seen Francis Byrne."

Patrick's change of expression betrayed his surprise. "Ave ye, now?" he murmured. Then he added craftily, "An be ye frinds still as iver?"

"Friends as ever," Hugh said. "And now let us be on our way."

"But thir be wan thin firther I maught tell ye."

Hugh stood rigid and silent, and Patrick withheld whatever else he had to say and began fumblingly to rebutton his jacket.

There was no doubt, Catherine thought, as to what further thing Patrick had yet to say. White Pawnee

Francis Byrne had enlisted Patrick's help and such knowledge as he might have from his prospecting with Hugh as to where copper might be.

From the door she watched the men go the familiar way, carrying their cumbersome gear, shovels and picks, and Hugh's gun. Patrick was trailing as though he hoped that the threat of snow might yet stop the day's search. And he was right, at least about the snow. Even as Catherine watched, big, loose flakes began to fall softly, slowly, impartially, upon the distant evergreens and the nearer leafless trees along the Ontonagon's banks. Winter had come, and Hugh faced Patrick's threatened desertion to Francis Byrne.

Seeing the snow, Emily and Larry clamored to forget lessons this morning and to go out to play. Yielding to the magic of the season's first snowfall, Catherine got out the box from the F. T. and J. General Store, and while Emily and Larry danced about impatiently, brought forth two bright red woolen jackets and caps. "Stay together. Do not wander far," she warned. She sat down, with little Mac and Madame Herries' aging Poo-poo her only company now, to remake for Emily her own plaid woolen dress, brought so long ago from Chapelizod.

She began to rip out the long sleeves, the careful seams. Poor little Emily. Except for her younger brothers, she had no companions, not even the Indian children, who had left Ontonagon for the winter. No schooling, beyond the lessons at home. No church. In frontier country, Indians fared better than white people. "Ah," Père Baraga had begged, "do not say this. With development, churches will come for all." But so far, it was true. Last September, across the peninsula base, at L'Anse, he had begun his new Indian mission to the Holy Name of Jesus.

Catherine laid the sleeves on the table and began to rip the blouse from the skirt. Much had happened elsewhere, beyond the Keweenaw Peninsula. Texas had been annexed, but though Lewis Cass had been first to speak out in favor of this, he had not benefited.

Like a dream, the scene in the Mansion House dining room recurred. Lewis Cass, then a contender for the Democratic nomination for President, had excused himself from the men he was dining with and strode to Hugh's and her table. Hugh had bounded to his feet. "General, my wife, Catherine." With an old-country bow and a "May I?" the general had kissed her hand. The Democratic Convention had met and nominated, not Cass, as Hugh and she had hoped, but a man unknown to them, James K. Polk, and he had been elected President. Would the treaty General Cass had initiated with the Indians, and which at last made it possible to mine copper, now prove of value to others but not to them, the first arrivals here?

The blouse separated from the skirt, Catherine turned to the side seams. And now Patrick threatened to desert Hugh for—of all people in this world—Francis Byrne! Catherine paused and watched the snow come down as if with the gentleness of compassion. Was Hugh too unyielding with Patrick? she mused. Perhaps a little indulgence now and again, the kind children respond to . . . But Hugh seemed to have grown hard lately and to be growing ever harder —sometimes, she regretted, even toward little Larry.

"Who is the lad like?" he asked every once in a while, puzzled that Larry did not react like himself.

"To be sure," she had told him more than once, "he is ever so like my brother George." But Hugh did not like that, either.

Where was George now? she wondered. The conflict his strange message had forecast had come to Ireland. O'Connell's meeting to defeat the Union had failed. Though the House of Lords had reversed his jail sentence and set him free, they had forever broken his power, his health, and his spirit. Well might they now let him go free. Catherine thought. But did George fight on still, and where? They would not hear until spring.

Catherine folded and laid down the four separate pieces and listened. She could no longer hear the children's successive cries, "One, two, three, here I come." She must go look, but she dared not leave Mac alone. She found Emily's outgrown winter clothing, outgrown now also by Larry. And again she got out the F. T. and J. General Store box and found the jacket and bonnet she had bought for herself. How gay she had been that day—mad, really—to choose for herself the same bright red she had chosen for them; because of her hair, she had never before worn red. Still, Hugh had encouraged her. " 'Twill look right cheerful against the white country."

With Mac's trusting hand in hers, and he so comical and appealing in the handed-down clothes, she set out, Poo-poo following. Mac lifted his face in delight and grabbed for the flakes with his unengaged hand. Catherine laughed at his pleasure. "You funny little boy," she said.

But Emily and Larry were nowhere about. They had done what they had never done before, wandered off on their own. Where ought she to look first? Down the river toward Patrick and Patricia's cabin? Farther up river, where their father and Patrick had gone to dig for copper? Or westward, in the cemetery the Indian children talked about? Most likely they would go there, Catherine decided, and she led Mac stumblingly through the woods.

Between the trees, before she came to the clearing, Catherine saw the new red jackets and caps flashing through the white, falling snow. Awed by their own daring, the children clustered over an Indian grave. A weight lifted from their mother, and she thought that the two might have been herself and George straying off to the Liffey, sharing in life's dawning mystery. The children looked up, inviting her to join in. Little Mac broke free, tottered over to them, and sat down in a drift. The others laughed at Mac, pulled him to his feet, took each other's hands, and circled about merrily. Then impulsively Emily and Larry started to run back to the cabin.

Half carrying Mac, and breathless from keeping up

with the children, Catherine came out of the woods and heard them shouting, "Patrick! There goes Patrick!"

Sure enough, he was shoving off down the Ontonagon. Had Hugh come home, too? There were no footmarks in the snow to the cabin. Patrick must have left Hugh alone . . .

From the dock Catherine called in her clear, strong voice, "Patrick! Oh, Patrick!"

But if he heard, he gave no sign. On Patrick went, down the Ontonagon, dark green and mirrorlike between the snow-covered banks.

Deserter, Catherine thought, crying inwardly. Weak, cowardly, faithless—to leave him there alone!

For hours it had gone on, the unwillingness to search, the objections, the indifferent tries, the complaining at the snow and the cold, the malicious unvoiced triumphs at each fresh failure. Then, like the black powder they used to dynamite, sudden violence had erupted within Hugh, and instead of rocks and earth, spewed forth splintering, fire-trailing words.

Patrick had half straightened, and his eyes at first had showed mild surprise. Then an answering violence erupted in him, and he was again the man Hugh had first encountered in steerage. He stepped up to Hugh, so close that their bodies touched. His tufted eyebrows seemed both to cajole and to threaten. In his pale blue eyes the flames jetted high.

Even though his outdoor work these last few years had enabled Hugh to grow stronger than he had ever been, he knew that physically he was no match for Patrick, who, if he chose, could trounce him and leave him injured and alone up here. But he did not move away. He stood, keeping the bodily contact, his eyes meeting and holding Patrick's. And in that eye contact Hugh was the stronger. Patrick was again a small boy before a punishing father. He faltered. Still, he decided he need not stay.

"Thir be thim who be aisier thin ye be to git on

with," he had said, and giving his shovel a petulant push, had discarded it and the rest of his gear, turned, and left.

Ought I to call him back? Hugh had questioned. Tell him it was myself I turned upon in mindless fury? That he himself at last also believed their search was useless, that he was sure they had wasted time here and was ready to quit and begin elsewhere? But he knew it was useless to call Patrick back. He had lost him. The truth was that he had lost him days before, when Patrick had first met with Francis Byrne and Byrne had persuaded him there were easier ways to get on in this tough country. But if it had not been Francis Byrne, Hugh realized, it would have been some other White Pawnee who would have taken Patrick from him. Deep down, he had always known— and had refused to face the truth—that Patrick was not a person he could count on to the end. He could never count on men like him, men who didn't own their own souls. They were ever in bondage to one or another. Hugh swung about, away from his disappearing, traitorous partner, and in anger drove his sharp, pointed staff into the ground.

It sank deep, up to the handle. What was this? He shoveled away the light covering of snow. It might mean . . . But he would not allow the thought. Too often in the past he had hoped. Still, he would see.

Through the falling snow he set to work spading. The mad hope that he could not quench drove him to too fast a pace. He fought for a slower, steadier rhythm, one that he could sustain however long he needed to. It was no use. He was desperate, and those who are desperate do what they must. He let himself go uncontrolled at the instinctive, fierce pace.

He dug deeper and deeper, passing from fatigue to a level of fresh energy, and again from exhaustion to another, unsuspected level of strength. At each new level he exulted as though he had found within himself a new and stronger man, one he was proud to know, glad to be. The snow ceased to fall, and a bright full moon shot up in the cold northern sky. Hugh lit his lantern, put it down by his rifle, and dug on. Within him there was a will that would not give up, that refused to surrender. From where did it come, this inner core of strength? His father? His mother? Aye, he was thankful to both for this, his inheritance, a determination bred deep in his bones.

He stopped in surprise. What was this? An opening of some sort. He lay down and peered within. He could not see. But when he enlarged the opening, beneath the bright moonlight a sizable cavern gaped before him. Hugh let himself down into a man-made cave big enough for him to move freely about. He climbed back up for his pick, lantern, and black powder. Then, deep in the cave again and holding his lantern high, he looked around. With his pick he felt about. A stone hammer! A milling stone! A piece of rock! Primitive Indian mining tools.

Again he lifted up the lantern and looked deep into the pit. At the bottom, resting on a cribbing of rotted logs about five feet above bedrock, was a large chunk of native copper. He had come upon a prehistoric mine, one of those rumored to be on the Keweenaw Peninsula, which Père Baraga, trusting his Chippewa friends, had never doubted existed.

But might it be only a cache? Hugh wondered. Other such caves had failed to reveal underground veins. He would try some of the black powder, see what it yielded. With powder set to ignite in the cavern's mouth, Hugh started to go up out of the cave. There, sitting on his rifle, as though carved in stone on the cavern's crest, a gaunt wolf waited!

Now that the children slept and she need not, for their sakes, pretend that all was well, Catherine's anxiety increased. Perhaps if she went on with Emily's dress . . . By the light of the single hurricane lamp, she unfolded the woolen pieces she had earlier ripped apart, laid on the table what had been half the skirt and over it the paper pattern made from one of

Nathaniel's old newspapers, and began. The scissors cut matter-of-factly through the cloth. She continued to cut—the other side of the skirt, both parts of the blouse. She picked up the sleeves.

A wolf's distant howl broke on the soundless night. Catherine dropped the sleeves. All-merciful God! She looked about wildly, as though seeking the One she called upon. Where was Hugh?

Hugh glanced from the pick in his left hand to the lantern in his right. Had Nathaniel warned him that a moving light traumatized a ferocious animal or merely made it follow its instinct? Whichever, he moved the lantern back and forth, up and down before the creature's gaze. As he did so, the powder he had set below ignited. He buried his head in his arms and waited. It was but a small blast, the first one, but it sufficed. The wolf rose and loped off.

The gun was still warm from the animal's body. Hugh picked it up and waited. From below came successive blasts, mightier ones. In the cold night, under the bright, distant stars, Hugh laughed loudly. He laughed at his escape from danger above and danger below. He laughed because he was sure nothing would happen to him before he had finished.

When the black powder had spent itself, and the earth and rock no longer spewed out of the cave, Hugh took his pick, lantern, and rifle and climbed in again. At the bottom of the pit, set off from the surrounding rock by its greenish-blue tinge, he saw a solid vein of pure, native copper many feet wide. This was no mere cache; this was a true prehistoric copper mine.

And it was his. All his. Thank God Patrick had not stayed to see—to see and possibly report to Byrne. True, Hugh's permit gave him permission to search nine square miles for nine years. Still, quarrels had broken out over other claims, and sometimes permits overlapped. He must refill the cavern, cover all signs of discovery, and mark it well so that he, and only he, could locate the site in the spring. When the ground was soft again, he would dig other pits nearby to see how far and how deep this vein ran. Nathaniel must come and see for himself.

Catherine snipped the thread. Emily's dress was finished. No further bit of sewing stood between her and the need to decide what she must do. When night gave way to morning, she would have to go look for Hugh. She remembered what she thought she had long since forgotten—the colonel running from the judge, left dead by the copper boulder several winters ago. She folded the dress, laid it on the table, and stood.

How stiff she was! But how could she be otherwise? For hours she had sat scarcely moving while the fire burned low and the cabin turned cold. Rubbing up against her legs was Poo-poo, confusing night and day and wanting to go out. How strange it was that all ordinary things still went on when it seemed they must stop. She tied on the red bonnet, struggled into the matching jacket, and led Poo-poo out.

A wounding, cold beauty gripped the pristine landscape. It was dawn. The world lay smothered in white, blind to night's mystical death and the new day's birth. But she was not asleep. She was awake and sharing it. She looked toward the way she must go later this morning and saw a figure, stooped under a double load, advancing. It was Hugh, carrying his own and Patrick's gear.

She ran to meet him, and he, seeing her, threw down his load and lifted his head. In the diminishing darkness she saw that his face, though drawn with exhaustion, shone with triumph.

PART SIX

The Ontonagon Country

(1845–1851)

Chapter 21

THE JUNE SUN, near midday luster, shone warm with promise upon the Ontonagon country. Another winter, its months passing in solemn Indian file, had gone by. Though the snow had stayed late into spring, it had finally left, and as Hugh had pledged through the winter, they at last all set out together to rediscover the ancient mine. Larry and Emily tagging closely, Hugh strode ahead, bearing mac. Catherine, slowed by her recollection of that portentous night, trailed behind. There were still times when she woke to the sound of a wolf's howl and turned in bed to feel Hugh there and to say a drowsy thanks.

"Hurry, Mother. Hurry!"

"Aye," she called. "I am hurrying."

Indeed, though pulled back by memories, she was walking as quickly as possible, as eager as they to discover what Hugh so often had described. Though the way was short, to her it seemed as long as those portages linking rivers on that endless trip northward.

Then suddenly they were there. Hugh had sighted the covered-over opening, put down Macaulay, and with the children's spirited help, was reopening the cave. Breathless and as excited as if all her life had been leading up to this moment, Catherine stood by, watching and waiting.

The opening made, Hugh scrambled in and reached upward to lift down in succession Mac, Emily, Larry, and finally Catherine. The children at first moved in awe about the roomy cavern and then stood by in silence while their father handed their mother, one by one, the Indian tools.

265

"Just think," she said, fingering the stone hammer, "that hundreds and hundreds of years ago . . ."

"Aye," Hugh said, taking it back from her, "an Indian held it so and worked here below just so." He tapped the cave wall, releasing bright-colored earth and rock. Then he handed the hammer back to his wife, and she passed it along to Larry.

"Maybe a son of the Indian chief also worked with this hammer," the boy said.

"Aye, I do not doubt that he did," his mother agreed, running her hand over the smooth milling stone, then passing this on to Emily.

"Shall we take these tools home with us?" Emily asked.

Catherine looked at Hugh.

"I have asked myself that very question," he said. "I do not doubt they will one day take their places in a museum. But I think I should like Nathaniel to see them here first, as I did." He paused, and Catherine joined him in his silent questioning: had the letter, sent by Père Baraga on an early trip to the Sault, perhaps found its way to Nathaniel?

The children, meanwhile, had discovered the bar of smelted copper on the rotting cribbing and cried to their mother to come see it, too.

"Aye, Kate," Hugh said. "They have found it. See for yourself, and see up above the size of that copper vein. 'Twas no doubt from that vein the Indians smelted this copper and hid it here, out of sight of some others."

"Why would they not share it?" Larry asked. To this his father—with his growing possessive love of the discovery that, happily, excluded Patrick—laughed such a laugh as only his wife understood, but not willingly.

"In what direction do you think the vein runs?" she asked, to break the children's puzzled silence.

"Ah, to know that, we must arbitrarily choose points in perhaps several directions at which to dig. You have seen now, so let us go."

He hoisted himself out of the cave and reached down in turn for each one.

"Was this where the wolf sat and waited?" Emily indicated a spot.

"Aye. Right there, on top of my gun. 'Twas a cold night, but the gun was warm when I picked it up."

She and Larry shuddered, but with pleasure, not fear. They were children; to them death was not real. However, the Indian mine was real, and they helped their father recover the opening and then, with many a backward glance, left loathfully, as even children leave secret treasure.

They had only just come out of the woods when a wild "Hello there!" startled them all, and someone waved from the dock.

"Why, 'tis Nathaniel!" Catherine exclaimed.

And so, Hugh saw, it was—an older, somewhat heavier Nathaniel, but still, in some indeterminate way, the schoolboy truant.

"There are others with him," Larry observed.

A younger man was climbing out of Nathaniel's canoe, and a slightly older man, though still young, too, from O-Kun-De-Kun's. So Hugh's letter had indeed reached Nathaniel. But was it not strange of him, to bring others without consulting Hugh? Were the two not partners? But no matter. As in earlier days, they hurried to greet him.

He hailed them blithely enough; a stranger looking on would have judged him overjoyed to see them again. But something unresolved in his manner caused Catherine to recall what she had perceived on his previous visit—that two persons now contended with Nathaniel and that he no longer was free to be the one they had first encountered. He met the children delightedly, exclaiming over Emily's and Larry's growth and welcoming little Mac by lifting him high overhead. Then he introduced the men he had brought with him from Boston, McKinley Martin and Peter Osborne.

Agreeable young men, Catherine judged them at

once. Tall, strongly built, and fair—though not so golden fair as Hugh had been—Peter Osborne was an engineer in his graceful, early twenties. His blue, disarming eyes were candid. Catherine knew that she liked young Mr. Osborne.

McKinley Martin, a geologist and, like Peter Osborne, Harvard-trained, was about ten years older. Not so tall as Peter and darker, but still not really dark, he was personable, too. His clear gray eyes were also friendly, but, unlike Peter's, they seemed to admit some problems without answers, and his slower, more complicated smile came somehow as a triumph. Over what? Catherine wondered, relinquishing his hand.

Though they were entering but a frontier cabin, they followed Nathaniel inside deferentially, full of praise of the Ontonagon land, its uncut forests, its invigorating air, its clean-tasting water. When Peter Osborne declared he had never drunk water so good, Mac ran and brought a dipperful. With thanks, the man took it carefully and drank slowly, nodding with satisfaction between sips and causing extreme appreciation to shine in his eyes. Ruddy-haired little Mac, his chubby hands resting on the visitor's knees and his warm eyes gleaming, stood enthralled.

Nathaniel, however, seemed impatient to be off to the mine site and unwilling to attend to Hugh's story of discovery, though it was obvious this interested the others exceedingly. When Hugh gave his estimate of the width of the copper vein, Nathaniel said briefly, "Well, we shall see." Catherine heard not the enthusiastic artist they had earlier responded to, but the contriving man of business. "We shall see," Nathaniel repeated, standing up, and his friends did likewise.

Reluctantly, as though there were matters he would first like to resolve before admitting others besides Nathaniel to the secret site, Hugh rose.

"You wish, then, to be off?"

"That we do!"

"May we go, too? May we go, too?" Emily and Larry clamored.

Their father demurred. "You have already been there today. Wasn't that enough?"

"No-oo!"

Nathaniel was silent, but Peter Osborne winked at the children, and McKinley Martin said, "Well, and why not?"

"Then Mac and I shall wait for you here," Catherine said, and turning to Nathaniel, she added, "I wish you had brought your wife to keep me company."

Nathaniel shook his head. "Ah, this country is not for her."

Suddenly Catherine realized what she long ago should have: he no longer was "their Nathaniel"; he was hers. Holding Mac and watching the four men start off, with the children running ahead, she puzzled as to why the Ontonagon country could not be his wife's also.

Turning from the doorway, Catherine wondered what would be the outcome of Nathaniel's coming this time and bringing with him the geologist and the engineer. She laid Mac down for his nap and then, more tired than she felt she had the right to be, stretched herself out beside him. They had traveled so far. Where was there to go from here?

The question stayed with her through the evening, despite the surface merriment. For the three Boston men returned jubilant at what they had seen—Nathaniel the most buoyant of all. Only Hugh was not.

"Up here," Nathaniel told Peter and McKinley, "we catch and cook our own dinner, you know."

So, to the children's delight, they went fishing.

"Like O-Kun-De-Kun," little Mac called from the canoe he shared with Peter Osborne.

From Nathaniel's canoe Catherine called back with affected gaiety, "Aye, like O-Kun-De-Kun." Her eyes went from Mac to Emily in McKinley Martin's canoe, and to Larry with his father.

"Look who caught the first fish!" Nathaniel shouted,

and all turned to see Catherine holding up a wriggling trout that paled and gleamed in the twilight mists.

Later, from the relative calm of the campsite where Peter Osborne cooked the fish, Nathaniel and McKinley Martin gave him unwelcome advice, so that Peter kept threatening good-naturedly to quit. Catherine looked back and laughed with the others at the children's near spills from the canoes. Then the young engineer struck a triumphant chef's pose and offered Catherine the first choice piece of baked trout. But for her husband's silence, she would have again felt like a girl on the banks of the Liffey. Whatever was it he brooded upon? she wondered. Something, she was sure, not to his liking, something to which he did not have the answer.

When they finished eating and the children had run off to play, they settled down to serious conversation, and Catherine thought, Now, perhaps, I may know. But first—was it not ever so?—they must talk not of what they wished, but of matters of general interest. Foremost of these was the fact that President Polk's election in 1844 had insured the annexation of Texas.

"It is Jackson all over again in the White House," said Nathaniel, an Easterner and a Whig. "Annexation is but a southern device for expanding slavery."

Whether in agreement or in deference to Nathaniel, the other two Boston men withheld comment.

But Hugh differed. "Our good friend Senator Cass, though a Northerner, favored the annexation of Texas."

"He has his eye on the Presidency still."

"That may be, but I do not forget our indebtedness to him. 'Twas he, you recall, who made it possible for us to survey and lay claims to this country."

Hugh sought to bring them around to the interest for which they had traveled west. Even so, they kept a fair distance, speaking first of the Cliff mine they had seen on a stop at Copper Harbor, where they had observed the Cliff methods for shattering rock and noted also the quarters for miners come from Pennsylvania, and more remotely from Wales and Ireland.

Catherine could no longer endure their avoiding the subject, and she asked, "Then what do you think of Hugh's mine? Is it worthy of development?"

"Aye, that it is," Martin said. "It's a true-enough prehistoric Indian mine, predating by hundreds of years the seventeenth-century French. And a vein of ore of unquestionable commercial value runs through the ground."

Catherine glanced at Nathaniel. He nodded. "I would like to leave McKinley and Peter here to build themselves cabins farther up the river, close to the site, and to build quarters for the miners who must come— to sink a shaft to follow the vein of ore, and then to put up a permanent refining plant . . . we await only Hugh's consent to my further plans."

The two young men looked away in embarrassment. Perhaps, Catherine thought, they had already been witnesses to Hugh's and Nathaniel's clash over those further plans. What might these be? Well, whatever, they were clearly Hugh's and Nathaniel's to resolve. She got up and went over to where McKinley and Peter sat a little apart from Hugh and Nathaniel. "And did you find what you saw of interest, then?" she asked, seeking to engage them in separate talk.

"Aye, that we did. It's a miracle!" McKinley exclaimed. "Until now the preglacial spewing of molten lava and the later glacial movements over the Great Lakes have been for me but words in books. Now I feel as though I myself had witnessed the upheaval, watched it cool and quiet, and experienced firsthand the deep and secret story of creation."

"Would you like to stay on as geologist?"

He closed his eyes briefly, and when he opened them, Catherine saw his admission of some problems without answers. She thought she also saw the hope of answers. Yet his slow, complicated smile somehow lacked triumph.

"But why will you not agree?" Nathaniel's words

were meant only for Hugh but were nevertheless heard by Catherine.

"Because the mine is mine and yours only," Hugh said.

"What good is it to you or to me, undeveloped?"

"I did not anticipate your forming a company. I thought the work was to be mine, the financing yours."

"And so it might have been once. Now I am married. You and I will still own a controlling interest."

"And these others? Who are they?"

"I have interested three, all men of means—men of important means."

"And their names?"

"Samuel Guilford, Joshua Bigelow, Wilfred Shaw."

"And should you and I differ, on whose side would they be?"

"I would hope on the side of whoever was right. They are men of probity, men of judgment."

"Sometimes men on both sides have these qualities, yet they differ. It is so now with President Polk and you. So, for that matter, with Lewis Cass, though he befriended us, and you. Each sees through his own eyes, from his own past and his own interests . . ."

"Then you will not agree?"

"Aye. I agree," Hugh said reluctantly.

Glancing at her husband, Catherine recalled how, when all else had failed, Hugh had gone to work for Francis Byrne. To be sure, though, Byrne and Nathaniel were in no way alike.

Nathaniel went on swiftly. "Then I'll go at once to Washington to buy the site from the land office, as we must do now. You'll stay here as superintendent. Back in Boston, I'll form the company to raise the needed capital."

"How will the five of us divide profits?"

"Each will share in proportion to what he invests, except that you will share equally with me. I shall invest for the two of us."

"By what name shall the mine go?"

Nathaniel stood and glanced toward where Catherine was sitting with his two friends. From his glance she knew that he still sought her esteem. "The Macaulay," he said.

Catherine got to her feet. "Then may the Macaulay reward us all."

Disappointment rose in Nathaniel's eyes, and Catherine knew she had robbed him of the pleasure he had sought in conferring her name on the mine. He could not know with what sorrow she relinquished for Hugh and herself the relationship they had cherished with him until now, or how lonely the future looked to her.

Chapter 22

IT HAD PROVED other than lonely. With development, the Macaulay in the spring of 1848, already in its third year and in time the most famed of the Keweenaw mass copper mines, drew from around the world geologists, museum people, and college professors. Standing with Hugh in the hallway of the spacious home which had replaced their former cabin, Catherine greeted them all this evening, welcoming with special pleasure McKinley and Elizabeth Martin, Peter and Susanne Osborne, now friends of long standing, and other Macaulay officials.

Emily and her friend Betsy Martin, and Mac and his friend Jonathan Osborne, moved among the guests, passing trays, smiling sociably, and politely answering the Misses Jenks, come from Boston to teach, bearing their sense of decorum and class distinctions, and perhaps also the furtive hope of a geologist husband to carry them off to some remote place as yet but a name in the children's geography books. Larry, however, was nowhere about, and when Catherine later went to the kitchen to confer with Patricia, Hugh sought her there. "Where is Larry?"

Catherine hesitated. A rift was widening between Hugh and Larry, and in her judgment it was not all her son's fault. Regrettably, she knew, it was Patrick who was usurping Hugh's place with their middle child.

"Well, where is he?"

"He's gone back down the river with Patrick."

Visibly angry, Hugh turned and started from the kitchen. Catherine caught his arm. "I asked Patrick to stay and help, too. But he was unwilling to do so."

"I see." The swinging door swished after Hugh.

"An why would he stay?" Patricia asked. "An 'im goin ivery day, an stayin late ivery day, savin wan, to help find th' mine, an gettin no share in it at all, now thit it be doin so fine."

That was the issue, and Larry, so like George in his sympathies for the unfortunate, was on Patrick's side. "Better straighten him out—early," Hugh had said meaningfully when Catherine tried to explain the resemblance.

She was silent now, and with Irish intuition Patricia spoke up. "Could ye nat spake to himsel in Pathrick's favor?"

"I have already done so."

"Well, ye maum try agin."

Catherine thought of the last time and of Hugh's hard refusal, but she said, "I will. I'll ask him the first thing tomorrow."

Remembering her promise, Catherine ran downstairs in order to catch Hugh before he hurried off to the Macaulay. The early morning sun sifted through the sheer curtains beneath the gracefully looped draperies and fell about the hallway where she and Hugh had greeted last night's guests. Perhaps the party will have put him in a responsive mood, she thought.

Throughout the house all was quiet, so quiet that Catherine heard the faint, liquid trickle of the spring that ran through the foundation, cooling the dairy cellar and the larger space filling with the Macaulay's gardens' harvest. Hugh must be outside already, looking over the currant and gooseberry bushes, bearing early this year, and the tender new fruit trees which must wait their time, making sure all was well with the new baby chickens; going into the big whitewashed barn to satisfy himself all was also well with the horse and cow he had brought by boat on his last trip to Detroit.

Then the back door opened. Catherine hurried from the hallway through the front parlor, opened wide the great double doors, and slipped into the back parlor with its square bay window filled with plants and canaries; again opened great double doors to the dining room and came through there into the kitchen.

"Oh, Hugh—" She stopped, disappointed. Last night's reception was clearly over for him, and he was again the superintendent on his way to the Macaulay.

"Yes?"

"There is something—"

"Can it not wait?"

"I promised Patricia."

"Well, and what is it, then?"

"Patrick wishes to speak to you. He feels he has a claim—"

Hugh did not reply.

"I promised Patricia you would see him today."

Already on his way out of the room, Hugh swung around, and Catherine could see why the men obeyed as they did. There was a little fear mixed into their loyalty. Just now, she felt it herself.

"Today!"

"The visitors are gone, are they not?"

"Aye, they are gone, and today we must recover the time they have cost us. We open a new level today, another sixty feet below. I shall need to remain close at hand. I won't have much time for Patrick."

"Still, I promised Patricia, and on my promise, he is making the trip up the river."

Hugh's laugh was short and grim. "For the future, please be less quick to make promises that have to do with my time. I must go, for I see Timmy has brought round the horse."

"You will see Patrick, will you not, for I promised?"

"Aye, since you promised—if he catches me. But I promise you that will not be easy for Patrick."

It was easier than Hugh had anticipated. Patrick, coached by Patricia, arrived at the shaft house early with the workable plan of waiting as long as need be. For Patrick, the voyage up the Ontonagon past the flourishing town of New Boston, where substantial frame houses replaced former Indian wigwams and later log cabins, had been melancholy. Luck had again outwitted him. Law had caught up with the White Pawnees, and Byrne had moved on. Nothing in the Ontonagon country had remained as Patrick had discovered it. Everywhere, not only in the saloons, there was a bustle of activity. Men's talk was lively and purposeful. One had to be quick to make the most of developments. Women made light of their problems —so much lay ahead. Children caught their parents' anticipation and strove to outdo one another.

But Patrick had no share in all this. With affection, he recalled the Ontonagon country as he had found it, as though fresh from the hand of God. Now that men were making and leaving their mark on all things, he discovered a proprietary feeling about the former quiet country, home to wildlife and the Indian. Traffic jostled the river, once so free to a solitary canoeist. An oversized freighting post, powered by ten men, made regular eighteen-mile trips upstream. When the

Ontonagon was at high levels, a small steamer made the two-hour-long passage against the swiftly running stream. Only by leaving early had he had the river to himself. On Lake Superior steamboats were replacing sailboats.

When he reached the Macaulay, the house over Shaft No. 1 assaulted him. It marked the spot where, that fateful autumn day, he had thrown down his shovel and left.

Timmy, a fugitive with a Boston stopover from Ireland's potato famine, greeted him at the entrance and waited uncertainly for his clue. Reading Timmy's mind, Patrick announced an appointment with Mr. Condon, "An auld frind, ye undirstand." Though Timmy protested that Mr. Condon was out, he indicated in what direction the office lay. As yet, the superintendent's office was a commonplace room, geared to needs. But to one shut out and wishing a share, the room looked impressive. Patrick took the chair beyond the desk and glanced morosely at the one where Hugh must sometimes sit.

The wait, interrupted from time to time by Timmy's glancing in, lengthened with the morning. At first Patrick ignored the other's intrusions, but, little by little feeling a growing need of company, he yielded to the inclination to talk. Timmy responded to him cautiously. Loyalty to Mr. Condon forbade giving away secrets about the mine. But when Patrick inquired concerning what had happened in Ireland since he left, that was another story altogether.

So Patrick heard again what he had already heard uncounted times from Irishmen on their way to hoped-for work in one of the Keweenaw mines. People were dying by the hundreds, by the thousands, by the hundreds of thousands. Nothing was being done to help them. Indeed, their deaths were what England's leaders sought as a solution to the "Irish problem."

The story, already a legend, had begun to bore Patrick when Timmy turned deftly to another aspect.

"Shure," he suggested, " 'twas our own fault as well."

"Be ye Irish, an do ye say this?"

His informer nodded sagely. He could vouch for it. Through the famine, the fight for repeal had persisted. Only there were two factions now, for even before O'Connell's death, the leaders of Young Ireland had insisted on physical force. Old Ireland, led by O'Connell's men, fought harder to defeat Young Ireland than they had fought either to win repeal or to relieve the famine. Young Ireland forgot the famine in trying to win repeal of the Union. Then there came one Finton Lalor, who made use of the famine to fight for agrarian revolution. The Young Irelanders themselves split over this.

To Patrick all this seemed over-complicated. Moreover, it seemed to excuse the chief villain, England, from blame, and he wished to keep England the central criminal.

"An be ye wan person, an do ye know all this?" he challenged.

"Was me brither not part of it all, on Young Ireland's side, th' side thit went with Finton Lalor?"

"Was he, now?" Patrick's eyes narrowed shrewdly, and caution shaped his next words. "An th' Irish thit ave found thir way to th' Macaulay—on whose side in all this would they be?"

"Thir be min heer on ivery side of thit fight, an they be ready to fight it still."

Patrick pulled his ear thoughtfully. "But fir a good fight, thir should be English. An heer we be, lackin thim altogither."

Timmy moved closer now. "Nat altogither."

"This be th' New World. Where would we be findin th' English?"

Timmy moved yet closer. "Back in Boston. Thim who owns th' mines heer." He caught himself. Had he overspoken, betrayed what he ought not? "To be shure," he hastily added, "they be peaceable min workin heer."

"Aye," Patrick agreed, "to be shure."

With Timmy's news to brood upon, waiting yielded to Patrick the pleasure of speculative connivance, for which he had an authentic taste. As a result, time seemed to speed by. Almost too soon, Superintendent Condon appeared.

Patrick stood, but Hugh gestured him to sit down. Peter Osborne came by just then and called in, "Ready to eat?" Then he saw Patrick, said, "Oh, excuse me," and went on.

Hugh sat down a little resentfully. He had looked forward to lunching with McKinley and Peter, to discussing the mining information some of yesterday's visitors had left behind. There had been this and other talk, besides, which interested them all—word of what was taking place beyond the Keweenaw. The Whigs had chosen General Zachary Taylor as their candidate for President; the Democrats, Senator Lewis Cass; but fervent antislavery men of both sides had bolted and formed a Free Soil Party with Van Buren as nominee. What would McKinley and Peter have to say about this? They still tended to follow Nathaniel in politics. And here, on Catherine's invitation, was Patrick.

Hugh took his lunch out of a drawer and looked at Patrick from across the desk. It struck him at once that it was here, on this very site, that Patrick had abandoned him. How the place had changed since then! Below Shaft No. 1 miners were releasing rich deposits of ore. Other shafts followed the curve of the vein, and below these there were more. Cars moved along rails, carrying ore to the central refining plant. And he, Hugh Condon, was at the exhilarating core of it all, issuing orders, expecting compliance, defeating resistance with a quick lift of an eyebrow.

"Well, Patrick—" He opened the box which he knew would contain choice fare from last night's reception. "Time for lunch." Without intending to, he had used the words with which years before he would interrupt their digging. Hugh handed over the box of sandwiches, and Patrick produced a wrapped package of his own.

" 'Tis lak auld times," Patrick said, "an yit nat altogither lak thim."

"No, they can never be quite the same."

"An yit they maught be more near to bein lak thin they be."

"Well, we must take them as they are."

"It be more plasant fir ye to do thin fir me."

"Then you must find the remedy."

"I be heer fir thit viry raison. Since we ave come at it so fast, I will tell ye straight out thit I an Pathricia thin ye be wrong nat to allow me a share in th' Macaulay." Patrick stopped and looked at Hugh.

"First of all, you must know the Macaulay is not mine to parcel out as I wish," Hugh answered slowly.

"Did ye nat find it?"

"Aye, that I did."

"Ye didna turn over th' whole of it, did ye, now, to th' Boston min?"

The question brought back to life Hugh's early resolution of that problem, a resolution that to his mind was still not wholly satisfactory and, though until now workable, was still susceptible to future differences. He said, "We formed a company, the Boston men and I."

"An ye ave a share in thit compiny, do ye nat?"

Hugh delayed answering. He held twenty-six shares, Nathaniel twenty-five; together they had the controlling fifty-one, and the other three Boston men divided equally between them the remaining forty-nine.

"I am not free to discuss the company, Patrick. You can surely understand that."

"I dinna ask ye to disciss th' compiny. I ask ye only to disciss yeer share in it."

"I am sorry I cannot."

"Ye will nat talk, thin, with an auld frind—wan who went ivery day with ye to th' mine an stayed late ivery day savin wan."

"I am talking with you, Patrick, but we must be

plain with each other. You left me and went with Byrne, and so forfeited any claim you might have had in my discovery."

Patrick hesitated. The plan Patricia had laid out was to push first his claim to a share, and failing that, to ask for a job. But from his talk with Timmy he had what now seemed to him a superior plan.

"Thin since ye will nat allow me a jist share, we maught talk about th' min come heer from Ireland to work. 'Tis said they dinna agree well among thirsels, an thit they tak th' Boston min fir th' English."

"The men agree very well on what is important. They need to work. And they are well pleased with what the Boston men pay them."

"An th' place where they live? Be they well plased with this, too?"

"They know we will improve things as soon as we can."

"They waited long in Ireland fir changes thit niver came."

"This is America. It is not Ireland."

"Aye, but to th' min it maught seem to be."

Hugh's eyebrow lifted in the way that put an end to fractious discussion, and he stood. "I must go."

"We maught finish lunch first."

"I have finished mine."

"Thin I maught finish mine."

"Finish it. Then you must go. I cannot welcome you again to Macaulay. If you wish to look for work elsewhere on the Keweenaw, I will give you the money to do so."

Patrick hesitated, and one part of his mind began rearranging his story for Patricia. There must be some explanation for her other than the truth. The truth would not do. Aggrieved, he reflected that the truth seldom did do.

"Thir be anither besides mesel who thins I ave a claim to th' mine ye were so free to give to th' Boston min, an this wan agrees with me thit ye had no right to give me share away."

"No doubt you have persuaded your wife."

"It be nat of her I spake. I spake of one of yeer own."

"It was a courtesy that Kate offered—my seeing you today."

"It be someone ither thin Kate thit I spake of."

Hugh waited, knowing the answer and yet fearing to hear it, as though Patrick's putting it into words could somehow define a conflict which he suspected was already there.

"It be yeer own bye, Larry."

Not since the day in New Orleans when he'd looked down at his countrymen working in the canal and heard Martin Arnaud's "Drive them" had he felt such fury come alive in his fists. But now his fury was toward one of those countrymen, a former "partner" in the Ontonagon country's early experiences. Hugh unfolded his tightened fists. With only the expressive lift of an eyebrow, he remained silent, staring at Patrick. As Hugh stood there, it seemed to Patrick that the distance between them grew increasingly wider and became the impassable gulf he had experienced all his life between the one in authority and himself. Slowly, with an awkwardness that carried back to boyhood submissions, he rose and without a word shuffled out of the room.

Hugh quickly crossed the floor and closed the door after Patrick. He needed to be alone. He hated to see Patrick as he had, hated to be the cause of it. For the memory of his own unequal approach was still buried deep and searing. "Mr. Eldon, may I see you today?" and the arrogant, telling reply, "You are seeing me now, are you not?" But what else could he have done just now? First Patrick had threatened to cause trouble at the Macaulay, then to provoke conflict between him and his son—really to aggravate the conflict he'd already created.

Still, he ought not to have behaved as he had. It was a mistake to show his concern. Why had he let Patrick provoke him into doing so? Well, in the first place, he supposed the concern was there. No doubt that was what had led him to react angrily last night when Kate told him Larry had gone down the river with Patrick. What complicated things further was that Kate always seemed to be on Larry's side. Nevertheless this was in the family, and he need not have exposed it to Patrick. He felt humiliated at having done so. Nowadays he always kept a distance between himself and the miners, and he knew they liked it that way and were the better employees for it. But Patrick had skillfully played upon their one-time relationship, had caused him to dwell upon it himself, and he had been quite ready to offer him work, had indeed been speculating as to what he might have for him. Then the stupid Irishman had threatened him with trouble among his workers, and when he had resisted that, had gone on disastrously further and threatened to alienate his son. Well, he would put a swift stop to that! The sooner the better. He was prepared to act.

But he had not expected the need to act to develop so soon. That very evening, after waiting a long time for Larry, they were forced to sit down to a late dinner without him.

Hugh restrained his rising anger until Emily and Mac had excused themselves and run out to the dock to watch for Larry's return.

"Did Larry not seek leave to go?" he asked Catherine.

"Aye, he did so."

"And you gave it?"

"I did."

"You know there are differences between Patrick and me. Patrick presses his point of view on the lad."

Catherine lifted her head in a way that suggested there were also differences between Hugh and her. "You did not heal these today? I had hoped that you would."

"They are worse."

Catherine looked down. There was much that she

would have liked to say. His success seemed to be making him hard, too hard and too driving. It was this that Larry, the most sensitive of their three children, was running from, and only an accident, in a way, that he was running to Patrick. Yet she could not bring herself to say this to Hugh.

Instead, she said, "I do not find Patrick wholly bad. Oh, I know you have not forgiven his desertion that day."

"Aye, I have forgiven that, though it might well have cost me my life, made a widow of you and orphans of the children."

"But he did not wish that to happen, or intend to cause it. He has not the quality that you have, Hugh. Indeed, few have it to the extent that you have. For him 'tis more natural to give up."

"I have said I no longer hold it against him."

"Then can we not be friends as before, in the way that we were when we took them as children, our children? Patricia suffers with her husband, and if he might have cost you your life, she saved me mine the night the colonel came, and I cannot forget it."

"I am sorry for her—and for you. But we cannot remain friends. Not because I will it so, but because of what Patrick has threatened."

"Patrick threatened? Oh, Hugh, I find that hard to believe!"

"Nevertheless, it is true, and because it is so, Larry must not go with him in the future."

" 'Twould be hard on the boy. He likes Patrick well."

"Aye, that is the danger."

"I see no danger in that. 'Twas Patrick who held him first, after you."

"I remember."

"Larry is not . . . like you, Hugh."

"Who, then, is he like? Is it Patrick?"

"No, not Patrick, either. I've told you before. He is ever so like George—ever ready to feel pity for others."

"And to fight?"

"Aye, I fear so—to fight if need be."

"Then let us change this lest he go the way of your brother—join irresponsible parties."

"You mean the Ribbon Men?"

"In George's case, yes."

'Twas George's membership with them that saved us once, Catherine thought, but she did not mention this to Hugh. For she accepted that he remembered only what he wished to and forgot what he didn't like. "In any case, it is Larry, not George, who concerns us now."

"So it is . . . and I will not have him go with Patrick again."

"There will be times, like today, when he needs to go."

"What need was there today?"

"As you know, Patrick has been meeting the boats and getting the mail. He has a letter for me."

"Why did Patrick not give it to me when we talked?"

"He said he forgot to bring it."

Hugh laughed mistrustfully. " 'Tis for another reason altogether that he took Larry."

"What might that reason be?"

"To turn the lad further against me. To complete what he has already begun."

"You could correct it by taking away Patrick's grievance. 'Tis that with which Larry sympathizes."

"I'll correct it by keeping Larry away from him. He is not to go with him again!"

The voices of the children floated on the night air, Larry's among them. Patrick had brought Larry back. Catherine followed Hugh to the hallway, and Hugh hurried to overtake Patrick, but he was already on his way home.

Hugh faced Larry. "I must speak to you."

"I must first give Mother her letter."

Hugh waited. It was ever so, he thought, and each was always first with the other.

Surprised that the letter came from London, not Chapelizod, Catherine stood in the hallway to read it.

I have not wanted to grieve you with the horrors of the potato famine, running into yet another year in Ireland. I never could have dreamed such suffering as I have seen. We turned Kemris House into a hospital. Jerry, Harriet, and I nursed the sick and dying day and night, until we felt such exhaustion that I, at least, sometimes wished I was one of those being carried out with no more to suffer. This was not to be. I cannot say why.

You would not believe it, but through it all, the fight for Repeal continued.

Catherine skipped over what came next—the fight between Old and Young Ireland, and between young Ireland's factions over Finton Lalor. All this she knew well. She went to what she foresaw was coming.

George and Tom followed the more violent Young Irelanders. Then, as perhaps you may know, last February revolutionists overthrew the French Government, and on the continent, government after government collapsed. Young Ireland took courage, as I suppose was natural, and its leaders united again.

There is little point in my recounting the happenings since. Suffice it to say that it was on a February day that George and Tom Kemris gave their lives.

What followed was altogether too wounding to grasp, and Catherine hurried through to the end.

I thought the Kemrises might resent me for George's influence over Tom—he was the leader

—but they have been kind. However, they could not bear that Harriet, their one remaining tie to the future, should stay at their house, and they urged her and Jerry to come to London. Jerry would not go without me, and so, though I should rather have stayed, as you see, I have come.

Now Lord Kemris wishes to make Jerry heir to his title as well as to his wealth, both of which our family refused. Jerry has consented. And now, in the evening of my life, I no longer quarrel with this.

Catherine glanced about the hallway where last evening she and Hugh had cordially welcomed guests. She put the letter down on a small table and ran out to the veranda that encircled the house. The wind set in motion the leaves of the young currant and gooseberry bushes and of the tender new fruit trees. In the distance, the Ontonagon sang. She hurried toward it. From habit, she stopped near the coop where the baby chickens struggled to survive. Out here all was quiet . . .

But there was no peace in Ireland, on the Continent, or—if last night's guests were to be believed—in America, where civil war threatened. Even here at home there was conflict between Hugh and Patrick, conflict involving Larry. She could not bear that Patrick and Patricia, feeling cheated, should be forced to move elsewhere again. Patricia, too, had lost her brother, and ever since the day she had reached for and shot off the gun, sending the colonel flying, there had been love between Patricia and her. What was she to do about this? About so much else? What was she to do about Hugh? Little by little, she was losing him to his ambition, to his thrust for wealth and power. Was there no way other than her mother's—not to quarrel with what would be? Her mother, though, was no longer young, and she herself still was. And George . . . George would have been thirty.

At this realization, the sense of loss struck again. Overhead, the moon moved swiftly through the screening clouds. Catherine peered into the coop, where the chickens clustered white as the moon and soft as the clouds. How tender the beginning of life was. Was it so that George could no longer feel all this?

Catherine was aware of a presence beside her. She turned and saw Larry. He did not speak, but she saw that he guessed. Somehow by his being there, sharing the moment with her, he helped. And yes, it was true: she would rather have him with her now than anyone else in the world.

After a while they started back to the house without speaking. Larry's thin, long arms dangled. He was young and rebellious, but in his own frustration he had come to share whatever sorrow her letter had brought.

"Father says I must not spend any more time with Patrick."

"I know that is his wish," Catherine said. But she could not bring herself to add, It is also mine. She said instead, "Your father has many problems with his work, and each day brings a fresh one."

Chapter 23

TIME BROUGHT FRESH PROBLEMS to Hugh. There was one that had stayed with him as an unhappy possibility ever since he had agreed to the formation of a company.

Hugh was at his desk during the July of 1851 when he broke the seal of Nathaniel's letter. Noting the date, Hugh's face glowed. The faster movement of the

Great Lakes steamers, combined with the railroad into Boston, had speeded mail delivery. It had been little more than two weeks since Nathaniel had written.

As he read, the brief radiance was quickly suffused by darkness.

So while I sympathize with your request for an assessment on all stockholders, I also share our officers' concern that the Macaulay is not paying dividends, whereas the Cliff, our most important competitor, has been doing so for two years. In any case, Samuel Guilford, Wilfred Shaw, and Joshua Bigelow have voted down the assessment. I appreciate that this comes as a blow to you. They, however, are adamant beyond my ability to persuade. If you think you can succeed where I have failed, I suggest you come here to try.

Anger seethed through Hugh. Why could Nathaniel and he not go ahead without the others' consent? Did the two of them not own a controlling share? No, Nathaniel was with them. Crumpling the letter, Hugh got up and pitched it across the room. He might have known.

On that first visit to Ontonagon, following his father's death, Nathaniel had wanted out. And there had been that later, complaining letter. Again he had wanted out. Had not Hugh himself made the trip to Detroit and met with Lewis Cass, Nathaniel would have quit at that point. That was nine years ago. And here it was all over again. Hugh should have known better than to yield to the company ownership. But what else could he have done? Without Nathaniel, he was stopped.

Who were these men he had never met—Guilford, Shaw, and Bigelow—who with Nathaniel held control? Contriving men of inherited wealth and cultivated caution, such as Nathaniel had grown to be. In their blue tailcoats and stock collars, they sat in their Boston offices venturing so much here and so much there, so much and no more. Better to pull out right away and invest somewhere else. The economy was expanding. There were plenty of places to make more. Maybe even another Keweenaw mine.

Hugh sat down again and stretched out in his chair. Suppose he talked to McKinley and Peter? They had agreed to his writing for the assessment. No, they would almost certainly comply with Nathaniel. They shared Boston and Harvard with him, strong and subtle bonds. It was obvious that in this, as in earlier crises, Hugh was alone.

Hugh sauntered out of the office into the hot summer day, alive with Keweenaw "eagles." Perspiration dampened his fair hair that was streaked with gray and retreating from his forehead. The mosquitoes struck at his moist face, forceful with the habit of authority, and he struck back at them.

Looking over his operation, he confidently decided all was proceeding in an orderly way and at the even pace he demanded. Too fast a pace, he told the men, was as bad as one that was too slow. Working too fast showed an active dislike of work; working too slow showed a passive dislike.

No fires such as those that had flared through other Keweenaw mines, snuffing out lives and delaying work, had burned through the Macaulay. There had been no cave-ins, pinning and crushing workers to death, and none of the dreaded air blasts, peculiar to Lake Superior mines. Nor had there been human outbursts, with one angry man pushing another off the working level to death below. When a miner, passing by, tipped his cap to him, Hugh knew he did so not in deference alone, but also in appreciation of the unrelaxed vigilance which made the Macaulay as safe as an underground mine could be. Was all of this to go unrewarded?

He looked to the farther distance where the newest shaft had struck a solid copper wall. Was it only a few weeks ago that the discovery had excited such wildly enthusiastic hope? There had been a limited exultant time and then at once a new problem. Cutting through the solid copper would disrupt schedules. Stockholders were clamoring for dividends. Other Keweenaw mines were making blatant promises. Besides the copper mines, iron mines were opening to the east. What was wrong with the Macaulay? Was it all it should be? Hugh had wanted to agree to a dividend. Instead, as a result of the delay, he had written and asked for the assessment. With the mosquitoes biting his face and arms he walked slowly back inside.

Picking up the crumpled letter, he sat down, smoothed it out, and read it again to the end.

... If you think you can succeed where I have failed, I suggest you come here to try.

Hugh rocked back on his chair, something Catherine would not allow at home. Suppose he did go? But how could he leave now with the mine at peak operation? Later, perhaps in the autumn ... But then there would be the rush to get copper shipments off before traffic halted on the lakes. Besides, in the fall he must get the winter supplies in for New Boston, growing with the Macaulay. For this he would trust no one except himself. There was the year the *John Jacob Astor*, carrying the winter supplies for the Copper Harbor area, had blown up in the harbor. Everyone there would have starved but for the few who had braved Lake Superior's ugly November moods to make the round trip in an open boat to the Sault.

By the late summer, Nathaniel's suggestion had become implanted in Hugh's mind, and it took only Père Baraga's visit to convince him. Twice a year the missionary walked the forty miles across the peninsula's base from L'Anse to his missions at the Ontonagon mines. After several days of performing his clerical duties, he relaxed for an evening with the Condons. The next morning he would be off by boat for Copper Harbor and the Cliff and other mining missions there, but New Boston was the last of his Ontonagon calls.

When Mac, Larry, then Emily, and finally Catherine—with the promise to consider sending Emily to Antonia's school for girls in Philadelphia—had gone off to bed, Père Baraga, perhaps sensing some unresolved conflict in Hugh, remained by the fire. Hugh was sunk in the Macaulay crisis. All over the Keweenaw, prospectors were abandoning mines to open up new, possibly more promising veins. The wild hope, the frequent failures, the occasional successes, infected the people like a fever, and the excitement reverberated across the continent in the counting rooms of Boston. There was no doubt—at least not in Hugh's mind—about the Macaulay's worth. But without the assessment he saw no way to continue beyond the current year. The question he sometimes asked himself between sleep and waking escaped into words. "What am I to do?"

Père Baraga did not answer at once. Strict inner discipline forbade speaking too quickly. A careless answer, taken seriously, could work as much harm as a dishonest or malicious one. When at last he spoke, his reply came as inevitably as the early evening star in the northern sky.

"You have no choice. You must make the trip."

Excitement quickened in Hugh. "But the mine, the shipments, the preparations for winter . . ."

Père Baraga smiled, and Hugh saw that he had grown more frail and that his penetrating eyes, perhaps seared by the blinding winter blizzards, had turned a gentler blue.

"Go, and take Catherine with you."

An overmastering longing to do so awakened in Hugh. It was nine years since they had journeyed to Detroit. "I shall ask her," Hugh said. "Once before she came with me on your suggestion. You remember?"

But Père Baraga shook his head, and it struck Hugh

that the priest had advanced beyond his peak vigor and could no longer recall everything clearly.

"Of course," Hugh continued, "that was before the Macaulay. Now all these men and their families look to me."

Père Baraga sighed. "I know. It is so with me. I look about and I say, 'I cannot leave. My poor Indians need me most.' But when the time I have set comes, I leave because the miners are also my trust.

"Last year I, too, ventured to Detroit to oversee the printing of my dictionary and other writings. Soon I, like you, will need money to continue, and so I must again cross the ocean to Europe to plead my poor Indians' cause to the Leopoldine Society."

He smiled his disarming smile, and behind it Hugh saw the joyful man who had leaped from the encircling Indians on the dock at Madeline Island. Père Baraga observed, "We do—not what we choose—but what we must. The trip to Boston . . . it is not so far as to Europe and not so wearing as it once was. Besides, it is there that this great new American nation first began to live. There you will see shrines dating back to the early struggle; I have paused there to look. This Keweenaw Peninsula you and I love is but a small part of America. I travel alone, but you will have Catherine."

The next day Hugh wrote Nathaniel he would come to Boston in September, and that evening he asked his wife to accompany him.

She answered him crossly. "I should like to, but how can I? Who is there to stay with the children— since you sent Patricia packing up north with her poor husband?"

PART SEVEN

The Boston Trip Interrupts the Ontonagon Years

(1851–1853)

Chapter 24

GRADUALLY SHE HAD SOFTENED and been kind, almost the Kate he remembered, when it came to getting ready and he tried on the suit, made by the local tailor from Boston. Standing before the mirror in their dressing room, with Kate sitting by, he felt as he had when setting out for Mass in Chapelizod, as a boy in his Sunday suit, and his mother calling after him, "Take care you get into no fight now, and you wearing your good Sunday suit." A father now himself, with a father's concern, he looked back affectionately to his parents, who had both died during the early Ontonagon years.

"Turn about," Catherine ordered, and he did so circumspectly.

She laughed and threw up her hands. "Ah, 'tis Hugh Condon you are still, I can see."

"Will they laugh at me in these clothes?"

"Indeed, they will not, and why should they?"

"You have just done so."

"Ah, to be sure, but I see what they cannot see."

"Still, they may think my new Boston-style clothes do not suit me."

"They must think as they please. My grandmother used to say—" She stopped, for it came to her that her mother was doubtless saying the same things to Jerry's children in London, and she wished her mother were with her to consult about Larry.

"Well, whatever it is, let us have it!"

"I remember well. 'Twas that each must find his dignity—not in what others say, but in himself."

Standing in the Boston and Wooster station, Hugh recalled Catherine's words and straightened in his new suit. But there was much here to distract him from concern about his appearance. Indeed, he was struck with delight at the Western Railroad's graceful diamond-stack, eight-wheeler engine with its brightly painted cab that had brought him from Albany. Beneath the dust and soot of the run, the gilded name-plate and ornamental brass work still showed. What good fortune to ride an all-passenger train, not a mixed train of passengers and "burthen." He turned from the engine to the car on whose roof, protected by a chaise top, the conductors and brakemen had sat.

If only Kate were here to enjoy it all with him! At the very end, she had confessed her longing to accompany him, and except for Larry, she might have. Emily could go to Betsy Martin's and Mac to Jonathan Osborne's, but there was nowhere for Larry to go, it seemed, now that Patrick and Patricia had left.

The engineer and fireman were climbing out of the cab. Hugh had talked briefly to them when they had stopped to "wood up" at intervals. Once the fireman had complained of the uneven lengths of the wood that forced him, while the train was still moving, to climb atop the tender, bucksaw in hand, and required the engineer both to feed the firebox and to watch the throttle. As they walked off, swaggering at their vital roles in connection with the mile-eating "iron horse," they waved to Hugh, and he waved back.

Where was Nathaniel? Most of the passengers had left, some welcomed by awed relatives or friends, others to board the six-and-a-half-cent-fare coach for their hotels or inns. Here he stood gaping about, feeling as new to Boston as, years earlier, he had felt to New Orleans.

Why had Nathaniel not come to welcome Hugh

to his native Boston, which came so often into his talk—sometimes hostilely, but more often affectionately? At the very least, Hugh had counted on his friend's welcome. What, precisely, had he written? Hugh pulled the letter from his pocket.

"Delighted!" it read, skipping a salutation. "Will meet you at station. Nat."

But there was a scribbled, forgotten postscript. "Should anything prevent me, take a hansom cab to the Revere House, where I have reserved rooms for you in my name."

Hugh picked up his greatcoat and new traveling bag and started out of the station to the corner of Albany and Kneeland.

The Revere House had a quieting restraint inside. Hugh looked about. Hotels had their own kind of weather. This one was cooler than those he remembered in Dublin and New Orleans. He might yet be wanting his greatcoat in here.

The desk clerk's appraising eyes held no welcome. "Good day, sir."

"You have a room for me."

The clerk waited.

Hugh reached for Nathaniel's letter and handed it to the clerk, who took it and held it before him like a shield over which he peered timidly, like a Macaulay employee, Hugh thought, caught in a misdemeanor.

"I trust my room is ready."

"Yes, sir. We will take you there directly. Mr. Avery left a message for you. Allow me to give it to you. We hope you will be comfortable with us. We wish you a pleasant stay."

There was a sitting room, bedroom, and dressing room. When Hugh was alone again, he picked up Nathaniel's message.

A thousand apologies. My wife insists on a trip to Philadelphia to see her parents, and we are on our way. Sam Guilford, Will Shaw, and Josh Bigelow will receive you in Will's office at ten on the morning after you arrive. Regret exceedingly I cannot show you Boston and Harvard. Nat.

The Boston weather was as fine as McKinley and Peter had promised for September. It was mid-afternoon still, with time before dinner to see those places that had come so often into their and Nathaniel's talk—the Old State House, Boston Common. Later—tomorrow—though Catherine had already written Antonia in Philadelphia, he would go, as he had promised Emily, to see the headmistress at the girls' school where the Martins had enrolled Betsy. And tomorrow he would also go to the address Timmy had given him, to deliver a message and money to Timmy's aged parents.

The walk about Boston relaxed him. Compared with Dublin, whose recorded history went back to the third century, and which, by the fifth, had achieved a Christian culture, Boston was a new, young city. And yet, compared with the Ontonagon mining towns, Boston showed a culture already two hundred years old and more.

Back in his rooms, he bathed in the iron tub that had been brought into his dressing room, and rested briefly. Tomorrow he would have to face by himself the Macaulay's three officials. Well, he would do so. Somehow in retrospect the combined boat-and-train trip from Michigan with the startled perception it brought of the nation's straining growth—and now this walk about Boston—had made him grasp how small a part of it all the Macaulay was, and had shrunk to manageable proportions his former consuming concern over the assessment. It was not until later, when going out of his room for a solitary dinner in the austere dining room he had glimpsed from the entrance, that the suspicion first struck Hugh that perhaps Nathaniel had not wished to be in Boston during his visit.

Looking up from locking his door, his key still in

his hand, he saw another man locking the neighboring door. It was none other than Lewis Cass! Hugh hesitated. But with instant recall, Senator Cass came forward, his hand outstretched in greeting. "My old friend! What an unexpected pleasure! By good chance, are you free to join me for dinner?"

The senator ordered briskly and leaned across the table to Hugh. "So tell me about our country." He ran his hand over his face as though to smooth the lines that current stresses were engraving there. "I spent some of my best years in Ontonagon."

"It is changing—rapidly. Thanks, in good measure, to you."

"Why thanks to me?"

Hugh looked up in surprise. "That Indian treaty of 1843 . . . I wrote to thank you."

"Ah, the one in ten who returned to give thanks." Disillusionment peered out of his eyes. Then he smiled. "Have you located your copper mine?"

"Aye, that I have, one of the best—the Macaulay."

The senator's features thinned. "Is that yours?"

" 'Twas my discovery. I am superintendent, and I share in the company developing it."

"Boston money?"

"Aye, 'tis that which brings me here."

"That's real country up there." The senator's tired face freshened, and a young man's imagination quickened his eyes. "You should do something, though, about that Sault impasse. I was there in the War of 1812. It was then the English destroyed the canal that the Northwestern Fur Company had built years before. With the tonnage going through these days and the promise of more to come, Michigan ought to rebuild. Do away with all that transshipping and delay. The present strap railroad is no answer."

Hugh's eyes burned a lighter hazel color. " 'Tis the very idea that came to me when I changed at the Sault. But what's there to do?"

The senator impatiently cut into the roast beef

the waiter had brought. "Get after the state legislature. I'll give you the name of the man to get action, but you'll have to keep after him."

"Would a letter serve?"

The senator looked sharply at Hugh and then laughed as a father might at a son's precocity. "I'll write the letter tonight. Return by way of Detroit. You will find your man there."

An almost unmanageable turbulence coursed through Hugh. Besides his plans for the Macaulay, might he not reveal to the owners tomorrow something of these more imaginative possibilities for development of the Upper Peninsula—development which would give an immense impetus to their interests there?

Not waiting for Hugh's comments, Cass continued. "Another thing. How are you getting your ore to Ontonagon? You are miles upriver near the site of the old copper boulder, are you not? Except in the spring, the Ontonagon's too slow."

"Aye, we are presently building a thirteen-mile plank road from New Boston to Ontonagon. The road company was created by legislative act last year, and we are financing it."

"Why not a railroad?"

"Up there?"

"Why not? The Sault Canal will take care of things between mid-May and mid-October, but you need railroads to unlock that country during those frozen winters."

The commotion inside Hugh crescendoed. Already the horse-drawn cars carrying ore to the smelting plant ran over rails brought from Detroit. Might this idea be of more immediate interest to the Macaulay officials—and so of even greater value than the canal at the Sault? And still Senator Cass, unknowingly presaging possible triumph for Hugh on the morrow, drove on.

"And a dock—you need an ore dock. One of the

lake ports will get it. Why not Ontonagon? Talk to my friend about a dock, too."

An ore dock at Ontonagon? Good God! What further might Senator Cass propose? Well, he'd have this also for Nathaniel's friends. Was it not perhaps providential after all that Nathaniel's wife had carried him off to Philadelphia? Still, Hugh would have liked to share these proposals with Nathaniel first, and now he could not do so. It was then he was sure of what had first been but a suspicion: Nathaniel had preferred not to be in Boston while Hugh was there on this mission. He not only doubted success, he expected failure. A sense of personal defeat dispelled Hugh's mounting elation.

Senator Cass, however, had not stopped. "Getting the ore out of the mines is just the beginning."

"Aye, I begin to see so, and I thank you."

Cass waved aside thanks. He smiled and looked utterly weary. The senator's exhaustion and the sorrow behind it swallowed Hugh's own disappointment, for he surmised that the man was experiencing a defeat far greater than his own.

"I, too, am here on business—my kind of business."

"I have followed your career with keen interest ever since we met in Detroit."

The senator nodded. "It was that day when I resolved to take my stand on popular sovereignty. But it did not win me the nomination in 1844, and that was the year—not 1848—in which I might have won. I still stand so. They criticize me for this and for favoring the Fugitive Slave Law. Last night, at Old South Meeting House, I debated these issues with Theodore Dwight Weld. I explained I had developed the doctrine of popular sovereignty not because I wished to see slavery extended into the states coming into the Union, but because this right of choice is in harmony with the Constitution. I explained further that in the light of the Constitution, no man ought to deny another what he has bought, paid for, and claims for his own."

Absorbed in his companion's argument, sympathizing and yet not wholly agreeing, Hugh asked, "Did your audience agree with you, sir?"

"They did not. They booed me and called for Mr. Weld."

"How did he answer you?"

"He argued that a deeper problem was involved —the question as to whether anyone had the right in the first place to buy or sell another human being. He asked whether anyone in the audience would willingly submit to being bought or sold and whether if robbed of his freedom, anyone listening would not do whatever was necessary to recover it. He ignored my issue of the Constitution. He is no lawyer, but the audience cheered everything he said."

Senator Cass leaned forward. "Of course, this is Boston, and Bostonians have mighty tender consciences toward the Negro in the South. But I ask you: how do they treat the destitute Irish here? Have you walked about South Cove and Harrison?"

Hugh started. That was the address Timmy had given him. "I must do so tomorrow."

"Yes, do. See how the immigrant Irish live *here!* I must continue to do as my own conscience dictates; I must argue my point of view as a lawyer who believes in the Constituiton."

Hugh reflected ardently. "Sir, you have helped me, and if I could, I should like to help you."

"Then tell me straight out, what are your thoughts on these questions?"

"Aye, but first you must realize that I am not a lawyer and also that I lack your close knowledge of the Constitution. What I say may have little sense. To me it seems that people act not from reason, but out of experience. Voyaging north from New Orleans on the Mississippi, I saw a fugitive slave dive from the paddle-wheel steamer into the river and strike out through that muddy, crocodile-infested water for freedom. Had I been on the shore and his captor, I could not have turned him back to the master who claimed him. You have talked and I have listened, wanting with all my heart to agree with you as a friend. I have asked myself whether experience does not have its own laws of reason and whether the slave, by escaping, was not obeying a higher law than the one protecting his master's property rights —and if the Constitution you revere does not somehow allow for this."

Hugh paused, realizing with consternation that Senator Cass was not fully in command of himself. Could a man like the senator break, even as Patrick had?

"Forgive me . . . forgive what I say. You must know these thoughts are the thoughts of an ignorant man, one who would not presume to dispute with you. But is it not a fact that here the law upholds the rights of one side and discounts those of the other? In Ireland this was so in a court of law regarding the rights of the English and those of the Irish. Again I judge solely out of my own experience."

"But a public man cannot change in midcourse, turn from what he has said all along—and said because he believed it. Yet what you say of experience . . . unsettles me. The law is experience, the history of experience." He pushed back his chair, and forgetting even that Hugh was still there, got up and walked dejectedly from the room.

Hugh remained behind, for the waiter had not yet presented their bill. It was the excuse he used because he was too shaken to move. Had he alienated the senator, lost his good will? Had Hugh forgotten his own objectives? Lost them in his arguments against slavery? He might well have done so. Suddenly he was filled with a chilling premonition that he had not escaped war by leaving Ireland and that here in America the issue of slavery would be settled only by bloody conflict. As he signed the bill his concern narrowed to his own immediate difficulties. Would Senator Cass deny him the promised letter or, more likely because of his turmoil, simply forget it?

Despite his anxiety a letter was under Hugh's door the next morning. Picking it up, Hugh saw it was addressed to the Honorable Edward Thompson, State Senator, Detroit, and was for the stated purpose of introducing Hugh Condon of Ontonagon. The only reference to Hugh's position on the Fugitive Slave Law was indirect and, at first, puzzling. After "Hugh Condon of Ontonagon," Senator Cass had written "to whom I have cause to be grateful."

Could it be that he, Hugh Condon, had brought influence to bear on such a man as Senator Lewis Cass, an influence which conceivably might affect the crisis tearing apart the nation? If only Kate were here to consult. Then clearly, as though she were, Hugh heard her say, "But what else could these words mean?" He put the letter in his inside pocket, next to Kate's note for Jerry. " 'Twill reach London much faster if you post it from Boston," Kate had said. He had deliberately left it unsealed, intending to add his own postscript in the event of his success in Boston. Kate had followed her mother in accepting Jerry's course, and perhaps, Hugh thought, it might please Jerry, now Lord Kemris, to know that his sister's husband had made advances of his own.

On Nathaniel's instructions, the clerk at Revere House had promptly notified Secretary Joshua Bigelow of Mr. Condon's arrival and made a ten o'clock appointment for Hugh this morning with the Macaulay officials at the Merchants Exchange. Before breakfasting, he would send a message to the headmistress and seek a late afternoon meeting, which might allow him time to locate a music store. If he won the assessment he sought, he might order a pianoforte for Catherine and Emily so that Miss Jenks might give lessons to them as she did to Elizabeth and Betsy Martin and to Susanne Osborne.

After finishing his meal, he set out for the home of

Timmy's parents. When he had located it, he regretted that he had not delayed breakfast, because he came close to sickening in the swarming, stinking Boston basement apartment. Cass was right. The Negroes in the South—at least Amelia and Antoine—lived better than the Irish did in Boston.

"I've come with a message from Timmy," he told the family, which consisted of Timmy's white-haired parents, in whose blue eyes lingered the fading memories of the Mourne Mountains; his brothers, who held forth with wild talk of leading an uprising; his nephews and nieces, the last but a pretty infant.

"From Timmy!" His mother clasped her hands thankfully. "Faith, an how be he?"

"Well." Then, appreciating Timmy's advantage over these others, Hugh added, "Very well."

"An be he workin these days?" his father inquired.

"Aye. For me."

"An phwat be he doin fir ye?" one of the brothers asked hopefully.

"His letter will tell you, I think." Hugh handed it to Timmy's mother. "And he also sent you this." From his pocketbook he withdrew Timmy's offering, and then he dipped in again for something of his own. "What message shall I bring him?"

"Tell 'im thit we be . . . fairly . . . an thit we send 'im our thanks an our love."

"Aye, I shall tell him." Hugh looked toward the brothers, silenced by their mother's reply. "And if it happens I succeed in my business here, I shall stop by again and see if some of you have a mind to follow Timmy, but you must give up all thought of leading an uprising and agree to be peaceable men."

Promptly at ten o'clock, Hugh entered Treasurer Wilfred Shaw's suite in the Merchants Exchange and found him and the other two officials awaiting him at one end of a narrow, immensely long, polished table. A single chair was at the other end. For me, Hugh thought. Perhaps it was because he had come directly from South Cove and Harrison and was still one with those he had found there that he felt as though he were again entering Mr. Eldon's Dublin office for the last, unequal confrontation.

The men rose correctly, and Hugh walked the length of the table and shook hands first with President Guilford, tallest of the three tall men, with appraising hazel eyes beneath tangled, graying dark brows; then with stouter, sandy-haired Secretary Bigelow, whose pale blue eyes were equivocating; and last with Treasurer Shaw, whose eyes were a clearer blue. As Hugh shook the hand of each, his habit of judging the men he employed came back to him, and he thought, Why, not one of these men is a match for Senator Lewis Cass—and my words last night had weight with him.

The three Macaulay officials sat down at their end of the table, and Hugh walked back to the chair at the other end, recalling the day at school when, because of some mischievousness, he had been told to sit far away from everyone else. What he'd muttered then on his way had brought murmurs of laughter from his classmates. Before seating himself, he said now what he'd said then. "I'm not in the habit of being so exclusive." Humor sparkled in Wilfred Shaw's eyes, and Hugh felt he'd lessened a little distance intended between the others and himself.

"Did you have time yesterday to look about Boston a bit?" Samuel Guilford asked, the others deferring to him.

"Aye," he said, "a little."

"Saw some of Boston's historic places?"

"Aye." Hugh looked down the table. Guilford's brows seemed to quiver expectantly. "I went to those places that are oftenest in our friend Nathaniel's talk —Boston Common, the Old State House, and the State House by Bulfinch."

The three pairs of eyes filled with one question: How had he, an immigrant Irishman, without inherited pride in Boston's history, reacted?

"And since I was passing by, I also went into Christ Church."

Wilfred Shaw's clear blue eyes deepened. "Did you, now? That is one of Boston's early churches—built in 1723."

"I took notice of the date, maybe because I recalled that Dublin's Christ Church was built in 1038."

Guilford, a little less formal now, thought to close the opening talk. "I am sorry not to have shown you a bit of our town, but our secretary"—he nodded toward Joshua Bigelow—"and I are leaving tomorrow for London, and time presses. I trust, though, you found your rooms at Revere House comfortable and the food to your liking?"

"I did. I also found agreeable company—an old friend from Michigan."

The men waited politely.

"Quite by chance, I met and dined with Senator Lewis Cass."

The Bostonians showed their surprise, and Samuel Guilford leaned over the table as though he would like to shorten the distance between him and Hugh. "You don't say?"

"Aye. The night before he debated the Fugitive Slave Law with Theodore Weld."

Guilford nodded. "We were there and heard him. Of course, we in Boston are opposed to this law."

"I understand so."

"It was no debate," Joshua Bigelow volunteered. "Weld murdered Cass."

"Aye, the senator said he had the unpopular side."

"Perhaps, then, he'll change his tune?"

"Senator Cass, if I read him rightly, is not a man to change his opinion because he is beaten in argument. He'll change only if he comes to see the issue differently."

"Will he do so now, do you think?" Shaw asked.

"I cannot speak for the senator or foresee what he will do. Though I myself differ from him on this matter,

I admire him greatly and am much in his debt, as all of us here are."

"In his debt?" the president questioned.

"Why, to be sure. Has Nathaniel not told you? Of course, that was before you interested yourself in the mine. 'Twas Senator Cass who was responsible for the Indian treaty of 1843, which permitted us to survey and lay claim to the area. He did this as a result of a visit I had paid him in Detroit. Without his action, there could be no Macaulay."

The silence that followed was replete with unspoken thoughts. Then Wilfred Shaw said, "Cass was a candidate then, was he not, for the Democratic nomination for President?"

"He was. He missed the nomination in '44, won it in '48, and lost the election; now he fights on in the Senate."

"Those who also ran recede quickly, but I recall Cass had a diversified career."

"Ohio frontiersman, U.S. brigadier general, governor of the Michigan Territory, secretary of war, ambassador to France."

Wilfred Shaw observed thoughtfully, "Even without capturing the Presidency, he's realized enough youthful dreams for half a dozen men."

"He has more dreams for the future and for that part of the country where your and my interests lie."

Like a man rising from some inner defeat, Samuel Guilford lifted his head. "What might these be?"

"First, in order to do away with all the transshipping and delay, the rebuilding of the Sault Canal."

"At whose expense?" Bigelow demanded. "Surely not ours!"

"No. That would exceed our capabilities, though we as well as many others should profit. This is a thing for the Michigan legislature. He also suggests a railroad."

"Up there? Is this not a wild, unrealizable dream?"

Hugh opened his hands expansively. "We already run cars on rails from the mine to the smelting plant.

You gentlemen do not know what you've got. A canal would serve through the months that Lake Superior is navigable. Senator Cass thinks we need a railroad to unlock the country through the long winters, to bring it into the nation."

"The thought staggers the imagination." Guilford shook his head. "From what source does this man draw his ideas?"

"From his vision of the nation we one day shall be. Talking to him, I felt a great urge to grow up to his vision. He has even another idea."

"Let us hear it," Samuel Guilford murmured in so weak a voice that Shaw and Bigelow laughed.

"He foresees that a Great Lakes dock must be built, and he proposes the site to be Ontonagon."

"And whose project would this be?"

"Why, he sees it as the legislature's."

"Were it here in Massachusetts. But we have no influence for things of this sort in Michigan."

"Senator Cass has, and he has given me a letter to the man he says can get action. I shall stop in Detroit to see this gentleman."

Again there was silence, heavy with swirling, reversing currents of thought. The silence persisted, and waiting through it, Hugh realized he controlled the meeting. No one spoke, and, as in Shaft House No. I, he felt compelled to take the initiative.

"Now, on this more immediate matter," he began, "of concern to us all—the assessment."

Like one called back to the present, Treasurer Wilfred Shaw looked up. "Yes, the assessment."

" 'Tis for this that I have broken from the Macaulay when there were many reasons I should stay."

This was ground they were better able to comprehend and to grapple with. "Other mines there, we hear —the Cliff, for one—are now paying dividends."

"Mines, like men, do not bear comparisons." Hugh was smiling. "These Keweenaw mines differ greatly. I would not trade the Macaulay for any one of the others."

"On what do you base this attachment?" Shaw was smiling now, too.

His smile, the first Hugh had won from any of the three, warmed Hugh as if it were the sun at last breaking through mist-filled Irish skies.

"As a boy in Chapelizod," he said reminiscently, "I often went to the races, and sometimes I would feel a great love for a particular horse. Why? Oh, to be sure, there were many reasons—a hard-to-define quality, the beauty he showed when he broke into a run. But was he a winner? I had to be sure.

"It is so now with the Macaulay. I am sure. Even during these development years, it has come close to paying its way with copper masses. In proportion to the labor and capital spent, it has already produced more copper than any other mine on the peninsula, including the Cliff. Only this solid copper wall we have met in sinking the newest shaft has delayed the payment of dividends. But even while delaying dividends, it has made our hopes many times greater. This is not the moment to tighten the purse strings."

"How will the money from the assessment be used?" Shaw asked precisely.

Hugh's earlier awareness of gaining—even winning —surged in his blood as it had when the horse he had picked reached out in the final stretch. Shaw had asked, "How will it be used?" not "How would it be used?"

"The Macaulay is a well-run mine. We have suffered no major accidents. We will continue to run it that way, with no cuts in operating costs which might lead to accidents or cause delays or spoil the accuracy of our assaying. We also will use a small amount for certain needs we have not as yet met—a company doctor, for one. As in all the mines, we are plagued by eye trouble."

"How long before we can declare a dividend?"

Treasurer Shaw, Hugh could see, was already on his side. Secretary Bigelow would follow where led. It was President Guilford he still needed. Suppose he assured them of dividends within a year? But he could not do this.

"I can but guess. We must cut through this copper wall, sink a new shaft, and see. It might be a year; it might be longer. With each of you, I share the hope that it may be in as short a time as possible."

"A year, maybe more than a year?" Joshua Bigelow frowned.

Hugh nodded. "To be sure, the delay is irksome. But once we are through this copper wall, which the assessment will assure, our profits will far exceed those of all the other mines."

Something in Guilford seemed to crumble, and then all at once to give way. "You have my consent."

Shaw next, and then Bigelow said, "Yes, and mine, too."

Triumph caught Hugh in a vise, and to break out of it, he pounded the table with his fists. "Well then, let us chalk up a long-delayed victory for the Indians!"

The tufts in Samuel Guilford's tangled brows seemed to curl and uncurl over his startled eyes. "The Indians!"

"Certainly. Did not Nathaniel tell you the Macaulay is the site of a prehistoric mine? When I first found the cave, I discovered Indian tools and a bar of smelted copper on centuries-old cribbing."

"By Jove!" Shaw exclaimed, and his clear blue eyes turned yet bluer with another dimensional perception. "You have taken us across the country, forward in time, and now backward. Speaking for myself, I feel more thoroughly exercised mentally than I've felt since my Harvard days."

"You gentlemen have been great, following me about as you have. I am impressed anew by your education. Perhaps one day my sons may go there. But now, from the bottom of my heart, I join the dead, triumphant Indians and thank you for the assessment."

"It is we," Samuel Guilford said, "who must thank you with more than words can convey for coming here when, as you said, there were many reasons why you should have stayed behind."

Hugh rose, and the three Macaulay officials rose, too, and walked toward him, their hands outstretched in friendship. "And you will let us know the outcome of your Detroit stopover?" Samuel Guilford paused, and Hugh knew he had been selected over Nathaniel as adviser. "Please let us know directly."

Chapter 25

THE OCTOBER WIND BLEW wine-sweet and chill from Lake Superior. Hugh sat in the bow of the canoe, his bag and folded greatcoat between him and the kneeling Kon-Te-Ka, son of O-Kun-De-Kun, who, with the strong, sure strokes learned from his father, was sending the canoe up the Ontonagon. The maples, elms, oaks, and birch, already leafless, showed their differing structures, and the dark, austere pines and spruce stood sentinel beneath a sky of deep and shadowing blue. He was home again.

Impatient during the homeward travel as he had been for reunion with Catherine and the children, now that he neared the moment, his thoughts turned back on his experiences. How venturesome his undertaking had been, diverted from likely failure to happy success, in good part, through his chance meeting with Senator Lewis Cass. Stopping in Detroit, Hugh had passed Cass's vision along to his close associate, State Senator Edward Thompson.

Thompson, a tall man whose stoop suggested habitual attentiveness, had come from his office to the reception room with the intention of merely extending a hearty handshake and then, with a few words of booming good will, sending Hugh on his way. But Senator Cass's letter had reversed any preconceived plan. Thompson's expression had quickly readjusted itself, and he gestured Hugh to precede him into the private room and closed the door softly.

"How is our good friend?"

"Better than ever I have seen him."

"You have known him long?"

"For many years."

The legislator thoughtfully attended to all Hugh had to say, and when he had finished, dropped his forehead into his right hand. "Senator Cass and I have long hoped for these developments," he conceded. "I'll go to work on this right away. We shall see what Michigan will spend for a canal at the Sault. Of course, the Federal Government should come in on this, too. No doubt Senator Cass had this in mind, and I'll hear further from him about it.

"What about upper Michigan? What will it give in return? The last county division, as I'm sure you know, has not worked. You need local government up there, and this costs taxes. Can you work it out? As Macaulay superintendent, you will be in line for township supervisor. No doubt you are already in charge?"

Hugh saw the men tipping their caps as they filed by on their way to work. "Aye, more or less."

Thompson shot him a covert glance. "There will be land to divide—government grants. Will you want yours in the Ontonagon country?"

Hugh deliberated. Senator Cass had said nothing of this. But apparently it was the way of things. He nodded. " 'Twould be best in this event to have mine close by."

How smoothly the canoe moved over even the shallower places. Kon-Te-Ka's paddle broke the water with no more noise than need be. It was the Sabbath, and quiet held. Hugh could but guess to what extent the plans set in motion in Detroit and in Washington would change everything. He foresaw that the variance would be great, destroying old ways, creating new ones. Still, he did not grasp that the pattern of life in the Ontonagon country would ultimately be set by the Boston men whose money developed the mines. Nor did he anticipate that in another generation this pattern would seem to many as destructive of human freedom as the slavery in the South against which the same Bostonians willed war. Though Hugh would help shape life in the copper country and prosper from it, even he in his time would question whether it was worth the price he had to pay.

But now, traveling the river beneath the blue and shadowing sky, beyond Nathaniel's receding cabin and his own early one, he looked to the future and to all he must do. Thanks to him, Timmy's two brothers were already on their way here, and uncounted others must follow, emptying at least to a degree those foul Boston houses. He must plan at once with McKinley and Peter to enlarge the work—open up yet another shaft and construct improved housing for the miners and their families. The winter supplies he'd purchased at his Sault stopover would arrive soon, and storage facilities ought to be built.

The voices of the children floated across the water, and there on the dock Emily and Mac anticipated him. Affection stirred in Hugh. What a story he had —one of success beyond what he had hoped, greater than he had dreamed.

Kon-Te-Ka secured the boat, and Hugh, lithe though less so than he once had been, stepped to the dock. Emily startled him. Despite their so-different coloring, how like her mother at Kate's early age Emily looked. Until now, he had not perceived this. She stood back and allowed her younger brother the first welcoming hug. But Hugh was surprised to see that his second son no longer was "little Mac." During his father's absence he seemed to have shot up and matured. Now it was Emily's turn, and she threw her arms about her father and inquired, "Did you order the pianoforte?"

"That I did, and a fine one. One I trust that will please your mother and you."

Then Emily clapped, and hugged her father again. "And did you see the headmistress at Betsy's Boston school?"

"Aye, that I did."

"You must not say 'aye,' Father. Miss Jenks says it's not right."

"Then tell your Miss Jenks the purest English is spoken in Dublin, and there we say 'aye.' "

Emily laughed her merry laugh. "I shall tell her, Father, and until I have her answer, you may say 'aye.' But what did the headmistress say about me?"

"She said, 'Aye.' "

Emily laughed again. "Oh, Father, she didn't say 'aye.' "

"She did—perhaps in courtesy to me."

"But what else did she say?"

"She said, 'A daughter of yours will be more than welcome, Mr. Condon.' "

"Then it's settled? May I run and tell Betsy and McKinley?"

"You may go, but you must not run; and you may tell Betsy, but not McKinley."

"Why may I not tell him as well?"

Hugh gazed at his daughter and for the first time perceived that she had already ceased to be his little girl and that her impulse was toward another. "You may tell Betsy today and McKinley tomorrow," he teased. "But remember . . . though the headmistress would welcome you, 'tis not settled you'll go to Boston. Your mother may have hinted to you, as she has to me, that she wishes you to go to Père Baraga's sister's school in Philadelphia."

"Aye," Emily said, forgetting herself and laughing at her own relapse, "she has 'hinted,' and not so subtly, either. But you will persuade her, won't you?"

"Aye, unless she persuades me. In any case, we shall talk, and you may tell your friends for now that, while 'tis not settled, the headmistress will welcome you warmly."

He watched Emily saunter off. Then her young hope that she, despite all, would have things her way triumphed, and she raced toward the home of her friends.

Hugh turned to Mac. "Are you not eager to know what present I bought you?"

"I want but one."

"And what might that be?"

"News that you may cut through the copper wall."

Hugh's head dropped to hide his emotion. His younger son's words came to him like a second victory, sweetening his homecoming. He lifted his head and looked at Mac with great love.

"I have won their consent, Mac," he said, "and a present is on the way for you, too."

Macaulay flipped a handspring. "It is present enough for me," he said, on his feet again, "to know that you have won over those Boston men."

Hugh glanced about. "Where is your brother?"

But Macaulay was doing a whole succession of handsprings right up to the house, and his father started to walk after him. No doubt Larry was inside with his mother. He was ever fond of her company, fonder of hers than of anyone's except, perhaps, of Patrick's and Patricia's.

Hugh went into the house, where Kate waited for him in the hallway. She was alone.

Her looks, like Emily's, surprised him, but differently. The bloom that had once been hers and was now Emily's was gone; in the short time of his absence her face had fined somehow, as though with suffering. He could but surmise that all had not gone as she wished. Nevertheless, she threw herself into his arms in a way that told him she had needed and missed him. He felt instant regret for what they had lost by her failure to accompany him. "You should have come, Kate."

"I might as well have done so."

Her answer, Hugh realized, could mean only one thing. She had stayed home for Larry. The children had failed to answer his inquiry. He stepped away from his wife. "Where is Larry?"

"He went north with Père Baraga on his missions tour. But his real purpose in going was his hope to somehow overtake Patrick and Patricia."

"Did you give your consent to his going?"

She lifted her head and looked directly at him. He caught the disturbance in her eyes. Did they also accuse him? "I did, for I knew that otherwise he would go on his own. He had grieved so over their departing. I thought 'twas better that he go this way."

Hugh was silent for so long that Catherine looked at him wonderingly. Finally he asked, "When will he return?"

"I can but hope when Père Baraga does."

Hugh was silent again.

"And you, did you meet with success?" Catherine tried hard to smile.

"Aye, that I did—and more." Hugh's triumphant laugh came with a surprising harshness. "The Macaulay officials not only agreed to the assessment, they are no longer content to have me advise them through Nathaniel. They wish me to advise them directly."

Surprised, Catherine asked, "And what will Nathaniel do?"

"Look after his family interests, I suppose. Besides the Macaulay, there are many. I shall be building our family fortune meanwhile." Hugh laughed again.

Hearing his laugh, Catherine felt the surge of her husband's ambition, stronger than ever before, freed from dependence on anyone but himself. She thought of how she had recovered him when failure had threatened and wondered whether she would lose him again to his thrust for achievement.

"But she wishes to go where her friends are going." As he had promised Emily he would, Hugh was presenting her point of view to her mother.

"I know. 'Tis an impulsive wish, an entirely natural one, but one I feel is not in harmony with her true character. Should she go there, her development will be somehow wrong for her."

"How? This is the school where Elizabeth Martin and Susanne Osborne went in their time. Was it wrong for them, and will it be wrong for Betsy?"

"I cannot answer that. No doubt it helped shape Elizabeth and Susanne . . . to make them what they are."

"Do you not approve? I thought you liked them well."

"I do. But their schooling—oh, no doubt other influences, too—has separated them from all but their own kind of people and they guard that separateness. They so seldom laugh. I remember Antonia as she greeted Monsieur Nicollet, the three of us, then Monsieurs Balthazar and Lawler, the half-breeds, and the Chippewa, in different languages and with equal courtesy. Her culture, I am sure, is more thorough and far-reaching than our friends', but it did not separate her from those not her own kind. She kept a merry laugh."

"But Emily has not Madame von Hoeffern's work to do. She will marry, live among people like the Martins and Osbornes. Aye, perhaps even the Guilfords and Bigelows and Shaws."

"It is not only what she shall do that concerns me, but also what she shall be."

"And what is it you wish her to be?"

"All that she has it in her to be. I wish her to remain open to life, to keep her courage—she is brave—and her loyalty toward all she loves, and I wish her to keep her joyous laugh."

"Are these qualities that the Boston school will snuff out?"

"They are qualities Antonia will see, I believe, and foster."

So in the end it had been settled, and the following year, in the fall of 1852, the McKinley Martins took Emily, Betsy, and McKinley Jr. to New York, where they parted. The Martins went on to Boston, Emily to Madame Antonia's school in Philadelphia.

The night before departure, Catherine and Emily had had a little talk. "But I would not have you go if it were to be unhappily," Catherine had said. "And," she added hesitantly, for it seemed to her that McKinley Jr. had his father's questioning habit but not his resolve, "I do think you should withhold your affection from McKinley for a time. You will meet many other young men while in Philadelphia."

"What if it should be that McKinley needs me more?"

A tremor like a premonition had stirred through Catherine. "You could not know this without knowing some others."

"Aye," Emily had declared firmly, "but I could."

But the departure by steamboat from Ontonagon was a merry one. Hugh and Catherine, pleased that Emily, on her first adventuresome trip from home, would be well looked after by the Martins and would have the company of her young friends, went down to the river to see the party off. Mac came along, too, looking ahead to the day when he hoped he himself would be leaving for school.

Excitement burned in Emily's eyes, and the pink that tinted her cheeks reminded Catherine of the color that excitement had brought to her own mother's face. How attractive she looked, really quite a young lady, in her dove-gray traveling outfit. Catherine sighed. Emily's departure seemed wholly happy. Unlike mine from Dublin, her mother thought.

The moment had come. Impulsively Emily threw her arms about her mother, then her father, then Mac. "Goodbye, goodbye," she cried, and got into the launch bound for the steamboat.

She waved, blew a kiss, then turned about and looked ahead toward the huge steamer. McKinley Jr. put his arm about her, and Betsy lifted her hands high and clapped. They were off.

But not all events were as fortuitous as Emily's departure. In the year that had passed since Hugh's Boston trip and the Detroit stopover, his responsibilities had expanded beyond what even he had foreseen. As time went on, they continued to increase and brought with them unanticipated problems. As New Boston Township's supervisor, he was locked in bitter controversy with the Ontonagon Township supervisor, who was bound that the copper on the docks, already taxed once at the mines, should be taxed again. Besides this, the adjoining mine had brought a case against the Macaulay to the State Supreme Court, claiming underground trespass. There was also the troublesome sand bar in the harbor that successive breakwaters had failed to relieve.

Besides these difficulties and those at the Macaulay with which Hugh wrestled daily and often intermittently through wakeful nights, another development in the spring of 1853 profoundly embittered him. It had come to his attention that his partners, despite the fact that the stockholders' investment had doubled since he had journeyed to Boston, had made a secret trip to Portage Lake to explore a possible venture in the new amygdaloid mines opening there and had apparently had no intention of letting him in on these prospects.

It was especially this last which made him so touchy nowadays. Nothing Catherine could say helped. She continued her efforts, however, in the increasingly rare intervals when they were together, and sometimes at night when, as now, tossing and muttering, he awakened her.

"But, Hugh, we already have much more than we thought we would have just a few years ago. There is your superintendent's pay, besides the return from your share in the Macaulay. And there is all the land given you. I do not quite understand why or how—but it is ours. Can you not be content with all you have?"

"That I cannot. Why should they not share with me as I have with them? These amygdaloid veins are in the true copper range, I have learned. One day the Macaulay will give out."

Catherine was more tired from the present contention than she had been from her struggles in the early Ontonagon days to bear Larry, then Mac, and to keep the cabin neat, the clothes washed, and the family fed and happy. She sighed inwardly and said, "But our wants, too, someday will come to an end. We already have more than we need."

"Emily, Larry, and Mac will have children."

"Can we not talk instead of tomorrow? As you know, I have long looked forward to the day."

"Aye, we may talk of it if it pleases you. But tomorrow will pass, and these problems I speak of will remain."

A new Catholic church, painted white and built like Protestant ones in New England, lifted a forty-six-foot steeple with its cross to the Ontonagon's changeful sky. Bishop Baraga arrived by steamboat from the seat of his diocese at the Sault to bless and to name the house of worship built on the Ontonagon River's bank. For the first time, this Easter of 1853, he would hear the organ delivered from Buffalo. He brought New Boston's first resident pastor, Fr. Martin Fox, chosen at St. Sulpice in Paris. It ought to be a day filled not with striving but with joy. Catherine planned to wear for the first time the hat Emily had sent her from Philadelphia.

My friends and I went shopping today. Guess what I bought? Though it is winter, the shop where Madame Antonia took us is already showing Easter hats. So I bought one for myself and one for you. Oh, yours is a wonder. Wait till you see. The shop's owner assured me it would reach

you in good time, and Madame Antonia says I
can count on her word. Afterward—although we
could hardly wait to get back to our rooms to try
on our new hats—we stopped for hot chocolate.
I wish I could see you when you put on your hat.
I will not describe it, but you shall see. My love
to you and to all. I'm so glad Larry has come
home.

Emily

P.S. My hat is lovely, too.

Catherine sat down at her dressing table. Carefully,
so as not to damage a single delicate violet, she lifted
the beautiful hat from the box and turned it about, ex-
amining it. What artistry had gone into its making!
The foundation was of pale green net, doubled for
strength. It was bound by a band of deeper green velvet, but the shade was so subdued one did not see it as
green at first. Then the long-stemmed violets both
dropped from the crown and were twisted about it.
The overall effect was of massed flowers in varying
muted shades: some pale, almost gray, and others
deep purple. In their centers were tiny red pistils,
tipped with white. Catherine continued to hold the hat,
now seeing not the hat but Emily, yielding, although
not without a struggle, her desire to go with Betsy Martin to the Boston school, in acceptance of her mother's
preference for Antonia's. She does seem happy, Catherine thought. She started to place the hat on her head
when Larry entered the room.

"You aren't going to wear that today!"

His mother hesitated. Since his return, Larry was
unaccountably touchy.

"I had planned to," she said, leaving open the possibility of change. "Why do you think I ought not?"

"The miners' wives do not have such fine hats. You
should be ashamed to wear it before them."

Catherine put it down. "Oh, do you think so,
Larry?"

"I do. Unless you don't care for their feelings."

"Oh, but I do care. You know how I share our fresh bread with those who are ill. Why, just yesterday I took my bread to Timmy and his brothers."

Larry waved that aside. "You do not really know how they live. I know—I lived with them."

Catherine drew in her breath. Always before, Larry had been silent about the period during which he had been gone from home, and she had always wondered.

"I know what they eat and how they eat. They do not eat our kind of food. How can they? They only earn thirty dollars a month. I know how they smell. They do not wash every day; they are too tired. Their clothes are dirty, too. They do not always have underclothes, as we do, but worst of all, they go deep into the mines, and they are afraid. I know. I was."

His mother froze. "You do not mean to say you went down into a mine, Larry?"

"I did. Patrick took me. I stayed the whole day. It is hot down there, hot as midsummer. Did you know a wind blows in our Lake Superior copper mines? Well, it does. Patrick says it dries out the timber supports and could cause a fire any day. It can start like a breeze and turn into a gale, even a hurricane. That's how it was the day I went down. It nearly blew me off the ledge where Patrick put me to work scraping at a copper vein."

"Oh, Larry!" his mother cried. "If you had slipped!" Seeing him fall through the mine's darkness to its imagined dank, abysmal depth, she went faint. Then anger roused her, anger like Hugh's at Patrick. "How wicked of Patrick to take you!"

"It wasn't wicked of Patrick. He goes down. And the sons of miners do, too. They start early. Maybe they are also afraid."

Catherine fought through her overwhelming distress for the right thing to say. The trouble was, Larry had brought her around to his point of view, made her see the lives of the miners his way, opened up social issues she had not been willing before now to see.

And she saw herself going weekly, as she did, with

her freshly baked soda bread to the cottages of the miners where there was illness. "Oh, I understand," Susanne Osborne or Elizabeth Martin had said more than once. "This is your day for the miners."

Larry had waved aside as trifling her taking the loaves, and now she remembered her visit yesterday to Timmy's cottage, dismal outside and within—the timid, unassertive young children, the disheveled wife and mother. However, before knocking she had been surprised to hear laughter inside and had been moved by the warm welcome. "Ah, it be Mrs. Condon. Come in. Come in." She had done so and heard—and forgotten when she left—that today, for the first time, an older son was going down into the mine. "Lake his father."

I must remember better what they tell me, Catherine decided, and whenever he will listen, tell Hugh.

She returned to her son. "How often did you go down, Larry?"

Larry laughed weakly. "Just that time."

"You did not want to go again?"

"No, it wasn't that. I promised Patrick to go again the next day. But Patricia woke me early, before he was up."

While Larry recounted what had taken place, his mother imagined Patricia speaking. " 'Tis home ye be goïn this day, Larry. Th' *Julia Palmer* be docked here, an 'tis sailin this mornin fir Ontonagon. So hurry off. Heer be th' money from Pathrick's wages fir yeer passige. Min ye, pay at th' dock. Ye may come agin whin ye be older, but now ye maught bide at home with yeer mither. An m' greetins to her."

And my greetings to *her,* Catherine thought. And my profound thanks. "I am glad you have told me this, Larry."

"Then you will not wear that hat today?"

"No, I will not."

"And you will try to help the miners? I mean in real ways, not just bringing bread."

Catherine's eyes filled with tears. What had previously seemed an errand of mercy now seemed an errand of shame.

"I shall try," she said, "but what can I do?"

"You can speak to Father."

Catherine sighed. "I shall do so, Larry, but I am afraid real changes must wait upon you. Perhaps when you have gone through school, you will know how to look after the miners' interests better than your father."

"I already know how to run things better than him, and I am not going away to school."

"What's this?" Hugh's voice had an edge to it. He had been on the way downstairs to talk with Macaulay about yet a third type of copper ore the youth claimed he had noticed. At Larry's words, Hugh had swung about and come into the room. "What is it you know how to do better than me?"

The dressing-table mirror reflected Catherine's frozen dread of the scene she would have given anything to avert and instead had provoked.

Hard and cold, Hugh confronted Larry, and catching them in her mirror, Catherine winced to see Larry wilt. Hugh laughed at his son's discomfort. "And what is this about not going away to school? Do you not know you must prepare if you are to go to Harvard College?"

"I do not want to go there," Larry mumbled.

"Then what do you want to do?"

Larry barely managed to say, "I want to go to Portage Lake to work in the mines."

"Like Patrick, I suppose?"

"Aye, like Patrick."

Hugh stepped closer to Larry, and Catherine cried out, " 'Tis a little boy's notion, Hugh! Leave him to it."

Hugh paid her no notice. Perhaps, she thought, he had not even heard.

"You see where his life has gotten Patrick?"

"That's because he was cheated."

Hugh's brow lifted in a way that Catherine could

not abide. "Hugh!" she pleaded. "You will end by ruining this day for us all!"

"And who cheated him?" Hugh persisted.

Larry dared not give the answer his father invited. Instead, he replied with a weakness his father had brought on and which sickened his mother. "The men who cheated you."

Hugh moved away, and Larry started to leave. "Don't go! Let us have this out. What makes you say they cheated me?"

"Didn't they?"

Hugh took a deep breath, and remembering his nighttime talk, Catherine held hers.

"Suppose they did? That is over and done with."

"It isn't finished for Patrick."

Then something seemed to give in Hugh. "Suppose I told you it really isn't that way for me, either. What would you say?"

Larry looked up timidly with hope. "I would like to help you if I could."

Hugh laughed again, but not, Catherine heard gratefully, so cruelly as before. "The best help you can give me is to get on with your studies—to try to do as well as your sister and brother."

Catherine saw Larry's underlip tremble as it used to when he began to cry as a toddler, and she knew that he wanted to protest, "But I am not either of them. I am myself. I am Larry." If only he had said that! Perhaps he still would. His lip steadied and his shoulders stiffened and a new determination leaped into his eyes, as though he were recalling his experience in the mine. But then his shoulders dropped, and he turned and left the room.

"Oh, Hugh," Catherine moaned, "need you have said that?"

"Said what, for God's sake?"

"About doing as well as his sister and brother. I have asked you so many times. How do we know? Perhaps he cannot."

"I thought you had other ideas as to that."

"I do. But we cannot be sure. Yet I believe Larry is as bright as the others, maybe brighter. He has been hurt. He is confused."

"You confuse him further by siding with him against me."

Catherine began to put the violet-covered hat away in its box. "There." She tried to change the subject. "After all, I shall not wear it."

"And why not?" Hugh inquired, also hoping to restore peace between them.

"Larry asked me not to. He said the miners' wives do not have hats like this one."

"Are you going to encourage him in his nonsense?"

"It is not nonsense to him."

"It is to me." Hugh's eyebrow lifted commandingly, and this time it was lifted against her. "I ask you to wear it!"

Trembling inwardly, she reached into a drawer for a veil. "Another time," she said, and tied the piece of lace about her head.

Hugh looked at her and saw, not the Kate whom until this moment he had loved through even the most recent stormy times, but her autocratic mother, frustrating him.

Catherine got up and said, "We must go." Just as her mother would have done, Hugh thought.

It was true enough. Mac, always dependable, had brought around the horse and buggy and was calling up the stairs to tell them so. He helped his mother into the buggy and stood back while his father stepped in after her.

"Where's Larry?"

"Never mind Larry. He seems to have disappeared. We shall go without him."

Inwardly Catherine cried out, but she knew her protest would do no good.

During the ride through the countryside, bright and gay with spring flowers, Catherine could not lift herself above the earlier conflict. With a child life mysteriously begins again for a parent, renewing the power both to suffer and to rejoice. But with Larry she endured so much. And with quickened insight she thought, How my mother must have suffered over George!

Perhaps George sometimes returned to her mother as he did to her, driving the jaunting car, his wrists lifted gracefully over the reins, his mouth curved sweetly in repose. Always when she thought of those occasions with George, it seemed as if they had been at the edge of some mysterious happiness. Was it perhaps in the memory of those who had loved them that the dead lived on? None of this, however, helped with Larry, and it was Larry she wished to help and somehow could not.

They arrived ahead of nearly everyone else and went into the church with its plastered white walls, high altar of carved white wood that supported statues, and the light burning before the tabernacle. Larry was already in the family pew. He must have cut through the fields, running all the way, preferring not to ride since *they* couldn't ride.

His mother sat beside him and touched his hand lightly. Quickly he pulled it away. She wanted him to notice the veil she was wearing instead of the hat, but he did not look at her. The church, meanwhile, was steadily filling. From where she sat, she noticed the Martins. The story, she remembered, was that although McKinley had been reared in his Catholic mother's faith, he had been married in his wife's church. Now, perhaps for the first time since then, he was again before the tabernacle with the vigil light burning. Did he feel the special presence of Christ? And she? What ought she to feel, defying her husband as she had done, deepening the estrangement that was growing between them? Yet at night—even last night after his insistence that he must share in the new amygdaloid mines, and her attempt to turn aside this fresh thrust of his ambition—they resolved their differences in love.

Behind Father Fox came Bishop Baraga, his frail form in bishop's dress, his face tanned to a half-breed's color, and his graying hair stirring slightly under his miter. A not-quite-audible whisper rippled a welcome through the congregation. Before the tabernacle, with Father Fox to his right and the altar boys to his left, the bishop sank briefly to his knees. Then he rose and, his expression tending toward abstraction, approached the altar railing. He looked upon the congregation out of eyes now seared by Lake Superior's snow and sleet blasts to the softest blue.

Though consecrated Titular Bishop of Amyzonia some years before, embracing all the Lake Superior country with his seat at Sault Ste. Marie, he was more accustomed to congregations of Indians or miners than to one like this with its township supervisors, professional men, merchants, and mining officials. He smiled gently, almost timidly. He had come back to the Ontonagon country where he had spent many years, and before dedicating the church and saying Mass, he wished to greet all his friends.

Afterward, he sat briefly in the special chair while the organist played "Ave Maria." It was in Mary's honor that the church would be called. From his chair the bishop looked about, his gentle smile inviting everyone present to enjoy the music. He rose and returned to the altar, and in his clear voice and measured diction, prayed aloud the solemn, centuries-old words:

> May the lord build us a dwelling
> and keep watch over the city.
> Unless the Lord build the house
> they labor in vain who build it.

Following the service there was a reception on the lawn, and the miners and their families lingered with the others. While Catherine introduced the Macaulay officials and their families to Father Fox, Hugh went with Bishop Baraga to meet the miners by name, for he would go first to them. Larry tagged along, his mother saw. To each, the bishop had something to say. When finally Hugh brought him back to the Martins, the Osbornes, and the other congregants, Larry stayed with the miners' families.

Why does he not return to us now? Catherine wondered. But watching Larry among them, she also saw that the men and their wives and children were as at ease with him as though he were one of them.

Chapter 26

ALTHOUGH NEITHER Elizabeth Martin nor Catherine Condon wanted a marriage uniting McKinley Jr. and Emily, the latter, with Betsy as go-between, were deep into a promising romance. For the decision to send Emily to Madame Antonia's Philadelphia school while McKinley studied in Boston had made their getting together a taunting dream, just barely realizable.

Twice already McKinley had made the exciting railway trip from Boston by way of New York to Philadelphia.

When he had come the first time, Emily had been nearly sick with longing for Larry and Mac and her parents, and for Betsy and McKinley and the wild, free days the three had known together.

"What joy it was," Emily recalled, "to canoe down the Ontonagon into Lake Superior shining in the summer sun! And to snowshoe across the white expansive land toward the eerie winter sunset!"

"It was so," McKinley had agreed.

They had fallen into a silence in which nostalgia for

their shared past subtly nourished dependency on each other.

When McKinley had arrived the second time, he had expected to find Emily still needing comfort. Instead, he found a buoyant girl fully alive to the new, opening life. All was going favorably: in the classroom, where the answers came to her easily; in her bedroom, where, in off hours, the young ladies from various other locations met to speculate and laugh about their unfolding futures; and at the Saturday-afternoon tea dances, when admiring young men from the nearby Academy sought her out.

"You will meet many other young men in Philadelphia," her mother had counseled, withholding, as Emily had divined, concern over McKinley's lack of resolve.

It was true, Emily had perceived during the second visit, that McKinley was not getting on as well as his family would expect, as well as she was.

Now he had come the third time, and her mood had changed once again. She knew now, firsthand, how America had struggled into being in Philadelphia and that the expanding nation was governed from Washington, where Madame Antonia had taken her and several other students for a long weekend. But she had still to see Boston, which, for all those bred in Keweenaw, was the hub of the universe from which streamed money and power. It was from Boston that Nathaniel came and to Boston that McKinley's mother hoped one day to return.

McKinley and she loitered about her school grounds, making tentative conversation, seeking each other again after months apart.

"It's strange," she said. "I was ever so lonely here at first."

"I remember," he replied, not without a tinge of regret, for he had been surer of her then. "And you no longer are?"

"I miss them, of course. I miss Larry and I worry about him because he does not fit into the life our parents have made. And I miss Mac, but there is no need to worry about him. He was the first who called to Father's attention the latest copper find. Father intends to make a lawyer of him, and he promises Father to look after his interests well."

"Do you sometimes miss the boy and girl we left behind up there?"

"Yes, I do, but I do not feel I can go back to the life I left there. For me, that is somehow over." She stopped. She could not tell him about her strange new stirrings of mind and body, her awakening to a mysterious life of her own, full of wonder. She had not even succeeded in broaching this subject to Madame Antonia, though she had come to understand why her mother held her in such high esteem.

All about the school grounds, flowering shrubs were in full, fragrant blossom, and they found a bench by an overhanging bush.

"How like your father you are," Emily observed.

"I fear it may be only in looks."

"To be sure; then you must be yourself in deeds."

They sat down in the shelter of the spreading shrub. "It is a bridal wreath," Emily said, lifting a drooping, flowering branch and making a wreath of it about her dark head.

McKinley bent over, put his head in his hands, and groaned.

"Whatever is the matter?" Emily lifted his head, held it between her hands, and looked into his troubled eyes.

"I cannot abide this waiting."

Emily laughed. "Forgive me, but I thought it was something worse. Time passes," she offered hopefully. "You see how the year has already come round to spring."

"But how many more times must it come round before I'll have done with schooling?"

"Many, I know," she sympathized. "Many more times for you than for me."

"You shall finish in June and return to Ontonagon, and I . . ." His eyes, gray like his father's, held unanswered questions. "Well, what am I to do without you?"

"It's a thought that worries me, too, McKinley, but you will get on."

He shook his head.

"Others do."

"It's somehow different with them than with me. Others may have some need of their own to get on. My only need to get on is for you." His slow smile signified relief at his hard-spoken truth.

"I shall wait for you, then," she said.

But he shook his head. "That will not do, either, with you in Ontonagon and me in faraway Boston. With both your mother and mine glad to have us apart and determined to keep us that way. No. I must have you close by, hear you laugh, know that all is well because you are so sure it is. May we not marry here this June, when our schools close for the summer?"

"Yes," Emily said, returning his kiss with passion she had never known before..

When the news of McKinley and Emily's marriage in the chapel at Madame Antonia's school reached the Condons from Boston—where, now alarmed at the audacious step they had taken, the young couple had repaired to—it threw them, as well as the Martins, into a panic-stricken state.

"I cannot believe it!" Catherine exclaimed to Hugh.

"Nor can I."

"She is so young!"

"Aye, and there is her pianoforte here, waiting for her to continue her lessons."

"To think of their doing it as they did! I wonder at Emily's treating us so." Then her daughter's unaccountable conduct triggered a memory, and Catherine saw herself with her mother by the window seat where the geraniums grew, and heard herself saying, "But whatever, it is Hugh whom I am marrying and America we will be going to."

"The boys, I see, are grieved, too," Hugh remarked sadly.

"How could she not know that, more than all else, we wish for her happiness?"

"Aye, her happiness means much to us."

"She was always an independent little person," her mother recalled. "Always sure of what she wanted to do. Always possessed of a sharply defined sense of herself. Sometimes I used to think it was her lonely childhood that made her so."

Her father nodded. "It was true she had no playmates here in the beginning."

"She was ever so fond of Patricia and Patrick."

"Let us not speak of them!"

"No, though I see no harm in merely mentioning Emily's early love of them."

"She has long since forgotten them, as she seems to have forgotten all of us."

"I marvel at Antonia. Why would she not let us know, seek our permission?"

"Perhaps she assumed we had given it. In any case, they are of legal age."

"Then you think it is irrevocable? That we must abide by it?"

"Let us see what McKinley and Elizabeth say."

They were not long in finding out. The Martins came calling, Elizabeth unable to dissemble her dismay. McKinley, an only son, was in but his freshman year at Harvard and had not yet settled on what he would do. Catherine discerned that in his mother's mind there was also the unhappy realization that he had married in a Catholic chapel while having been reared in the Congregational faith, thereby no doubt committing his children to a Catholic upbringing, something she herself had overcome.

"I'm amazed at Emily," Elizabeth said, as though it had been all Emily's doing and McKinley an innocent victim.

"So are we," Catherine answered. She could not resist adding, "And we are also amazed at McKinley."

"The question is," Hugh said, "what are we to do about the young scalawags?"

"Yes," Martin agreed, "that is the question."

The four sat apart, staring ahead as if the question had assumed tangible proportions that they could stare down.

After a little while Hugh remarked reflectively, "Kate's mother was not happy about her marrying me and coming to America. To her, that was the ultimate disaster."

And McKinley said, "Nor were Betsy's family pleased at her marrying me. From their point of view, there were lots of things wrong with me."

At the men's humble admissions, a laugh escaped Catherine, drawing in first McKinley, then Hugh, and finally Elizabeth, and they all sat laughing together. They were young again, in love, and defiant. Who was to tell them what to do? Or to forbid them? Not their aged, unaware parents.

Besides, Catherine considered, what parent could know the mysterious future? It had to be risked—as she had chosen to do—and grown into, as she had done.

When the healing laughter died away, Hugh asked again, "The question still is, what are we to do about the young scalawags?" But now he said "scalawags" indulgently.

"Finance them, I suppose," McKinley replied. "See the young man through school. We'd have done so in any case."

"We, of course, will carry Emily," Hugh stated.

"Well, between us," Catherine said, "they should manage—frugally."

"It appears Emily has taken refuge with Betsy for the time being," Elizabeth said. "My family will help them locate rooms and settle in."

Then, for the first time that evening, it occurred to Catherine to offer refreshments.

Tea was steeping in Catherine's favorite china pot

and the dining table was spread with cold sliced chicken, newly baked soda bread, last year's cucumber pickles, and fresh gooseberry pie, but when Catherine went to announce all was ready, she could scarcely pull them out of their intense conversation.

"So they sought your advice as geologist, did they, on the new Portage Lake mines?"

Oh, Hugh, Catherine pleaded inwardly, can you not, at least for tonight, let this be?

But Elizabeth, only slightly less intense than Hugh, Catherine noted, spoke before her husband could answer. "But *only* as geologist."

Hugh smiled grimly, and Catherine saw that, like herself, he had not missed the bitterness in Elizabeth's comment. "With never the thought to reward you, I suppose, for your help in establishing the value of this amygdaloid ore?"

McKinley shook his head.

"And no suggestion at all about letting you in?"

"None whatsoever," Elizabeth cut in sharply. "After all these years up here!"

"Perhaps you know that although they have profited hugely from my early discovery, they have delayed in inviting me in on this new mine of theirs."

Elizabeth moved forward tautly in her chair, and her husband said, "I did not know. I have wondered."

The tea would be oversteeped, but what could she do? Catherine sat down and waited.

In his driving way, Hugh persisted. "Have you given them a written report on this ore? You know it is the true copper range; the mass mines, like the Macaulay, are but outcroppings."

The geologist nodded. "So far I've given only an oral report. I have yet to complete my written one."

"Well, now that we are related through our children, I shall let you in on a secret—one I have not yet shared with my partners. You are first to hear of it."

"Yes?" Elizabeth's face became drawn, and her pale eyes sparkled hard and bright, like diamonds.

McKinley waited, more relaxed than his wife.

"There's a third type of copper ore in the area of their discovery. Mac came upon a piece, brought it home to me, and led me back afterward to the spot where he had found it. I lost no time, you may be sure, in establishing my claim. 'Tis hard to describe, but Mac says 'tis a kind of puddingstone."

"You don't say? Then it must be conglomerate. This type of ore is also part of the true copper range."

"I want you to go there with me, see what you think. Delay writing your report until then. You may have something of surprise to drop into it. When they learn, seemingly by chance, that I have something even better than they do, they may think it worth their while to bargain with me on this new mine of theirs."

"The Quincy, they're planning to call it," Elizabeth supplied while her husband considered.

"Well, what do you say? If I win, you share."

"I must think about it."

Catherine saw again the young McKinley she had instantly liked when he had first come to the Ontonagon country, and she felt more affection for him than she had yet to feel for his wife. Her heart went out with love to his son, irresolute like his father, and she thought, Perhaps it is just that, before deciding, he, too, needs to weigh the right and the wrong of a problem.

"Well, there is a war ahead," observed Hugh, always close to the point of his interest. "The Government will have greater need than ever we dreamed of for this copper of ours and will offer many times more than it presently does. Do not think overlong."

PART EIGHT

The Keweenaw Peninsula During the Civil War

(1861–1865)

Chapter 27

THE WAR BETWEEN THE NORTH and the South erupted April 21, 1861. The conflict propelled Hugh into explosive activity, and a week later, with Mac, he prepared to set out in the early morning for the Portage Lake area. Catherine insisted they first have at least a hasty breakfast and sat down with them in the predawn.

"Would you not have liked to sleep longer this morning?" Catherine sought her mother's share in their youngest offspring.

"No, Mother. I have been awake a long time and am eager to be off."

"What is it you will do?"

But Mac, ever so like his father, was caught up in Hugh's fever of excitement, so that Catherine's questioning elicited as little information from her son as from her husband.

Still, she knew Hugh's overall plan—to go down the river, board an early steamer bound for Portage Lake, and order a stopover midway between Eagle Harbor and Portage Lake. There he would oversee the new conglomerate mine that he had located when the army had first begun to lay the new military road across the peninsula. This, Catherine recalled, had to do with the puddingstone-ore discovery of Mac's that her husband had long ago revealed to the Martins and, with McKinley's help, had used as a bargaining lever with the Bostonians on their amygaloid holdings. And now Hugh had again sent McKinley on the voyage to Portage Lake to discuss with the men, due in from Boston, the situation at the Quincy, in which Hugh held important interests. If all went well and Hugh made good connections, he would be back the following day. But he couldn't be sure. For, as happened so often, there were fresh problems at the Quincy and elsewhere on the Keweenaw.

"And what might these problems be?" Catherine asked.

"We must first arrange to send a company of light infantry to take part in the Union fight. Then we must find a way to replace the miners we shall lose to the war, and also the workers on the still-uncompleted military road, which should have been finished long before now. In addition to all this, the revolt that was brewing at the Quincy has broken out. Some of the troublemakers there will go to war. But others will remain. We must deal with them."

Catherine put her hand to her throat. She could feel a lump of apprehension gathering there. "Not harshly, I trust, if our old friend Patrick be among them."

"As harshly as need be." Hugh got up abruptly. "War is no time to coddle seditionists."

Catherine went with them to the dock and saw them start off. They were soon out of sight, but she lingered, enjoying the tentative feel of the coming spring and waiting for the sunrise. There was no one in the house to draw her back now. Even Peggy, who helped as Patricia used to do, had asked to leave because of the war for a few days' visit to her family. And, unlike Hugh, for whom the war served to whet a single and ever-stronger drive for control of the Keweenaw Peninsula, Catherine felt the pull of disparate emotions.

Which side one was on seemed to her a matter of chance rather than of choice. She was a "Northerner," but had they stayed in New Orleans, she would have been a "Southerner" like Madame Herries. Was the war to come between friends of long standing, perhaps, as in Ireland, even between families? Although

infrequently, Madame Herries and she still exchanged
letters, but she no longer read Madame Herries' letters aloud to Hugh. "She is so foolish, Kate," he
would say. "She lives in an unreal world." It was true,
Catherine knew, that Madame Herries dwelled in a
world of fantasy. But sometimes a certain perceptive-
ness, even truth, would steal into her observations. It
was this mingling of absurdity with truth that from
the start had amused Catherine. Besides, she was
still fond of the old friend who had indulged her and
made possible the school for the channel children.
Yes, she must write her.

There were also those whom Hugh would enlist
for the company of light infantry. What of them?
Some, she surmised, would respond as a way out of
drudgery in the mines or on the military road. Others
would do so because they were young and restless and
driven to seek the untried and to test themselves. Still
others would enlist because they wished to redress
what they judged the evil of slavery. Whatever their
motives or their mixture of motives, all were going to
fight other young men like themselves, to maim and
kill or to be maimed and killed.

What course would Emily's husband—reading law
in a Boston office and the father of little McKinley III
—follow? "We call him Mac, both for his father and
for our Mac," Emily had written. Larry, unwillingly at
Harvard, did not write but let Emily include news of
him in her letters home.

At the thought of Larry, apprehension seized his
mother. What would he do now that there was war?
She remembered him the day he had reluctantly set
off for the East.

As they had done when Emily set out, Hugh and
Catherine had gone downriver with Larry. He had
been dressed like the young gentleman his father
wished him to be, and he had fine new leather traveling bags filled with clothes to last him the year.

"He ought to appreciate all we are doing for him
and the opportunity that lies ahead," Hugh had said.

"Aye, that is so," Catherine had answered. "Perhaps in time he will."

She had always been aware that in her husband's mind was the thought of how much better Larry fared than he had. Yet she had known that Larry was setting out for college not because he wished to do so but because his father wished him to, and at heart he was a dutiful son.

He had kissed her goodbye, kissed his father, and without the anticipatory excitement that Emily had revealed, climbed into the launch that sputtered off toward the steamboat.

The sunrise had started, and Catherine watched while it spread ever-varying color over the eastern sky and then paled to morning's early light. Then she turned and went back to the empty house.

She returned later, when it was time for the steamer to go by. There was no longer the hope of a letter from her mother. She had died in familiar Chapelizod while there on a visit with Jerry to see about restoring Kemris House, and when there, they had looked in on their own former place. "Quite," Jerry had written, "as it used to be." At his letter, Catherine had once again been in that house, a young Kate, accepting from her mother what it seemed she still had to give—the gift of the past, enfolding a future which had beckoned with the promise of joy, beauty, majesty. Now Catherine's hope was for a letter from her daughter.

It was rewarded today. She opened Emily's letter as she walked back to the house and read rapidly at first. She stopped dumbstruck when she came to the part about Larry. He had left Cambridge, Emily wrote, and no one knew where he had gone.

This was the day for the afternoon quilting bee, and the ladies arrived promptly at two o'clock, shattering the quiet with their talk and questioning what project ought to replace quilting now that the war had come. Three or four possibly more valuable undertakings stayed alive briefly in the room until, buoyed by the excited camaraderie the war evoked, they left, looking forward with greater than usual eagerness to getting together the following week.

Elizabeth Martin lingered in the hallway after everyone else had departed. "What do you suppose Larry will do?"

Catherine hesitated. Did Elizabeth already know he was no longer in Cambridge? "We must wait and see."

The echoes of the women's chatter faded away. Evening came, and Catherine was alone. She got out Emily's letter but no number of rereadings altered the fact: Larry had disappeared without letting anybody know where he had gone. She put more wood on the fire. Outside, the late April wind tossed the branches of the full-grown fruit trees. Through the quiet within, the spring that cooled the basement cellar trickled noisily. But she was not afraid to be alone. Nobody but friends came to the front door. And tonight doubtless all were locked with their families in war talk. There was not even a knock at the back door, announcing a miner in distress. There was only the sound of loneliness.

Had time ever passed so slowly before? Yes, that night in the cabin . . . the night the wolf had howled, and fearing for Hugh's life, she had sewed tensely until morning.

Catherine started. Was that not the door opening? Who, at this hour? It must be her imagination. No! Someone was closing the door softly. Someone was hesitating in the hall. She stiffened in her chair, pinioned by a not-quite-erased terror. Patricia—brave Patricia—was not here. Catherine forced herself to call out, "Who is it?" As if in a nightmare, there was no response. She waited rigidly while the intruder walked along the hallway and into the living room . . .

Larry!

Despite whatever unfavorable circumstances had brought him, a cry of pure joy broke from his mother.

"Larry!" She went to embrace him with unspeakable relief.

He winced at the pressure against his right arm, and she drew back. "Have you hurt yourself in some way?"

"Just a little . . . stiffness." His eyes twinkled with his old affectionate concern in order to spare her worry over him.

"Larry," she said again.

"Now . . . no crying."

"No crying," she promised, and because she must do one or the other, she laughed as she sat down.

"That's better." He pulled up a chair and sat across from her.

"Well," his mother said, "and what now?"

"I do not know," Larry answered.

She paid attention then to his untidy look. "Where did you go after Harvard?"

He grimaced and was once again a little boy discovering that "Mother knows all." "You heard, then?"

"Emily wrote."

He dropped his head and sighed. "It was no good, Mother. I never wanted that."

" 'Twill disappoint your father greatly."

"Yes, I fear so."

"Where are your clothes, your luggage, your books?"

He lifted his hands in an empty gesture. "Lost."

"Where have you been keeping yourself?"

"I stopped at Portage Lake . . . with my old friends there."

"Patrick?"

"Yes, and Patricia."

Catherine put her hand to her throat. The lump she had felt gathering like apprehension this morning seemed to have been growing steadily through the day and was now threatening to choke her. " 'Tis there your father has gone to put down the revolt said to be brewing."

"What business of his is the Quincy?"

"As much his business as the Macaulay—or almost so, for he is not superintendent there."

Larry went so limp that his mother feared for a moment he would fall off his chair.

"Then it is true. I had not believed it until now."

"What is true, Larry?"

"That my father sent word ahead with McKinley Martin that Superintendent Lester was to deal with the uprising in whatever way seemed best to him."

Remembering Hugh's words in the eerie predawn, Catherine could not speak over the lump in her throat. After a while she was able to ask, "And was Patrick among those who revolted?"

"Yes, he was. It was he who led the march on the stamp mill, which the miners wish to take over and run to suit themselves." Larry lifted his head and, for the first time, spoke proudly. "I marched with them."

"Oh, Larry! You did not do so! You would not march against your father!"

"I did not know then that I was. But now I am proud I did. I would march against anyone who would license what Tom Lester did, even my father."

The fear that she, too, might side with Larry against Hugh prevented Catherine from asking what Lester had done. She asked instead, "What of McKinley Martin? Was he not there?"

Larry shook his head. "He had already left to return to the Macaulay, I heard. It was said they fear repercussions here."

Oh, I trust not, Catherine thought. But she did not voice her opinion. For it struck her that in this, she and Larry were on opposite sides. Though he stood against his father, she could not bear that he should also stand against her.

The spring, unnoticed during their talk, trickled loudly through their silence.

"It is a pleasant sound," Larry said at last. "I used to like to listen to it at night before falling asleep."

"Then perhaps you may listen again."

Larry shook his head. "When will Father return?"

"Soon. Possibly tomorrow. As you know, he wastes little time. Why do you ask?"

"I don't want to be here when he comes."

"Where will you go?"

He lifted his hands uncertainly, in the gesture that went back to his boyhood. "There is the war."

"Do not speak of the war. We will think and talk of your future—all of us together."

A silence followed like a separation. Catherine thought of earlier talks in which she had pleaded with him and he had rejected what she said. It was useless to open this up again. Besides, she could not deny that those who went down into the mines fared badly, while those who profited by their work fared well. Perhaps in Larry's mind the conflict had been irreparable ever since the day he had urged her not to wear the hat. Well, she had crossed Hugh that day and humored Larry.

Larry stood up. "Mother, there is something I must tell you, something I must ask you. It is for this I have come home. Besides," he added quickly, "wishing to see you."

"Ask me."

"Patricia is expecting a baby."

"Patricia? Oh, Larry, this cannot be. She is no longer young. Why, she must be in her late forties."

"It is so, Mother. She told me. She fears she may not live. She made me promise to ask you, in that case, to take the baby to raise."

"I, take the baby? But what of Patrick, the father?"

"It is doubtful he will recover from the injury he got when he led the march on the stamp mill. Patricia believes he won't."

"Oh, let us hope that he will. And let us hope that Patricia also will survive."

"But if they don't?"

"Oh, Larry, I am no longer young. A new baby? This one would not be my own. Suppose he were different?"

"Am I not different? And do you not love me?"

"Aye, that I do."

"Then will you give me this promise?"

"Aye. Should these double misfortunes arise, I promise to do as you ask."

Larry sighed tiredly. "Now I must sleep."

He allowed her to kiss him good night, but he winced again at her touch on his arm and then started out of the room. He stopped and called back to her, "When you write Emily, thank her for all the kindness she showed me in Boston. And tell Mac he may have whatever he wishes that is mine." But his mother refused to face the suggestion that lay behind these statements.

"If your arm is still stiff, you should put heat to it," she called after him.

His laugh, not a merry one, came for an answer. "It's not heat my arm will be needing."

The late morning sun streamed through the window and fell as lucid as water upon the table.

" 'Twas Mac's idea," Hugh said, "and it worked—the more credit to him. Let him sleep now. The superintendents from all the big mines as well as the men from Boston were there, and Mac sat down like one of us to the meeting. First, everyone agreed to send a company of light infantry to share in the Union fight. Then I rose and made Mac's proposal—that we raise a fund to bring four hundred miners from Sweden and get them to sign a paper promising to repay transport out of their wages. Once again, all agreed.

"Well, then I said let us pass the hat! That, too, was Mac's idea—not to delay but to get their commitment at once. In no time at all, those present subscribed a fund of ninety thousand. So 'tis done. Those four hundred will replace the men who go off to the war and will free us from the need to coddle any troublemakers who remain."

"Has not Superintendent Lester already dealt roughly with them?"

"Aye, that he has."

Determination to know conquered the earlier fear of deciding against her husband that had kept her from questioning Larry further, and she asked, "What, then, did Tom Lester do?"

"I would rather not tell you, Kate. 'Tis not a thing for a woman to hear."

"Did the miners' wives not hear of it?"

"Aye, they did."

"Then tell me."

Reluctantly, Hugh did so. "They ran a hose to the mill boilers and turned live steam and scalding water down on the uprisers. I am sorry to tell you Patrick led the revolt and that he was scalded . . . badly."

"Aye, and someone besides Patrick."

A flash of intuition leaped into Hugh's eyes, and he got to his feet. "Then it is true. Peter told me McKinley thought he had seen Larry. I laughed and said he knew well that Larry was in Boston at his books." Hugh sat down again in his chair. "Why would my son do this to me?"

"You must answer that question yourself, for, though Larry has been here, he has left."

Anger restored Hugh's vigor. "I am glad that he has. I thank him for going before McKinley could catch a second look at his face."

The wrath which had brought back his forcefulness also blinded him momentarily, and he did not see his sickened wife get up and walk out of the room. When he looked about and found that she had left him, he feared that the relationship which had begun in far-away Chapelizod and survived through the years was now broken.

Chapter 28

LITTLE BY LITTLE, the war drew them together again, the enormity of its tragedies swallowing, even for Catherine, the evil happening at the Quincy. In time she also came to accept that neither her husband nor Martin had sanctioned what Lester had done and that he alone had been responsible. Then the fortuitous fact that Patrick had survived the burns and Patricia had delivered a son helped to repair the break. Early in 1862, a penciled letter advising Catherine of these events arrived from Patricia, its heavy pressure revealing an immense effort and its misspelled words the familiar dialect. There was a postscript.

"I trist Larry give ye m' missage. His name be Hugh."

Catherine handed her husband the letter when he came back from putting another log on the fire. The February night was cold.

"And did Larry give you some message?"

Catherine was slow to answer. There was one hurt the intervening months had not healed and for which she still held Hugh accountable. Always there was Larry. Though letters came from Emily and from Mac, at Harvard since September preparing to study law, they had no word from Larry.

"He did."

Hugh waited.

"In the event of her and Patrick's death, she wished me to take the baby. Larry asked me to promise I would."

Accustomed though he was to surprises, Hugh shook his head over this. "Did you do so?"

"Aye."

An angry answer to challenge simmered in Hugh's eyes and then went out. "Well, let us be glad that both parents survive! I've enough to trouble me presently."

Catherine knew this was so. Despite the copper mines' well-organized contribution to the war, problems persisted, and they were all his. There was always the threat that the far-from-unanimous Union support on the Keweenaw might extend into copper production. From time to time, when off work and drinking, some miners could be overheard chanting the Civil War version of the Lord's Prayer:

Father Abraham, who art in Washington, thy Kingdom come and overthrow the Republic; thy will be done, and the laws perish.

And some of the men brought from Sweden to replace the miners had violated their agreements and gone off to the war.

From Ireland, where James Stephens had started a new revolutionary journal, *The Irish People,* the persisting conflict reached across the Atlantic. One O'Mahoney, who had escaped in 1848 from English vengeance, had established the Fenian Brotherhood in America, held a Chicago convention, and hoped after the war to enlist Irish Union fighters, money, and arms to invade Canada, and then to carry the Irish-American fight against the English overseas. There were those, Hugh knew well, who would not be slow to question whether his own background made him perhaps a little suspect.

Yet, through it all, he carried on relentlessly. For the most part, taught by the disastrous lesson at the Quincy, the miners rebelled no more but instead worked to "win the war in the mines." The Federal forces needed bronze cannon, copper canteens, brass buttons; with the demand, copper rose to thirty, forty, fifty cents a pound. At the Macaulay, the Quincy, and the new Hecla conglomerate mine, men worked three shifts a day for wages which climbed from thirty to a hundred dollars a month.

Stimulated by the war, new developments speeded the output of copper: the light portable drill, the circular bin, the steam-powered stamp. From the boom the Keweenaw had realized enough to make itself over in the years that would follow. To get the emergency copper more speedily, the U.S. Government had already deepened the Ontonagon Harbor. Congress was considering the laws needed to set in motion a vast postwar development: a Homestead Act, giving one-hundred-and-sixty-acre farms to settlers, and a Railroad Act, subsidizing a railway westward from Omaha, Nebraska.

So, along with its disasters, the war promised a way to an improved life. In New Boston and elsewhere, those not immediately stricken by deaths of loved ones responded animatedly to the hoped-for after-war world. In constant touch with his Boston associates and, through them, close to the Union's requirements, Hugh was central both to the war efforts and to plans for the future.

There were times when Catherine, busy with her own war effort, wondered from what source Hugh drew his power. She knew only that it was there, deep in his subconscious, not to be denied. Watching him, Catherine felt her earlier confidence and love for her husband revive. To be sure, she told herself, he was no ordinary man.

Then, in January of 1863, a letter came which reopened the unhealed wound between them. The Quincy superintendent, perhaps seeking to assuage an old guilt, wrote them that Patricia had not been long in following her husband to his grave and that among her effects was a letter from Mrs. Condon, promising to take their son in the event of their death. Meanwhile, Lester's wife was caring for the little tyke, a year old.

"What do you say to Tom Lester's letter?" Catherine asked.

"I have already told you my answer. Surely you do not intend to take this infant to rear."

"Indeed, I have every such intention."

"How can you do so without my consent?"

"I have already written and promised—and, you see, Mr. Lester's letter is addressed to us both."

"I'll have a talk with Tom, man to man."

"I'll write his wife, anyway. I doubt she wishes to take charge of the baby."

Ignoring her, Hugh was listening with evident concern to the firing of the big guns.

" 'Tis the cannon sent in case of attack from Canada, but I do not think the English are coming, Kate."

She would not be thrown off by his attempt to change the subject. "I promised Larry." She paused and then, close to breaking, added, "Larry is also your son."

"Have I ever denied it? When he comes home, we shall talk over our differences. First I'll listen to him. Then perhaps he'll listen to me."

"He will not come home."

"You must not say that, Kate! You know we both want him to."

Hugh threw down his napkin and got up from the table, his face brightening perceptively.

"News takes time to reach not only their ears but their understanding. They are celebrating, a week late, Lincoln's Emancipation Proclamation. I must go stop them lest one thing lead to another." He started from the dining room.

"You forget, I think, that Dolly is lame and cannot pull the cutter."

"I shall go on snowshoes, as I used to do." He hesitated in the archway and turned about. "Will you not come with me as far as the office—for the exercise and the air—as you used to?"

"That I will not! I must stay to write to Mrs. Lester."

Always when his wife defied him, Hugh saw her mother, whom he had never forgiven for preferring Tom Kemris to him. Across his face dislike flicked like a whip. He turned on his heel and left.

Catherine sat on alone. That long-ago talk with Hugh, about where Emily should go to school, came back to her. Protesting the Boston school where Elizabeth Martin and Susanne Osborne had gone, Catherine had said, "But their schooling—oh, no doubt other influences, too—has separated them from all but their own kind of people, and they guard that separateness. And they so seldom laugh."

Now she realized that, with the children away, the laughter had gone from her and Hugh's life, too. Where has it gone? she wondered. Then she recalled that on her occasional visits to a miner's cottage with freshly baked bread—she continued to do so despite Larry's disparagement—she would interrupt laughter. So, she questioned, is this where laughter lives still?

Crunching over the snow to the rhythm of the distant cannon's booming, Hugh thought, Well, whatever they are up to, I am glad to be out in this cold afternoon. It surprised him, as winter days that first year had done. The sun threw a sparkling brightness over the shadows cast by the trees, and he paused to enjoy the vista as he used to do. But it was bitter cold, colder than he had ever felt it before. He hurried on.

By the time he reached his office, the cannon had ceased firing. Did they guess he was coming? No matter. He must go inside briefly to warm himself before going on.

In his room the fire, which was not allowed to go out, was burning in the stove, and from down the hallway came the sound of Timmy's shuffling feet. Hugh tossed aside his fur mittens, and flexing his numbed toes and rubbing his chilled hands, stood looking about.

The superintendent's office reflected the opulence which the war had brought to the Macaulay. Hugh glanced toward the box by the door in which mail, brought during the winter from Green Bay by pony relays in forty hours, was placed throughout the week.

To his surprise there was a letter. He had seen Friday's mail and had not expected more before Monday, even Tuesday. What might this be?

"Dear Mr. Condon," Hugh read, and dropped to the signature, "George B. Meade, Major General of Volunteers," before reading on:

The news of war's outbreak caught up with me somewhat late in the spring of 1861, when I was conducting an army survey of the Great Lakes area. I put the United States Cutter *Floyd* in the Ontonagon slough and hurried east. Quite by coincidence, a young man offered to accompany me as an aide, and I accepted his offer. He was my first volunteer.

He was with me throughout my command of the Second Brigade of the Pennsylvania Reserves in the Army of the Potomac. When I was wounded at Frazier's Farm, he remained with me until I recovered. Then he returned with me to the second battle of Bull Run. He was with me during the battles at South Mountain, at Antietam, northwest of Washington, in September, and at Fredericksburg, near Richmond, in December. It was here, on December 13, while carrying a message for me to Major General Burnside, that he was shot and killed. I miss him sorely.

The War Department will notify you officially of his death, if it has not done so already. I write to offer my deep, personal sympathy to you and his mother and to tell you that, in every respect, Lieutenant Lawrence Condon proved himself a young man whom a father might proudly call son.

The cannon blasts had resumed and were still in Hugh's ears as he set off again, but their noise was remote now. In his mind there was no clue to their meaning, nor was there any sense of purpose to his walking.

From his office he had somehow gone in the direction opposite from what he had intended, past his home, down the Ontonagon, past the old cabin. If he kept on, before long he would come to the smelter of the Marquis de Pontalba, maybe encounter him on his sled with his dogs Nero, Hero, and Plato. He ought to turn about and go home, bring Major General Meade's letter to Kate.

The afternoon wind seared his eyes, and he looked about for some place to rest. He thought of the caves which the river had hollowed out of the soft sandstone banks. He would leave his snowshoes standing upright in a snowbank and climb down. Once, he remembered, he had done so with Larry when he was perhaps nine or ten. But he had forgotten how steep the banks were, almost perpendicular, and how high. Close to one hundred feet, he remembered Larry had guessed. Climbing down more cautiously than he used to do, slipping and stopping his fall by catching hold of a sapling that had rooted itself in the bank, Hugh thought, I should not have come here. I may have trouble getting back.

The cave proved roomy enough for a hundred men. Could this be the one Larry and he had come to that day? He looked about, and his eyes riveted on an immense pillar of ice, high as the wall of the cave and shaped like a pyramid. It must have been formed, Hugh thought, by a stream falling over the bluff, freezing as it fell. Then he saw that the stream had kept a small channel through the center, where the water shone like pure silver through the crystal-like ice. Never in all his Ontonagon days and years had he seen a sight of such living beauty.

From deep within came the cry for another to share it, for Larry. But Larry was gone . . . For Kate.

But because he opposed her taking Patricia's baby, she had turned from him. Doubtless the general's letter would separate her from him forever. . . . He shook his head forlornly. From childhood on, they had been close, in love while still in their teens. The whole of their lives together flashed through his mind.

Then, as though by some sleight of hand—was it Larry's?—the fabric of those days flipped over, and he saw the other side of the pattern he had been weaving.

Twilight was engulfing the cave, isolating it. The snow began to fall softly. It had fallen so early that other night when, deserted by Patrick, he had searched by himself for the mine. Had there been another side to that too? Might he have called Patrick back? If he had done so, would Patrick have come? Hard though the digging had been, had Hugh actually preferred to be alone, to have the discovery all his, should it come? Later, though he had not known what course Lester would pursue, he had sent word to him through Mc-Kinley to be as tough as necessary. Lester's ruthlessness had alienated Larry, sent him from home and to war, taken him from his mother. And at the time, Hugh had preferred to have his son go rather than stay to oppose him and, as he had thought then, disgrace him.

Had he, then, always made the wrong decision? But didn't a man have the right to get on? And in getting on, had he not been useful to others? What of the hundreds, even thousands, of men over the years to whom the Keweenaw mines had given and would give employment? How was a man to know how to choose? Hugh glanced around the now darkened cave and up the walls that the darkness made yet more forbidding. No matter. He must climb up, get back to Kate, bring her the letter.

But the pillar of ice that had first attracted him drew him back. Larry seemed to be beside him, marveling, too . . . and pressing his own differing view as to how one ought to choose. Attending to his son, Hugh entered an altered world, thinking that perhaps it was the one where Larry now lived, where time's familiar values gave way to those beyond time, and a magnetism he had never known before seized and held him.

The experience passed, and only the water continued to trickle through the small central channel of ice in the pyramid. Hugh felt a paralyzing numbness, and he moved stiffly toward the wall of the cave and started to climb awkwardly. But the saplings on the way up would barely support his ascending weight. At last, as he had feared, one of them gave, and he fell into the deep snow below. The snow was yielding, inviting, restful, and he was more tired than he had ever been.

Celeste Delfie, Marquis de Pontalba, his mustache waxed and wearing his full-length coat of Russian sable, passed by on his sled, saw the outline of snowshoes through the disguising snow, and called to his dogs to stop. Sure enough, he observed, there were not-quite-covered footprints to the cave down below, and there at the bottom lay a man. He knew a gradual descent farther off, a way by which the dogs could easily pull him on his sled.

"Why, it is Mr. Condon!" he exclaimed to the surrounding walls of the cave. Only his echo answered him, but he knew what to do, and he lifted Mr. Condon onto his sled. Then, driving the dogs and running along beside, he brought him back up the frozen Ontonagon to his home.

When Hugh opened his eyes, he was in bed, but he closed them again, content to be where he was, and slept on. "Exhaustion, shock, exposure," Dr. Ahearn had said. "We must wait and see."

Still, he *had* opened his eyes, and Catherine had caught in that instant a flicker of his old fighting light. A January thaw was tentatively relaxing winter's grip on the Ontonagon country, and, beside herself with relief, Catherine ran out into the great white brightness that spread all about. She had long since found and read—and copied for Emily and Mac, for Jerry and Bishop Baraga—Major General Meade's letter. But she had known before that that Larry would never come home again. Often before she had differed from Hugh and accepted his way, had understood well that he could do no more than fight. But she had not excused his conflict with Larry and held him accountable. Now she looked about the snowbound country, and it seemed to her that Larry was with her still and that he was also with Hugh, that he had found the way to be with them both.

The winter sun, sparkling on the snow, was strong enough to thaw the earth's frozen surface. Yet how gentle it was, Catherine thought, gentle as forgiveness. Mysteriously, like nature's obscure movement toward spring, it brought hope.

She went back to the bedroom. When Hugh opened his eyes again, Kate, her former self, no longer willing the distance between them, was beside his bed, her eyes wide with anticipation. With a great effort, he caught her hand. "I was bringing you a letter."

She nodded. "I found it."

He was silent, accepting. Then he asked, "Do you still wish to take the little boy?"

"That I do . . . when you are better."

Hugh nodded and rested again.

Chapter 29

WAS IT POSSIBLE, Catherine wondered, that since that January thaw, two Christmases had come and gone? She snuggled deep beneath the beaver blanket. Hugh slapped the reins, and Dolly, shod against slipping on the ice and with shades to protect her eyes from the glare of the late afternoon sun, started off.

The sleigh bells pealed out their bright promise of merriment. The Condons were at last on their way to the Washington's Birthday Soldiers' Benefit Ball at Bigelow House this February 22, 1865.

They were late. Hugh had been delayed at the shaft house, and when he had finally returned and dressed, they still had to take three-year-old Hugh to the Agassizes for the night. Priscilla Agassiz was a sister of Billy Shaw, whom Betsy Martin had married, and Priscilla's husband, Alexander, a son of Louis Agassiz, the famed naturalist and Harvard lecturer, was in New Boston to learn all he could from the Macaulay, still considered the Keweenaw's best-run mass copper mine.

Hugh had waited outside in the cutter while Catherine took the little boy in.

"Did he fret at your leaving?" Hugh asked when she returned.

Catherine laughed. "Not at all. Children always prefer other children for company. Besides, Priscilla started at once to read Mr. Longfellow's 'Hiawatha.' I caught but the two opening lines:

> By the shores of Gitche Gumee
> By the shining Big Sea Water . . ."

"I am glad he was content to remain there," Hugh said.

"So am I."

". . . And this one would not be my own. Suppose he were different?" Catherine had said that night to Larry. How little she—or, for that matter, Hugh— had foreseen. He was as winsome as her own children had been, maybe even a little bit more so. Perhaps somewhat surprised, Elizabeth Martin had said, "But he would steal anyone's heart!"

And so he had done from the moment on that spring day in 1863 when Nathaniel, who had come to inspect his investments and had found himself stranded at Portage Lake, had brought him, then a year and a half, to Hugh and Catherine. From the start he was a charmer. Nathaniel, too, had found him so. Catherine could only imagine what lineage lay behind his parents or what they, born out of their time and place, might have been. All knew him now as Hugh Condon, Jr. When he smiled and laughed, as he did much of the time, it was Catherine's smile and laugh he gave back to her. He bustled about after Hugh, imitating his swift gait and incisive gestures.

He had drawn Hugh and Catherine together again in a love such as they had known when their own children were little.

"Is he all right?" Hugh had asked the night before, hurrying into the living room from his day at the shaft house.

"Of course he is all right. Why would he not be?" Catherine had laughed. And little Hugh, hearing her laugh, had laughed, too.

"Well, and what did you do today?" Hugh had asked, picking up the toddler.

For an answer, his small son had put his arms around Hugh's neck, hugged him tightly, and set a wet kiss on his cheek.

Hugh had put him down and gone to embrace his wife. "Well, Kate," he said, releasing her, "and what did you do today?"

"Need you ask?"

Hugh had known he need not. All was well with her, too.

"Perhaps Nathaniel stranded himself on purpose," Catherine said now to Hugh, resuming a recurrent topic of discussion. "Both when he brought little Hugh to us and again last autumn, he seemed to have recovered his early love of this country."

"Aye, he did so."

"He seemed also to have recovered his own early self."

Hugh gave Kate a mischievous glance. "Aye, it takes a man a while to free himself from a wife."

Catherine laughed. And a wife from her husband, she thought. But she said, "If only he had been left in the Ontonagon country and could come tonight to the Benefit Ball!"

They had reached the plank road which led straight to Ontonagon and which, since the last heavy fall, the snowplow had opened. Dolly's rhythm was even, and the sleigh bells softened to crystal-ball tones.

How pleasant, Catherine thought, to start out. . . . It had ever been so. All journeys began hopefully.

"I am sorry I was late," Hugh apologized.

Catherine turned to him. Though he had recovered well from his exposure two winters ago, the hardships of many years had somehow triumphed during the time he lay defenseless, so that now he looked his full age. His helplessness, the first he had ever known, had brought other changes besides. Now he strove always to please her and was repentant for small things. He need not be so. The forgiveness that had come that day with the January thaw had never left, and Larry had stayed with them both.

" 'Twas the money's coming from Boston for the men's monthly pay, was it not, and the need to pay those who claimed they must have it at once?"

But Hugh now also strove to stay close to the truth, and after a pause, he said, " 'Twas more than that which detained me, Kate. Another matter altogether."

She looked at him in alarm. "I thought we had finished with these surprises."

He laughed his low laugh. " 'Tis a calm, clear night, Kate. Do you think the wind will not blow again?"

"Has it to do with Emily? Or with Mac? Or—" She thought of her brother's last letter, telling of the trouble brewing once more in Ireland. "Or with Jerry?"

"You know well that Jerry by now is more English than Irish. But you are right. It has to do with the trouble he wrote of, though it is here now, thanks to the Fenian Brotherhood."

"How does that concern us?"

" 'Twas O'Mahoney who delayed me. He seeks funds for the Irish fight against the English overseas."

"How does it happen that he came here, and to you?"

"George spoke to him often of you . . . and sometimes of me. In Chicago someone told him of the Macaulay and its great earnings."

Catherine tensed. Over the years she had hoped that somehow good would come of George's death. The sleigh bells rang brightly with hope. "You offered to help?"

Hugh shook his head. "I refused."

She looked at him in disbelief. "Why, Hugh? Why?"

"What he wishes to do, he wishes to do out of hate. I do not like hate for a motive. More important, we have seen America divide between the North and the South and known the cost in lives and suffering. Are we to divide it again many times over between those who have come here from Europe?"

"You told him this?"

"Aye, it was this that delayed me. I talked to him patiently, with whatever kindness is in me."

"Did he listen? Did he heed you?"

"No."

"Perhaps you invited him, then, to the Benefit Ball?"

"I did not. 'Twould but furnish him the opportunity he seeks to arouse others." The breath from Hugh's sigh hung in the cold air. "For your sake, Kate, and for many reasons besides, I should have liked to do otherwise."

"I should have done otherwise. And yet, perhaps in this you are right."

Hugh threw her a relieved smile and slapped the reins on Dolly's rump. A sweet peace fell upon them.

The melting snow revealed patches of muddy earth where the land fell away, the trees stood gaunt and black, and yet the cutter slid no less lightly over the road through the country that rose, fell away, and rose again.

Like waves, Catherine thought. And then, once again, with the winds from the Irish Sea filling her sails, tacking a little to east and west, rising and falling, the *Independence* made her way out of the enclosing arms of the bay, through the roaring of the North and South Bulls, into the chopping Irish Sea, and the sun spilled again with happiness.

It was hoped that at the Soldiers' Benefit Ball they would raise thousands of dollars for the wounded men of Company A of the Twenty-seventh Michigan Infantry . . . or for their families. Many in the company had died at Vicksburg in July of 1863, when Grant won the great final victory in the West while General Meade was winning at Gettysburg. And still others were likely to die or to live out shattered lives, for the remnant of the Twenty-seventh Michigan Infantry was currently matched with Grant against Lee in the great line bending from Richmond to Petersburg.

"Let us hope the ball will succeed," Catherine said.

"Aye, let us hope so."

They were silent, reviewing the reasons why it might not fare well. Many in the area had not really favored the war, and more than one man of fighting age who could afford to had paid three hundred dollars to engage another to go in his stead. In the 1864 election the upper Michigan vote had favored McClellan.

"Two to one, was it not," Catherine asked, "for McClellan over Lincoln?"

"Feeling is changing, though, with the promise of certain victory. 'Tis a long time since I have heard miners chanting the parody on the Lord's Prayer." Hugh gave his low laugh. "Lincoln may yet come out of it a great hero."

Catherine was silent, reflecting. Besides all the Macaulay officials and their families, there were many who they were sure would be at the ball . . . and others who they knew could not be. David Plummer, for one. He had resigned as Ontonagon's sheriff to captain Company A of the Twenty-seventh Michigan Infantry. Young Waite was another. Risen from first lieutenant to colonel, he was fighting now at Petersburg under Grant. Still others might come or might not.

Would Ontonagon Township's supervisor put aside his resentment at defeat in the old tax matter and come? Would National's superintendent forgive the beating in Michigan's Supreme Court and take his invited place in the receiving line? Would Jay Hubbell, who had vowed to take the case to the U.S. Supreme Court for National, drop his bitterness and join them tonight? And what of the Marquis de Pontalba, who usually preferred to dine alone on the red squirrel he paid boys to catch? They had invited him to dinner after he rescued Hugh, but he had declined. Would little Johnnie Death, the sixteen-year-old, back from the war hopelessly crippled, manage to get there?

Catherine glanced at Hugh. What was he thinking about? Of the men lost to the war? Perhaps of the future? The Macaulay would one day give out, but the Quincy and the Hecla would go on—beyond his lifetime, possibly even beyond the lives of his children. The Keweenaw Peninsula would share in the promised great postwar development.

They were approaching Ontonagon now, and the sun was going down. On the town's outskirts was the Ursuline convent, which last year Bishop Baraga had come to bless. How frail he had seemed then, Catherine recalled, and what an effort it had cost him to talk. At the close of his dedication he had said, "In the evening of life we shall be judged by how we loved."

Catherine listened to the murmuring of the lake. The Indians, Joseph Nicollet had told them, said the lake was a woman and talked to herself. What was she saying? No matter. The ice reaching from the shore into the distance muffled her voice. Above the lake's awesome expanse, serene and silent in its beauty, the rose-toned sunset held. Gradually it faded to an eerie line of light just above the horizon, and there was once more that shattering moment when Lake Superior first lay before them, shining and immense.

Lights shone from all of the Bigelow House's five stories. The brightness fell on the bridge over the Ontonagon slough and on the hollow beneath, where in the growing darkness General Meade's cutter waited out the war's end. For Catherine, three-year-old Hugh seemed to stand guard over the memory of Larry's enlistment there. Their sleigh glided up to Bigelow House. From within, someone sprang to take the reins from Hugh, and others threw wide the doors to the great entrance hall.

All waited there. Ah, they all had come: National's superintendent; Jay Hubbell, National's lawyer; the township's supervisor. And there, seated because he no longer could stand, was little Johnnie Death.

As though out of nowhere, Nathaniel sprang forward, and with his great festive sense, gave the signal. The fiddles began and everyone sang, "For he's a jolly good fellow . . ."

The voices rang through the hallway, filling it and all the rooms about with tribute to the man who had done so much for the Ontonagon country and for all of the Keweenaw Peninsula, and to whom everyone looked to do still more in the great days that would follow the war. Catherine looked from Hugh to the singing crowd—larger than they had hoped—and back to Hugh. He had fought many fights and won most of them, yet the people gathered here did not know of the battle he had fought and won and ever since wished he had lost. But Catherine knew, knew how it had colored both past successes and failures, and how it would temper all that lay ahead. Those who had fought with him and those who had fought against him sang louder and louder in tribute. All had come with long-pent-up emotion to the Soldiers' Benefit Ball to celebrate the Union victory, bound to come soon. And had not Hugh Condon also given a son to the Union cause?

About the Author

MARIE LOUISELL NOWINSON claims Duluth, Minnesota, as her home town. She was graduated from the University of Minnesota, where she majored in composition and journalism. Her first published novel, *The Legacy of Gabriel Martel,* won a Christopher award.

Stimulated by her mother's autobiography, beginning with her great-grandparents, Marie wrote a fictionalized account of the early part of her story. *Winds of Change* is the result. She researched early nineteenth-century Irish history at Trinity College in Dublin and American history in this country.

She lives in Highland Park on Chicago's North Shore with her husband, Richard. They are the parents of a son, Peter Ewing.

Alice Chetwynd Ley...
The First Lady of Romance

_____THE BEAU AND THE BLUESTOCKING   25613—1.50
Alethea's sheltered life could never have prepared her for the outrageous Beau Devenish or London in 1780!

_____THE GEORGIAN RAKE   25810 1.50
In England of 1750, one did not defy the social code...but Amanda would do _anything_ to prevent her sister's marriage to hellrake Charles Barsett.

_____THE MASTER AND THE MAIDEN   25560 1.25
Amid the violence of Yorkshire's Industrial Revolution, a young governess risks her future by clashing with the iron-willed master of Liversedge.

_____THE JEWELLED SNUFF BOX   25809 1.25
Set against the backdrop of Georgian England, lovely and innocent Jane Spencer falls in love with a nameless stranger who holds the key to her destiny.

_____THE TOAST OF THE TOWN   25308 1.25
Georgiana Eversley—admired and pursued by all the men around her, except one. Vowing to change this Buckinghamshire doctor's mind—she ignores propriety and eventually must pay the price.

_____THE CLANDESTINE BETROTHAL   25726 1.25
In Regency England an unspoken vow awakens young Susan to womanhood when she finds herself trapped in a lie and engaged in name only to Beau Eversley.

_____A SEASON AT BRIGHTON   24940 1.25
Reckless, impetuous Catherine Denham was too anxious to become a woman to remember to be a lady...something one never forgot in Regency England.

_____THE COURTING OF JOANNA   25149 1.50
While England is threatened by Napoleon's invasion, romance blooms between daring, spirited Joanna Feniton and a man who could destroy her future...and the future of England!

BB **BALLANTINE MAIL SALES**
Box 100, Westminster, MD 21157

Please send me the BALLANTINE or DEL REY BOOKS I have checked above. I am enclosing $.......... (add 35¢ per copy to cover postage and handling). Send check or money order — no cash or C.O.D.'s please. Prices and numbers are subject to change without notice.

Name_____

Address_____

City_____ State_____ Zip Code_____
Allow at least 4 weeks for delivery.   L-28

Available at your bookstore or use this coupon.

A Gift of Romance

Six novels of passion ... fire ... and triumph!

NEW FROM BALLANTINE!

FALCONER, John Cheever   27300 $2.25

The unforgettable story of a substantial, middle-class man and the passions that propel him into murder, prison, and an undreamed-of liberation. "CHEEVER'S TRIUMPH . . . A GREAT AMERICAN NOVEL."—*Newsweek*

GOODBYE, W. H. Manville   27118 $2.25

What happens when a woman turns a sexual fantasy into a fatal reality? The erotic thriller of the year! "Powerful."— *Village Voice.* "Hypnotic."—*Cosmopolitan.*

THE CAMERA NEVER BLINKS, Dan Rather
with Mickey Herskowitz   27423 $2.25

In this candid book, the co-editor of "60 Minutes" sketches vivid portraits of numerous personalities including JFK, LBJ and Nixon, and discusses his famous colleagues.

THE DRAGONS OF EDEN, Carl Sagan 26031 $2.25

An exciting and witty exploration of mankind's intelligence from pre-recorded time to the fantasy of a future race, by America's most appealing scientific spokesman.

VALENTINA, Fern Michaels   26011 $1.95

Sold into slavery in the Third Crusade, Valentina becomes a queen, only to find herself a slave to love.

THE BLACK DEATH, Gwyneth Cravens
and John S. Marr   27155 $2.50

A totally plausible novel of the panic that strikes when the bubonic plague devastates New York.

THE FLOWER OF THE STORM,
Beatrice Coogan   27368 $2.50

Love, pride and high drama set against the turbulent background of 19th century Ireland as a beautiful young woman fights for her inheritance and the man she loves.

THE JUDGMENT OF DEKE HUNTER,
George V. Higgins   25862 $1.95

Tough, dirty, shrewd, telling! "The best novel Higgins has written. Deke Hunter should have as many friends as Eddie Coyle."—*Kirkus Reviews*

LG-2